CU00978084

Water, Water, Everywhere, . . .

Water, Water, Everywhere, . . .

By

Bill Higgins

Blackie & Co
Publishers Ltd

A BLACKIE & CO PUBLISHERS PAPERBACK

© Copyright 2003
Bill Higgins

First published in 2003

A CIP catalogue record for this title is
available from the British Library

ISBN 1 903138 83 3

**Blackie & Co Publishers Ltd
107-111 Fleet Street
LONDON EC4A 2AB**

To my wife Ish, with love

I would like to give credit to Dr Brian Jordan for his excellent work on the book cover design, and to Mercedes Crespo, who took my photograph.

Water, water, every where,
And all the boards did shrink;
Water, water, every where,
Nor any drop to drink.

Samuel Taylor Coleridge
(*The Rime of the Ancient Mariner*)

CHAPTER ONE

The tree lined Mall in London has seen more than its share of pomp and splendour over the years. Occasionally bedecked with bunting and flag draped - the flags to flutter and flatter a visiting president or monarch of some powerful nation or banana republic - it is instantly recognised by millions of people worldwide. Gracefully wedged between two of central London's breath-giving lungs, the soothing and tranquil greenery of St James's Park and Green Park, the Mall derives its grace and splendour from its sheer extravagance of space. However, at times it is little more than a bustling early morning thoroughfare, with fast moving traffic conveying London's workers to their office desks and shop counters. As the day moves on, the colour, hustle and bustle of the *Mall* changes. Tourists in their thousands, from every corner of the world go there to see the *Trooping of the Colour,* and the *Changing of the Guard* at Buckingham Palace. But only such outsiders have time to stop and stare. As ever, at seven-forty five on any weekday morning, London's lifeblood swarms through the *Mall* in the rush hour traffic, anxious to get to its destination. As it flows through its plane tree-lined sweep, few of the drivers, or their dozing passengers, spare a glance at the graceful scenery and still leafless trees a few steps away. Had they done so on the morning of the third of March, they would've spotted a man in the distance scattering bread upon the placid waters of the lake in St James's Park. An everyday occurrence, most would have thought; after all the lake was the habitat of various forms of birdlife; pelicans, swans, ducks, sea birds and every type of goose from Hawaiian to Emperor, rarely seen together elsewhere. The observant few may also have been aware that *Joe Public* was expressly forbidden from feeding the Park's prized pelicans, a role of the especially qualified badge-carrying personnel of the *Royal Parks Department.* But then as the traffic roared on, most would've probably envied the man for being able to spend his time there, and in any event feeding the ducks was hardly a major crime.

WPC Pam Jordan was on the home straight of her beat that morning, enjoying the solitude as she made her way across St James's Park; a welcome respite from the noisy nearby streets. She glanced up at the sky, through trees that were beginning to display fresh green buds on the stark winter branches, reminding her that spring was not so far away. A smile crossed her chilled, pale cheeks, and a warm, pleasurable spasm rippled through her as she remembered the reason for her feelings of joy. She was seeing him tonight. Nothing like a new man in your life to keep you warm and excited on a cold morning. She would've been back at Buckingham Palace Road Station a few minutes ago if she hadn't met that nice American couple laden down with maps and guidebooks, who'd asked her for directions to the US Embassy. She had enjoyed their chat, mainly about how much they loved London and the *London Bobbies* as they'd put it, and she'd directed them to Grosvenor Square. It had been the highlight of an otherwise uneventful back shift. She'd be finished just after eight; a nice cup of tea, then off home to bed. Thanks to her efforts at international diplomacy, she was now a few minutes later than usual when she reached the bridge over the lake, and the incessant traffic noise behind her had dwindled to a low hum.

At the east-end of the *Mall* a few hundred metres away from the lake in St James's Park, an unimposing building close to Admiralty House houses the Metropolitan Police Control Room, the nerve centre of the Security Branch's surveillance of Buckingham Palace and its immediate surroundings. Sergeant Ron Lander surveyed a bank of VDU screens in front of him, and for the want of nothing more compelling to look at, idly watched a man at the edge of the lake evidently feeding the ducks. Naughty, naughty, Lander thought, but he hardly rated the event as a *High-Risk* situation. Like WPC Jordan, Lander was minutes away from completing a long and lonely night's shift. He carried on completing his shift report, and forgot about the duck feeder. Let someone else trot out the standard caution, he thought, knowing that it was impossible to restrict the public from feeding the birdlife in the park. He stood up and stretched his shoulders, facing the array of surveillance technology; CCTV, motion detection, infrared display for night use, fence monitoring, barrier controls, etc., all automatically recorded, ensuring that nothing was missed at any hour of the day or night. As he casually glanced at the screens he wondered when his tardy replacement, Eric Smith, would appear. He could still see the man and an array of birds, ducks, and even two pelicans close to him. It was a breach of *The Royal and other Parks and Gardens Regulations 1977* to feed the pelicans. I'll let Smith deal with it if he ever gets here, he thought. Serves him bloody right when he knows I'm playing golf this morning, Lander said to himself. He returned to his paperwork, and signed off his otherwise uneventful shift report, failing to notice the man eventually stroll away from the water's edge.

As Pam Jordan went to cross the bridge, she as usual playfully mimicked the birds, although she'd checked beforehand that nobody else could hear her.

'Hi duckies, us early birds are up and going as usual I see,' she said lightly, and added playfully, 'the early bird gets the worm you know.' But she had no sooner said it than she suddenly became aware that something was wrong. There was a different sound from the usually chirpy inhabitants of the lake; only a piercing eerie hum now surrounded her. It took a few seconds to penetrate but, looking around the grass banks of the lake she saw that there were dead or dying geese, ducks, birds, fish, even pelicans, lying everywhere, including a number of dead fish floating belly up on the surface of the lake.

'Bloody hell!' she gasped, looking in horror at the feathers and dead birds splayed around everywhere. She was also now conscious that the screeching sound coming from the dying creatures was so loud that it completely drowned out the normal rush hour traffic noise around her. What a bloody mess she thought, but there was nobody in sight, only the never-ending traffic at the edges of the park. The feeling of nausea swept through her as she saw the pain and agony that the poor creatures were going through, their ruptured and destroyed intestines being vomited up in front of her. She was relieved when her training kicked in. Was she herself in any danger she thought? Not that she could see as she glanced around. Maybe there'd been some kind of sewer gas leak? But she couldn't smell anything. She struggled to regain her composure, then used her radio to call up her station. There'd be hell to pay for this she thought as she waited for a reply, knowing how much care and attention went into looking after the various species of birdlife. Her radio responded and she clinically reported the facts of the incident in constabulary tones, in spite of her hand shaking uncontrollably. She had to sit down somewhere, anywhere, before she fell down. She slumped down on the bridge, her back resting on the metal railings. She tried hard not to look at the dying birds, and using her recently acquired copper's cynicism, tried even harder not to hear their screeches of pain. The radio operator at Buckingham Palace Road, in his way of providing her with a feeling of support, advised her to stay calm, and keep her radio open for further instructions. He also told her to remain on location till backup arrived. It was 0807hrs and WPC Jordan felt annoyed because she should've finished her shift seven minutes ago. 'Bastards,' she groaned.

CHAPTER TWO

For more than a few months before WPC Jordan had stumbled upon the dead and dying birds in St James's Park, diplomats in the West had become more and more concerned about Iraq and the ruling regime in that country. It was daily news in national and international newspapers, as well as radio and television. Saddam Hussein, it was claimed, continued his attempt to build an arsenal of weapons of mass destruction, and Western diplomats warned their governments that with each day Saddam became more of a threat to the rest of the world. They advised their governments to resist the demand from campaigners to lift international sanctions against Iraq. Instead they advocated that the governments of the Western Allies, mainly Britain and the US, should use force on Saddam to remove him from power.

As always, Saddam enjoyed his place in the worldwide media attention. He was used to taunting the Allies; particularly the US which he loved to treat with contempt. In the late nineties he'd seen the full might of American naval and air power aimed at Iraq, and himself in particular. He did however survive, and continued to plague the US.

Now, at the beginning of March with spring again approaching, the world watched and waited. Would Saddam continue to allow the UN Weapons Inspectors to function in Iraq? The game of cat and mouse continues between the US and Hussein, with Hussein taking the initiative, always at some cost to his more powerful adversary. The current Bush administration in the United States found itself caught between the history of its past relationship with Iraq, and the current need to rid the world of terrorism. Consequently, although ready to pounce on Iraq after the Afghanistan War, the USA was hampered by its European Allies, which were less inclined to connect Saddam with international terrorism. As a consequence, and after much deliberation, the earlier imposed sanctions on Iraq remained in place, preventing Saddam from selling at will Iraq's most valuable commodity: oil. In addition the import of necessities such as medical supplies and food were still not permitted. With such restrictions in place, the Allies live in hope that an internal revolt by the people of Iraq will occur soon, and that Saddam will be toppled from within.

Far removed from Baghdad and the machinations of Saddam Hussein, Abdullah Kadri threw the last piece of a stale bread roll into the mud-coloured water. It was two minutes to eight in the morning. Kadri then walked casually away from the lake before crossing the Mall at the nearest set of traffic lights. He made his way out of the St James's Park and through to Piccadilly, merging into the hustle and bustle of people hurrying to and from Green Park Tube Station. Taking the packed escalator down into the Station, he welcomed the breeze in his face as he descended. He took a train to Kings Cross, where he would change to the Northern Line and go on to the Angel in Islington. The journey would be no more than fifteen minutes. Kadri hated being cooped up with the morning rush hour commuters: Infidels, as he thought of them; dregs of humanity. They disgusted him. As the train left the platform he positioned himself close to the sliding doors, cursing silently, and trying not to breathe in too much of the foul-smelling air all around him. Kadri was fanatical about cleanliness, as he was about his worship of Allah. As an Islamic fundamentalist, he was convinced that all infidels were born unclean, and remained that way throughout their lives. He closed his eyes, and opened his mind, visualise the presence of Allah. In his inner peace his thoughts returned to his actions of a few minutes ago in St James's Park. He'd carried out his instructions to perfection. He'd removed the tight-fitting seal from the flask he'd been given the day before by his fellow countryman, and thrown it, together with some bread towards the water fountain in the lake. As he watched the flask sink under the water, he threw in more bread, encouraging the various birdlife swimming on the water's surface to go in that direction. Suddenly he became aware that the train had stopped, and saw that he'd reached Kings Cross. He got out and headed to the Northern Line service. When he got there, he saw on the digital display that the train to the Angel, the nearest Tube Station to the upmarket restaurant, Fred's in Islington where he worked as a waiter, wasn't due for another four minutes. As he stood on the virtually empty platform, his mind now focused on what he'd get to do when he reached the restaurant. He'd begun working there only six weeks before, after becoming bored in his last job as a security guard with the Airports Authority. Now, apart from serving tables, he was responsible for putting the rubbish out for collection: empty wine bottles, boxes, and the by now rotting leftovers from the previous night customers. It was the lowest of low tasks, and he hated the indignity of it. Handling the filth of the infidels disgusted him. When the train arrived he got on. One stop later at the Angel he got off and took the escalator up to street level, and breathed deeply at what passes for fresh air in that part of London. It was raining again, as it nearly always did, he thought. He joined the hustling throng on the filthy, wet pavements, and a few minutes later he arrived at Fred's restaurant. He walked carefully down the steep, moss-covered steps at the rear of the building. Using the key he'd been grudgingly entrusted with, he opened the much kicked and battered black basement door. The rubbish awaited him and soon he started pulling out the first of many garbage bags. Empty bottles clanked and rattled, and the smell of the other filth made him retch. Kadri closed his mind to the task, and quickly pulled the bags up the pavement level. When he'd finished he went to the staff area at the back of the basement to wash the filth from his hands, and to change into a white shirt and black trousers: his waiter's uniform. For the rest of the morning he was kept busy, due to the early arrival of a ten man Strike Committee from the local Water Utility whose headquarters were close by and who were taking advantage of an expense account lunch.

When Constable Eric Smith eventually turned up for his shift at the Met Control Room, he joked with his sergeant, 'Wish it was me who was golfing this morning Ron.' He quickly keyed-in his security number into his desktop computer at precisely 0805hrs. Five minutes late, he noted with a little guilt, which he quickly overcame. Lander laughed, and said something derogatory about Smith's golf before he left the Control Room. Smith started to scroll through the report of the last shift on the screen. As he read the empty log Lander had left him he thought, 'old Ron makes a mountain out of a bloody molehill'. As he was settling into his seat the speaker on the console next to him activated, picking up a nearby Police radio transmission. It was a woman's voice reporting some incident, and she sounded alarmed. Smith instantly focused on the screens in front of him to see if she was in camera range. There, he spotted her: a WPC alongside a bridge; the small bridge over the lake in St James's Park. Looking at the other monitors he saw very few people near her. It seemed to Smith that the woman wasn't in a threatening position. He zoomed in on the camera covering the bridge and saw that she was surrounded with what looked like dead birds. God, he muttered to himself, Lander's here all night and nothing happens, and I've only got off the blooming bus and the shit hits the fan. He began scrolling back through the past night's camera footage. A few minutes later he was looking at a man at the edge of the lake in the park. The man appeared to be feeding the ducks, all of which looked to be healthy, and very much alive at the time. He glanced at the digital clock on the machine and saw that the film had been recorded around seven-forty five that morning - barely twenty minutes ago.

Later that same morning, the early edition of the *Evening Standard* newspaper carried a short front-page story. **DEAD AS A DODO** blazed the headline. Outrage was expressed in the article at some mindless vandals who'd fed poison to the ducks and swans in St James's Park. A photograph showed the lake, and dozens of dead birds floating on the water, and countless others lying dead on the grass slopes around the lake. The article predicted public outcry, vigorously challenging the Government to find the mindless perpetrators.

Although some of the Strike Committee had read the early editions of the *Standard* before arriving at *Fred's* for lunch, none thought the subject of poisoned ducks worth discussion. Their current and most pressing worry was future pay claims for them and their Union members. They wrestled instead with such weighty matters, as whether their salaries would be tied solely to the *K* factor, a factor determined by *OFWAT* every year or so, which was meant to keep water prices affordable to the public. The factor of course could be a negative number as well as a positive one - as they had recently been reminded, and that thought worried the Committee. Huge profits and recent large pay rises to executives throughout the water industry had caused *OFWAT's* Director General to make formal complaints to the privatised water companies in England and Wales, and public reaction had been understandably hostile. That matter did trouble the Strike Committee, because it would affect their and their members' pockets - and that was a matter of real concern, not dead birds in some park on the other side of London. Later editions of the *Standard* published that evening, as well as *Carlton Television* and

Capital FM newscasts, did however expand upon the earlier story of the dead birdlife. The later reports stated that all forms of birdlife in and around the lake in St James's Park had been poisoned, including a large number of seabirds that frequented that stretch of water on their journey to and from the Thames Estuary. Literally hundreds of birds and other species, including the popular pelicans, had been killed. The reports also added that surprisingly for such restricted waters, there was also a number of dead fish including some Rudd, and adding a touch of colour to the grim words, said that *their golden, gleaming bodies, with bright red fins*, could be seen floating all over the lake. A spokesperson from Buckingham Palace expressed Her Majesty's, 'anger and disgust at the outrage that had occurred on her doorstep,' and confirmed that the Government and the Security Forces had assured Her Majesty that they would look into the incident in the park at the highest level.

CHAPTER THREE

The day after the St James's incident, Abdullah Kadri came out of the Angel Tube Station at Upper Street, again heading to *Fred's* restaurant. He walked with a feeling of purpose and felt like a soldier of Allah. He'd read some of the morning newspapers, most reporting on what was being called *The Outrage,* and had read that, as planned, Her Majesty the Queen had been distressed by the incident. He was in good spirits, his ego bolstered by his recent success. The week before, Kadri had left *Fred's* restaurant at one o'clock in the morning after a long and hard double shift, and met a stranger as if by chance. The man, tall and heavily built had said that he was a stranger to London, and that he was looking for John Street, which he understood, was close by. The men chatted for a few moments, and Kadri directed the man to John Street a few blocks away. Although Kadri hadn't instigated the subject during their conversation, the other man raised the subject of how badly Britain and the US were treating the people of Iraq. Kadri had agreed with much of what the man had said, and had enjoyed the short conversation. Both Kadri and the other man, who'd introduced himself as Ali Ciddiqui, agreed to meet again, around noon the next day at a restaurant in Soho. Both men it seemed wished to develop their friendship, and their common interest -- *Revenge for Iraq.*

Abdullah Kadri was an insignificant individual, thirty-six years of age, slightly built, with fair, thinning brown hair, no more than one hundred and seventy centimetres tall. His English was particularly good, as in his youth he'd attended the *Foundation Preparatory School* in old Baghdad, known simply as the *English School.* He was also a loner. His arrival in England just after the end of the Gulf War followed the completion of his Degree in Chemical Engineering at the then badly war damaged Baghdad University. During his time as a student, the ruthless *Iraqi Foreign Espionage Department of the Ministry of Industry and Military Industrialisation* had recruited him as a spy. Kadri had been sent to London as soon as his degree course had been finished, and as soon as the UK Government allowed, under the pretext of furthering his Chemical Engineering knowledge with industrial experience. In fact his actual instructions were to disappear as soon as he arrived in London, and wait to be re-activated at some future date. He followed his instructions and had taken on a new identity in London, and with it an adopted Turkish nationality. His sole purpose in life from then on had been revenge for the humiliation suffered by Iraq at the hands of the Western Allies, Britain and the United States of America. He waited impatiently for his call to arms. Retaliation his only desire.

Ali Ciddiqui, the man Kadri had met, was a card-carrying member of the Diplomatic Branch of the *Embassy of the Republic of Armenia.* An Iraqi by birth, and trained by the dreaded *Amn-al-Amn,* the Iraqi Secret Police, Ciddiqui had been earmarked to provide great service to the Iraqi regime and up to this time had served it well. Through the *Amn-al-Amn,* Ciddiqui had acquired the false diplomatic position and his identity in co-operation with some sympathetic Armenian government officials who shared Iraq's dislike for the Western Allies. Ciddiqui was the opposite of Abdullah Kadri. He was tall; one hundred kilograms in weight, forty-four years old, with a head of thick, black, heavily gelled hair. He was an extrovert, smoked Havana cigars and was a noted womaniser. His suits were expensive, and he only wore Swiss white cotton shirts, with thickly cut silk ties. A heavy diamond-encrusted gold watch on his wrist sparkled, as did his highly polished, black skin shoes. He portrayed an overall figure of excess in every way. In the diplomatic circles in which he occasionally mixed, Ciddiqui was looked on as a *nouveau riche* playboy, lacking in culture; a typical product of the rich oilfields of his unsophisticated, adopted country. As a consequence, not too many people paid much attention to his boisterous, and vulgar behaviour, assuming that what you saw was what you got. A brash, and none too intelligent diplomat, hell bent on having a good time while the oil revenues lasted. Such an assessment couldn't have been further from the truth, as Ciddiqui was one of Baghdad's top field agents, with an extremely high success rate in his covert operations. With his love of the good life in the West, no one suspected his intense hatred of the people of Britain and the USA: the *Eternal Enemies of Allah,* as he believed.

Following the Vice-President of Iraq, Taha Yassin Ramadan's vow that Baghdad's resistance to the Allies would continue after years of damaging sanctions applied on his country, Ciddiqui had been especially chosen by a splinter branch of the *Iraqi Foreign Espionage Department* to set up and activate a plot against Britain. Ramadan had also strongly advocated that Iraq should strike back where and whenever possible. On this remit, and following the last of many political shambles involving the United Nations Weapons Inspectors, a Major General in the Iraqi Army took it upon himself, mainly to bolster his position with His Excellency Saddam Hussein in the future, to strike back at the Allies. He chose Britain. His target, the most basic commodity: water. He reasoned that the British were to blame for the humiliations forced on Iraq, preventing the supply of medicines, fresh food, and other life supporting items into the country. Iraq had recently suffered the worst drought in some fifty years, with water levels in the mighty Tigris and Euphrates rivers so low that people had been able to cross the wide expanses of each river on foot. The Major General had witnessed the suffering of the people of Baghdad as a consequence, and it was his most fervent wish to bring that same suffering to Britain, and its infidel population. His plan was to implement an action of retaliation on the 17th July; the anniversary of the Ba'ath 1968 Coup. He hoped it'd be the kind of gift that would please Hussein, and that when the success of the action became known, Saddam would bestow further honours on him and his family.

Ciddiqui and Kadri met up again the following morning as arranged, in a small, seedy-looking café in Soho. Ciddiqui ordered strong black coffee for both men and when it was served, took out a large cigar and lit it with great flourish. Kadri was impressed and more than happy to be seen in the company of his new well-informed friend. During their long and wide-ranging conversation, the men again touched on the subject of sanctions imposed on Iraq by the Western Allies. Both became agitated by the topic, and in the heat of their debate, Kadri admitted he'd been born in Iraq.
'A fellow Iraqi my friend,' was all Ciddiqui said as he offered his hand to Kadri. They shook hands warmly, and the content of their conversation became more concentrated on revenge as it progressed. Ciddiqui had been fully briefed by the *Amn-al-Amn* on the man facing him. Both men had been born in the old Karsh district of Baghdad, close to the River Tigris, and both were passionate

believers in the political and military claims of the Iraqi regime. *Kuwait, and some other puppet Gulf States, are the rightful territories of Iraq,* they had agreed wholeheartedly. They talked of how to achieve these aims, and the need to retaliate. It was during this part of the discussion that Kadri heard Ciddiqui use coded passwords that he'd memorised ever since coming to Britain. The words were, *Ma Ma, Fi Kul Makaan,* translated into English meaning, *Water Water, Everywhere...* Kadri knew he'd met his activator, and that the time had come for revenge.

The men met again in the café two days later, and this time Ciddiqui instructed Kadri on his first assignment. The Plan, Ciddiqui explained was to bring death and chaos to the British by causing continuing disruption to the supposedly safe environment that the population in Britain took for granted. They were to prove to the population and the authorities responsible for the safekeeping of public utilities, that such beliefs were fragile and could be destroyed with ease. Retaliation was to begin now and they, Ciddiqui said, had been chosen to strike the first blow. As Ali Ciddiqui described The Plan, the first stage of which he called The Appetiser, he said that it would be simple and inexpensive to put into effect. It would also cause great offence to the British, taking place on their Queen's doorstep.

'This is all you have to do Abdullah,' Ciddiqui said holding up a dull, stainless steel container. 'Take this flask. It contains Hydrocyanic Acid. At seven-thirty tomorrow morning go to St James's Park near Buckingham Palace. There, open the flask and place it close to the water jet in the lake. Nothing more complicated - simple as that.' He handed Kadri the flask, and said that the liquid would kill all of the birdlife that lived in and around the lake within the hour and most of it within minutes. Ciddiqui smiled at the thought then added that the British Queen would be upset by the incident, especially as it had taken place in a Royal Park. The authorities would create a great fuss, but would eventually blame the incident on an act of vandalism to cover up their lack of clues. Kadri, from his knowledge of industrial chemistry, knew that the acid Ciddiqui had mentioned was extremely poisonous. In Iraq some years before, Kadri had worked with the deadly product in the manufacture of chemical weapons in a secret processing plant in the desert. He also remembered that the chemical formula for the liquid was simply HCN. When Ciddiqui had finished his briefing, Kadri said that he'd be honoured to carry out the wishes of Allah, and praised the genius of His Excellency's advisors for the simplicity of the planned action.

CHAPTER FOUR

In Britain at the time of the St James's Park incident, the subject of water was much in the public's mind. The Director-General of OFWAT had disclosed to the media that he would mount a fresh inquiry into the finances of the privatised water companies, and would do so before the present price controls expired in 2004. The DG also said that he intended to make sure that cost savings made by the companies should benefit the customers rather than the shareholders. His statement was made just after a report in *The Times* claimed that the water companies had collectively made in excess of £15 billion total profits since privatisation in 1989.

'Customers have seen prices rising for far too long, with minimal re-investment by the water companies,' the DG sternly added.

As if by reply to the Director-General, a well-respected University professor completed a report on behalf of the Department of Transport, Local Government and Regions, proposing that at least six new major reservoirs would be needed in South-East England to ensure sustained water supplies throughout the twenty-first century. It was made clear in the report that as demand rose as a result of global warming, and the increase in single parent households, present water supplies could not cope without the addition of the proposed storage facilities. Ever mindful of the environmentalists, such as the *Friends of the Earth* and the *Anti-Reservoir Campaigners*, the DTLR urged that in the first instance the cash-rich privatised water companies should tackle problems such as water main leaks, and demand management. Water it seemed, was now a matter of concern to everyone, friend and foe alike.

To the public some things never changed. Most of what was being reported in the media had been aired many times over the past decade. The water companies the media claimed, *had reaped the wind* since the heady days of entering the *World of Privatisation* during the late eighties and fortunes had been made by some, mainly at the cost to the consumer. But things had changed at least to those perceptive enough to see that water was now in the forefront of big business and politics - international as well as national. The public had discovered that water was something that could now be taken away from them. Hosepipe bans and water rationing were common events and, as a result of recent flooding, even contaminated water supplies threatened the normally stable and reliable commodity. As the UK's public and the media debated the subject of water, in Baghdad Saddam Hussein's high-ranking Major-General's thoughts had turned from planning to action; action that would satisfy his need for revenge against the Western Allies. He approved the plan, *Ma Ma, Fi Kul Makaan,* confirming that it should take place in Britain. Time would be needed to implement it and brief the operatives who were already in their strategic positions. The pompous British he decided should be first to taste Iraq's revenge, and taste it drinking their own water.

CHAPTER FIVE

As the media to a man was still calling for Government action to find the culprits of the St James's Park incident, the Deputy Pathologist from the Royal Society for the Protection of Birds, Dr John Greenstreet, telephoned Deputy Assistant Commissioner Mike Hughes at Scotland Yard. Hughes, a tall, heavy-set individual, and a previous Head of the *Protection Business Group* at the Yard, which included *Royalty Protection*, was responsible within the *Met* for the investigation into the incident at the Park. For the past two days Greenstreet had been conducting tests on the dead birdlife, as well as having water samples analysed from various locations within the lake. As Greenstreet explained the results of his tests to Hughes, trying to keep the technical details to a minimum, Hughes jotted down a few pertinent points he thought of particular importance.

'Deputy Assistant Commissioner, in summary, the toxicological analysis leads me to conclude that the birdlife was poisoned by a very volatile and poisonous liquid called Hydrocyanic Acid, or HCN for short.'

'You're saying that someone simply poured a quantity of this HCN or whatever you call it into the water,' Hughes asked, 'and then walked away and all of those poor creatures died almost instantly. Is that it?'

Before waiting for a reply Hughes added, 'Dr Greenstreet, we've examined every minute of film from the surveillance cameras covering the park and lake, and I have to say we haven't seen anyone putting large quantities of anything into the water - apart from handfuls of bread that is.'

'I'm not saying it was a large quantity of HCN that was used Sir. A litre, no more than that would've been enough.'

'A litre. As little as that?'

'Unfortunately yes. You see HCN's a very potent poison, and positioned close to the suction connection for the fountain it would spread throughout the lake in minutes.'

'Doctor where would someone get HCN, and what is it normally used for?'

'Well I'm not an expert on the uses of the substance, but I do know that one major use is in the production of *Acrylonitrile* - a starting compound for various products to produce cyanide compounds, such

17

as sodium and potassium cyanide. Both these compounds are used in recovering gold and silver from ores. However great care is needed when handling the substance, as even the fumes are lethal. Several of these cyanide compounds are also employed in the electroplating of metals with silver, gold and platinum that feature in the microelectronics industry. Micro-chips in computers and such like.'

Hughes listened, his mind taking in Greenstreet's information.

'Is it possible that the HCN could've got into the lake accidentally?' hughes asked.

'I don't think so. You see my water sample locations covered the entire surface area of the lake, and the concentration of HCN within the water at every location is fairly consistent. I would have to say that the HCN was placed very purposefully to gain maximum diffusion. If a container of HCN accidentally fell into the lake, or was even casually thrown in, then there would've been a very high concentration recorded only in the area where the container came to rest. It's a lethal liquid - that I do know, and one that distorted then dissolved the internal organs of the unfortunate creatures. For example, a litre of HCN discharged into a public swimming pool would make a lethal concoction, and because of the normally efficient circulation and diffusion of pool water, most of the bathers would be violently ill or worse within minutes. Child fatalities would almost certainly be very high.'

'As little as a litre?' Hughes questioned.

'Possibly less, maybe seventy, or seventy-five centilitres, but certainly a litre - that would be sufficient to produce a very high death count.'

Greenstreet finished by saying he'd dispatch a full report on his findings to Scotland Yard within the hour. Hughes thanked him for his help before replacing his telephone. He recalled that the Assistant Commissioner *Specialist Operations* had phoned him earlier that day and asked bluntly, 'Mike, what the hell's happening with your investigation into this incident at St James's Park? I'm getting big stick from above about it. Get it sorted out ASAP would you Mike?'

He'd wait till he had the report in his hands he thought before going to see the AC. Now as he thought over the conversation he'd had with Greenstreet a few minutes ago, he realised the potential for disaster was immense. It didn't have the hallmark of any of the usual terrorist groups, but the more he thought about it, the less comfortable he became. He lifted his telephone and asked his secretary to get Commander Hall to come to his room in ten minutes. He then telephoned the Yard's Pharmaceutical Department and asked them to tell him everything they knew about HCN. What Jim Bannistair, the *Met's* pharmacist told him confirmed his worst fears.

When the incident at the park had first occurred, and because of the Royal connection with St James's Park, Hughes had been given responsibility within the *Met* for the investigation. His first action had been to close the park to the public, and have the lake drained as quickly as possible to prevent further loss of birdlife. He was aware that in the circumstances it wasn't possible to drain the water off into the public sewers and he'd brought in a specialist Hazardous Waste Disposal firm. The company operated a fleet of tankers non-stop for twenty-eight hours, causing major disruption to traffic throughout the West End of London while the operation was underway. The dead and the dying birdlife were collected and water samples were taken from a number of recorded locations on the lake and then delivered to the RSPB in Bedfordshire for detailed analysis. When the lake was empty, everything found on the bed was collected and delivered to Scotland Yard. As the hours went by, the proceeds grew numerous. Everything from a kitchen sink to a small ship's anchor as well as dozens of cans, bottles and more than one supermarket trolley, was collected from the muddy sediment. Each item was bagged and tagged, with a description of the item and location on a grid plan showing where it had been collected.

As he waited on Hall, Hughes picked up a recent memo from the specialist waste contractor. The memo confirmed that geese, swans, ducks, seagulls and a wide variety of other birds were still dying at the lake as they continued to fly in from other nearby areas. The memo also stated that as it was proving difficult to keep wildlife away from the muddy waste, netting should be erected over the entire area. Hughes signed his approval, and put the signed copy in his out-basket. As he was about to pick up another letter he was interrupted by the arrival of Hall. Hall was Hughes' right hand man, and had been promoted into Hughes' job a year earlier when the latter had been made a Deputy Assistant Commissioner.

'Come in Chris and take a seat,' Hughes said motioning towards a chair opposite him. Hughes related the contents of the telephone call he'd had with Dr Greenstreet from the RSPB.

'Chris I think, in fact I'm bloody certain, we've got a real problem with this St James's Park incident. From what Greenstreet tells me, I'm sure it was deliberate. From what I know of the stuff they... HCN that's its chemical name...I'm sure we've got some terrorist action here. This stuff you see, this HCN, you don't pick up at the local pharmacy. It's a very serious product - mainly industrial use, with restricted government sales and distribution procedures. In other words, it's bloody difficult to get your hands on it.'

'Real IRA Sir?'

'No, no I don't think it's them Chris. No, I don't think so, not them. That bloody lot would've confirmed it by now in their usual cocky way to get maximum publicity.' Hughes got up and stood at his office window. As he gazed out he said, 'What Greenstreet said about somebody putting this stuff into a public swimming pool horrifies me Chris. It would be so bloody simple for someone to do that, or even put it into a river without drawing too much attention to themself. Can you imagine the horror of hundreds of kids and parents who normally use public pools every day, getting caught like those suffering birds? It's unthinkable and it would amount to nothing less than mass murder.'

'What've we got to start with Sir? Can we be sure it wasn't an accident?'

'This was no accident. Bannistair at Pharmacy agrees with Greenstreet that HCN is a highly lethal chemical that needs professional handling. It's a deadly poison we're talking about; Christ even the fumes are lethal.' Hughes went silent for a minute or so then, as if refocused, he said, 'Chris I want you to take on this investigation. We'll keep it within *Protection* as I've the feeling it's got some way to go. It could even be aimed in some way at the Royal family.'

'Where do we start Sir?'

Hughes thought for a moment then said, 'We've a hell of a lot of items retrieved from the lake, and I'd think there must be something amongst them that'll help. Nothing's been physically touched, except by whoever put it in the lake in the first place. It's now sealed in plastic bags. Remember what Greenstreet said about the placement of a container of some kind close to the fountain, something that would contain about a litre or two of HCN. Check first of all what's been found near the fountain. That's a good place to start.'

'Right Sir. I'll clear the decks and focus on it as of now. I also know we've got umpteen hours of CCTV film, and the Admiralty House Unit may have missed something. I'll get the film checked in more detail. What about the suppliers and the end users of the HCN, from what you say there aren't too many of them?'

'Not according to Greenstreet and Bannistair, but have them checked out, and Chris get on to it right away. In the meantime I'll inform *Security Group* to issue an immediate alert to all local councils in the Greater London area that operate swimming pools. The public should be restricted from taking cans or bottles of any kind into the buildings whether they like it or not. The councils will also need to step up security of these premises after hours. Private swimming clubs and fitness centres as well. The more I think about it, the more I begin to see the potential for bloody disaster. I want you to report back to me every four hours for the next few days no matter what Chris. I'll advise the Commissioner to inform the Home Secretary, and the health authorities of the risks.'

Hall said he'd set up a team to deal with the incident immediately, and suggested that they use the code name *Operation Hydro* for future reference to the incident. As he went back to his own office, his mind started to focus on whom he'd bring in to his team set-up.

After Hall left, Hughes returned to his paperwork. An hour or so later his secretary brought him a large envelope that had been handed in for his attention. He opened it. It was Greenstreet's report, and he quickly read. It was clinically factual and contained a terrifying 'What If' scenario. Picking up his telephone he asked his secretary to get him the Assistant Commissioner right away. Once he was put through, he explained the content of the report, and the other matters he'd discussed with Hall. The AC told Hughes to send him a copy immediately, and added that he'd set up a series of meetings that afternoon involving the health authorities within the Greater London area to apprise them of the dangers.

'What do we do about the press Sir?' Hughes asked, 'I have them on the telephone every half hour or so wondering what's happening with the St James's incident.'

21

'When I speak with the Commissioner in a few minutes,' the AC stated, 'I'll ask him to put pressure on the media to play down the matter in the meantime to minimise public anxiety. I'm sure there are still some in that profession who understand the need for restricted information in the public good in matters of this nature - at least I hope there are?'

As he hung up on Hughes, the AC speed dialled the Commissioner, and quickly explained the situation, stressing the concerns regarding public safety, including the need to minimise public anxiety.

'I'll speak with the Home Secretary as soon as possible,' the Commissioner said, as he gathered the seriousness of the situation. 'Keep me informed as it will go all the way up to the House.'

The Commissioner of the Metropolitan Police telephoned the Home Secretary and apprised him of the situation, and of his fears of further incidents. The men exchanged thoughts and concerns, and the Minister confirmed that he'd speak to Downing Street and ask to see the Prime Minister as soon as possible. The circumstances being what they were, the men met fifteen minutes later and agreed a plan of action, including the need to consider the possible cost to the Public Purse.

'This could escalate Prime Minister, and the cost could be considerable.'

'It has to be sorted whatever the cost Minister, and we must be seen trying to do so. Now remember, make sure that you make the most of it when the time is right,' the PM replied, forever political.

A week or so passed with no further related incidents, and as early spring made itself felt in London in the arrival of some fine, warm weather, the public and media interest in the *Dead Ducks in St James's Park* incident subsided. A short statement had appeared in most of the national daily newspapers a week or so after the event, stating that following tests conducted on the dead wildlife, it had been established that *'the various species had been poisoned by persons unknown.'* The tabloid press found other matters to indulged itself with instead, items such as *Possible al-Quaeda terrorist attacks in London; Sleaze in Politics; Profits made by farmers as a consequence of the Foot and Mouth Epidemic two years after the end of the last reported case; the struggle of the Euro and the performance of David Seaman, Arsenal and England's No.1 goalkeeper.* In fact editors of all of the national newspapers and television companies had been advised through the usual Home Office channels, that the story of the *Dead Ducks* should be dropped for the time being. The editors, aware that an instruction of this nature usually meant that there was more to the incident than met the eye, usually something affecting National Security, backed off and reluctantly waited.

CHAPTER SIX

Abdullah Kadri stood on the pavement and watched with dispassionate interest as one by one the tramps choked and shuddered in their death throes, unable even to scream. Kadri's face creased in a twisted smile at the sight of the last surviving individual: a filthy, unshaven youth whose eyeballs were bulging to bursting point as he gave out his last strangled gasp of foul-smelling breath. Now a half dozen or so bodies lay silent like rag dolls amongst the garbage and urine-soaked cardboard boxes the dropouts called home. Kadri had planned the last hour or so two days before, and had enjoyed watching the gruesome outcome.

When he'd returned to his flat two weeks ago with the flask of HCN that his fellow Iraqi, Ali Ciddiqui, had given him to use in St James's Park, Kadri decided he'd keep some for his own future use. He had filled a small bottle with HCN and put it into a concealed cupboard he'd recently constructed in his flat. Now, two weeks later, he'd become impatient waiting for further instructions from Ali Ciddiqui. To break his boredom he decided to take the initiative and dispose of some of the tramps - box-dwellers as he called them - that he walked past every day outside Russell Square Tube Station, a short walk from his flat in Tavistock Place. He hated going anywhere near them, their rough language, their acceptance of their pitiful place in life and worst of all the smell of urine that surrounded the collection of soiled bedding and cardboard boxes where they spent most of their days and nights. He bought two bottles of *Hooch,* a mixture of pure alcohol and the dregs of discarded sherry casks from a van that parked every day near the Royal Mail Sorting Office in Parringdon Road. The van was known to supply postal workers and other locals with cheap drink and had done so for some years. Kadri poured some of the *Hooch* from one of the bottles, and added back the HCN. He put the empty HCN bottle and the bottle with the now 'doctored' *Hooch* back into his cupboard and the bottle of 'un-doctored' *Hooch* into his rucksack. He'd give this latter bottle to the tramps later that night on his way home from the restaurant. As it turned out, it was in the early hours of the morning before he got back to Russell Square, and the tramps, when they realised what he was giving them, shouted their gruff thanks to him before passing the bottle around amongst themselves. He walked away, trying desperately to get the smell of their filthy bodies and sleeping quarters out of his nostrils. The next night as he came out the Tube Station, he repeated the gesture, only this time he gave them the 'doctored' *Hooch*. Again they gulped at it, telling him he was, 'just like a brother, and their best friend in London'. Kadri left them to it, although this time he only crossed the road, out of range of the foul smell from their stinking camp. Now from across the street, and as he'd anticipated but still enjoyed seeing it, within minutes the group became progressively more incoherent, gasping for breath, and clutching their stomachs in agony. He thought of it as a silent puppet show, and the thought made him laugh out loud. After a few minutes they all died and the camp lay silent. No sound, no movement. It was just one thirty five in the morning and Kadri, feeling good within himself, walked away.

CHAPTER SEVEN

It was now two weeks since the incident in the St James's Park, and Operation Hydro had been up and running in Scotland Yard as planned. Fortunately no further incidents had occurred, although the extra security measures were still in place, with the associated heavy cost and inconvenience to the public and authorities alike.

Hughes and Hall were going through the motions of their daily meeting regarding Operation Hydro. The investigation it seemed had ground to a halt. As both men paused for a moment, Hughes stirred his coffee pensively.

Hall, more as a way of breaking the uncomfortable silence than out of any desire to converse, asked, 'Did you see the bulletin board this morning Sir - the item about the six deaths; the vagrants at Russell Square? Odd circumstances: the poor devils seem to have had something to eat or drink that didn't agree with them. No doubt drugs related.'

'No Chris I didn't see it. Where did you say this happened?'

'Outside Russell Square Tube Station Sir. I've asked to have a look at the file report later this morning.'

'Do that Chris. I know that those kind of people take and drink anything, but for six of them to die at once is, to say the least, a bit odd!'

Even as Hughes and Hall were speaking, the Newsreader at Capital Radio was announcing that a suburb of *Cardboard City*, the Russell Square area of London, had been the death scene, and that the six males had apparently drank themselves to death. As it would turn out, this unintended pun was not too far from the truth. A later report appeared in the *Evening Standard* adding that the Police were treating the matter as *Suspicious*.

Later that day at around five o'clock, and after he'd read the file report on the deaths of the six men, Hall had gone to the office of the District Pathologist, Dr Duncan Ferguson, in Middlesex Hospital.

In the cold, grey and sombre setting of the Pathology Department, Hall and Ferguson were now discussing the recently completed *post-mortems* of the dead men. 'Doctor, in your reports you say all the bodies contained a moderate level of alcohol, as well as a lethal

26

quantity, in human terms, of prussic acid. You're saying they were poisoned, or they jointly committed suicide. Would that be correct?'

'You have a way with words Commander, but to answer your questions I'd have to say that it's unlikely that the six of them jointly agreed to commit suicide,' Ferguson replied with a smile. 'So yes, I suspect that they were poisoned - whether knowing or unknowingly. I can't be more specific.' Ferguson went on to confirm that there was no other cause - or causes - that would have led to the simultaneous deaths of all of the victims, estimated to have taken place around one or two o'clock that morning. He also went on to say that he'd established that all of the deceased had been in poor health, some much worse than others but none likely, as he put it, 'to pop off of their own free will in the next day or so without a push'.

As their discussions reached an end, Hall thanked Ferguson for his findings, and asked that a final copy of the report be dispatched to him as soon as possible. As he came out of the mortuary, he welcomed the moderately mild temperature and the smell of fresh air. Making his way back to Scotland Yard, he pondered what sort of person would get pleasure out of poisoning the vagrants? What were the chances of it being the same person or persons who'd poisoned the birdlife in St James's Park he wondered? He was aware that *Fingerprints* had been unable to get a clear set of prints from the numerous bottles that'd been picked up around the dead men, although *Forensics* had identified the bottle that had contained the 'doctored' *Hooch*. When he got back to the Yard, Hall decided that he'd check the earlier report from the RSPB. There might be some connection between the two incidents he thought, although he felt it would be a long shot. Ferguson he recalled had named the lethal component of the liquid contents found in the stomachs and bladders of the six dead men: prussic acid.

Now an hour after he'd left the mortuary, Hall was reading the RSPB report, and in it he noted that the poison used in St James's Park incident, was known and called hydrocyanic acid. His initial reaction was that prussic and hydrocyanic were two different acids, and that the incidents were not related after all. He'd decided to check. He picked up his telephone and dialled the *Met's* pharmacist, Jim Bannistair, whom he knew well. Hall explained the situation to him.

'One and the same old boy. Hydrocyanic acid is the posh name within the chemical world for prussic acid: its more common name,' Bannistair replied.

CHAPTER EIGHT

Ali Ciddiqui was having morning coffee and reading *The Times* newspaper in the sumptuous ground floor lounge of the Carlton Hotel in Belgravia. He was waiting on a fellow member of the Armenian Diplomatic Corp who'd requested to meet him to discuss some problem related to their diplomatic duties. Ciddiqui had agreed to meet the man at eleven o'clock, and had positioned himself close to the regular table used by his one-time mentor in Baghdad, Colonel Safa al-Dabobie, although the Colonel had yet to arrive.

Colonel Safa, unbeknown to the British Authorities, was a senior officer in the Iraqi Secret Police, and he and Ciddiqui met in Hotel lounge every week. Sometimes they spoke to one another if Safa required to pass on some instruction or other, however on most occasions Safa ignored Ali Ciddiqui. Safa, like many other wealthy people from the Middle East, lived in London during the summer months, enjoying the warmth but not oppressive heat of his homeland. They enjoyed living in the best hotels, with the many forbidden fruits such as alcohol, women of pleasure and other commodities not readily available to them in their homelands. Safa held a false Jordanian passport, giving him excellent diplomatic credibility in Britain and in the United States.

As Ciddiqui sipped his strong, black coffee, his attention was drawn to an article half way down the front page of the newspaper. The article stated that six men, vagrants as they were defined, had been found dead in the early hours of the morning in suspicious circumstances near Russell Square Tube station. The deceased it was stated, all white males, had been sleeping rough there for a number of weeks. Ciddiqui passed over the item with little further thought; other than to think that it would be six fewer down and outs on London's pavements from now on. He turned to an article concerning the continuing appeal by the convicted man involved in the Lockerbie/Pan Am terrorist attack, a subject that provided him with more pleasurable reading.

'Good morning,' the tall, dark-skinned man said brightly as he stood over Ciddiqui and waited to be invited to sit down.

Ciddiqui looked up from his newspaper to see his vaguely familiar colleague from the Armenian Embassy. 'Good morning to you too my friend,' Ciddiqui replied, folding his newspaper, and placing it on the side table. He stood up, and shook the man's hand in a warm show of affection that belied his true emotions. 'Sit here,' he instructed, motioning the man to sit on the other side of him, leaving himself with an unrestricted view of the adjacent table. 'You would like some coffee I'm sure?' he asked, signalling for the hovering waiter to attend to their needs. Soon the men were in deep discussion, although Ciddiqui could barely conceal his lack of interest. A few minutes later, as the two men continued their unequal conversation, Colonel Safa entered the lounge and sat at his reserved table, adjacent to Ali Ciddiqui. Following a few yards behind, although ostensibly unconnected, Safa's personal bodyguard also came into the room, and sat in a remote corner of the sumptuous room. As the Ciddiqui's companion droned on about the state of the Armenian economy, and the restrictions imposed on civil service salaries including his own, Ali Ciddiqui felt a gentle tap on his shoulder.

'Please forgive me for interrupting your conversation, but did you drop this envelope?' Safa asked. 'It was lying at the side of my chair.'

Ciddiqui looked at the large, heavy envelope and reacted quickly. 'Thank you, it must have fallen from my lap. Thank you so much.'

After a brief pause in his diatribe about his personal grievances, and his country's plight, Ciddiqui's colleague continued as though nothing had happened. Five minutes later, with the man threatening to get passionately into his subject, Ciddiqui made his excuses on the pretext that he had an early lunch engagement and left the lounge carrying the heavy envelope. He walked quickly back to his apartment a few minutes away, and as soon as he closed his apartment door behind him, Ali Ciddiqui opened the envelope. He took out a bound document headed *Ma Ma, Fi Kul Makaan*, as well as a large amount of US dollars, and other maps and papers. A hand-written memo was attached to the cover sheet of the document. It stated that an *unauthorised event* had taken place in the early hours of the morning in which six people had died as a result of poisoning. Ali Ciddiqui remembered seeing the article in *The Times* less than an hour ago but he hadn't given it too much thought. The memo continued, stating that a *friendly source* at the hospital where the bodies had been taken, confirmed that the men had died as a result of drinking an unknown substance, but possibly a substance similar to that used in the incident at St James's Park. Ciddiqui felt himself begin to sweat. He continued reading the memo, and saw that in the circumstances, and to put the matter beyond doubt, he was instructed to terminally close any possible link between himself and Abdullah Kadri without further delay. He placed the document down on his coffee table, his hand visibly shaking. He sat still for a few minutes before picking up his telephone. He carefully checked a number in his personal directory before dialling it. The telephone rang a few times before it was answered. Instantly he recognised the Kurdish guttural sounding tones of the man at the other end of the line. Ciddiqui gave short precise instructions for the immediate liquidation of his errant colleague. Name, description, location, date and time for the event to take place. He asked the man to confirm that the instructions were clear, and when he was assured that they were, Ciddiqui replaced the telephone. He poured himself a large malt whisky, before settling back down on his soft, leather sofa to read the document that Colonel Safa had given him. He was relieved to see no further distressing instructions were included for him to execute, and his excitement rose even higher when he read that the plan, *Ma Ma, Fi Kul Makaan,* was now approved, and instructions to proceed were confirmed. He rose from the sofa and refilled his glass before returning to his seat. He began to read in detail the various stages of the plan. He read that he was instructed to visit the targeted locations immediately, and verify the strategic viability of each. It would be his sole responsibility to approve the selected strategic locations, locations where the plan was judged by him to have major impact. Feelings of fear crept through Ali Ciddiqui at the mention of sole responsibility, knowing what that meant to the likes of Colonel Safa who saw failure of any sort as punishable by the slowest, and most painful death. He forced himself to read on, and noted that the operators of the plan, who were already in position, were to be briefed by him as soon as possible. Their names, a brief resume of their past individual achievements in the employment of the Iraqi Secret Police, character references, their present locations in the UK, and contact telephone numbers were all provided. Three sealed envelopes, each marked with a location code name were also bound into the document. The targeted locations were defined as *Locations Alpha+Beta, Gamma,* and *Delta.* Ciddiqui looked at his watch and saw that it was ten minutes to twelve. He lifted his glass of malt and drank it slowly, thinking about the task ahead. He had been instructed to act immediately. He pressed an intercom button on the wall beside him, which was connected to the downstairs Reception. When the concierge replied, he asked the man to arrange for a car to take him to Heathrow Airport as soon as possible. He packed some things but soon realised he'd have to buy clothes more suitable for his purposes when he got to his destination. He'd just finished packing a few things when the concierge rang to say the car was waiting. Ciddiqui collected his things, made sure he had his other forged passport and driving licence - the Turkish ones - and his charge cards, then locked up his apartment, and took the lift to the ground floor. As he passed Reception, he told the concierge that he'd be back in a few days time. Climbing into the back of the black Mercedes S class saloon, he instructed the driver to take him to Heathrow Airport, Terminal 1, as quickly as possible.

As the black Mercedes saloon with Ali Ciddiqui inside arrived at Heathrow, Commander Chris Hall had just finished addressing a hastily convened meeting in Scotland Yard. DAC Hughes was looking hard at the younger man.
'Chris, you're trying to put these two incidents together, but can you really? Have you sourced the supply of the HCN, or the prussic acid? Do we know that it's of the same bulk supply? How can you be sure of the connection?'
Hall nodded in acknowledgement of the difficulties. 'Sir there's been only one major purchaser of HCN in the past six months, apart that is from the Ministry of Defence. You also know the MOD; they'll tell us nothing and hide behind their usual statement that it's, *in the interests of national security...* Anyway I think *they're* unlikely to be going around the country poisoning people and wildlife,' Hall stated positively. 'On the other hand, the only other listed purchaser is a company called Kiremla Ltd, based in Croydon. They bought a total of one thousand five hundred litres, 1.5 tonnes of the stuff, three months ago. Now the UK's only stockist of HCN, call it prussic acid if you like, is Zenecal Chemicals. They're based in Hatfield, and have stated that as far as they knew Kiremla specialised in recycling microchips for the computer industry. Zenecal said also that Kiremla completed all the necessary paperwork, even arranged for uplifting

the product and paid for it by bankers' draft on the same day no less. It seems, from what Zenecal say, that Kiremla appeared to be genuine in every aspect. Due to the nature of HCN, and the government regulations concerning the sale of the stuff, Zenecal are confident that their stocks have been correctly recorded, and that no one else has been supplied since, nor has any of the product gone missing.' Hall paused and walked over to the window. His voice now an octave or two lower, he added, 'The only problem, Sir, is when I asked the local Police force in Croydon to look in on Kiremla, the address given on their paperwork couldn't be found, and they're not listed in BT's telephone directory.' He paused again before saying, 'On checking with Companies House they told me that Kiremla Limited used to be a Scottish company, listed in Edinburgh, with a Glasgow head office. Further checking of the listed directors, who incidentally were two women, established that they were engaged in the leasing of cars, office equipment and office space, and certainly not microchips. One is now living in Spain, and the other is still in Glasgow. When interviewed - and catching up with the one who moved to Spain proved difficult - the women were more than surprised to hear the company's name mentioned again. Both confirmed that they'd had no connection with the company for years, and as far as they knew it was closed down.' Hall grimaced, then added, 'Companies House confirmed all of that last part I'm afraid Sir.'

Hughes shook his head, and said, 'The old story I suppose Chris - a shell company used to screen the real motives.'

'Probably Sir. Anyway it succeeded in keeping us fairly busy over the past two weeks I can tell you, and ended up getting us nowhere.'

'Fifteen hundred litres is a bloody lot of poison. You could kill half of London with that amount.' Hughes said as he rose from his chair and paced the room. 'Whoever they are, this Kiremla lot, from what you're now saying they may've been involved in the incident at St James's and it could be they've just killed six people as well.' He stopped to look out of his office window then asked, 'What the hell are they going to do next, kill more people? Is that what they're trading in now, poisoning people?'

Hughes sat down again. 'Chris I've had a problem with this matter since the start. The incident in the park for example - what was the point of it? What was their message, whoever they are - let's call them Kiremla? What point were they trying to get over? I mean if you wanted to kill a few ducks and birds they could've fed them some rat poison on some bread, or something similar; something you can buy in a hardware store. You don't have to get into restricted chemicals to do that. Now we have six people dead. What next I ask?' The men remained silent for a moment or two as they considered the question. Hughes broke the silence; 'I want you to have all major supermarket chains advised that they'd better be on the lookout for the possibility of tampering with their stocks. The sooner they get up to speed on this HCN situation the better, before we have a massacre on our hands.'

'I'll set that up with their security people right away Sir,' Hall said, scribbling on his notepad.

'Good,' Hughes said pensively. Again he got to his feet and paced around the room struggling with the uncertainty of the situation. 'Chris if you're right about the connection between these two incidents, and let's take the view that you are for the moment, then I want you to double up your efforts to find Kiremla before they really put the boot in. A major disaster is on the cards here if we're not careful.'

'I agree Sir. There must be something that we can trace them back with; the paperwork given to Zenecal for example. We'll bring all that in and take a good look at it. There must be some thing that will help us.'

'Right Chris, now we've had two weeks to locate the man caught in the film by the security cameras in the park. If we take the film as proof, then he was the first person to appear at the lake that morning, and the birdlife was alive when he first appeared. And still was when he left. It was only just after that, that they began dying in numbers. There must be something he can tell us? As far as finding out who put the HCN into the lake, well he's got to be the prime suspect although the film doesn't confirm that. But two weeks later and we've still haven't traced him for God's sake!' Hughes shouted. He paced around the room in frustration. 'With all the bloody computers and photographic equipment we have in this place, I'm sure we can produce a good close-up ID photograph from that film of him surely.'

'We can Sir, I'm sure that won't be a problem. But for the record Sir,' Hall said, feeling that Hughes was getting around to blaming him for the lack of progress with the investigation, 'up until those deaths at Russell Square we were concentrating on the whereabouts of Kiremla and the HCN. If we assume that both matters are related, then I agree we must locate the man as a matter of priority. The man, Kiremla, and the HCN are interlinked I'm sure.'

'Chris, I'm not blaming you in any way. It's just the fact that, and it's not a time for jokes either, but we seem to be like the poisoned birdlife - dead in the water.' Hughes continued to pace around the room making Hall feel like an errant schoolboy. 'We have no real line of active inquiry going at this time. We need to get some results now, not in ten days time. Get on with it Chris otherwise the Commissioner will be forced to take the investigation out of our hands, and you can imagine the implications of that I'm sure?'

'Got the message loud and clear Sir. I'll have the Yard's *Photographic and Graphics Services* onto it right away and a digitised photograph in every police station in London by this evening.'

CHAPTER NINE

Arriving at London's Heathrow Airport, Ali Ciddiqui, using the assumed name of Sayid Taleb and the Turkish nationality displayed on his forged driving licence, went to the British Airways ticket desk in Terminal 1 and bought a ticket for the 1415 BA Shuttle to Glasgow. He also arranged to hire a car on his arrival at Glasgow. He went to Gate 5, and waited a few minutes before the flight was called. Along with over a hundred others, he walked to the waiting aircraft. Showing his boarding pass, he was directed to his seat: row three left, and ten minutes later the flight left for Glasgow.

The BA Boeing 757 aircraft flew over Scotland's largest city, making its final approach into Glasgow's International Airport, one hour after leaving London. Ciddiqui glanced out of the cabin window: vivid coloured green fields everywhere. Not like Baghdad, he thought, which was normally scorched and burned brown by the sun. Beneath him he saw lakes, as he thought of them, in all shapes and sizes, glistened in the afternoon sun. The plane passed over a river just before smoothly touching down on the runway. During the flight he'd read, for a second time, the document Colonel Safa had given him. It contained a full itinerary for the next four days, including route maps showing the various locations where the plan, *Ma Ma, Fi Kul Makaan* would take place.

When he arrived in Glasgow his instructions were to make his way to a small town called Aberfoyle about fifty kilometres miles north of Glasgow. From a map, Ali Ciddiqui saw that the town was near to an area called *The Trossachs,* in the Queen Elizabeth Forest Park. As the plane jolted to a halt at the pier attached to the terminal building, Ciddiqui stood up, opened the overhead locker and took out his suit carrier. Being at the front, he was able to leave as soon as the doors had been opened. He followed the signs to the Arrivals Hall, surprised by the size of the building. He spotted the sign to the Hertz desk and followed it. When he reached the desk he handed his car voucher to a bright, cheerful girl who welcomed him to Scotland. She keyed-in the voucher number into her computer, and asked him for his driving licence. He handed her both his licence and passport. Seeing that his passport was of Turkish issue, the girl smiled and said that she'd been to Turkey on holiday a year ago, to a place called Side, adding in her friendly Glaswegian tongue, 'it was brilliant so it was.' Ali Ciddiqui intending not to get into conversation, said he'd never been there, and bluntly asked if he could have the car as quickly as possible as he had a journey to make that evening. The girl's smile temporarily vanished as she set about completing the paperwork, although a little less cheerfully. Spotting on her computer that the car was due to be returned by Mr Taleb to Hertz at Newcastle Airport she said, 'Sir there's a supplement for returning the car to Newcastle Airport. I have to ask you if you're aware of that?'

'Yes, yes I am,' Ciddiqui growled back, adding impatiently. 'Look, just give me the papers to sign, I don't want to be here all night.'

'It's my job to advise you of any additional charges Sir,' she said keeping a smile on her face as she passed the paperwork across the desk. She'd be pleased to see the back of this one she thought.

Ciddiqui signed the paperwork and took his copy together with the car keys. The girl then directed him to the Hertz Hire Car compound outside the terminal building, telling him that the car was a silver Mondeo, and wished him a nice visit. When he found the hired car, Ali Ciddiqui put his luggage in the boot, hung up his jacket and climbed in. He left the open map on the passenger seat before heading off in the general direction of the M8 motorway towards Greenock. After five or ten minutes the motorway split and he followed a sign to the M898 that brought him to a toll point. He paid the charge and drove across a towering bridge spanning a river. From the map Ciddiqui saw it was the River Clyde. Again, as he crossed the bridge, he was struck by the vivid green background of the hills on the north side of the river. As he came off the bridge, he took the A82 lane, the West Highland Highway to Crianlarich. He drove a further thirty kilometres or so before joining the A81 to Aberfoyle, arriving ten minutes later. The journey had taken him just under an hour. He needed to find a hotel, and spotted a sign to the Covenanters Plaza Hotel and which he followed. The hotel was located on the edge of the small town. He parked, went in and asked if he could have a room for two nights.

'No problem Sir. We can do that for you,' the receptionist replied enthusiastically. She handed Ali Ciddiqui a registration card saying, 'If you would just complete this for me, Sir, I'll get you organised.' She continued her cheerful conversation with him as she completed the reservation details on her computer, asking if he'd come up to Scotland on business or pleasure? Before he had the chance to reply, she added that she hoped he'd also have time to take in some of the local scenery during his stay. Ciddiqui muttered a reply, not wishing to get into any conversation. He filled in the card, and handed it back. The girl gave him his room key, and told a younger female colleague who'd joined her to take Mr Taleb to his room.

'Nice to have you with us Mr Taleb, and I hope you enjoy your stay. Karen here will take you up to your room. If you need anything else just give Reception a call on zero. We're here to help at any time,' she said. The younger woman then led Ciddiqui to a medium sized room on the first floor. He unpacked the few things he'd brought with him, and lay down on the high, extremely soft bed for a few minutes to gather his thoughts. He glanced at his watch and saw that it was five to five. He hadn't eaten since breakfast having refused the *Deli Bag* offered to him on the Shuttle. He also became aware that since receiving the document from Colonel Safa earlier that morning, his appetite had been subdued. He called Room Service and ordered an early dinner. He needed to think quietly before he making contact with the first of the operators. He ran a bath, soaked in it ten minutes or so, and came out just as there was a knock on his door.

'Room Service,' a male voice said.

'Just a moment,' Ciddiqui shouted as he pulled on his dressing gown. He opened the door and allowed the waiter to bring the trolley into his room. He signed for the meal and gave the young man two, one-pound coins, closing the door behind him. His appetite had returned. He ate hungrily. Opening the Colonel's briefing document, he concentrated on the plan. He'd make a telephone call to the first contact at 1830hrs precisely, a pre-arranged time when the operators would be at their contact number. Again he read the instructions for the meeting. This would be the initial phase of the plan, to take place at the designated locations of *Alpha+Beta*. It would involve two operators, one named Hamid Pasha, and the other Mohammed Bejyi, both currently employed as waiters at the Beneagles Hotel, forty-five kilometres or so from Aberfoyle. He checked his watch, and then dialled the number.

After two short rings a male voice answered, 'Hello?'

'Is that Hamid Pasha?' Ciddiqui asked.

'Speaking.'

'Mr Pasha, good to speak to you. Now listen,' Ciddiqui paused before adding, '*Ma Ma, Fi Kul Makaan,*' the password the operators would recognise.

'Who's speaking?' Pasha asked, his voice taking on a more questioning tone.

'*Ma Ma, Fi Kul Makaan,*' Ciddiqui repeated slowly.

A few seconds silence at the other end, then the man replied saying he was overcome with excitement to hear those words. Ali Ciddiqui let the man continue for a moment or two, then interrupted, 'I understand your keenness to serve Allah but now you must listen to what I have to say. We will meet tomorrow. At the Trossachs Pier car park, near Loch Catrine. Do you know where that is Mr Pasha?' Ciddiqui asked, pronouncing the *h* in Loch as *k*.

'Yes, yes I do.'

'Good. We'll meet at three-thirty and enjoy a sail on the Loch. I will tell you news of your family. Do you understand me Mr Pasha? Is that clear?'

Pasha said he did, and that he looked forward to the meeting. Ali Ciddiqui closed the conversation, and both men in their national manner, wished each other a pleasant night of undisturbed sleep.

Ciddiqui spent the next few hours studying the map and the terrain around the targeted areas. Early tomorrow morning he'd visit the targeted locations *Alpha+Beta.* He switched on the TV and tried to relax, but found that he couldn't concentrate. He undressed and went to bed. As he switched off his bedside lamp he saw that it was approaching ten-thirty, and for the first time in many hours, his thoughts focused on Abdullah Kadri. His instructions would be coming to a conclusion shortly.

'Imbecile! You could've jeopardised the entire plan,' he muttered pulling the duvet up around him. Angry or not, he was asleep within a few minutes.

At twenty-past one in the morning as Ciddiqui slept soundly in his warm, soft bed, Abdullah Kadri, six hundred and eighty kilometres south in Islington, had just finished working at *Fred's* restaurant. He'd collected the rubbish from the usual places, and stacked it behind the *Fire Escape* door in the basement for removal in the morning. Going out the back door he pulled it closed behind him. He started to climb up the steps to street level but never made it. Halfway up his head was fiercely pulled back by his own hair, and his throat was quickly cut from ear to ear. The only sound was Kadri drowning in his own blood now flowing freely from his fatal wound, as it mixed with the last of the air in his lungs.

Ali Ciddiqui awoke early, showered and ordered black coffee. He opened his heavy curtains. It was a beautiful morning, with just a touch of early morning mist hanging in the chilled, spring air. He was feeling good, the night's rest having refreshed him.

There was a knock on his door, 'Room Service!'

He unlocked the door and opened it.

'Good morning Sir,' the young girl said, carrying a copy of the *Herald* newspaper and small pot of coffee into the room.

Ciddiqui grunted a reply as he stood by the door till she'd found a place to put the pot down. As she bent down to place it on a low table he enjoyed the view of the girl's youthful body, and the line of her underwear showing clearly through her service uniform.

His lustful thoughts were jarred when she asked, 'Is thur anythin else a can da fur ye Sir? Ur ye sure ye'd no like some toast an at?'

Ciddiqui smiled, eventually working out what she'd said.

'No, that's fine thank you,' he replied, his eyes remaining on her as she left the room. Ali Ciddiqui was beginning to miss his Personal Assistant, Hala Najid, who apart from looking after his secretarial requirements also satisfied his other manly needs. He drank two cups of the hot, watery coffee, and glanced at the newspaper. The newspaper it seemed found nothing more important in the wider world than that of the new status of the *Loch Lomond and the Trossachs National Park*. He threw the paper aside, and put on the casual clothes he'd brought with him. He looked at the map again, following the route to, *Location Alpha*. He'd calculated it would be a short drive, eighteen kilometres or so. Picking up what he needed, he left the room, and put the *Do Not Disturb* notice on the door handle. It was ten past nine as he went downstairs, and as he passed Reception he said, 'I'll be back early this evening. Would you make sure my room remains undisturbed.'

'Don't you want your room serviced Sir?'

'No, don't bother,' Ciddiqui said abruptly.

The girl smiled and told him to enjoy his day. Mr Taleb was proving a difficult customer she thought as her telephone rang.

She picked it up and automatically responded, 'Covenanters Plaza Hotel. Tracey speaking, can I help you?'

Ali Ciddiqui reversed out of the car park, then drove off towards the centre of Aberfoyle a short distance away. He needed to buy heavy walking shoes, and some waterproof clothing. A few minutes later he pulled over and parked in front of a large *All Weather Clothing* store. Going in he said to the nearest sales assistant, 'I'd like to buy a pair of heavy walking boots please.'

'OK Sir, what shoe size do you take?'

'A nine and a half.'

'Then I'd say you'd take a ten in walking boots Sir, as you'll be wearing a thick pair of socks with them. Put these on,' the girl said, handing Ciddiqui a pair of dark green, woollen socks. 'I'll get your size from our stockroom Sir. Won't be a minute.'

She returned soon with the boots that Ciddiqui put on and walked across the carpeted floor. They felt cumbersome and inflexible.

'They're fine. I'll take them, and you'd better give me a pair of the socks as well. I also need a waterproof jacket and trousers. My size is large.'

'We've a good price on these Barbour jackets Sir, and I can give you a matching pair of waterproof trousers,' the girl offered as she lifted a jacket off a long rail of hanging clothes. 'Go through to the fitting room over there and try it on.'

'If they're large they'll fit. Just give me the bill for all of these things, the jacket and trousers as well. Would you hurry please?'

'Fine Sir, but are you sure you don't want to try the jacket and trousers on before you go. It's really the best way you know,' the girl advised.

'Just get them for me and the bill, or do I have to go somewhere else?'

'OK Sir, just come this way,' the girl replied, carrying the clothes Ciddiqui had just bought as she made her way towards a cash register to make up the bill.

'How would you like to pay Sir?'

'Cash,' Ciddiqui retorted.

'Fine Sir,' she said cheerfully, trying to lighten the gloom that had taken over the transaction with her customer.

Ciddiqui ignore the girl's gesture, and seeing the amount of one hundred and fourteen pounds displayed on the register, handed over six twenty pound notes. He lifted the goods the girl had put into a large plastic bag, collected his change and left the store.

As the door closed behind him, the girl said to one of her colleagues, 'What a miserable faced customer he turned out to be. Some o' these tourists think they own the place, don't they. Cheek! Anyway he spent more than a hundred pounds - that's no bad fur this time in the morning. It gets my sales bonus up for the week, which is brilliant.'

'Aye you're lucky - at least he did spend some money,' her colleague replied, 'most o'them tourists come in and only look.'

Soon the girls went back to fixing the racks, generally trying to keep busy till their coffee break, and the early, rude customer was quickly forgotten.

Ciddiqui put his purchases into the back of his car, checked to make sure he was heading in the right direction and drove off towards Loch Catrine: *Location Alpha* in the plan. He'd calculated that it would take him around twenty minutes on the single-track road from Aberfoyle. Twenty-one minutes later, after an uneventful, though bumpy drive, he parked at the edge of Loch Catrine, under a sign that stated *Stronachlachar Pier*. He got out and walked to the edge of the pier, looking out across the water. The beauty and silence of the place stunned him as he stood there in the stillness, the feeling of being alone in the world surrounding him. From the document he knew that a small steam ship, the S.S. Sir Walter Burns, called regularly at the pier, but he also was aware that the ship wasn't due at the pier till nearer midday. The ship, one hundred years old, apparently the last of its kind in Britain to sail on fresh water, retained its original engine of a design ahead of its time. For some unexplained reason, he looked forward to sailing on it later that day. As he looked at the vast expanse of pure water, Ciddiqui knew that Loch Catrine provided most of the drinking water to Glasgow, Scotland's largest city, as well as a large part of the West and Central parts of Scotland. It had done so for over one hundred and fifty years. Queen Victoria, the late, great grandmother of the present Queen, had performed the opening ceremony a short distance away from where he now stood. The spot was near the Loyal Cottage, a typical solid; Victorian building constructed purely for the occasion, a photograph of which had been incorporated into the document.

Huge water sluices about two kilometres from the pier were also part of that complex. The sluices at Loyal Cottage had been designated *Location Alpha*. Ciddiqui opened the document at the section dealing with this phase of the plan. He saw that 4.3 cubic meters/second, up to one hundred million gallons of water every day, were taken from the loch to supply Glasgow and other areas with drinking water. He marvelled at the quantity. One hundred million gallons! From the sluices, the water travelled forty-two kilometres south, before being discharged into the Mugdoch and Craigmaddy reservoirs in Millguy on the outskirts of Glasgow. Those reservoirs were designated *Location Beta* in the plan. He looked around, still in many ways overwhelmed, and impressed by the grand scale of the civil engineering works all around him. Going back to the car, he changed into his boots and waterproof jacket, then walked along the track close to the water's edge towards Loyal Cottage. After a few minutes he spotted the building. As he approached it, the track cut inland towards a stone-built tower. Ciddiqui had read that the tower was the airshaft of the outgoing aqueducts, and those two tunnels, one 2.4m and the other 3.0m in diameter, passed directly beneath him. The tunnels drew water from the Loch, carrying it towards the *Frenik Control Chamber* two kilometres away, and from there to Millguy forty kilometres further south. He heard them before he saw them, the sound of the rushing water increasing with his each step towards the sluices. When he reached them he looked down into the frothing, turbulent water in the draw-off basins, and knew instantly that the operators would find no difficulty putting the HCN into them. Again he was surprised by the lack of any visual security or protection. Nothing, apart from a single wooden sign on which it stated, *Private Keep Out*. Nothing else. He grunted, thinking that the infidels would live to regret it. From the document he'd read that the water from Loch Catrine was considered to be so pure that treatment at source wasn't considered necessary. Security it seemed was considered to be similar he thought, as he looked around and shook his head in disbelief. Even the surfaced track leading to the draw-off points was unrestricted. When he was completely satisfied that the operators would have no problems implementing the plan, he went back to the pier. He checked his watch. Fifteen minutes to eleven. Feeling on top of things he got back into his car and drove off to his next destination: *Location Beta*, the reservoirs at Millguy on the outskirts of Glasgow. As he drove away from Loch Catrine on the winding, twisting and narrow roadway, he recalled reading that the twin reservoirs in Millguy, when full held six million cubic meters of water, the equivalent of twelve days' water supply for Glasgow. He was thinking how lucky Glasgow was to have that amount of pure water available, when suddenly a van travelling at high speed came round a bend straight at him. He swerved, avoiding a head-on collision by no more than a few centimetres, before skidding into the ditch at the side of the narrow road. As the blue van went past, and now disappeared around a bend behind him, he'd caught sight of the name displayed on the side, *West of Scotia Water.* Cursing as he got out, still shaking from the ordeal, he said softly, 'Allah has preserved me for greater things.' When he'd got himself together again, he got back into the car, reversed out of the ditch back onto the narrow road with some difficulty, before heading towards Millguy. Twenty-five minutes later he approached the village from the north, and noted on his map that the reservoirs were now positioned high above him on his right. Again he was struck by the apparent lack of protection and security, as in a number of places he saw open gates leading directly to the reservoirs off the public roadway. Cars were parked on the grass verge at the side of the roadway, the occupants obviously able to, and had accessed the area around the reservoirs. A few hundred metres further on, he pulled up alongside two women who were standing at one of the gated entrances to the reservoirs. The gate was locked he noticed by a simply domestic padlock and chain.

Putting the window down he asked in a pleasant voice, 'Excuse me, how do I get into the grounds around the reservoirs?'

Both women replied at once, anxious to help a stranger. He gathered from what they said that all he had to do was continue on from where he now was, turn right at the top of the roadway, and on his right, he'd come to a vehicle entrance to the whole area.

'You can then just drive in and park,' one of the women helpfully added.

'You'll see the offices when you get up to the top of the hill once you've gone through the gates,' the other contributed.

Ciddiqui smiled and thanked them, then drove off as directed. He spotted the gates the woman had mentioned, and an adjacent notice board, marked *Water Authority Vehicles Only.* Carrying on as the women had suggested, and ignoring the sign, he was prepared to pretend that he'd missed it if questioned. Suddenly a blue van appeared at the top of the drive heading towards him. He stopped, flashing his lights at the van, and reversed back a few metres into a passing bay. The van quickly came down the track and as it passed, the driver waved his gratitude before speeding off. Ciddiqui noticed that the van had the same name on it as the one that had almost killed him less than an hour ago. He continued up the drive, and on reaching the top, was taken aback by the vast expanse of water that constituted Mugdoch and Craigmaddy Reservoirs before him. The view was impressive. He could see most of what was the City of Glasgow. On his left and right, he noticed some low, rectangular buildings, as well as a small Victorian building close to the water's edge of similar construction as that of Loyal Cottage. A sign directed him to the Visitors Car Park. He parked in the only available space. On the Victorian building a sign stating *Reception* was fixed on the main door. He went into the building, and stood at the unattended reception desk, the sounds of a chiming clock the only noise. He pressed a bell on the desk in front of him. The noise of the bell jarred the silent room. He waited a few moments, taking in the domestic ambience of the room. In Baghdad he thought, a facility of this type would've been heavily guarded, with no public access.

A young woman suddenly came into the room from an adjacent office. 'Good morning Sir, can I help you?' she asked in a quiet, European dialect.

'Good morning,' Ciddiqui said back, smiling confidently at the woman. 'I hope you can - you see I'm from Turkey, visiting Scotland on holiday, and I'm most interested in the wonderful waterworks I see all around your lovely country. This morning I went to visit the beautiful Lake Catrine. It is so beautiful.'

'Yes it is, I think so too,' the woman replied softly, smiling back at Ali Ciddiqui.

'That is the place, Lake Catrine, where all the water here, in these reservoirs, comes from I understand?' Ciddiqui asked acting the slightly naive tourist.

'That's correct, but in Scotland we don't call these large areas of water lakes, they're called lochs. The Scots are, how you say?' she said trying for the right word, 'touchy about it.'

'Ah yes lochs, not lakes. I will remember that.' Ciddiqui looked around the desk in front of him and asked, 'Do you have any publications you can give me that tells the story of these wonderful waterworks? How they were built? For example, how is the water treated before it is fed into the water pipes to serve the public? You see I also work with the water in Turkey, my homeland.'

The woman nodded, then frowned, 'Um, we used to have some details like that. Hold on one moment Sir and I'll see if I can find you something.' She went to the back of the room and searched through a dusty pile of books and other papers lying on a table. 'Yes here it is, it's the last one we have I think,' she said returning to the desk. 'We're having new books printed shortly I'm told, but you can have this old one, and nothing much will have changed over the years I'm sure.

'Thank you so much,' Ciddiqui enthused as he took the book. 'I'll have much enjoyment from this. Thank you so much,' he said, looking at the book titled, *'Water Supply from Loch Catrine to Glasgow and environs.'* He opened the book and saw that it contained a scale map of the infrastructure of the complete network of the water supply and line of aqueducts. How much more foolish can they get, he thought?

'It's my pleasure,' the woman said, smiling pleasantly at Ciddiqui, 'and if you'd like you can take a walk around the reservoirs. It's a nice day, and such a beautiful place,' she added.

'Can I?'

'Yes, all our facilities are open to the public,' the girl said proudly.

'How wonderful, that is wonderful,' Ciddiqui replied, then adding, 'I'll do that, thank you.'

As he left the stuffy, overheated old building, he noticed that the other buildings on his right were much newer, and appeared to be equipment and control rooms. He followed a sign leading him in the direction of the reservoirs. From the document he'd read that water taken through the drawn-off towers was un-treated due to its inherent purity. Now, standing at the edge of the reservoirs he could see why. The water was crystal clear. He examined the approaches to the towers, and decided that the best route for the operators would be from the other side of the reservoirs, the tree-lined shore some two hundred metres to the north, where they would be concealed until the last moment. After he'd walked all the way around one of the reservoirs, a distance of two and a half kilometres, he decided he'd seen enough to know that the operation could go ahead as planned.

He returned to his car and drove out of the complex the way he'd come in. Again no one approached him, or even appeared to notice that he was there. Going back towards Aberfoyle, his mind was absorbed in the details of what he had just seen. Security was lax; it was he thought, a disaster waiting to happen. Shortly he arrived back at Aberfoyle, which was a busier place than it had been earlier in the day. He drove through the town, this time taking the twisting, bumpy road, up into the hills, and sign posted *The Trossachs and Loch Catrine Pier*. As he drove he passed a noticed stating; *You are now Entering Queen Elizabeth Forest Park*. Ciddiqui laughed, marvelling at the perception and planning of *Ma Ma, Fi Kul Makaan*. He was going to strike at the very centre of the lands named after the British Queen. He checked his watch. It was almost three o'clock. He'd have time to park, and find a place to wait and watch the operators arrive at the car park. After a few more minutes he spotted a road sign to *The Trossachs*, and he drove towards a long, narrow car park. At the pay booth he handed a one-pound coin to the attendant who instructed him to drive further up the car park, and park near the pier entrance. He did so, got out of the car, locked it and crossed over to another Victorian building that housed the *Trossachs Tea Room*. Going inside, he climbed some stairs and took a seat at a window facing back out towards the car park. The night before during the telephone conversation with Pasha, the man had said they'd be driving a dark green Range Rover, with a small Turkish flag displayed on the windscreen. Knowing he'd have no difficulty spotting the vehicle from where he now sat, Ciddiqui ordered tea, and waited.

Ten or fifteen minutes later Ciddiqui spotted an old classic two door, dark green Range Rover entering the car park. The driver paid the attendant, parked and both he and his passenger climbed out. The men walked to the pier entrance and stood together facing the parked cars. Ciddiqui studied them carefully, aware that they were both in their early thirties, and appeared to be strong and fit young men. He paid for his tea although he'd hardly touched it, went downstairs and crossed the car park, walking towards the men.

As he got within hailing distance he shouted, 'Hello my friends, how are you both? Did you have a good drive down?'

The men turned, a little surprised, then nodded, but before they could say anything Ciddiqui added, '*Ma Ma, Fi Kul Makaan.*'

Taken aback by Ciddiqui's sudden arrival, the taller of the two men, Hamid Pasha, managed to shake hands a little too vigorously before saying, 'It's good to see you too. I'm Hamid Pasha.' The other man smiled and nodded his head as if he too was glad to see Ali Ciddiqui. Ciddiqui knew both their names and identities from his notes and photographs.

'Our sailing trip, the one I promised you, well the boat leaves shortly,' Ciddiqui said, indicating that it was time to move on. 'I'll collect the tickets. You wait here.' Ciddiqui went to the pier ticket office and asked for three tickets for the next trip.

'You'll have to hurry Sir,' the ticket attendant stated, 'the Walter Burns is about to leave in a few minutes, and that'll be it fur the day. Get on board now if you don't want left behind.'

Taking the tickets and his change, he waved to the other two men to come and join him. All three then climbed the gangway to the small, colourful ship, the aged S.S. Sir Walter Burns. The boat, no more than a third full, left the pier a few minutes later on its one hour round trip of Loch Catrine.

'Sit here,' Ciddiqui instructed the two men, motioning towards two or three rows of empty seats at the stern of the ship. The men sat down casually, and remained silent for a few minutes while they took in the scenery as the boat made its way out into the wider expanses of the loch.

'The water is so clear. I've read that the quality is so good that it only requires a primary filter to remove leaves, bits of trees and other things before you can drink it. I wish we had water like that at home, don't you my friends?'

The men nodded slowly in agreement, looking all around them.

'Water, water, every where, nor any drop to drink,' Hamid Pasha replied, laughing aloud at his own joke.

Ciddiqui smiled, although the smile never got beyond his mouth. He opened up the large photographic bag he'd carried with him, taking out a heavy brown envelope, marked *Location Alpha+Beta*.

'Your instructions,' he said, passing it to Hamid Pasha. 'Make yourselves familiar with all of them as there can be no mistakes. You'll get sufficient notice to allow you to prepare for your actions. Remember the locations and timings are critical to the success of the plan. You must also fully understand the physical and technical difficulties involved. We demand total commitment from you, and expect nothing less than total success. Ciddiqui paused, then added, 'I'm sure you understand the consequences of failure?' allowing the last few words to hang in the air.

The two men nodded sombrely, the laughter and frivolity no longer evident on their faces.

Pasha stiffened up before replying for both men. 'You can be sure of our commitment. It is with honour and pride that we serve. We'll succeed, have no fear. We are only too anxious to get started, the need for action has been building up for too long.'

Ciddiqui again smiled, and in a more friendly tone added, 'The plan is very simple but ingenious. The consequences are beyond your wildest imagination.' He glancing around to make sure that they were still not being overheard. 'All the instructions you need are defined in the document I've just given to you. The prime action is to discharge the chemical substance, let us call it *The Juice of Allah*. Discharge it into the draw-off sluices from this loch. You will find the sluices adjacent to the Loyal Cottage by the side of the loch, which I'll point out to you when we sail past them shortly. The sluices are your targets. This chemical substance when mixed with water at the entry point to the sluices, will transform into a deadly, highly poisonous acid, and will be sucked into the sluices and piped to the holding reservoirs in Millguy outside Glasgow. Don't worry about all these names; there are maps in abundance showing these locations in the document. Everything you need is contained in your instructions, which you can read later.' He paused allowing the men to digest what he'd told them so far. He then continued, 'A few minutes after you discharge *The Juice of Allah* into the sluices, the polluted water will then pass through a number of control chambers on its way to the reservoirs at the next target location, *Location Beta*. The engineers who operate these chambers may or may not detect that the water quality in the mains between the chamber and Loch Catrine has gone outwith the normal parameters of their quality control system. If they do, then alarm bells will begin to ring, and they'll make the quick assumption that the entire supply of water from Loch Catrine to the reservoirs has been contaminated. The only action available to them at that time, and before the polluted water reaches the reservoirs in Millguy, will be to shut down the main supply from Loch Catrine. As a consequence, they'll leave the Glasgow relying on the water already stored at Millguy in the two holding reservoirs.' Ciddiqui paused again and looked at the two men sitting opposite him. He added, 'If they don't detect the quality change it won't matter, it'll save them some heartache that's all.' He then continued, 'In normal circumstances that wouldn't be a problem, as the quantity of water in the two reservoirs can serve Glasgow for up to twelve days without any make-up from Loch Catrine. So our action would appear to be a mere inconvenience you might reasonably think, and something that their sophisticated equipment, and engineers, would put right very quickly.'

'May I ask a question?' Pasha said.

Ciddiqui nodded.

'Surely they'd close down the water supply to the reservoirs from the loch, then drain off the contaminated water in the mains between the Loch and Millguy. They could then simply reopen the supply to the reservoirs when they've established that the water is no longer polluted. That shouldn't be too difficult, should it?' Pasha asked, a puzzled frown on his face.

Ali Ciddiqui smiled at Pasha, 'Of course they can, and they might think that is all they've got to do. No doubt in the past they've done that perhaps as a result of their own mistakes, who knows? But knowing the British mind, they'll want to know what caused the water to be contaminated in the first instance. It's their nature. They'll call out the police, and their armed forces. This area will be swamped by hordes of the infidels looking for someone to blame. Yes, they may close down the supply from Loch Catrine to Millguy the instant their sophisticated computer systems tell them to, thinking that they've plenty of time to sort out the problem. The public wouldn't even be aware of it. The fact that they've got twelve days supply safely stored in the Millguy reservoirs is what they'd count on. Twelve days to sort it out, wouldn't you think that way?' Lowering his voice yet again he continued, 'But that won't happen, and the reason it won't happen is that you'll give them a second problem to handle, a much bigger and immediate problem. That is the spark of genius behind the plan, the trigger to its very success if you like. You see you'll repeat what you did at Loch Catrine, only this time you'll do it at *Location Beta:* the reservoirs in Millguy.' The men listened as Ciddiqui elaborated the cunning deception of the plan, and laughingly he said, '...the earliest the infidels will know about the second problem will be when they hear about thousands of people dying after drinking water from their water taps, water from their precious, safe Millguy reservoirs. A mouthful of the water, or simply cleaning their teeth using water from their taps will be enough. When news of the first deaths becomes public, and there will be thousands who'll die very quickly, the authorities and the police won't be able to keep it quiet. Water will be declared undrinkable in all of Glasgow. No one will touch it. Panic will set in. The entire public water supply will then be shut off, depriving the infidels of the most precious commodity they took for granted all of their filthy lives. Bodies will be found everywhere, in houses, streets, cars, and most of them in Millguy and Beersden, the so-called wealthy suburbs of Glasgow. It will cause alarm on a massive scale, and be worldwide news within the hour. Iraq will hear of our success, and you'll be honoured my friends. A million people without water of any kind, panic and fear on a grand scale, and civil unrest like never before. It will cause the structure of their society to crumble and fall around them. No one will feel safe at home, and by the early hours of the morning people will have taken to the streets. They'll demand action from their blundering authorities. But nothing will happen because they'll be too busy collecting the dead and the dying.'

Ali Ciddiqui looked at the two men of whom much was expected. He continued saying; 'The fools will be deceived into thinking that the water in Loch Catrine, and in the holding reservoirs at Millguy is all contaminated. By the time they can prove otherwise, they'll be dealing with chaos and unrest on a vast scale. Bodies will be piled high in hastily arranged mortuaries. Uncontaminated water, bottled water in supermarkets, bars and restaurants, water in streams, anywhere where it hasn't already been taken forcibly by the desperate public, will then be commandeered by the police and army.' Ciddiqui smiled, 'Water will then be as precious as gold - only more so. You can live without gold, but you cannot live long without water.' Ciddiqui rose to his feet and stood by the rail at the stern of the ship. His eyes were moist with emotion. 'How ingenious of our leaders who have prepared this plan. The British and the Americans, those who have deprived us of our rightful possession of our lands, such people deserve to die. We can serve Allah, and by bringing this action into being Allah will be blessed by the countless deaths of the infidels, and Iraq by the chance to taste cold, sweet, revenge.'

Only the smooth sounds of the small ship cutting through the calm waters of Loch Catrine broke the silence that now surrounded the men. Hamid Pasha took it upon himself to respond. 'Allah be praised,' he whispered, bowing his head in reverence, a gesture that his colleague, Mohammed Bejyi silently repeated.

What Ali Ciddiqui had omitted to tell the two men as he described a stark picture of success, was the fact that they too would die within a few hours of carrying out their actions. The inhalation of the fumes given off when they discharged *The Juice of Allah* into the water at both locations would see to that. He visualised that they'd probably be driving away from Millguy when they'd become violently sick, and their deaths would follow quickly afterwards. When their bodies were eventually discovered, probably in their crashed car, they'd be treated as just another two victims of water poisoning. Such a clean way of disposing of the evidence he thought. At that moment the S.S. Sir Walter Burns swung around on the return leg of the short cruise, and brought Ciddiqui back to the present. Looking towards the near shore, he pointed to a Victorian building at the water's edge. 'That's Loyal Cottage: that's *Location Alpha.*'

The men silently stared at the building, which was surrounded by dense, dark green shrubbery. 'And that stone wall that you can see marks the position of the sluices,' he added.

A minute went past as the men studied the location in silence. Pasha finally asked, 'What about security? Is the facility fenced off?'

'There is none, and there are no fences. They are fools I tell you. You'll have no problem. They take everything for granted, especially their precious water.'

The men remained silent as the ship steadily sailed past their first target.

'When you have finished at *Location Alpha*, you must then drive quickly to *Location Beta* in Millguy outside Glasgow. Again you'll have no difficulties getting into the complex. You'll need a small inflatable boat to transport *The Juice of Allah* precisely alongside the submerged draw-off tower in the reservoir.' He looking at each man in turn, 'As I've said, you must be precise otherwise it will have minimum effect, a few deaths, but not nearly enough to make the plan a success. There is no point discharging the liquid into the

52

wider expanse of the reservoir, as it would quickly become diluted. It must be discharged directly into the draw-off tower. Do you understand that, it is of major importance?'

Both men nodded in agreement.

Hamid Pasha asked nervously, 'When do we begin?'

'Patience my friend,' Ciddiqui replied, 'this is not a single, individual action. Our advisers have co-ordinated nation-wide strikes throughout Britain. Your instructions will tell you all you need to know. How to get to the targets, everything. Read them carefully. They'll also tell you where you'll pick-up *The Juice of Allah*, the HCN. Everything you need to know, and to succeed is in them.'

Mohammed Bejyi spoke for the first time, more a statement than anything else. He said, 'We won't fail. You have our word on that. Praise be to Allah.'

Ciddiqui looked hard at the man. 'You had better not, because remember this and remember it well. If you do, we will find you, in the driest of deserts, the wettest rainforest, or the most populated of cities. There will be no hiding places, no hiding place at all if you fail.' Ciddiqui then added, 'Be well aware that the date and time of your actions are arranged to coincide with others elsewhere. That is a key requirement of the plan. At precisely midnight on the chosen date you act. No sooner, and no later. Is that fully understood?'

'When will we know that date?' Bejyi asked.

'Buy *The Times* newspaper each day. Look in the *Personal Columns.* Soon I assure you, the words *Water, Water Everywhere* will appear, and a date will be stated. You strike on the midnight hour of that date, and as I've already said, not sooner, and not later. That date and time has been chosen carefully to cause most confusion, and with it more deaths. As soldiers of Allah, go forth now and prepare. Everything has been thought through for your protection, and your ultimate safe return to Iraq where you'll be welcomed back as heroes.'

The two young men fell into their own silent thoughts for remained of the boat trip. Eventually all three men rose to their feet and made towards the middle of the ship, where Ali Ciddiqui professed keen interest on the efficient, non-polluting, marine engine cooling system. When the small ship was skilfully berthed alongside Trossachs Pier, Ciddiqui shook hands with the two men and wished them well. As they parted he said that in case of an emergency, then they should put a notice in *The Times,* using the location code names Alpha+Beta, and he'd contact them. They separated in the car park, with Pasha and Bejyi climbing back into their old Range Rover then driving off. Ali Ciddiqui waited a few minutes before he too drove back to his hotel in Aberfoyle.

CHAPTER TEN

Commander Chris Hall left his home, a semi-detached house in Mitcham, South London, at six in the morning to drive to Scotland Yard.

Hall, tall, dark and 'drop dead gorgeous' in the eyes of his female colleagues at the Yard, was thirty-five years old, and he and his wife Amanda had two children, Emma and Gregory, aged six and three respectively. He had reached the rank of Commander in the Metropolitan Police twelve months ago, having previously graduated at the University of the South Bank, taking a degree in Management Studies. He had then added an MA in Business Studies, before joining The Met ten years ago. He had progressed quickly through the ranks, and was well liked by his colleagues, both those below and above him. In the Met's Sports Club, where his main sporting interest was squash, his natural sporting talent was admired and envied by more than a few of his colleagues.

Hall arrived at the Yard just before six-thirty, and went to his office. He glanced at the department bulletin board as he went past, which had been up-dated a few minutes before. He read through a list of incidents that had taken place overnight, thinking it was the usual things. Nothing changed much from night to night in London. The last item caught his eye. A male found dead in the early hours of the morning in Islington. A life was a life after all. From what he read he thought it was probably drug related. He carried on to his office. The digitised photographs were lying on his desk. He knew the photographs would've been circulated to all stations in the metropolitan area by now. They clearly showed the face of the man who was in the park the morning the birdlife had been poisoned. As he studied them he thought at least they could now identify the man, if they could trace his whereabouts. He put the photographs in his out basket and picked up the case file to read the updates. The phone rang, and he got caught up in a series of calls regarding a forthcoming pro-al-Qaeda demonstration outside Downing Street. The morning passed quickly, and he was beginning to think of an early lunch when his telephone rang again. It was the Desk Sergeant at Tolpuddle Street Police Station, Islington. It seemed that the station had filed a report on the death of a male, and wished to discuss the matter with him. The sergeant asked Hall to hold; adding that he'd be putting him through to his Chief Inspector, John Hamilton.

''Commander Hall?'

'Good morning Chief Inspector, what can I do for you?'

'Sir I understand you're handling the St James's Park case, the poisoning of the birdlife?'

'For my sins I've got myself immersed in the case you might say. What can I do for you Chief Inspector?' Hall asked.

'Well I may have something of interest for you Sir,' Hamilton replied a little excitedly. 'You'll no doubt have read about the murder in Islington early this morning?'

'Yes I did see it on the bulletin when I came in.'

'It was one of my men who found the body. A male, in his early thirties as far as we can guess. The body was discovered in an external basement at the rear of a restaurant,' Hamilton stated flatly.

'Go on Chief Inspector.'

'Anyway Sir,' Hamilton continued, 'the constable called in and we immediately arranged for *Forensics* to provide the usual murder scene set-up, the caravan, the whole set-up. The constable remained on the scene until everything was in place Sir. Apparently the deceased's fatal injuries were all to the throat Sir. Horrible sight I'm told.'

'We've all seen them more than once I'm sure Chief Inspector,' Hall said, wishing Hamilton would get on with it.

'Well yes. Anyway as a result of being there so long it seems my constable took particular note of the deceased's facial details, more than usual that is, Sir. He came back to the station a short time ago. Couldn't sleep, he says, for thinking about the murder. Needs therapy he thinks. I suspect he's hinting at getting a few days off if you ask me Sir. Anyway when he came back he saw that photograph on our bulletin board. The one of the man in St James's Park that's just been circulated. Well, Sir, he thinks, my constable that is, he thinks the deceased maybe one and the same man.'

'Where is the deceased at this time Chief Inspector?'

'Forensics have apparently completed their primary work at the murder scene Sir, and the body was taken to the mortuary at University College Hospital, Gower Street, not too far from our station.' Before Hall could reply Hamilton added, 'I'm going there now Sir, would you like to join me?'

Hall was already standing at his desk, having risen from his seat during the telephone conversation. 'I'll meet you there in twenty minutes Hamilton,' he said lifting his jacket from the back of his chair, and going out his door.

'Lorna get me a car at the rear exit ASAP. I'm off to the University College Hospital, Gower Street. I should be back about two o'clock all being well. Will you be good and order me a toasted sandwich, whole-wheat bread and tuna. Just leave it on my desk; I'll get it when I come back. Would you also contact the Photographic Department? Tell them to send someone to meet me at the hospital mortuary, now, not in an hour's time.'

'Some people get all the good jobs. Do you think you'll still feel like eating a sandwich when you get back after that visit?

'You better get me a sick bag as well then,' he added with a grimace.

'Off you go. I'll have the car at the door when you get down there, and maybe David Bailey waiting for you at the hospital. Make sure you straighten your tie.'

Hall smiled as he went to the lift. Lorna McBride, his secretary had worked for him since his promotion, and was now beginning to know exactly how he operated. She seemed to know what he was going to do or say sometimes before he did. He was very comfortable with that. Going into the empty lift he pressed the -2 button in his stride. He then realised he'd forgotten to take a copy of the photograph of the man he left lying on his desk. When he got out of the lift he picked up an internal phone and called his secretary.

'I know. You've forgotten the photograph. I've sent someone down with it. I guess that's who you're hoping to see when you get to the mortuary?'

Hall laughed. 'I suppose you might as well handle this case as you seem to be one step ahead of me at the moment. Anyway thanks Lorna, I'll see you later. Don't forget the sandwich.'

The Lift door opened, and an office assistant handed him a large envelope, marked diagonally *PHOTOGRAPHS - DO NOT BEND.* He thanked the girl and made his way to the rear exit. The car was waiting for him. The driver, a sergeant from Traffic whom Hall knew by face only, stood at the rear door. Hall got into the car, and the driver said, more of a statement than a question, 'University College Hospital on Gower Street Sir. Correct?'

'Yes Sergeant,' Hall replied, 'and I'd like you to wait for me there. I don't intend to be too long.'

As he sat in the car, he wondered if the man in the photograph he had was that of the person now lying in the mortuary at the UCH? The traffic was heavy, and the driver used his knowledge of London's lesser-known back streets and lanes to get them from the Yard to the UCH in quick time. They soon pulled up in the ambulance bay and the sergeant jumped out.

'I'll be parked close by Sir,' the sergeant stated briskly, holding the rear door open.

Hall entered the main hospital building and went to the reception just inside the doorway.

'Can I help you Sir?' the black receptionist asked.

'Good afternoon. My name's Hall, Commander Hall, Metropolitan Police, Scotland Yard. I've arranged to meet a Chief Inspector Hamilton. Can you tell me if he's arrived yet?'

'Yes Commander he has. He said to send you down to the mortuary when you got here. If you follow the signs you'll have no problem finding it,' the woman said, indicating the overhead signboard. Hall thanked her, and went off in the direction the woman had pointed. He saw the sign to the mortuary and followed it. It led him outside to a separate small building with frosted glass windows that didn't appear to have been cleaned for years. He went in and found himself in another reception area. Voices could be heard on the other side of a door. Hall knocked. A voice replied, 'Come on in if you can stand the sight of blood.'

Opening the door he went into a cold room.

The voice turned out to be that of the Resident Pathologist who continued speaking as Hall came into the room. 'The victim died within a few seconds of the fatal wounds to his throat. It's the deepest cut I've seen of this type in a long time Chief Inspector.'

'Ah, Commander Hall,' said the policeman standing alongside the Pathologist. 'Chief Inspector John Hamilton,' he said, then added, 'and this is the Resident Pathologist at the UCH, Dr Bill White,' turning to the green-attired and rubber-booted figure standing next to him.

'Good to meet you Commander,' White replied, shaking Hall's hand. Hall noticed that the man's hand was icy cold.

Hamilton continued, 'Dr White's just finished the PM on the body Sir.'

Hall looked at the pathologist.

'If you'd like to follow me gentlemen we can take a look at the body. I hope you're both ready for this; it's not the prettiest sight I've seen, but then they rarely ever are I find,' White said. He went through two more double doors, both policemen following slowly behind. They came into a large, cold room where the main feature was a centrally located marble table. The surfaces of the room, including the ceiling were hard and washable, and a large floor gully was positioned centrally beneath the table. White closed the doors and pressed a button on a wall mounted control panel. An electric motor buzzed noisily somewhere, and a drawer-like unit projected itself slowly from what looked like a giant filing cabinet. The buzzing ceased and the unit stopped, projecting two metres or so into the room.

'Well here's your man from Camden Passage - not that he'll be going back there again,' White said, removing a loose-fitting white sheet that covered the body.

Hall ignored the unnecessary insensitive comment, and looked at the dead man's face. He walked around the body to look from the other side. He took the photograph out of the envelope and compared the face. The resemblance was more than uncanny. It had to be the same man.

'Doctor have you shaved the face at all?'

'No, he'd no moustache, beard, anything like that; no earrings. My only difficulty dealing with him was to keep his head on his shoulders. You see the cut was so deep and long, there wasn't much left to keep him together Commander.'

Hall looked at the naked man. The head was now firmly back in place. Except for the dark brown cut across the throat, he looked as if he was asleep. There was a knock on the door. White repeated the response he'd made when Hall arrived, obviously his stock reply. The door opened tentatively, and a small, stocky built man came into the room, carrying a camera and other photographic equipment. The man introduced himself, and, unable to take his eyes off the dead body, asked Hall what was required by way of photographs.

'I'd like you to take a few close ups of the man's face,' Hall replied, positioning himself where he wanted the photographs taken from.

'Can do Sir; that's the easy part. It's developing the close ups in the dark room that'll be the hard bit,' the man said in an attempt at some black humour.

The men stood in uncomfortable silence for a few seconds. White spoke first. 'Well gentlemen, is there any more I can do for you, or have you seen enough? Mostly you see one you've seen them all. But this one it seems was caught by surprise. I've taken all the necessary details and samples. I'll send a copy of my report to Scotland Yard Commander, and to you too Chief Inspector. You should have it tomorrow, unless we get a run of these cases. Maybe business is looking up?' White said with a dry laugh.

Hall again ignored the man's attempt at humour. He thanked White for his time, and asked the photographer to have the photographs delivered to him as soon as possible, and to send two copies to Chief Inspector Hamilton. Hall and Hamilton left the building together, and made their way back to the main entrance. Neither spoke. When they got there, Hall thanked Hamilton, then added; 'We may have something after all Hamilton. I need to have the photographs analysed in a similar manner to the first one, then we'll see. Thanks again for your help, and please send me the name and number of the PC who spotted the similarity. That was good basic police work Chief Inspector.'

"I will Sir, I will. As it just happens Sir, the constable in question is assisting with the inquiry, and is continuing with the questioning of the restaurant staff at the scene of the incident as we speak. I'll tell him you were grateful for his good work Sir. It's maybe the therapy he needs, and it'll be good for his morale.'

Hall and Hamilton shook hands, the latter said that when the questioning of the restaurant staff was completed, he'd sent a copy of the report to Hall at Scotland Yard. The two policemen then went to their respective waiting cars.

CHAPTER ELEVEN

Keelder Water, situated in North-East England within Northumberland's North Tyne Valley, is one of the largest man-made lakes in northern Europe. It forms part of the United Kingdom's first example of a regional water grid. Water released from there supplies Tyneside, Wearside and Teesside, the latter over eighty miles away.

Ali Ciddiqui turned off the A68 just beyond Troughend, after spotting the sign to Bellingham, a small hamlet on the edge of the Northumberland National Park. Ciddiqui had left Aberfoyle in Scotland early that morning and had now been driving for almost four hours. Ten minutes later he drove into Bellingham, a short distance from Keelder Water. He was hungry, and pulled over outside Riverdale Hall, a hotel on the edge of the village. He was glad of the opportunity to stretch his legs as he walked into the hotel. He asked the receptionist if he could have some lunch.

'It's only a Ploughman's Lunch in the bar today if that's OK Sir?' the receptionist replied loudly.

'That's fine. Can you now tell me where the toilets are please?'

'Take a right and go straight down the hall Sir.'

When Ciddiqui got back to the bar he was alone. As he waited for his lunch, he looked at a map he'd brought in with him. He was ten kilometres from Keelder Water. He'd go directly to the Visitor Centre there, just beyond Stannersburn according to the map. His lunch arrived and he ate quickly. He asked for the bill, which he paid at Reception. He was anxious to see the location of the dam and reservoir at Keelder. It concerned him that it might be too large a facility for the plan at this time. Colonel Safa's brief had left him with two options in the North of England. Keelder Water was one, and the other a less prominent target but with potential for equal impact, an air shaft on Skylock Hill near Durham. He drove off towards Keelder. Twelve minutes later, Tower Whene Visitors Centre on the edge of Keelder Water came into view. He parked and headed to the visitors centre. Going into the centre he spotted numerous brochures and books describing the Keelder facility. Some of the books provided detailed technical data, and reminded him of the similar situation in Scotland. He picked up two brochures and a small book, and paid for them as he left. As he came out, the Keelder Water Cruiser, packed full of day-trippers, sailed past. Back in his car he glanced through the book he'd picked up, and saw that it provided some useful information. The Valve Tower at Keelder for example, with its distinctive triangular top, measured seventy metres in height, and was stated to be higher than Nelson's column in Trafalgar Square. Also, the glazed operational island gallery was fifteen metres above the water level of the reservoir. From his own briefing notes he knew that access to the gallery was from a four metre wide subterranean road that led through the massive structure and formed part of a giant concrete culvert, and a lift from the base went all the way to the top. The location was one of the preferred targets of *Location Gamma*. After reading all the information he had on the facility, Ciddiqui was not convinced that a strike here would produce the desired results. Five hundred litres of HCN, *The Juice of Allah,* would be of little significance he thought, and was unlikely to produce any fatalities. He'd look at the alternative, the air shaft at Vaskerley at the foot of Skylock Hill, just outside Consett, and forty kilometres further south. Keelder could wait, he decided. A one-off spectacular strike would be the way to attack it. Once he'd made the decision he retraced his route back to Bellingham, before joining the A6079. As he passed, he spotted the Roman Fort on Hadrian's Wall, then picked up the A68 south towards Consett. Running low on fuel he pulled in to a service station a few miles from Vaskerley. He filled up. As he paid his bill he asked the pump attendant, 'Is the road up to Vaskerley accessible in my car, that's it at pump two, or do I need a four-wheeled drive?'

'As long as you stay on the track you'll manage to the village in the Mondeo Sir. Mind how you go up there though, it's quite steep.'

Ciddiqui thanked the man and got back into his car. Once back on the main road and after a few minutes he saw the sign to Healeyfield and Vaskerley. He followed the sign into a narrow road that rose steeply into the hills. He passed a few cottages, then realised that he'd just gone through Healeyfield. From his map he knew he should now be looking for a small pond on his right, followed by a right hand bend on the road. The village of Vaskerley would be just below Skylock Hill, a bleak area of County Durham. The road was in terrible condition, and he hit more than one pothole before he spotted the pond and some cottages above it on the hillside. He pulled over onto the grass verge when the road all but ceased to exist. The rain had started and he decided to put on his waterproof jacket and boots. Outside the car it was much colder than it had been down at the service station. The wind had also picked up. He pulled on his Barbour and zipped it up to his chin, then changed his shoes and socks for those he'd bought in Aberfoyle the day before. Checking his map, he set off on a much-worn footpath in the general direction of the air shaft. Ciddiqui saw occasional signs of heavy tyre tracks adjacent on the footpath, four-wheel drive he thought, noticing that they also seemed to be heading in the direction of the shaft. As he climbed higher on the rough hillside, he decided four-wheel drive was the only way to deal with the terrain and steep hill. The hill became too much for him, and he had stop for a break. He sat down on the damp, rough grass to get his breath back. After a few minutes he carried on, and to his relief he soon spotted the air shaft. It had been constructed at the lowest point of a gully, and although from his line of sight he was looking down on it, he estimated that the top of the shaft projected four metres above the surrounding hillside. A black painted steel ladder was fixed to the shaft wall, starting about two metres above ground level. A padlocked heavy-duty galvanised open-barred steel frame was erected on the top. As he approached the shaft, he realised he'd no means of getting to the bottom of the ladder. He walked around the shaft and checked his brief. It was one of two similar shafts, the other being at Sharnberry a few kilometres away. Both were located at the high points in the three metre diameter, thirty-two kilometre-long underground tunnels that connected the rivers Tyne, Wear, and the Tees beneath the hills of West Durham. The brief stated that the tunnel system, which he thought must be beneath his feet, had a direct pipeline to nearby North Wood Water Treatment Works, a facility that served the towns of Consett, Stanley and south Gateshead. Apparently the thousands of people who lived there were supplied with drinking water from North Wood. As he surveyed the landscape, and its remoteness, he decided that the strike could be achieved with maximum effect at this location. The hardest part would be transporting *The Juice of Allah* up the steep hillside he thought. The operators would need some sort of tank attached to a trailer, something with a low centre of gravity that could be pulled up the steep incline by a four-wheel drive vehicle. Once satisfied with his decision he retraced his steps back to his car, took off his wet jacket and changed his shoes. Five minutes later he was heading towards Durham. As he crossed the River Wear and drove into the city, he saw the Marriott Royal County Hotel at the edge of the river and decided to get a room there. Driving through an archway into the hotel car park he eventually found a space. He was glad to get out of the car, and as he stretched his cramped shoulders, he repeated a prayer to Allah. He locked the car and went into the hotel reception and asked if he could have a room for two nights.

'Yes we can do that Sir. Smoking or non-smoking?' the over friendly receptionist asked.

'Smoking please.'

Ciddiqui was asked to sign the register - and how he'd like to pay before being handed an electronic door key. A Guest Relations staff member took him a moment or two later to his room, which backed onto the river. He thanked her, closed the bedroom door then stretched out on the bed. He was tired after his long drive and hill climb, and unintentionally fell asleep for forty minutes or so before awakening with a jolt just after six-thirty. He felt refreshed. He opened his briefcase and took out the document. He looked for the section dealing with *Location Gamma*. Opening it, he saw the names and the contact telephone number of the operators on the summary sheet as well as other details. The men were students at Durham University, both reading Biology. He lifted his telephone, dialled nine and then their number.

After two short rings a male voice said, 'Hello?'

'I'd like to speak to Niazi Bey,' Ciddiqui asked.

'I'm Niazi Bey. Who's calling?'

'*Ma Ma, Fi Kul Makaan,*' Ciddiqui said slowly using the coded password. He followed that with an instruction that brooked no question, 'Meet me tomorrow morning at nine o'clock. I have news of your family and we've much to talk about. I'm staying in the Royal County Hotel and we can meet in Reception. I'll be seated inside to the right of the doorway. We will walk in the hills later so bring some waterproof clothes and strong shoes.'

After a short pause Niazi Bey responded saying, 'I am delighted to hear from you. We have waited a long time; too long. We look forward to seeing you tomorrow as arranged.'

Ciddiqui replaced the telephone, then decided to freshen up and have dinner. Lifting the telephone again, he dialled the restaurant and asked for a table for one at eight pm.

Twenty-four hours after Commander Hall had seen the body in the mortuary at the UCH; he was studying the photographs of the dead man taken after he'd left. The more he looked at them, and the digitised photographs processed from the earlier video film, the more he was convinced that the two sets of photographs were of one and the same man.

'Lorna would you try and set up a meeting with DAC Hughes. Tell him I've something interesting to show him.'

His secretary appeared at his open office door, 'What time would you like me to make the meeting? Five OK? Remember you've a squash match tonight. Oh by the way, this folder was hand-delivered for you a short time ago. It's from a Chief Inspector Hamilton. I think you him met at University College Hospital yesterday,' she added, placing the folder on his desk.

'Thanks Lorna, and yes, five would be great. Now would you bring me a cup of coffee before I pass out, but set up the meeting first, you know how busy the DAC is at the best of times.'

Hall opened the folder. It contained a copy of a photograph of the dead man he'd been looking at a few minutes ago. There was also a four-page typed statement, and a hand-written memo attached to it. The memo had been signed by Hamilton, and stated,

Commander Hall,

I attach a copy of a statement taken from a Mr Franco Mazzini at nine a.m. today. He stated that the man in the attached photograph worked for him in Fred's restaurant in Islington, although he added that he hasn't seen or heard from the man for two days now. Mr Mazzini is the maitre d' and can be contacted at 020 7459 0000.

PS Mazzini is not aware of the connection between the man in the attached photograph, and the St James's Park incident.

Hall read the statement twice, then picked up his telephone and dialled the number.

'...Restaurant, can I help you?' asked an urgent female voice at the other end of the line so urgent that Hall didn't hear the name of the restaurant.

'Is that Fred's Restaurant?'

'Yes, Fiona speaking.'

'Can I speak to Mr Mazzini please?'

'Can I say who is calling?' the woman again asked urgently.

'Commander Hall, Scotland Yard.'

There was a slight pause before the voice said rather more cautiously, 'Just hold a moment please, and I'll put you through to Mr Mazzini.'

The line went dead, then a male voice with an unmistakable Italian accent asked, 'Commander Hall, how can I help you?'

'Mr Mazzini, I'd like to talk to you about the statement you made at Islington Police Station earlier today. Are you available later today Sir?'

'Anytime after three o'clock Commander, but tell me, why Abdullah? He was a nice quiet boy, cause no trouble to anyone. Why has this happened? Can you tell me Commander?'

'You'll have to wait till we meet Mr Mazzini before I can answer your questions. For one thing we can't be certain as yet that the man in the photograph is the man you call Abdullah Kadri. There are a number of things to be investigated before we can do that. I'll see you at three o'clock. We can talk then,' Hall said firmly.

'OK Commander, OK, then you can tell me about Abdullah.'

'We'll speak at three o'clock Mr Mazzini.'

As he put down his telephone, Hall remembered that he'd asked for a five o'clock meeting with Hughes. It shouldn't be a problem he thought, as he'd be back from Islington by that time. He picked the photographs off his desk, and looked again at the digitised photocopies taken from the film. It's got to be the same man, I'm sure of it he thought. 'Lorna, have you managed to set up the meeting with the DAC yet?'

'Five o'clock it is Sir,' she replied, then asked, 'However he did say he's only got a twenty minute slot. He's got a meeting at the Home Secretary's office at five-thirty.'

As he listened to his secretary, he was thinking that maybe, just maybe; he might at last have some good news for Hughes before his five-thirty meeting. He shouted back, 'Five's fine, now some coffee please. I'm in need of some stimulant. Will you also get me my usual sandwich when you're at it.' Hall paused before asking, 'What time did you say my squash match was tonight?'

66

'The court's booked for you lot at six-fifteen, and you're scheduled to play around seven o'clock,' she replied. 'I've heard you've been drawn against Bannistair, so you better not eat too many sandwiches before you play.'

Hall smiled thinking the Yard's grapevine had been working overtime. Bannistair was a good player, although he'd beaten him as many times as he'd lost to him over the years they'd known each other. Honours even, he thought.

'You can tell the gossips to put a bet on me. Now where's the coffee and sandwich? If I don't get them soon I'll not be able to get to the low balls in the corners. What's happened to the service in this place anyway?' he said with good humour. His mood had improved immensely since the recent turn of events in the St James's Park case.

As Hall contemplated his lunch, Ali Ciddiqui, Niazi Bey and his associate Hussein Mabeirig had driven from Durham and were now parked outside Vaskerley. The three men had met as arranged in the Marriott Royal County Hotel. Ciddiqui had briefed the two men on their part in the plan: *Ma Ma, Fi Kul Makaan*. As they got out of the car Ciddiqui stated, 'As you can see you'll need a four-wheel drive vehicle and a low loader trailer as I said earlier to get you all the way up to the air shaft. You've got enough money in the package so make good use of it. Any old Land Rover will do though; they're reliable enough even after hundreds of thousands of kilometres. It's one of the few things the British seem to get right, and remember,' he cautioned, 'you're supposed to be poor students, so don't buy anything that's going to draw too much attention to yourselves.'

The men nodded, still a little apprehensive of the stranger. Ciddiqui opened the boot and the men took out their boots and heavy jackets.

'We climb from here,' Ciddiqui said, leading the two younger men up towards the air shaft. From where they'd parked it was a twenty-minute climb, and soon the younger men caught up with him. Ciddiqui struggled on in silence, the only sound apart from his heavy breathing was the group's footsteps on the rocks and rough grass. A few minutes later they reached the top of a short steep rise, and looked down into a shallow valley. 'That's the air shaft. That's your target: *Location Gamma*,' Ciddiqui managed to say as he gasped for breath. The three men now looked down at the stone built structure about two hundred metres away.

'At the bottom of the shaft a water supply from the underground tunnel is taken directly to North Wood Water Treatment Plant. You'll have to ensure that you discharge the HCN, *The Juice of Allah,* down into the shaft as quickly as possible. A pumped method giving a good flow rate is essential to prevent diluting the liquid HCN too much, and powered off your vehicle. Within a few minutes it will reach the towns of Consett, Stanley and South Gateshead.'

'When do we begin?' Bey asked.

'Be patient,' Ciddiqui warned, 'Buy *The Times* every day and look for the message *Water Water, Everywhere.* It will be printed in English, in the *Personal Column,* and the date will be stated. You'll strike on the midnight hour of the given day.'

Both men nodded their heads in acknowledgement.

'As I was explaining,' Ciddiqui said irritability, 'as a consequence of your actions many of the infidels down there will die very quickly. Death and panic in Consett, Stanley and south Gateshead, and the water company will have to shut down the supply. The police and the army will be called. Bodies will be found everywhere, even for days afterwards.' He paused before adding, 'It'll be international news within the hour. All of Iraq will hear of our success and you can be sure you will be honoured on your return.'

'The plan will be successful, you have our word on that,' Bey said. He opened the file Ali Ciddiqui had given him then said, 'We'll take a closer look at the shaft now and familiarise ourselves, but I can see no problem.' He turned the pages, pausing occasionally to read some specific paragraph. 'One further question though, how much notice will we get of the date of *Ma Ma?*'

'You'll get all the time you'll need.'

The men nodded but said nothing, and went towards the air shaft.

Ciddiqui got to his feet again and walked towards the shaft, watching as the two men shouted back and forth as they considered their assignment.

When they reached the shaft, Bey with his colleague's help began to climb up to the point where he gripped the ladder fixed to the shaft's stone wall. Once he got a hold on the ladder he quickly climbed up to the top of the structure. Standing on top of the shaft he shouted to Ciddiqui, 'I see no problem here.'

'That is good my friend because failure cannot be tolerated.'

Bey came down the ladder, then dropped down the last two metres. The two men rejoined Ciddiqui. Bey said, 'We'll be ready to strike on the given date, Allah will be praised.'

'Your confidence reassures me. Now if you've seen all that you need to see at this stage, then I suggest we get off the hillside.' He was anxious to get back down the hillside in case they drew to much attention to themselves from the nearby village.

'Yes we've seen all we need to see. Let's go.' Bey said

The men walked back down Skylock Hill towards their parked car they could see in the distance. They changed back into their other shoes and jackets and got back into the car. Ciddiqui drove back down through the village, towards the main road then turned towards Durham, as the two men in the back continued to discuss their brief. Ciddiqui noticed they occasionally reverted to their native Arabic tongue as they exchanged views. When they reached the outskirts of Durham, Ciddiqui said, 'You must remember that the date and time for your strike has been carefully co-ordinated to coincide with others. The plan will only achieve maximum impact in Britain if you do exactly as instructed. That is essential. Are you clear about that?' The men confirmed that they understood, and Bey asked, 'If we need to contact you, how do we find you?'

Ciddiqui told the men to use the designated code name *Location Gamma*, and put a message in *The Times Personal Column*. He added, 'I'll contact you if you do that, but you've got your brief, you'll have no need to meet or speak with me again.' As they crossed the bridge over the River Wear on the edge of the inner City of Durham, Ciddiqui said assuringly, 'Everything's been arranged for your success. Your instructions, your funds, everything. There can be no question of failure.' He stopped the car close to the University buildings to let the men out, then added, 'Go forth and prepare. I wish you both the blessings of Allah.'

Bey and Mabeirig got out and with little more than a casual wave Ciddiqui drove off into the moving traffic, back towards his hotel. It was precisely seven-thirty. He contemplated driving directly to Newcastle's Woolsington Airport and catching the London flight to Heathrow which was due to depart at 2035. However, feeling exhausted, he decided against it. He'd have a quiet dinner at the hotel, and early in the morning he'd return the hired car to Newcastle Airport, before taking a British Airways flight to London. As he drove towards his hotel he felt that his plans were now well established in both Scotland, and in the North-East of England. He allowed himself to relax as he headed to the hotel, thinking it was about time that Hala, his PA, attended to his more urgent physical needs. His lustful thoughts caused him to almost miss the entrance to the hotel car park, and he braked suddenly, causing the cars behind to screech to a halt. Ignoring them, he drove through the archway, and again with some difficulty found a parking space. When he'd switched off the ignition, he stretched his shoulders and arms with a feeling of satisfaction. As he got out of the car still stretching his aching shoulders, he shouted aloud, 'Glory be to Allah, Glory be to Allah.' His sudden outburst startled a man who'd been sitting in the car that Ciddiqui had parked next to. The man, who'd left his car window partly opened, hadn't been spotted by Ali Ciddiqui, and as Ciddiqui walked towards the Hotel entrance, DC Falconer took careful note of him.

CHAPTER TWELVE

While Ali Ciddiqui, Bey and Mabeirig had been climbing Skylock Hill in Northeast England, Chris Hall arrived at *Fred's* restaurant in Camden Passage, Islington. Hall and Franco Mazzini, the Maitre d' Restaurant this time were looking at the digitised photographs of *The Man in the Park,* taken from the video film. Mazzini was unaware of the connection between the photograph and that of St James's Park.

'I'm sure it's Abdullah, Commander, I recognise him anywhere. I tell him that he must've had a British father - his English so good, and the colour of his hair. He says back to me, 'I'm Turkish Mr Mazzini, from Adana, close to the Mediterranean Sea. My mother she comes from Pervari in the east of my country. She is good to me. I speak good English because she sends me to the nuns who taught in our village. I am lucky compared to my poor parents.''

Hall and Mazzini remained quiet for a moment in the small, stuffy office at the back of the restaurant. It was after three o'clock in the afternoon, and with the pleasant spring weather a number of people were still lunching outside on the patio area, the sound of their laughter filling the silence in the back office.

'Mr Mazzini you're convinced that this photograph is a positive likeness to Abdullah Kadri? If you are, then I'll have to ask you to come with me to the mortuary to see if you can identify the body of the man murdered at the rear of the restaurant two nights ago.'

'From that photograph I'm sure Commander. I recognise him anywhere but I hope the body is not Abdullah's. I hope he is still alive, and he comes back to work for me soon. Of course I'll come to see the body Commander, of course.' Mazzini put his head in his hands, then added, 'If the body is Abdullah, then you must find who did this terrible thing.'

'No one else has reported Abdullah Kadri missing other than you Mr Mazzini, and we've been unable to make any contact with any friends or relatives of the murdered man. If you are able to identify the deceased as Abdullah Kadri, then you can be assure that we'll do everything in our power to find out who caused his death,' Hall replied.

'OK Commander, I understand that.'

'So far Mr Mazzini you've been a great help. Now if it's convenient, we'll go to the University College Hospital mortuary and see if you can identify the deceased. I must also say that if you do, then I'll have to ask you to come back with me to Scotland Yard. You can make a further statement there. Do you understand that Sir?' Hall asked.

'No problem. I'm very happy to do that. I go and tell my staff that I go with you, and that I will be back later. Just one minute Commander, just one minute.'

Both men stood up and looked forward to leaving the hot, stuffy room.

Hall played the cut drop shot to the left-hand corner of the squash court. Bannistair tried desperately to pass in front of him, stretching to reach the ball as it ricocheted off the front and then the sidewall of the court. He never made it, although as usual he gave it his best shot. Hall had just made his starting time at the squash court forty minutes before, and was now playing in the semi-final of the Yard's Squash Challenge Cup, an event he'd yet to win.

'Well done Chris,' Bannistair said breathlessly, sitting down on his hunkers in the corner. 'That was tough going,' he added, his head now resting on his knees, and his face drawn and white from the effort he'd put into his game. 'That last shot was easily your best backhand tonight,' Bannistair said between deep breaths.

Hall, equally breathless replied, 'I thought I had you earlier Jim, but you produced a few surprises. Our usual climax Jim. Anyway I did enjoy it, and now the final next week with McDade.'

Bannistair still breathing heavily, and suffering the taste of defeat said, 'I met him the other day. Said he hoped I'd beat you as you've an Indian Sign on him at the moment.'

Hall laughed thinking of McDade's remark. Both men eventually struggled to their feet and went to the locker room. They showered quickly, then dressed. As was usual when they played squash together, they'd arranged to meet their wives and children for dinner afterwards, at their favourite Chinese restaurant, the *China Temple* in Streatham.

Earlier that same afternoon Hall's five o'clock meeting with DAC Hughes had started ten minutes late as a result of his visit to the

UCH mortuary. Mazzini and he had then gone on to Scotland Yard, where Mazzini made a further statement. The time however had been well spent, and Hall was able to report to Hughes before he left for his meeting at the Home Secretary's Office that Mazzini had positively identified the murdered man as Abdullah Kadri, a waiter who worked in his restaurant. Mazzini had also provided Kadri's address: 14 Tavistock Place, Camden, London, and stated that as far as he knew, Kadri had no known relatives in Britain. He had also added that he thought Kadri had recently become acquainted with a fellow countryman from Turkey, but he was unaware of the man's name or whereabouts. Hall told Hughes that after Mazzini had made his statement, he'd called the Yard's Fingerprint Bureau and took them to Kadri's address at Tavistock Place. He added that he'd left them there to carry on with their work.

'We should've an Interim Report from the Bureau tomorrow morning Sir,' he said, as Hughes pulled on his jacket and headed for his waiting car.

CHAPTER THIRTEEN

It was raining the proverbial cats and dogs when Ali Ciddiqui came out of Heathrow Airport after his flight from Newcastle. He went straight to the taxi rank outside Terminal One's arrivals hall, and was soon heading into central London. He'd slept well, and although he'd had an early rise to catch the flight, he was feeling good. The plan's operations at locations *Alpha, Beta, and Gamma* were now set up.

'One mission left,' he said aloud as he relaxed in the back of the cab, causing the driver to look at him in his rear view mirror. Ciddiqui closed his eyes and settled back in his seat with a smile on his face as his thoughts turned to the evening and the rest of the weekend ahead. He drifted off to sleep contentedly, as the cab rushed towards London on the relatively quiet, traffic-free, M4 motorway.

CHAPTER FOURTEEN

It was a beautiful crisp spring Tuesday morning as Ali Ciddiqui left Cliveden; a Hotel set in the National Trust grounds near Cookham in Buckinghamshire where he'd spent the night. He walked across the sweeping driveway towards his car, dressed in his tweeds, and looking the picture of the perfect English country gentleman. The crunching sound his footsteps made on the gravel pleased him. After his weekend of passion in London, Ciddiqui was now keen to get the final stage of the plan *Ma Ma, Fi Kul Makaan,* in place. Yesterday morning he'd booked a room in the Cliveden for that night, then set up a meeting at the Themes Water Farmore Water Advanced Treatment Works near Oxford. Now, as the young assistant hall porter was putting his luggage in the boot of his car, Ciddiqui was anxious to be on his way.

'Have a good day Sir, and don't forget to turn left when you get to the end of the driveway. The M40 is only ten minutes away from that point,' the young man said, pausing slightly to received a tip from Ciddiqui,

'I shall, I shall' Ciddiqui replied as he got into his car, feeling the usual excitement rise within him at the beginning of a mission. He reversed out of the parking area and drove slowly past the *Fountain of Love,* an ornate water fountain positioned in the centre of the roundabout at the head of the hotel driveway. He turned right in the direction of the exit, towards the M40 motorway and Oxford.

Farmore Countryside Walk and Redhill Nature Reserve is situated to the west of Oxford, near the village of Farmore. When Ciddiqui arrived there, he drove into the public car park next to the nature reserve gatehouse and parked. It was cold when he got out. The drive had taken him little more than half-an-hour in spite of some road widening works on the motorway. He paid for a ticket, and asked the attendant how to get to the Water Treatment Works. Told to 'take a left and then a right and keep walking until you see water,' he thanked the man, and walked off in the direction of the River Thames. From his brief, Ciddiqui knew that Farmore Advanced Water Treatment Works covered an area of approximately 400 acres, with the capacity to treat over 100 million litres of raw water every day. The works supplies drinking water for more than half a million people within the area of Oxford, Banbury, Thame, and west as far as Swindon. It was a perfect target. A few minutes later Ciddiqui spotted the warden's office. He went into the small building and said he had an appointment with Customer Services. The day before he'd arranged the appointment, saying that he worked in the water industry in Turkey, his homeland, and that he was on a visit to the UK. He asked if it would be possible to see the workings of an advanced water treatment facility, like Farmore.

'Someone from Customer Services will be with you shortly Sir,' the warden's assistant told him, and asked him to take a seat meanwhile. A few minutes later a young man appeared, introduced himself as Iain Taylor saying that he'd be pleased to take 'Mr Taleb on a fact-finding mission.' Ciddiqui repeated his cover story to Taylor adding that, 'Here in the United Kingdom Mr Taylor you've such wonderful facilities for the production of your drinking water. You're the envy of the world in that respect. How I wish we had such skills in my country,' Ciddiqui said with more than a degree of truth.

'Well Mr Taleb,' Taylor said using the name Ciddiqui had given when he'd set up the visit, 'it's taken over one hundred years for this country to reach this standard, and even now we're spending vast sums of money improving our Clean and Dirty Water facilities. If our company can be of help to you in any way, don't hesitate to ask.'

'That's very kind of you Mr Taylor. I'll report your offer when I get back to Turkey you can be sure. But tell me this, how do you protect your water? How do you prevent pollution from getting into the water? So far I've seen no security or detection equipment anywhere!'

'Until recently it's been unnecessary to protect, as you say Mr Taleb, our source,' Taylor replied smugly. 'We've many automated systems in place, and can monitor most functions. However there is now a need for better permanent monitoring of all ground and surface waters to facilitate immediate responses to hazards. We're working very hard on that as we speak I can assure you. The need to design low cost probes that are easy to install, and which favour the multiplication of measuring stations, those sort of things. At this precise moment,' Taylor said warming to his subject and unbeknown to him, reaching Ali Ciddiqui's boredom level. 'There's no device available between large high-cost automated measuring stations, and portable point sampling monitors. There is presently no sensor available that could for example, measure simultaneously physico-chemical changes or pollutant concentration across a river or reservoir, or along a pipeline for that matter. There is a great need for research into the development of a low cost, robust sensor capable of multi-point monitoring, vertically and spatially in large bodies of water, such as here at Farmore.'

'Really?' Ciddiqui replied, trying to display a keen interest and keep the boredom from his voice.

'I believe that fibre optic technology will in time allow us to do all of those things Mr Taleb, however we're still a few years away from every day use of such technology,' Taylor added with a hint of sadness in his voice.

As Taylor boringly talked on, Ciddiqui allowed his thoughts to marvel again at the simplicity of plan *Ma Ma, Fi Kul Makaan.* It was inexpensive, easy to implement, and success could be virtually guaranteed. During a brief pause in Taylor's continuing dialogue Ciddiqui asked lightly, 'You mean, Mr Taylor, that someone can simply come along here and dump a pollutant into the reservoir and you've no way of detecting it until it's passed through the system and into the water mains?'

'Well yes and no,' Taylor said backtracking. 'You see we'd get feedback from some of our current methods, such as *Validation and Harmonisation of Measurement Procedures.* But that could be too late to allow the shut down of a pipeline supplying drinking water to a large section of the community. In other words I'm afraid it'd be the general public, who after drinking the water, would be first to tell us about the problem. What we really need to do Mr Taleb,' Taylor said again warming to his subject, 'is utilise a Hydrogel; that's a device being developed and tested at the University of Strathclyde's Chemistry and Optoelectronics Departments in Glasgow. The Hydrogel utilises fibre optics to measure the level of acidity in the water, taking the form of an alarm sensor, or a sensor to measure the range of pH levels.'

At the mention of Glasgow, Ciddiqui wondered how far the university had gone with the development work. He asked, 'Are any of these test facilities currently in use within public supply water systems, for example in the Glasgow area? If so, I'd like to see them.'

'Mr Taleb the subject is a special one for me, and if there was an installation of that kind in use outside of a laboratory, even under preliminary testing conditions, then I think I'd know about it. You can be assured at this time, no such facility exists and is unlikely to for a few more years.'

Taylor's words gave Ciddiqui some relief, and they continued walking around the facility for a further twenty minutes or so before arriving back at the warden's office. Ali Ciddiqui had now decided that the operation at Farmore, *Location Delta,* would be carried out along similar lines to those of *Location Beta* in Scotland, with the liquid HCN being discharged close to the draw-off point within one of the reservoirs. It was simple to execute, and guaranteed to provide maximum impact. Having seen enough, he thanked Taylor for his time. He added, 'On my return to Turkey I'll speak with the Minister of Works, and tell him of the hospitality I've received from Themes Water, and you in particular Mr Taylor.' There could be some business created between our countries, and the advanced water company, Themes Water. Taylor shook him by the hand and wished him well as they parted, handing over a collection of publications about the Farmore facility, describing the construction, and details of the plant and equipment.

'If there's anything else I can do to assist you, Mr Taleb, please give me a call. Here's my card. It's been my pleasure,' Taylor said warmly.

Ciddiqui returned the handshake, but didn't offer a business card. 'I'll write to you when I get back to Turkey Mr Taylor, once I've spoken with my Minister. Thank you again for your valuable time. You've been most helpful.'

As Ciddiqui went back to his car in the nature reserve car park, he passed the visitors' car park in front of the treatment works and noticed that it was under closed circuit television scrutiny. He was glad he'd decided to park in the nature reserve, well away from the prying eyes of these cameras. It was the only form of security he'd seen all morning. The strike at *Location Delta* didn't look as if it would be any more difficult than the other operations, and as before, security was cursory.

CHAPTER FIFTEEN

'Chris after the Bureau efforts at the Kadri's flat we've got nothing new! I can't believe it. If we're certain that it was him who used the HCN in St James's Park, then there must be some trace of the bloody stuff in his flat?'

Hughes and Hall had just read through the Bureau's interim report on the search at Abdullah Kadri's flat in Tavistock Place. Hughes got up and walked around his room to burn off some of his frustration. He poured himself another coffee, the fifth that morning, before sitting down again. He said, 'Get the Bureau to try again Chris, and tell them not to bloody well come back without something we can use. There's got to be something there; there must be for Christ sake!'

'I'll get them back this morning Sir, and I'll go with them. You're right, there must be something in the place, something we just haven't found yet. But I've got to say the flat was as clean as a whistle when I went there yesterday, and I mean really clean. According to this report,' Hall said, putting his hand on the document lying on the table, 'the only prints that the Bureau found were Kadri's. He must've cut his left thumb sometime in the past; it left a distinctive vertical line. They're the only prints they found. Nothing even in the fridge was past its sell-by date. The place was *that* clean!'

Hughes shook his head, then with more than a degree of frustration said, 'Chris, get the Super at the Bureau to meet me here at two o'clock this afternoon. You come along as well. I want to stress the urgency of this case, and the fact that we're now back to square one. The meeting I had at the Home Office last night was no picnic I assure you. I was asked right out by the Minister if I thought that we should hand the case over to Security Business Group here at the Yard, as it appeared according to the Minister, and I quote, 'that you're getting nowhere with it Mike.' You can imagine the repercussions that would have?' Hughes was back up on his feet again, 'If the Bureau don't come up with something we can use soon, well we're dead in the water just like the bloody ducks in the Park, and that's not a joke.'

Hall looked at Hughes and shook his head in acknowledgement of the situation. He said, 'I'll press the Bureau hard Sir. Oh by the way it's David Loudoun who's the Super handling it. I'll get him up here at two.'

'OK Chris,' Hughes said more evenly, although his mind had moved on. 'Chris, what about the HCN? Surely nobody can hide fifteen hundred litres of that stuff without drawing attention to themselves? What have you got on that so far?'

'Well again I've nothing firm to go on. I've had half my team solely on it for what seems like weeks now, and still nothing.' This time it was Hall who got up from the table and walked around the room. 'We've searched all the usual, and some unusual, channels for anything on Kiremla. Nothing I'm afraid, and the HCN? Well the stuff has just disappeared into thin air.' Hall was beginning to feel the case had got the better of him. He offered, 'Maybe you should replace me Sir? Give someone else a chance, a fresh mind so to speak. It could be that I've missed the obvious clues on this one?'

'Don't be daft Chris, I feel just the same as you. That would get us nowhere. Look, I'll see you and Loudoun at two. Let's hope we can come up with something soon. I've got to report to a Parliamentary Committee on Royalty Protection on our progress with the St James's incident next week. Her Majesty is still upset by the loss of the birdlife it seems. At the rate we're going you might have a new boss this time next week. Get back to Kadri's flat, there must be something there, there just has to be.'

'Thanks for your vote of confidence Sir. I'll have David Loudoun here at two sharp, and in the meantime I'll see what we can find at Tavistock Place.'

Hall left the Hughes' office feeling less confident than he cared to admit. He hated the feeling, knowing he needed something positive to happen soon.

Ali Ciddiqui turned off the television. He'd driven back to London from Farmore an hour or so ago, and gone straight up to his apartment. He'd picked up *The Times,* and glanced through it, spotting that a television programme, a documentary on the subject of water, was coming on in ten minutes. He switched on, and settled down to watch it. When the programme had started it begun by showing people in the suburbs of Glasgow a few years earlier. The people were collecting water in pots and pans from large plastic water containers located at street corners. According to the programme presenter the local water supply had become contaminated from a small diesel oil spill at a nearby water treatment works. The presenter, a blond female, twenty something, stated that no more than a few litres of diesel had been *inadvertently discharged* into the facility there, and that 22,000 homes had been affected within an area comprising Millguy, Beersden and Clydebank, suburbs to the north and west of the city. The woman also stated that schools had been closed, hospitals had struggled to continue, and businesses, particularly those which relied on heavy usage of water such as butchers, catering, florists, hairdressers, and even a whisky distillery, had all been uncertain if they could remain open for business at that time. She added that the documentary was being screened again today, in response to recent press criticisms of Themes Water's lack of action, over a two to three year period, regarding the condition of their water facility at Grimsbury. Diesel oil had similarly leaked from a vehicle parked there, and the diesel had got into the water source. The incident was similar to the one in Scotland a few years before. As he now stared at the blank screen, Ciddiqui's thoughts were concentrated on only one thing. Would water companies now tighten up their security arrangements UK wide as a consequence of the re-run of this documentary? What could they do to prevent plan *Ma Ma, Fi Kul Makaan,* from succeeding? He played the matter over and over in his mind, but after twenty minutes or so, he decided that in the time frame now available, there was no way the planned action could be stopped. He was aware that for water companies to ensure the safety of their water resources, they'd need to spend millions of pounds, and it would take years to do the work properly. The construction of defensive barriers, new security systems, quality monitoring, and all the other systems that would be needed would take time, time they didn't have.

'Nothing; there is nothing they can do,' he shouted, causing his PA in the room next door to look up from her desk.

His thoughts went back to other parts of the documentary the positive parts as far as he was concerned. It had been claimed that the lack of a critical decision at an early stage had delayed the public being informed of the contamination incident for some hours. This in turn had allowed the contaminated water to flow through the pipework distribution for distances of up to twenty kilometres from the contamination source. And as Taylor had advised earlier that day, it was a member of the public who'd initially reported the contamination, experiencing the foul smell of diesel oil after drawing water from a tap at his home. As Ciddiqui visualised the carnage that would've resulted had the twenty kilometres of piping contained the *Juice of Allah*, he paused to reflect on the thousands of people who'd been affected by the simple diesel spill. People who'd had to queue for hours with their assortment of pots and pans in squally, wet weather on the streets of Glasgow for their allocation of fresh water. At least after that incident they were still alive. If events went to plan, then these same people, and many thousands more like them would soon be dead. They're so arrogant he thought. Their utilities; water, gas, electricity, and fresh air, they take for granted. How dare they insult Iraq? It will be their downfall. Nevertheless Ciddiqui decided he'd watch out for the next news bulletin to see if the subject of water and the diesel spill appeared again.

He went to his study; the feelings of doubt having left him. He checked his watch and seeing that it was approaching six-thirty, decided it was time to contact the operator who would make the last strike: the one at *Location Delta.* It was the last piece of the jigsaw before the deaths of the British would begin. He dialled the Carlton Hotel. When his call was answered he said, 'May I speak with Mr Farraj Rasid please, he'll be in the Health Club at this time.'

Ciddiqui was aware that Rasid's instructions were to be there every day around this time, and if unable to do so, he was to leave a contact number. He heard the woman repeat his request to the club receptionist. The call was then transferred to another extension.

'May I ask who is calling?' a male voice asked in an American English dialect.

Rasid, Ciddiqui knew had spent a few years in Washington prior to the Gulf War, where he'd maintained a low profile. Before coming to Britain he'd worked as an Air Traffic Controller at Dulles International Airport. He'd been trained by the US Military in the late eighties under an exchange deal brought about by the governments of the US and Iraq at that time, but had failed to land a job. He found Americans came first in all the job intakes, a situation that had incensed him ever since. Eventually he got employment with the US Air Traffic Control Organisation serving his employers well, and was missed when he left to go to Europe a few years later, allegedly to be close to his dying mother in London. The real reason behind Rasid's departure was that Iraqi Intelligence had secretly advised him to leave the US just prior to the start of hostilities in Afghanistan. Thanks to his US experience, and the credibility that went with the job, he was employed instantly by the National Air Traffic Control Authority, the *NATA,* in the UK when he arrived. He was now stationed at London's International Heathrow Airport.

'You have no reason to know my name,' Ciddiqui replied, 'you need only know that the plan *Ma Ma, Fi Kul Makaan* is being activated.' He smiled knowing that the Rasid would be taken aback with the information, but offered no opportunity for the man to ask further questions. 'You're familiar with the meaning of the plan I'm sure?' he asked Rasid dismissively.

'I am,' Rasid stated positively, 'and I've waited a long time to hear these words. Indeed I'm honoured to participate.'

'Good, then meet me tomorrow morning at 10.30 am at the information desk on the ground floor in Terminal 1,' Ciddiqui said in a tone, which implied that there was no alternative. 'I'll recognise you,' he added, looking at a recent photograph of Rasid in his briefing document. 'And do not, and I repeat, do not be late.'

'I'll be there at 10.30.'

'Goodbye for now then Mr Rasid, I'll see you tomorrow morning.'

Ciddiqui replaced his telephone, and flexed his shoulder muscles as he sat back in his chair. 'What I need right now is some relaxation,' he said. He turned towards the opened door to the office suite in his apartment, and said softly, 'Hala my lovely, please come and soothe your tireless lover. Leave your work for an hour or so, I need you now.' He closed his eyes, a smile spreading over his tanned face, and his excitement climbed as he heard her getting up from her desk to come and join him.

Three days before Ali Ciddiqui had spoken with Farraj Rasid, Hall had returned to Abdullah Kadri's flat in Tavistock Place. With him were officers from the Fingerprint Bureau, as well as some from Forensics. They'd been going through the contents of the two-roomed apartment for the umpteenth time. Hall walked through the square hall that separated the rooms, still struck by its clinical cleanliness. As he passed through a doorway, he paused to look at the woodwork around a doorframe. No chips in the paintwork and no dents in the woodwork either. He was about to walk away when he spotted two small holes on one side of the opposite frame. Each hole was about two millimetres in diameter, about seventy-five millimetres apart, and one above the other. The first hole was approximately a metre up from floor level. At first he though they were nail holes that hadn't been filled. He saw that the holes appeared to go straight through the full thickness of the frame, as if the nails had been removed. He gripped the side of the doorframe, now realising that one side was wider than the other side, and pulled. But it was well constructed, and fixed firmly to the wall. From his inside pocket he took out a plastic toothpick he'd picked up from his favourite Chinese restaurant, and pushed it into the top hole. To his surprise the hole was so deep the toothpick went in its entire length, about fifty millimetres or so.

'Jim will you take a look at this?' he shouted to the nearest officer, 'Those two holes just seem so out of place on this otherwise unmarked frame.'

Johnston from Forensics whom Hall had just spoken to, looked closely at the holes before touching the edges with his fine rubber glove covered finger. 'Holes are as clean as a whistle Sir,' Johnston said, taking a pen torch from his pocket, and shining the beam into the small aperture. He then held a small magnifying glass over one of the holes. 'Don't think they're nail holes. If they were then when the nails were pulled out, fifty mil or so, more than likely the edges of the holes would've split outwards.' He bent down and lifted a thin rod about four hundred millimetres long from his case and inserted it into the top hole. It penetrated around half of its length before stopping. Johnston slid his thumb down the rod to the point where it went into the doorframe, then withdrew the rod. He measured how deep it had gone in. 'One-fifty mil Sir.' He reinserted the rod into the hole. Hall watched as Johnston pressed a little more firmly. 'There's a bit of give in there, as if I'm pressing against something flexible Sir,' Johnston said taking the metal rod out of the hole again.

'Try the other hole Jim.'

Johnston put the rod into the bottom hole. 'Same depth and feel Sir. Feel it for yourself you'll see what I mean,' Johnston said as he left the steel rod in the hole, and moved aside.

At first Hall pushed gently, then a little more firmly. He felt the flexible movement Johnston had described, like pushing against a spring. 'Jim do you have another rod or a screwdriver, or something similar? Let's see what happens when we press both at the same time.'

'Here we go Sir,' Johnston replied as he put a thin, wooden-handled, steel-shafted rod into the other hole. 'I found two of these in a drawer but I couldn't think what use the deceased had had for them.'

'Push together Jim,' Hall said, as he took hold of the wooden-handled rod.

Both men felt it at the same instant; it was as if the flexible, spring-like tension had been released. The steel rod with the wooden handle had gone into the hole the full length, and only the handle had stopped it going any further.

'Hey, how did you do that?' said the voice of the Prints man in the adjacent bedroom, as he backed away from doorframe he'd been dusting for fingerprints.

Hall stuck his head around the door, curious to see what had happened. The doorframe on the other side of the doorway had sprung open, revealing a tall, narrow, shallow-shelved cupboard. In the cupboard was a small clear glass bottle about the size of the wine bottles served by airlines. The bottle appeared to be empty.

Farraj Rasid tried hard to appear calm and composed as he stood amongst a dozen or so people, some with printed cards with the names of people, or companies held up on front of them. He'd positioned himself, as instructed at the information desk in the busy ground floor arrivals hall at Heathrow Airport, Terminal One. He'd used the excuse of an early lunch break to get away from his control desk, and now a few minutes early, was feeling nervous about meeting his nameless contact. From fifteen metres away Ciddiqui observed Rasid for a moment or two before slowly coming up behind him. 'Good morning Mr Rasid, I hope you had a nice flight? If you would follow me please we'll go to the car.' To anyone standing next to Rasid and if they'd cared to listen, the meeting and greeting would've seemed perfectly normal. Ciddiqui made his way towards the pay machines at the exit, where he inserted his parking ticket, and paid the fee. He then walked briskly away from the terminal building, Rasid following close behind. They crossed the road and went down some steps to the lower floor of the covered car park. No words were spoken during the short walk. When Ciddiqui reached his car he opened the rear passenger door, and indicated with his other hand that Rasid should get inside. He then went round to the driver's side and climbed in. It was perfectly normal behaviour; something that takes place many times, in any hour, and every day of the week at London's Heathrow Airport. Once he'd settled into his seat, and only then, Ciddiqui looked into his rear view mirror. He made direct eye contact with Rasid then asked, 'You are ready to commit to *Ma Ma, Fi Kul Makaan?*'

Farraj Rasid moved forward in his seat, and whispered, 'I'm honoured to be chosen to undertake Allah's work. Please be kind enough to give me my instructions, and allow me to proceed as soon as possible.'

'There is little haste,' Ciddiqui replied casually. 'It's not a race against time. We have to plan and co-ordinate our actions with others. It is the wish of Allah to make this plan as devastating as possible to the British nation; to achieve many deaths, and inflict suffering and pain on the infidels. To do this we must have co-ordinated action. Iraq must never forgive or forget what the British, and their allies the Americans have done to our people. We need revenge.' He paused to let his words sink in, then added, 'If you fail, then the kindness of Allah will not ease your suffering. Do I make myself clear Mr Rasid?'

Rasid had involuntary sat back in his seat as Ciddiqui spoke, and now leaned forward again saying quietly, 'I will not fail. Please proceed with the instruction, and let me begin my task. Your name please, I don't know your name?'

'My name is of no interest to you. You don't need such details.' Ciddiqui took a large heavy envelope from his briefcase and added, 'Your instructions are here. All you need to know.' He turned and put the envelope on the seat next to Rasid. 'In the envelope you will find enough money, maps and contact names within this package to assist you to fulfil your task. Your target, called *Location Delta*, is the Farmore Advanced Water Treatment Works near Oxford. 100 million litres of water are treated there daily then distributed as drinking water to towns and villages all around. Your part in the plan requires you to inject into the water system a highly poisonous chemical called HCN, or if you prefer *The Juice of Allah*. You must ensure that it is discharged directly into the draw-off tower in one of the reservoirs at Farmore. From your instructions you'll also find out where to collect the HCN. Do you have any questions?'

Rasid paused before saying, 'I'm a little surprised by my chosen target. I did think that, as a consequence of my work, my task may have involved passenger aircraft, or should I say the destruction of them. But I'm not ungrateful. Any means of causing pain and suffering to the Allies will also be my cause, and my honour to fulfil. Please continue with my instructions.'

Ciddiqui smiled and turned around to look at Rasid. 'Then we have nothing to worry about have we?' he asked. 'You'll find your operations take place during the hours of darkness. You require access to the waters of the reservoir at Farmore. Water is the chosen means of revenge to pay back the West for the insults they've imposed upon our people. Read your operational plan carefully. Farmore Plant is the initial target, and through it the people of Oxford, and surrounding towns and villages. Once they've tasted our wrath, we'll see how clever they are in their Ivory Towers.' He paused as they both shared a moment of anticipated pleasure. Continuing he said, 'You'll need a small boat. There's a sailing club at the reservoir, and any number of boats lying around. Take one to suit your needs.' He carried on giving Rasid details and procedures he'd need when moving the HCN around at Farmore, just as he had done with the operators in Scotland. When he'd finished he asked, 'Have I made myself clear?'

'Perfectly clear,' Rasid replied courteously.

Ciddiqui nodded at Rasid's response, then continued, 'As I've said you will have to carry out the strike on your own, an added difficulty but not impossible. Your intended colleague failed to *live* up to his ideals and as a consequence of his indiscretion he no longer lives under the goodness and watchful eye of Allah.' Ciddiqui hesitated, then added, 'When you complete the strike at *Location Delta,* thousands of the infidels will die. As you might expect, the media will report the event worldwide. You will become a soldier of Allah.' For a moment or two both men were silent, and Ciddiqui could see that Rasid's eyes were moist. He broke the tension. 'Go forth and prepare. There is work to be done, and you must be ready on the given day and time. Remember; buy *The Times* every day. In the *Personal Column* you'll see the message, *Water Water,*

Everywhere. It will be in English, and also the date of your operation will be confirmed. You must strike on the midnight hour of that day and not before. I ask again, is that clear?'

Rasid bowed his head slightly towards Ciddiqui. 'As I've said to you I am honoured to be chosen, I won't fail.'

'You're not expected to fail. Failure is unthinkable.'

'I will succeed, and Allah be with you,' Rasid replied, opening the car door and getting out. Once in the car park, he turned back towards Ali Ciddiqui, nodded slightly, then carrying the large heavy envelope under his arm, walked back in the direction of the control tower. Ciddiqui sat in his car for a few minutes of reflection. He'd now activated all of the operators. Death and pain were but a short time away for many of the British, but for the first time nagging doubts had grown in his mind. As a result of the political pressure that was currently being forced upon it, he hoped Iraq wouldn't back down. The combined forces of evil, as Ciddiqui referred to the governments of the USA and Great Britain, were manoeuvring for position, and bringing great pressure to bear on Iraq. He quickly tried to be dismissive of his negative thoughts, and to replace them positively. 'Iraq will never back down,' he muttered under his breath. 'Osama bin Laden has only just begun Islam's response to the so called Allies. The World Trade Centre strike in New York is only a small tasting of the terror that has still to come. Iraq will complete the banquet!' As he was about to start his car, his attention was drawn to two tall, elderly and scraggy men, pulling heavy cases towards the taxi rank, dressed in navy blue raincoats, who were being followed by their overweight and badly dressed wives. 'Americans!' he said with venom, looking at the group twenty metres or so away from him. 'They are fools; infidels who think that their wasteful lifestyle can go on forever. We'll strike soon at their natural and utility resources, just as we're about to do in so-called Great Britain. Their time is short. We have plans for all of their filthy US cities, and their fat, arrogant people.' He turned the key in the ignition and drove towards the exit barrier. Inserting his parking ticket, he waited for the barrier to lift. Instead a computerised voice from the speaker on the barrier column beside him instructed him that his parking ticket time had expired. He was instructed to return to a parking space, and go to the pay office where a supplementary charge was due. His anger flared and he cursed blindly. He put the car in reverse, blasted his horn at the car behind him, waving the helpless woman driver to get out of his way. When she'd done so he drove into a vacant space and got out, slamming the car door shut behind him. Ten minutes or so later he returned having paid the supplementary charge. His anger was still high as he drifted out of the car park, and into the airport *Through Car Lane*. The blast of the horn from a black taxicab he'd cut out in front of quickly brought him back to his senses. He cursed the driver, ignored the man's rude hand gestures, and accelerated towards the tunnel under the main airport runway, heading in the direction of the M4 and London. He needed to relax now that he'd completed his briefings. He'd take his PA to dinner. They'd go to Santini's in Ebury Street. She loved the sophisticated Italian food there, and he knew he'd be well rewarded afterwards. Soon the troubles of the past few minutes were forgotten, his mind occupied by his plans for later that evening.

CHAPTER SIXTEEN

After finding the bottle in Abdullah Kadri's flat, Hall had it sent to Dr Greenstreet at the RSPB in Bedfordshire. Hall hoped that Greenstreet would find some connection with the bottle and the poisoning of the birdlife in St James's Park a few weeks ago.

Twenty-four hours later, he opened Greenstreet's reply. As usual, he read the conclusions of the report first, and saw that his hunches had been correct. The bottle contained traces of hydrocyanic acid. He quickly read through the rest of the report, then asked his secretary to arrange a meeting with Mike Hughes. He shouted through to her, 'Tell him that at last I have some good news for him.'

She phoned him back within a few minutes. 'The DAC will see you now Sir.'

Hall went straight to Hughes' office, and relayed the contents of Greenstreet's report. Hall then said, 'We now know for certain that Kadri was the man in the park; we know he had access to some if not all of the HCN. He may also have given some of it to those poor beggars who died at Russell Square. The two questions remaining are what has he done with the rest of the HCN, and does he have any accomplices? That wound to his throat wasn't the clumsy work of some violent mugger; that was a professional job. I'd guess that Kadri had some bad friends, and he'd probably stepped out of line or something.'

'Maybe Chris and we'll find out in due course. But now I want you to go back to *Fred's* restaurant. Get the entire management and staff together. There must be something they haven't told us yet about bloody Kadri. They worked with him for Christ's sake. They haven't told us anything about him. The man can't have been that bloody invisible. Nobody could be. Give them a real grilling this time. They must know more than they've told us so far. And don't forget, whoever is in possession of the HCN has the potential to wipe out half of London,' he added sombrely.

'Will do Sir.' Hall rose, and after lifting his notes and other papers, made his way back to his office, from where he telephoned *Fred's* restaurant. He spoke to Mazzini, the *maitre d'*, and told him that he and his entire staff had to make themselves available for further questioning in one hour's time.

'But Commander, I have to close the restaurant. We have many bookings already Sir. What can I do Commander?' the man protested.

'We can do this the easy way or the hard way Mr Mazzini. You either do it the way I've suggested, or you and your staff can get yourselves in here to Scotland Yard in one hour's time. This is a murder inquiry, not a bloody picnic. Now I guess you'll do it my way. I'll be there in one hour's time, so get your people rounded up.'

'I'm sorry Commander, I do as you say. I'm sorry. You come here. We'll be ready for you Sir.'

'That's more like it Mr Mazzini. Now I want everyone there; even those who may have the day off. You understand? Everybody Mr Mazzini.'

'I understand Commander. I have everybody when you come.'

Later that same afternoon, Hall stood up in frustration. He and his interview team had been in *Fred's* restaurant for three hours and they seemed to be getting nowhere. When they arrived, Mazzini had put up a notice on the door of the premises, stating that the restaurant was closed for the rest of that day. He'd also contacted his pre-booked clientele and apologised to them that he had to turn them away that day.

Now he looked around the dining room at the tired-looking group. A waiter was actually asleep in a seat. Hall shook him, told him to stand up. The man, the most recently employed member of staff, had already been questioned, but Hall decided to make an example of him to the rest.

'Mr Patrick you and Abdullah Kadri worked closely together. You both started early and finished late. You more than the rest had the chance to get to know Kadri,' Hall said, lifting up a clear polythene bag containing the bottle picked up in Kadri's flat. He handed it to Patrick, and said, 'I'd like you to look at this please. Do you recognise it?'

The waiter looked at the shape of the bottle, and replied casually, 'It looks like one of the bottles we use here for olive oil.'

'Are you sure? Are there more bottles like this in the restaurant?'

The waiter, with little interest, replied, 'Yes, maybe twenty or thirty. We've at least one for each table.'

Hall watched the man closely, then said, 'If I tell you Abdullah Kadri had taken one home would you be surprised?'

'Not really, Abdullah poured olive oil on everything. Bread, salad, anything, even toast. He loved the stuff, don't ask me why? He said it was the one thing he missed most, apart from the weather, about Turkey. One day, a week or so ago, he came in to the restaurant and said he'd met a friend; a fellow countryman. The man had given him a big flask of olive oil. Told him it came from an area near the village where Aby, I mean Abdullah had been born. Aby was quite excited about it I remember,' Patrick said, and laughed at the thought of it.

'Did you see the flask?'

'Yes I saw it. It was metal, shiny like, probably stainless steel. I don't know, but maybe Aby took this bottle home to use for the oil,' Patrick said, holding up the bottle in the bag. 'It would've been easier than using the big flask. And the seal on the top of those bottles is very good; they never leak.'

Hall asked firmly, 'Why didn't you tell us about Abdullah Kadri's friend before? We've asked you a number of times if he'd any friends. You said,' Hall looked down at the notes taken earlier, 'you said, and I'm reading this from your previous statement Mr Patrick, "I don't think he had any friends, at least I've never seen him with any."' Hall paused. 'Why did you make that statement Mr Patrick?'

The man shifted uncomfortably in his chair, now fully alert. 'Well yes I did say that, but it's true I'd never seen him with anybody. I forgot about the guy from Turkey until you gave me that bottle. It was a while ago and I had just started working at the restaurant. What's the problem? I've told you all I know about Aby.'

'The information you have just given could be very important Mr Patrick. If there's anything else that you're holding back Mr Patrick it could be very serious for you. I must remind you that this is a murder inquiry, and that you're still under oath. Is that clear?'

'Yes, yes,' Patrick replied, looking at the floor.

'You're sure that you never saw Abdullah Kadri's fellow countryman Mr Patrick?'

The silence lasted about ten seconds. 'No, I never saw the man. I've never been with Abdullah anywhere other than at the restaurant. That's the only place, and that's the truth,' Patrick replied, and beginning to feel uneasy about his predicament.

Hall let him wait before he asked, 'Did Abdullah Kadri tell you anything about this man? Surely you both had some conversations about things outside the restaurant? Did he say the man was tall, short, young, old, anything about the man's likes or dislikes? Surely he said something?'

Patrick's face flushed deeper and looking more and more apprehensive he replied, 'Well yes, he did say that the man was rich. A big man, about forty or so. One day he said they'd gone for an expensive lunch and the man paid for it all. Aby said he saw that the man had plenty of money in his wallet. His gold watch even had diamonds around the face, Aby said.'

'Did he say anything else about the man? Was his skin dark or light? Hair colour? Did he say what age he thought the man was?'

'I told you. About forty or so Aby said.' Patrick was now very alert and worried. He paused before adding, 'I think I remember him saying that he was tanned, with dark hair, big, but I don't know if he meant heavy, or tall. That's all I know believe me Sir.'

'Mr Patrick, for a man who thought he'd nothing to tell us, you've been most helpful. That'll do for the moment, but we'll want to see you again. Don't attempt to go too far until you've cleared it with us. If you think of anything else, anything at all, then you must get in touch with me; it's very important. Do you understand that?' Hall got back up from the table leaving the pathetic-looking Patrick sitting there.

'Yes, I understand that,' Patrick called after him.

Hall closed the interviews. He said, 'You may go now Mr Patrick. Your information, no matter how hard it's been to get at, may turn out to be very useful.'

David Patrick rose slowly and looked around sheepishly at his fellow workers, unsure of what to do next. He was guided towards the door by the WDC who'd been taking notes throughout the interview. She too was ready to stretch her legs and have a breath of fresh air. Hall sat back down again after Patrick had left the room.

DS Bartram, who'd been sitting at the back of the room said, 'Sir, I'll get one of the bottles from the kitchen so we can compare it. But, I'm sorry to say we didn't find any flasks at Kadri's flat Sir.'

'OK Dick,' Hall said, his mind thinking beyond the subject of the bottle. Hall was sure the bottles would match. He'd have to take another look at the items picked up from the lake. From what he'd just heard, he hoped he'd find a stainless steel flask. If it had been in the lake, why hadn't he spotted it? How could he have missed it he was thinking? If he could find it, he knew that any fingerprints would still be intact, even after being under water for some time.

He got up from the table, 'Dick, bring the two bottles back to the Yard. We can let this lot go for now. Speaking directly to Mazzini he said, 'Mr Mazzini, thanks for your co-operation today. It's been a great help.' He turned towards the rest of the restaurant staff and said, 'Thanks to you all as well. Although I have to say had Mr Patrick been open with us from the start, he could have saved us all a lot of time. We'll get ourselves out of here now, and let you lot get back to work.'

'No problem Commander,' Mazzini replied, 'anything to help you find out who murdered poor Abdullah - anything.'

Hall acknowledged Mazzini's words, then told his team to return to the Yard. He asked Bartram to come to his office in one hour's time. He was still thinking about the flask that Patrick had mentioned.

CHAPTER SEVENTEEN

Strathclyde Central Division Fire Chief, John Hamilton, was looking at the derelict property in Washington Street, Glasgow, and just beginning to feel that he and his crew of three brigades had done a good job of containing the fire. Fifty years ago, the area had been a thriving working class district, comprising aged tenement buildings housing countless thousands of people in unsanitary conditions, alongside a number of heavy industrial engineering workshops, and whisky bonds. Today the area was extensively redeveloped, and most but not all of the old buildings had been demolished; hotels, commercial offices, and high rise housing blocks taking up the cleared spaces. The fire had taken place within one of the old buildings where demolition work had been taking place.

'Looks like you caught it in time John,' the Chief Inspector of Strathclyde Police Force said, as he watched the fire crews pulling back some of their equipment.

'Aye we were lucky this time. One of your lads saw some youths running away from the premises John, just before there was any visible sign of smoke. That was a great help. Pass on my thanks for that please would you? It could've been a hellava lot worse, and fortunately nobody got hurt. Did you catch any of them by the way?' Hamilton asked.

'Aye we did,' Anderson replied, 'Druggies' of course. They couldn't even tell us their names. All out of their minds I have to say. Knew nothing about a fire they said. All we can do is lock them up overnight for their own good. They'll be out again the next morning. These new drug laws are something else I tell you, something else.'

'John, we live in changing times I'm afraid. I'm just glad that we got out of here without my lads getting hurt. These old buildings are a nightmare I can tell you,' Hamilton said with feeling.

'I take it the adjacent property...?' Anderson asked, looking at the old stone building fifty metres away. It appeared in better condition, although looking closely at it, he thought it would be the same sort of age as that of the building where the fire had taken occurred.

'We think there's maybe some water damage internally John, but nothing more than that,' Hamilton replied. The men looked across at the building. Above the main vehicle entrance, a newly painted sign boldly stated the *Isosceles Centre*. 'From our records it's a Self

95

Storage facility, one of those indefinable businesses, storing God knows what!' Hamilton said. 'That was a concern I must say. If you don't know what you're fighting in a fire, anything can happen. Even when you know what's in the premises it's bad enough. These companies are supposed to keep accurate records of what's stored in the secure units, but even with heavy fines most of them don't. Dodgy places like that especially,' he said nodding in the direction of the Isosceles Centre.

'I've still got the key holder for the building in one of our police cars John,' Anderson said, 'though, can you believe he tells me he doesn't have access to the individual units? At least we can take a look and see if the damage is serious or not. Give me a shout when you're ready John and I'll bring the key holder as well.' Anderson moved away and back up towards Argyle Street, where a crowd of people had gathered at the police barriers even at two in the morning, had gathered to watch the Fire Brigade at work.

Daylight was breaking when Anderson, accompanied by Fire Chief Hamilton and Mr McPhail, the key holder, entered the Isosceles Centre. Hamilton stressed to the other two men not to touch any electrical appliances or light switches in the building, as he thought there might be water damage to the electrical circuits. The three men cautiously went into the main high-arched roofed area of the old building, and Anderson spotted immediately that there was water on the floor area. Each of them shone their torches on the compact storage units, which were stacked five high, one on top of the other, to a height of fifteen metres. The units at ground level had large, full-width double doors, not unlike garage doors, and the upper units had smaller doors, accessed off a multi-level steel gantry that ran the length of the building. Each unit resembled a giant safe, with an electronic keycard facility on the front. The units were arranged in rows, facing each other across a four-metre wide corridor. A heavy steel structure supported the units, and above the topmost unit, steel beams spanned the corridor, incorporating lifting equipment. One or two of the units had water dripping from them, visible even in the torchlight.

'How many units do you have here Mr McPhail?' Anderson asked the key holder.

'Oh, we've around two hundred and forty-five currently in use, and forty empty at the moment,' McPhail replied, stepping over a pool of deep water. 'I can give ye' a list of names of the users if you like,' the man offered. 'We keep good records at the centre, not like some o' those other places,' he added.

'Aye we'll need those Mr McPhail,' Anderson replied, 'particularly those where there may be water damage, and possible insurance claims. You'll have to advise all of those unit holders of that possibility I presume, and we'll need copies of the responses for our records.'

The men continued to look around, their eyes now more accustomed to the dark interior of the building. They saw that water had come into the property through a high level broken window. Anderson also noticed that the interior of the building was served by surveillance cameras, one or two of which appeared to have been caught in the incoming water. That apart, there appeared to be very little damage within the building itself.

The men walked around for a few more minutes before Inspector John Anderson asked the Caretaker, 'Mr McPhail I suppose you'll want to begin the cleaning up as soon as possible?'

'Aye a' would that Inspector.'

'First things first though Mr McPhail. The Fire Chief's men will have to check your electrical systems before you can switch them on again. Am I right John?' Anderson asked.

'We can start on that within the hour I'm sure. By the looks of it I don't expect to find much wrong with them that wasn't wrong before the water got to them,' Hamilton replied smiling.

'OK Mr McPhail, while that's going on you might as well come back with me to the Station. You can make a statement there and we'll get that out of the way at least,' Anderson summed up, as the men stepped back out of the dark building and into the early morning sunlight.

CHAPTER EIGHTEEN

In London the sun was also rising. Ali Ciddiqui hadn't slept well; a normal weekly occurrence he experienced when he was about to meet Colonel Safa al-Dabobie. He'd showered and shaved early, and was now scanning the *Personnel* column of *The Times,* as he had done each morning since he'd briefed the operators. There were no messages. Silently he praised Allah. When he went to the Carlton Hotel later that morning, he hoped he'd receive some further instructions. He poured himself another cup of strong coffee and switched on his television, tuning to Sky News. As the sound came through he heard, '.... Hussein would appear to have gained the initiative again,' said the attractive news announcer. 'The revised Russian plan has ensured that the UN inspectors remain in Iraq, including the numerous palaces, which had been the source of the latest diplomatic row. The governments of the USA and the UK have expressed doubts of Saddam's promises...' Ciddiqui stopped listening and finished his coffee. He knew that Saddam would keep them guessing for as long as it suited him and that he'd achieve his goal in the end. Ciddiqui planned to figure large in Saddam Hussein's cause. He dressed quickly and left his apartment to walk the short distance to the hotel across Sloane Street. He enjoyed the cool morning air as soon as he stepped out of his building, and a few minutes later the top-hatted doorman outside the hotel greeted him.

'Good morning Sir, and a nice one too don't you think?' the man said, recognising Ciddiqui as a regular user of the hotel, and a friend of some of it's wealthier clientele.

'Good morning Tony. Yes, it's a great morning. I think I'll go to the park later to see the spring flowers, and of course the pretty girls that the sun always seems to bring out on a day like this,' Ali replied with a smile and a wink. It was a false touch of humour by him; humour that he didn't possess at that moment. He went through the door held open by the doorman, and as always walked into Reception. He smiled warmly at Erika, the tall, blond receptionist, and told her that if there were any urgent messages for him, he could be found in the ground floor Grand Lounge.

The girl smiled warmly, and said in continental English, 'Thank you Mr Ciddiqui, it will be my pleasure.'

Ciddiqui mirrored her smile, and held her stare a moment longer admiring her large, pale blue eyes. He then went into the lounge. He opened a newspaper he'd picked up from a nearby table as he sat down. Glancing idly through the pages, his anxiety now again getting the better of him, he caught sight of an article on page four on the subject of *Low Water Pressure Hindering Firemen*. The article reported that National Fire Chiefs were allegedly claiming that privatised water companies had reduced water pressure in the mains to combat leakage rather than spend more money to repair, or replace the aged water mains. In the article, one of the Fire Chiefs was quoted as having said, ' In the town centre where I have the responsibility, the water pressure is so low that members of the public who live, or work five floors or more above ground level are in grave danger. They have to be aware that my fire fighters cannot guarantee to get sufficient water up to that level to tackle any sizeable blaze.' The article reported that a meeting was due to take place soon between the Home Office, local government, and the private water companies representatives to address the safety concerns. Ciddiqui smiled and sat back in his comfortable chair, relaxing a little, and thinking of the added problems he'd give to all of these organisations. As he basked prematurely in his planned moments of glory, Colonel Safa al-Dabobie entered the room, followed as always by his minder, Ivan Beria. The latter, a Russian, had been recruited by Safa at the time of the fall of the KGB, and was a highly trained professional killer.

'Mr Ciddiqui I understand. Permit me to interrupt your quiet meditations, but please don't get up,' Safa said, standing over Ali Ciddiqui, and smiling at Ali's obvious unease. He extended his hand towards Ciddiqui adding, 'My name is Safa; Colonel Safa al-Dabobie. If it's convenient I would like to have a few moments of your precious time?' Ali Ciddiqui was shaken. He'd never had any previous direct discussion with Safa, let alone one in the middle of the hotel lounge. He tried hard to recover quickly; first standing a little too much to attention, then by asking Safa to take a chair beside him. Both men eventually sat down and Safa spoke first.

'I understand that you are an Armenian Diplomat Mr Ciddiqui? How is the lively city of Yerevan? I have fond memories of my times there.'

Recovering a little from the direct approach of Colonel Safa; an approach that had thrown him, Ciddiqui replied, 'Colonel I'm delighted to meet you. I'm at your disposal for as long as you require. If you wish we can resort to more private surroundings?' he added with a wave of his hand in a desperate attempt to get out of this public domain.

Safa smiled with his mouth, his eyes remained cold and unreadable. He was enjoying the play before the kill, and it didn't matter if the kill, as it was at this time, was purely hypothetical. He could see from Ciddiqui's eyes that the man was afraid. Safa liked that. Because other peoples' fear was his pleasure, and this man was pleasing him.

'I think not Mr Ciddiqui. I have only a small matter to discuss, albeit with major implications,' Safa replied smoothly. 'It will only take a few moments of your valuable time I assure you.' He paused, then added, 'And I must not forget. I have a gift for you, from someone we should both be honoured to serve.' Safa handed Ciddiqui a package about the size of a telephone directory. With an amused smile he said, 'I promised to pass this to you when I met our mutual friend last week.'

Ciddiqui took the package; his hands were shaking slightly which Safa noted. Ciddiqui wondered if it was a bomb? He made to open the box knowing that Safa would stop him if it contained a bomb.

'By all means you may open it now, but our mutual friend told me it was something that you would appreciate in privacy.' Safa motioned with his hand towards the other people sitting around the lounge. The option of opening the box no longer applied.

Ciddiqui inclined his head in reply, now more sure than ever that the package contained some device to cause him pain. He managed to say, 'Thank you for bringing me this gift. When you see our mutual friend please give him my most humble regards. Indeed I'm honoured to be called his friend.'

Safa allowed his mouth to smile by way of a reply. 'The other matter I referred to is of little importance,' Safa said again leading the conversation forward. 'It is merely to say that our two countries are indeed fortunate to have diplomats such as you and I to attend to their affairs. Let us trust that in the future we may have many more informal meetings, preferably in locations like this,' he added, with a sweep of his hand towards the opulent décor of the lounge. 'It's so much better than the prison that people in our business, who fail, generally end up in.' Looking directly into Ciddiqui's eyes he added, 'No windows, no view of the sky. To die in such a place would be the only escape. Indeed for you or I to fail, a quick death would surely be more preferable don't you think?' He arose out of his chair, bowed slightly to Ciddiqui, then walked out of the room. Only three minutes had passed since he'd entered.

Ali Ciddiqui sat very still for a moment or two, although that was an involuntary action on his part. As he did so, he failed to notice Ivan Beria leave the lounge behind Safa. When he'd regained his composure, he got up and left the hotel, carrying the package under his arm.

CHAPTER NINETEEN

The Rat & Carrot was noisy. The noise was mostly coming from a group of off-duty male and female police officers. It was eight-thirty in the evening, and Chris Hall was footing the bill, having one hour earlier beaten Bob McDade in the final of the Scotland Yard Squash Championships. McDade, a stern Scot from Glasgow, and a Superintendent in the River Police, at Waterloo Pier [UW], had held the title for the past three years. Hall's supporters were toasting everything they could think of, including the mighty River Thames, which that day had been exceptionally choppy, and had ensured that McDade's land legs had not quite returned in time for the match.

'Speech, speech' they shouted, 'let's hear from the champion.'
Smiling, Hall got to his feet with more than a little pride. He held up his hands to try to quieten them for a moment.
'Let the champ speak!' someone shouted above the din.
'Right you lot, quiet for a minute, that's all this'll take,' Hall shouted at the top of his voice.
Another cheer went up, and again he tried to quieten them. 'Let me say first of all that the match with Bob was as hard as it should've been for a final, and...quiet, and...,' A roar from the friendly crowd drowned him out yet again as they clapped and cheered.
'Please let me finish,' he shouted above the renewed shouting that followed his opening remarks. 'Bob was a great opponent, and a great sportsman, he's... quiet please...' again he tried before his voice was lost in the friendly banter.
'Speech, speech,' they now shouted towards McDade, having been satisfied from what they'd got from Hall. 'Come on Bob, let's hear from the loser. Tell us why you lost?' they shouted, laughing and enjoying every minute.
McDade, a smile on his weathered face, got to his feet. He started to say, 'It was the river that beat me.., hey let me finish..,' before he too was shouted down in great mirth.
'River Police beaten by rough water,' some of the crowd shouted as they all laughed at McDade's expense, which he took in good spirit. It was just as well, as a minute or two later they poured their drinks over him singing at the top of their voices, 'The River Police get wet at last, the River Police get wet at last,' as they enjoyed every minute of the fun.

The squash final had been a close run thing earlier that evening, with Hall winning the last game by the narrowest of margins. A beautiful executed lob shot from Hall that died in the left-hand corner of the court, and gave McDade no chance, saw to that. As a consequence, Hall was now the Yard's Squash Champion, and he was proud of it!

The morning after the night before, as his alarm went off at 0545 hours; Hall was feeling a little fragile. He groaned as he stretched to reach the clock and turn off the alarm.

'I can't believe it's that time already,' he mumbled as he fell back on to his pillow. Amanda, his wife, was also now awake, guessed how he must feel. She had heard him arrive home just after one-thirty in the morning, and knew that although Chris wouldn't have been drinking anything other than fruit juice, after only four hour's sleep he wouldn't be at his best.

'Well it's your own fault,' she said sleepily. 'You didn't come home till after one o'clock.'

'I just want to lie here for another ten minutes, then I'll be OK,' he said, pulling the duvet up around his shoulders, and turning on his side.

After a moment or two, Amanda said, 'Chris have you remembered what you told me last night, or should I say early this morning. Apart from telling me you won the Squash Championship last night, you said you'd an eight o'clock meeting this morning.'

Hall groaned into his pillow.

'You'd better get up and have your shower or you'll never be in time,' Amanda added.

He was suddenly awake. Yes, he did have a reason to be there early this morning. He got out of bed, heading to the bathroom. Amanda heard the shower being turned on and then the sound of the scales as he stepped on them to weigh himself, something he did every morning. He was now fully awake, and into his normal morning routine.

He shouted above the sound of the shower, 'Amanda did I tell you that both bottles matched? And that we found a metal flask in the Lake in St James's?'

'Yes you did darling, at nearly two o'clock in the morning if I remember right,' she replied with a note of slight sarcasm, and wishing that he'd just do his normal things and let her sleep for another forty minutes or so.

'I'm sure we'll find prints on the flask,' he shouted as he stepped into the shower, 'and I bet the prints match those on the bottle.'

Amanda could hear that he sounded confident, and she liked that. The St James's case had become almost an obsession recently, and she knew that he needed something to break sooner rather than later. But she was too sleepy to reply.

Hall finished his shower, shaved and ate a light breakfast. He dressed quickly and kissed Amanda as she stretched out for her last few minutes in bed that morning, before he left to drive to Scotland Yard. He couldn't wait to get there. He knew that the Lab would've completed their tests, and that Prints would also have produced their findings. Prior to the squash match last night, he'd put together all the pieces they had so far. The flask had been there all along, but not tagged. A note attached by the contractor responsible for collecting the other items stated that as the cap for the flask had not yet been recovered, the flask would remain untagged meantime. Then it had been put aside, and never included with the other items, as the cap hadn't been found. Then Bartram, one of his assigned sergeants, had come into his office with the two matching bottles, one from Kadri's flat, and one from the restaurant. The bottles were identical. He sent the bottles and the flask, to the Yard's Fingerprint Bureau, and asked them to give it priority. They said they would, and that he'd have their report by eight o'clock next morning. Hall's adrenaline had been high yesterday evening, and that had helped him beat McDade. He was now hoping that he'd also beat the odds on the St James's case, starting today, as drove through Elephant and Castle on his way into the Yard.

CHAPTER TWENTY

Ali Ciddiqui again hadn't slept well. He had experienced repeated nightmares, in which he found himself drowning in deep, dark water, water that was poisoned with chemicals that would burn its way through his stomach and intestines. This fear would subconsciously caused him to stop breathing, and in a panic he'd woken up with his heart pounding, gasping for breath. Four times last night he'd suffered the same nightmare; each one seemed to get more realistic. At five-thirty in the morning he decided to get out of bed and replay the video that Colonel Safa had given him in the hotel the day before. He hoped the film would help him erase the nightmares from his mind. He pulled on his towelling robe, went into his study and put on his television and VCR. The film had automatically reversed after being allowed to run to the end when he'd last played it, although he'd stopped watching before the end. When it started, he was again looking at the face of an Iraqi army Major General. The man was smiling, and speaking in the softest of plausible voices, but his eyes, his dark, black eyes looked as cold as ice. Ciddiqui shivered involuntarily, knowing why, but not wanting to admit it. He knew and feared the man. The man was a known psychopath in Iraq; allowed to indulge his every whim. He'd watched the film three times yesterday, and the message was clear. *Ma Ma, Fi Kul Makaan,* was to be brought forward. In the short film the Major General spoke with a building passion, starting in a measured way. However after describing the alleged atrocities inflicted on the people of Iraq by the Allies, the USA and Great Britain, he screamed for revenge. His message was clear: he demanded the death of all those who'd hurt Iraq. None of the infidels was to be spared. *Ma Ma, Fi Kul Makaan,* was to take place in the United Kingdom at midnight on the 27th April; less than one month away. Ciddiqui reaction to the date when he first saw it was that celebrations would already be underway in Baghdad at that time, where the new day of the 28th, Saddam Hussein's birthday, would already be three hours old. *Ma Ma, Fi Kul Makaan* was planned to take place on that day, the Major General now decreed. He stopped the film before it ended, and in doing so he failed, once again, to see the instruction contained in the last few frames, specific instructions displayed in bold Arabic symbols. It read: *Destroy After Viewing.*

Now as he sat in the quietness of his room, his coffee getting cold beside him, he didn't feel much better. Fear still gripping his stomach. He picked up the notes he'd taken yesterday as he'd watched the film for the first time. They were sparse and irrelevant. Only one item, the date of *Ma Ma, Fi Kul Makaan,* was important. Yesterday, when he'd come back from the Carlton Hotel with the *gift,* as Colonel Safa had put it, he had cautiously and apprehensively opened it. Inside, much to his relief, he found only a video film. He poured himself some fresh orange juice, and put on two slices of rye bread to toast. As he did so, he heard his morning newspaper being put through his letterbox. He went into the hall and lifted the newspaper, then poured some more hot Turkish blend coffee. He glanced through *The Times,* as he ate his breakfast. By now he was feeling a little better. The horrors of the night before, and the deep, black water, fading from his consciousness.

CHAPTER TWENTY-ONE

As Ali Ciddiqui finished his breakfast, Commander Chris Hall parked his Range Rover Vogue in the Yard's secure car park. A few minutes later he was at his desk. The Bureau's report he was anxious to see was already there. He opened it at the executive summary as was his habit, leaving the detail for later. He was right. As he read the one-page summary he saw that if proof was needed, he had it. The flask had retained Kadri's fingerprints, and the prints match those on the bottle from Kadri's flat. Kadri had put the flask and the poison in the lake, and from what he now knew, Kadri had more than likely poisoned the six men at Russell Square tube station. 'Mike Hughes is going to love this,' he thought.

'Lorna,' he shouted to his secretary, 'would you set up a meeting with Mike Hughes as soon as you can. Mid morning if possible. Tell him I've some good news regarding St James's. That will get him going.'

'Someone's sounding bright and cheery this morning. Did you have a good game then last night?' she asked, not yet knowing the result of the squash final.

In his haste to get at the report, and after reading the contents, he'd forgotten all about the match.

'You're looking at the Yard's new squash champion,' he said as he went through to his secretary's office. 'I won would you believe?'

'Well done Sir. Congratulations.'

'I bet old McDade will be feeling a bit low on the river this morning,' Hall said mischievously.

'Those River Police think they're the answer to every girl's prayers you know. It must be to do with all that water if you ask me!' Lorna said with feeling. 'I must give Superintendent McDade's secretary a phone and hear what she's got to say for herself. I'll enjoy that,' she added.

'Now, now, no scratching if you please,' Hall said with forced formality. 'Get that meeting with the DAC set-up ASAP,' he said, returning to his room and closing his door. He picked up the report from his desk and began reading the detail. His phone rang. 'Sir the DAC will see you now, and he said he means NOW.'

'Great I'm on my way. See you later Lorna.'

'Look are you sure you don't have a phone number for Kiremla Ltd?' asked the frustrated caretaker of the Isosceles Centre in Glasgow. 'They've taken space in our premises, and they pay their rent, so they must be listed somewhere,' the man complained to Directory Enquiries.

'I'm sorry Sir, I've checked, including new entries, and there's no such name listed. Are you sure that you have the right name and the correct spelling?'

The caretaker, Willie McPhail, had had a bad day, following a rough night. He crashed the telephone down without replying. 'Bloody outfit doesn't exist she's telling me. They pays their rent but they don't exist. I can't believe it,' McPhail said aloud. 'The only bleeding outfit that I can't get hold of,' he said rising to his feet in his small dark office as he poured himself another glass of whisky; his third that morning. McPhail had made contact with all of the names on the list of firms and individuals who were renting space in the Isosceles Centre, and who might have incurred water damage, with the exception of Kiremla Ltd. He'd had enough. He'd tell the police he'd informed everyone. They'd be none the wiser he thought. As he was about to tick the name Kiremla on his list, he remembered he'd let two men into Kiremla's unit the day before the fire? 'How could I forget that?' he asked himself, shaking his head. He picked up the book of entries.

'Aye, there they are,' he muttered, looking at the illegible signatures of the two men. 'Bloody can't write if you ask me. Foreigners as well ah think. Didna say very much either if I remember richt. A lot a bloody help this'll be,' he sighed, contemplating taking the page out and destroying it. Just then his telephone rang. He sighed, then picked it up, '*Isosceles Centre*, how can I help you?'

'Mr McPhail, Chief Inspector Anderson, Strathclyde Police here. We met when the building next to you experienced some fire damage just over a week ago.'

'Aye Inspector, I remember ye,' McPhail replied warily.

'Well Mr McPhail, you were good enough at the time to tell me that you'd be contacting the firms who rent space in the centre,' Anderson said, leaving the question unasked.

McPhail replied instantly, 'I've just about been in touch wi them all. One outfit gein me some trouble. Called Kiremla Ltd, or somethin like that Chief Inspector.'

Anderson listened. 'Well that's not bad considering the number of people using the place. What did you say the firm's name was? I'll see if our boys can come up with something. We've got all these expensive computers at Headquarters here that the public think we only use to catch motorists,' Anderson replied lightly.

McPhail hesitated before continuing, 'K-I-R-E-M-L-A Limited, Kiremla, Chief Inspector.' Did yi get that? Oh, an bye the way, two men frae that outfit came in here the day before the fire to take something ot o' their unit. I jist let them in, it's no my business whit they dae when thuy'r there. They jist drove in wi their caur, used the overheed crane, loaded up, and left.'

'Did you get their names or the registration number of the vehicle Mr McPhail? That could help us find out where they're based,' Anderson asked pointedly.

McPhail paused. 'Aye, I got thur signatures in my entry record, bit a canny read them. It's just a scrall if you ask me. A didn'a get the motor number, but it wis a jeep or something.'

'Well that's something Mr McPhail. I'll have to ask you to bring the entry book into the station at Finnestone, we'll see what we can make of it,' Anderson replied. 'Oh, by the way, do you have any reports of damage as yet?'

'No not yet, but then I've only had a few o' them in to look at thur places. It might tak another few days,' McPhail stated flatly.

'OK Mr McPhail, but I would ask you to keep up the pressure on all the people who've still to check their premises. I'd like to wrap up this incident inside the next week to ten days, and your help would be appreciated.'

McPhail was thinking that he'd like to see it wrapped up quicker than that, tomorrow if possible. He didn't need the police sniffing about the place if he could avoid it.

'Aye Inspector I'm the same, the sooner the better eh. I'll see whit a can do fur you. I'll bring the book in to you on my way hame tonight. Is that time enough?'

'If I'm not here when you come in Mr McPhail, just leave the information with the sergeant at the Desk. Thanks for your help so far.'

'Good Morning Sir,' Hall said brightly as he went into Hughes' office, Hughes' secretary having waved him straight through when he'd appeared at her desk.

'Morning Chris,' Hughes replied before rising from his seat. 'Chris let me introduce you to Mr Peter O'Brien,' he added, as a tall, slim man about Hall's age got up from a seat at Hughes' conference table. 'Peter's the Private Secretary, the PS in other words, to the Home Secretary who's had our St James's case to contend with Chris. Peter, Commander Chris Hall.' O'Brien and Hall shook hands, each making strong eye contact. Hughes continued, 'I think it is time you both met in view of the current circumstances associated with the incident.'

The younger men exchanged a few pleasantries, then sat down.

'Chris, Peter's here this morning in connection with another matter, albeit similar in many ways to that of the St James's incident,' Hughes stated. 'This other matter may not have any connection with the St James's Park, but Peter will give you the full details.'

Hall looked at O'Brien as Hughes continued. 'We'll talk about St James's afterwards Chris, although I hear you're anxious to pass on some good news. We could do with some of that,' he added, smiling to both men.

Hall nodded; thinking whatever it was that O'Brien was going to tell him, it must be important, as the DAC was prepared to wait for some good news. O'Brien was now opening his brief case and took out two files. Hall noticed the Home Office badge on the case, and the secure lock. O'Brien opened one of the documents, took out two sheets of paper, and passed one each to Hughes and Hall. O'Brien then said, 'Gentlemen, Her Majesty's Government has issued an APW, an *All Ports Warning,* he added almost apologetically. As you will know, that's a warning stepping up security to the equivalent of *Red Alert* at Scotland Yard. The reason being, it seems there's a possible threat of the deadly bacterium anthrax being smuggled into Britain. Through our ports, sea and air that is, and possibly even the channel tunnel. We're treating the threat as serious, hence this hastily convened meeting.' He looked directly at Hall, then added, 'We've had intelligence reports from Baghdad that suggest Hussein is considering using anthrax as a weapon of terrorism by sending it to

London, possibly disguised, can you believe as tax-free perfume and cosmetics for both men and women?'

Hall glanced back to the sheet O'Brien had given him. It was a proposed press release from HM Government, stating that the public should be informed of the general facts concerning the danger. They were also to be assured that steps were being taken, in co-operation with other countries, to deal with the threat. It was a typical *Told You So* cover, Hall thought.

'Anthrax is easy to propagate,' O'Brien continued. 'It diffuses nicely into the atmosphere. It's easy to handle, and it kills slowly enough for those infected to spread it around before it's noticed. All in all, it's the terrorists' ideal weapon.'

O'Brien cleared his throat, 'Now the point of my coming here this morning,' O'Brien said, 'was to ask you to run with this anthrax situation along with the HCN concern. You could be up to speed on the issue faster than any other team we could put together starting now. At this time we don't expect there will be an immediate saturation of the bacteria, in whatever form, after shave or otherwise, and for all we know it may even be scaremongering on Hussein's part to keep our hands full.'

O'Brien looked at both men assessing their reaction. Neither said anything.

'What I propose Commander, is that you and your team continue with the St James's incident as required, and if necessary, and I will be the judge of that, take on the anthrax threat in parallel.' O'Brien looked directly at Hall. 'Is that something you feel you could take on board Commander?'

Hall rose to his feet, and started to walk around the room. Hughes looked towards O'Brien, a smile on his face, and added, 'Chris walks around all the time in here Peter. It helps him to think, he tells me,' Hughes said, trying to lighten the atmosphere.

'Before I give Mr O'Brien my answer Sir, I'd like to bring both of you up to date regarding St James's.' Hall continued walking. He stopped at the electronic wallboard. 'What do we have?' he asked. Picking up a pen he started to write down on the left-hand side of the board the known facts. As a sub-heading he wrote the name Kadri. Underneath the name he printed the following: spoke English, murdered, About thirty years of age, HCN bottle and flask. He continued with more details of where Kadri lived, worked, no passport found, friends (one, not traced), nationality, allegedly Turkish. He added in another sub-heading: appears in film taken at St James's Park; more than likely involved in the deaths of the six people.

'OK so far?' he asked, looking around at the other two men.

'Carry on Commander,' O'Brien said with a trace of impatience in his voice.

Hall continued, specifically addressing Hughes, 'Sir one or two of the items listed above have only just come to light. That's the reason why I requested this meeting. The flask for example, we now have identification of the fingerprints on it, and they're Kadri's.'

O'Brien interrupted saying, 'Tell me Commander. Where do you think Mr Kadri obtained the HCN? That product, as you well know, is restricted.'

Hall hesitated before replying. 'One of the two missing items on my list of facts Mr O'Brien. The other is the identity of Kadri's alleged friend. We'll come back to those St James's items in a moment. Let's now have a look at the other column. What have we got there to work with there?' he asked. He wrote down the word anthrax, and below that started writing down the headings O'Brien had spoken of a few minutes before. Air, sea and channel ports, UK tourists' tax-free goods, and the Middle East connection in Iraq. 'That's it!' he said.

The three men were quiet for a moment, then Hughes said, 'Chris, you've only another few minutes to finish. Peter doesn't have all day you know.'

'My first reaction,' Hall said, 'is that we need one major link between the events. It could be Kadri's and his friend and fellow countryman's alleged birthplace. Stated to be Turkey, but *what-if...?* Just for the moment let us assume that both men were born elsewhere. Say in Iraq or Afghanistan for example.' Hall paused, 'If that was the case, then we've much more to work with. Both countries feel they have good reason to strike back at the Western Allies. Let's not forget also that we already know that fifteen hundred litres of HCN are still out there somewhere. A vast quantity of deadly poison, and a threat to the British public. All consistent with what our intelligence people tell us about the recent mutterings of the Iraqi regime. Now Mr O'Brien you tell us this anthrax situation may be connected to Iraq!'

It was O'Brien's turn to get to get up from his seat. He walked over to Hall and put his hand on Hall's shoulder. Turning to Hughes he said, 'Yes, I'm impressed Deputy Assistant Commissioner. Your man Chris here; if I may call you that?' he said looking back and smiling at Hall, 'your man has come to a fairly accurate conclusion very quickly, very quickly indeed, and one with which I concur.'

'Thank you Peter, I was almost sure he would, other wise I wouldn't have put Chris forward to you.'

O'Brien nodded, then continued addressing both men. 'Please be seated gentlemen. I came here this morning primarily in connection with the anthrax incident. However we've had some, let me say,' he paused for a second or two then added, 'some *loose* information from an unusual source in relation to the St James's affair. The information came from a British citizen, a dental surgeon. A Dr Bruce Miller, a Scotsman who recently moved his home to Turkey. He and his wife now live in a lovely town called Adana, on the Turkish Mediterranean coast. I've been there. It's beautiful! You see his wife was born there, and Miller met her while serving with the Royal Air Force in Cyprus, during his National Service days in the late fifties. He has just retired, and he and his wife, lucky people, intend to spend their winters in that lovely part of the world,' O'Brien said with look of appreciation. After a slight pause he added, 'Let me continue. For a number of years Dr Miller ran a dental practice here in London, Wick Square to be exact, just behind Russell Square.'

Both Hughes and Hall nodded their knowledge of the location.

'Now the point of the story,' O'Brien said, 'is that Kadri was a patient of Miller's. Recently Kadri required a visit to Dr Miller with some tooth problem or other. During his last visit, and apparently amid some delicate root canal work, Kadri uttered some obscenity, not directly at Dr Miller you understand, but to the world in general. According to Miller the words Kadri said are not in the Turkish language. Arabic, Miller said. Words that would never've been spoken by any Turk. Something to do with male national pride more than dialect I understand. Now that is a very important point let me tell you.' O'Brien looked at Hughes, then Hall. He sat down, then said, 'You see during Kadri's first visit to Dr Miller's surgery, he told Miller that he'd been born and lived most of his life in Turkey, not too far from the town of Adana. Naturally Miller remembered this, his own wife coming from there. Apparently on reflection since he recently returned to Turkey, and following discussions with his wife, Miller has reportedly said the words Kadri used were Arabic, with an Iraqi dialect. Words, he said that were more likely to be used by a city dweller, as opposed to a man from the countryside. Baghdad more than likely Miller stated. You see Dr Miller, during his National Service, also spent some time in Iraq, particular in Baghdad.'

Hughes and Hall both attempted to speak at once, Hall conceded the opportunity to the DAC.

'How can we substantiate Dr Miller's statements Peter?' Hughes asked. 'If Miller has now retired it may be difficult. Does he still have any dental records for example?'

O'Brien smiled. 'Better than that Mike. The dental records of Mr Abdullah Kadri will be with you some time this afternoon. You see Dr Miller was here in London a week or so ago, on some personal business. He and his wife were entertaining a young chap, a Dr Andrew Wilson, who is apparently buying Miller's practice from him. They had dinner at Fred's restaurant in Islington where Kadri worked, apparently a place Miller and his wife used regularly when they lived here in London. They'd been there the week before as well when they'd just arrived back in London and had been served by Kadri. Anyway during the course of the most recent visit there, Miller asked after the waiter he knew as Abdullah, only to be told the unfortunate news that the man had met an untimely death. Well it's not quite something you like to discuss over your *Brochette of Salmon Teriyaki*, I'm sure you understand. However another waiter explained to Miller that the police were, how do I say this kindly Mike? *Baffled!* I think that's the word that was used.'

Hughes and Hall shuffled uncomfortably in their seats.

O'Brien cleared his throat before continuing, 'Miller and his wife were due to return to Turkey the next day, and had little time to think again about the poor unfortunate waiter. Miller however didn't put the event out of his mind entirely. He'd been puzzled at the time by Kadri's outburst in Arabic, and thereafter a little uneasy about the man's claim to have come from Adana. Shortly after his return to Turkey, Miller had occasion to be in the capital city of Ankara, a frightfully warm place in the summer; temperatures in the middle forties if I remember correctly,' O'Brien detoured. 'Anyway where was I? Yes Dr Miller had flown to Ankara on some business matter, and while waiting to be taken back to the airport later that evening, he'd gone to a bar for a drink. It so happened that the bar was opposite our Embassy there, and no doubt the sight of the Union Jack flying above the building stirred Miller's nationalistic memories. Anyway he was good enough to put aside his initial thoughts that he must have been mistaken and he went in to the Embassy and simply reported to a Desk Officer there more or less what I've just told you over the last few minutes. He did say to the officer however, that he hoped the information might help to catch whoever murdered Kadri. You'll now see why I was impressed with your quick conclusion Commander,' O'Brien stated.

Hughes and Hall glanced at each other, knowing the implications of what they'd just heard.

O'Brien said quietly, 'Yes, we have some reason to believe that Mr Kadri, or whatever his real name is, may not have been Turkish at all? He was more than likely to have been an Iraqi.'

Hughes broke the silence that had followed O'Brien's revelation by asking, 'How can we be of help Peter?'

O'Brien smiled, then looking at Hall replied, 'What do you say Chris, are you prepared to handle both incidents?'

'With Deputy Assistant Commissioner Hughes' permission Peter I'd be more than willing to take both the anthrax threat and St James's HCN Case.'

'You have it Chris,' Hughes replied. The men stood up and shook hands. O'Brien asked that Hall report through Hughes for the sake of protocol, and invited Hall to meet him at the Home Office in two days time for further briefing. He then excused himself saying, 'Parliamentary business and the worries of the world gentlemen.' Hughes escorted him back to his chauffeured driven car. Hall meanwhile sat down, wondering just what he'd let himself in for. When Hughes returned, he pressed his intercom and said, 'Could we have some coffee please?'

CHAPTER TWENTY-TWO

Ali Ciddiqui had just signed the fax he was having sent to *The Times.* The message simply stated, *Water Water, Everywhere, April 27th.* 'Make sure they are aware that it must be in the *Personal Column* tomorrow,' he said to his PA. He was feeling better today than of late, his mind more relaxed. When she returned a few minutes later saying that the fax had gone, he said, 'I would like to take you to dinner tonight; would you like that Hala?'

'Yes Ali I would, but only if you're going to be in a better mood than you've been of late,' she said. 'You've not been nice to me recently. It's as if you've something, or someone, more important on your mind.'

Putting on his most hurt facial expression, Ciddiqui responded, and trying to sound more relaxed than he felt at her mention of *more important things,* said, 'That could never be my lovely.' He knew he'd have to put Colonel Safa out of his thoughts. He looked up at her, then said enthusiastically; 'We'll go to Grassini's at the Carlton Hotel tonight. Would you like that?'

'If you promise to be nice to me Ali. No sulking, promise?'

'Of course I'll be nice to you, and I promise. You'll be overwhelmed with my love and kindness. I'll even buy you a present; a surprise. Would you like that?' he asked, getting up from his chair and putting his arms around her waist from behind.

'You smell delicious,' he said quietly into her ear and gently drew his lips down the nape of her neck. She moaned with pleasure.

Pressing her body back into him, her eyes closed, she replied in an enticing voice, 'Yes, let's go to Grassini's, then when you take me home I'll open my present. I may find something for you as well if you're good,' she hinted, pulling her body away from him, and leaving him in no doubt that he should wait till later to continue.

Ali Ciddiqui smiled, and looked at his watch. 'If you say so my lovely. Until tonight, anyway I must go out now. When I pass the hotel I'll ask them to reserve our table in Grassini's.' He kissed her neck once more before leaving the apartment. His first destination after leaving his apartment was Cartier, the jewellers in Sloane Street. He was already looking forward to the late evening.

As Ciddiqui crossed Cadogan Place in Belgravia, McPhail the caretaker of the Isosceles Centre, carrying a brown envelope went into Cranston Hill Police Station in Glasgow. He asked the Desk Sergeant if he could speak to Inspector John Anderson. The Desk Sergeant asked McPhail his name, then picked up his telephone and spoke to someone. Replacing the phone he said, 'Take a seat Sir, the Chief Inspector will be with you in a few minutes.'

McPhail sat down on the uncomfortable, straight-backed chair and picked up a magazine the front page of which was headed, *Drugs Rule Britannia*. An article in the magazine described the current situation throughout the length and breadth of the UK. McPhail had barely started to read the article when a young woman dressed in civilian clothes appeared at his side. She asked him to follow her, saying that Chief Inspector Anderson would see him now. She walked through the ground floor corridor, and climbed the stairs to the first floor level. She knocked on a door bearing the Chief Inspector's name.

'Mr McPhail for you now Sir,' she said holding the door open to allow McPhail to go through, smiling as she did so.

'Ah Mr McPhail, take a seat,' Anderson said as he motioned with his hand to the chair facing his heavily laden desk. 'This paperwork never seems to get any less no matter how long I work at it,' Anderson said resignedly, and pushing some files aside to make room between. 'I thought computers were supposed to make it all easier for us, at least that's what they told me,' he said smiling trying to put McPhail at ease. 'Now Mr McPhail I take it you've brought me the entry records and signatures we talked about the other day? We should be able to resolve this with little trouble I hope. Let me get back to the real issues; the local drug problem for example.'

McPhail sat up straight in his chair. He never felt comfortable with the police around, let alone sitting inside a police station. 'Aye, I've broat the entry book. You'll no be able tae read the signatures Inspector, at least ah couldn'a,' he said, and coughing to clear his throat as he reluctantly handed over his records.

Anderson took the book, which he thought was surprisingly clean, and placed it on his desk. He lifted a form from the side of his desk and looking at McPhail said, 'I hope this is the last of these. It'll only take me a minute or two with your help to fill this in Mr McPhail, and I might have to ask you a question or two. OK?'

McPhail didn't like that sound of that one bit. He reluctantly replied, 'Aye.'

Anderson looked at the insurance claim form then said, 'Mr McPhail, you say that two men called at the centre the day before the fire. They uplifted some heavy objects from the unit they rent; the Kiremla unit that is. Is that correct?'

'Aye, they loaded up their caur, a jeep thing as I remember it, then left. A didna see if thur wus anything left in the storage unit.'

'I take it you have duplicate keys for all the units Mr McPhail?'

McPhail rocked in his seat, then replied 'Naw, we didna keep spare keys Inspector. The management didna believe in't. Ta dae wi the insurance they said.'

'I must warn you Mr McPhail,' Anderson replied looking at the uncomfortable McPhail, 'it's against the law for the owners of facilities such as the centre, not to be in possession of at least a master key. But we'll come back to that later.' He continued filling in the last few parts of the claim form before saying, 'Now Mr McPhail, would you please sign just here,' he said turning it round and pointing to the line for signature. 'The form states that you willingly offered me access to your records, and copies of the signatures of the men who opened up the Kiremla storage unit. It also gives permission to the police to gain access to the premises to assist with their inquires should we ever need to. Saves us the trouble of getting a search warrant Mr McPhail, and it might help your bosses regarding the master key, although I can't promise anything if you know what I mean.'

McPhail took the pen Anderson offered him, and scrolled his name on the line Anderson had pointed to.

'Now,' Anderson said sternly, 'we'll need to get into that unit to check that it's suffered no damage. It's the only unit outstanding from the insurance company report on that fire next door to you.'

McPhail shook his head in resigned agreement.

'What we'll do Mr McPhail, is that I'll have some of my lads come round their tomorrow morning, and maybe by then you'll have found your master key. What time would suit Mr McPhail?'

McPhail coughed noisily, then replied, 'Anytime, it disnae matter, anytime.'

Anderson stood up making sure that McPhail knew it was time to leave.

'Thanks for your help. We'll no doubt need to talk again,' he said taking McPhail back into the general office area.

McPhail hesitated as he reached the door then said, 'Oh Inspector, a've jist thought o' something. We've got security cameras at the centre. They were pit in a few months ago. Only work when ye put oon the lights in any o' the units. Whit a mean is, we might hae some film o' the men who came in that day. Wid you like t'see it?'

Anderson paused, thinking what did it matter, but replied anyway saying, 'That's a good idea in view of what took place the next day, the fire I mean. You could pass the film over to my lads when they get there tomorrow. We'll take a look at it Mr McPhail.'

'Right Chief Inspector,' McPhail answered, getting Anderson's rank correct for once. 'A'll dae that. It's always nice tae help the polis,' he added.

The young woman holding open the door smiled at McPhail, having been party to the last minute or so's dialogue between him and the Chief Inspector. She asked him to follow her, saying she'd see him back downstairs. As soon as he was outside the building, McPhail muttered to himself about doing bloody police work as well as his own.

DAC Hughes and Chris Hall had spent the past two hours discussing the consequences of their earlier meeting with PS O'Brien from the Home Office. They'd discussed manning requirements, which Hall suggested could be, if required, supplemented by other forces from outside the Metropolitan area. Hughes and Hall both felt that the HCN and the anthrax issues were bound to take on a wider profile than that of only the Greater London area.

'Right Sir, I'll get that going right away. Oh by the way, I take it that if I do need some outside, or even inside help, that I'll have your authority to call it in whenever? If I want someone working alongside me from the *Anti-Terrorist Branch* for example, can I have them?'

'Chris you can have the whole of the Met's *Security Business Group* as far as I'm concerned. And I'm sure the Minister will agree to you having any other business group as well. Just as long as we sort this thing out quickly. Just get on with it. You and I will meet on a daily basis to discuss progress, etc. I also think we should warn all National Police forces, Scottish, Welsh and our Northern Ireland counterparts. Send them the description of Kadri's unknown acquaintance. Make it clear that that the man is probably from the Middle East, more than likely Iraq. Pass on any information, no matter how little we have on Kiremla. Give them everything Chris. I think we'll need all the help we can get on this. Hughes paused then added, 'By the way, phone that dentist in Islington to make sure he knows we're waiting on the dental records he promised to send us.'

'OK Sir, will do. I still think we should put the heavy hand on that company up in Hatfield - Zenecal Chemicals - who released the HCN to Kiremla in the first place. A short, sharp fright will do them no harm, apart from scaring the hell out of them.'

'Just make sure it's done properly,' Hughes said cautiously, 'no muck-up's or any damage to people or property. You know what I mean. It's one thing scaring them into action, but we don't want the media down our necks as well. We've managed to keep them quiet for sometime now but that won't last forever, mark my words.'

Hall nodded in agreement. "Right Sir, I've got the picture. I'll see you tomorrow. What time shall we schedule for these daily meetings?'

Hughes considered the question. 'Make it late afternoon, say four o'clock. No more than thirty minutes tops, OK! Now get on with it before we have some real catastrophe to content with. Birds and ducks are one thing, and some people may say the same about the down and outs at Russell Square, but who knows what they may do next time!'

As Hall left Hughes' office he thought through the past few hours. There was still no evident motive for the each of the events that had actually taken place. Wildlife, and six people poisoned, and now a nation-wide threat of anthrax. What were these events leading up to he wondered? When he got back to his office he asked his secretary, 'Would you get me Chief Inspector Iain Marshall of the *Anti-Terrorist Branch* please. And will you try and get my wife. Tell her I'm going to be late tonight. Say I said the DAC's starting to get excited about something. She'll know what I mean.' He went to a filing cabinet and took out a document folder containing blank *All-Forces Alert* notices. He started to draft the *Alert* message he'd circulate throughout the UK. He paused for a moment, then remembered he'd still to contact the dentist and get Kadri's dental records. 'Lorna would you also get me a Dr Andrew Wilson. I don't have his number, but it's Wick Square, near Russell Square. If he's engaged ask him to call me back as soon as he can please.'

'If it's the dental records of Mr Kadri you're after Sir, they arrived about ten minutes ago. I'm having them photocopied just now. Is that OK?'

'Thanks Lorna. Look, I want this AFA to go out asap,' Hall said. 'It's to be faxed to the full list on the cover sheet. Oh, and those phone calls. Would you get them right away please Lorna?'

Lorna McBride didn't reply, she had returned to her desk, and was halfway through dialling the *Anti-Terrorist Branch* as Hall was still speaking.

Hall's phone rang in his office. He went through and lifted it. 'Sir, I've got Chief Inspector Marshall of the *Anti-Terrorist Branch* on the telephone for you now. I'll put you through.'

'Thanks Lorna.' Hall swivelled his chair until he was looking out of his office window. He heard the line being put through, then said cheerily, 'Chris Hall here Iain, how you doing mate? Still chasing those black spotted balls and those fruit cakes out there?'

'I'm in the pink my friend, although my squash is not as good as yours I hear,' Marshall replied. 'Congratulations on your win the other night; long may you reign. I met old Bob on an exercise this morning. He's still miffed at losing his crown. He's telling me that next year he'll apply for shore duties a day before his matches, so that his sea legs don't sink him. You can imagine how that went down with the boys. He got rollicked well and truly I can tell you.'

Hall laughed, then said, 'Iain, I'm on the scrounge.'

'Just like any other policemen!' Marshall retorted in his quick sense of humour.

'Hall laughed, then said, 'Iain, seriously, I'd like to have your man Ian Day seconded to me for a few weeks. Something special we're on here needs some particular intensive attention. If you can oblige I'll get the papers put in place in due course, but I thought I'd speak to you first to make sure there'd be no problem.'

Marshall hesitated a few seconds, then replied, 'Day's my best man Chris, but you can have him for a few weeks. Some here would say have him for a few years, if you know what I mean?'

They both laughed, as each recalled one or two moments of Day's sense of humour.

'Iain I appreciate this. I know what its like to lose your key man, even for a week or two, and even if it happens to be Day.'

'We've just concluded a major training programme Chris, so he's in sparkling form. Well you know him; you know what he's like. When would you like him to start?'

'Ask him to pop his head in here later today if possible, we can have a chat. This is not an ordinary case Iain, and I think he may have to give it some thought. Heavy hours, not that that will be much different to what he's used to, but there are other factors which I'll explain to him when I see him.'

'No problem, always pleased to help out an old mate in time of need, as they say Chris.'

'Iain you know the saying, *A friend in need,... is a pest.*'

The men laughed, then Marshall said, 'Consider it done Chris.'

'Thanks, that's one I owe you. I'll get the paperwork done to back up the action in the next day or so. Take care my friend, and look after yourself out there. Thanks again.'

Hall replaced his telephone. It rang instantly. His secretary told him that Mrs Hall had got his message, and that the photocopies were back. She then asked for the AFA so that she could dispatch it.

Hall thanked her, then said he'd have the AFA ready shortly if the phones would just stop ringing. He then asked her to book the first floor conference room tonight for a five o'clock meeting, and to phone Inspectors Dobbie, Johnston, and the Met Pharmacist, Jim Bannistair, and ask them to attend the meeting. He added that he expected an Inspector Day from the *Anti-Terrorist Branch* to drop in late afternoon, and that he should be brought to the meeting as soon as he arrived. 'Oh and Lorna, I'd like you to come as well. Take the minutes, that sort of thing.' He had a feeling that his planned actions would more than likely be subjected to closer scrutiny than usual.

When he put down his telephone, his secretary brought up his diary on her computer screen, noting that he already had a half-hour meeting with the DAC at four o'clock, which just moments ago been changed to eight pm. She amended the entry and copied it to him, highlighting the change. She'd be working late that night, she figured. Picking up the phone she dialled her husband and asked him to pick her up at the Yard a little after eight - hoping he'd take the bait and take her to dinner somewhere on the way home.

Hall completed the AFA and passed it through to be distributed throughout the UK. As his mind now started to focus on the various strengths of his team and life-threatening matters such as anthrax and HCN, a sharp crash of thunder brought him back to his immediate senses. The weather in the UK over the past few days had been the worst of its kind ever recorded for the time of the year. In middle England entire towns had been flooded and cut-off, rail lines deep in water, roads submerged, and thousands of kilometres of riverbanks had burst. It seemed there was water everywhere. He'd glanced through *The Times* earlier, and had read that chiefs of the privatised water companies in the some of the affected areas were quoted as saying, 'It's the wrong kind of rain that has fallen........ ' They said what they wanted was lighter, gentle rain, over a longer period of time, instead of the deluges that had taken place. It seemed as if they were never happy - or more importantly, never prepared. The companies took themselves seriously but not their customers. Companies were still predicting water shortages during the coming summer months in regions where televised news reports and the press coverage were showing hundreds of people being rescued by boat from their homes. In some severe cases the floodwater was at eaves level. *The Times* had stated that an industry that made statements about, *the kind of rain...*, could not be taken seriously, and asked what were the privatised companies providing in terms of security and protection of the water capacity they already had in their possession? Public confidence in the water industry was at an all time low. As he looked out of his window at the current deluge, he was reminded of press comments. He shrugged, not my problem Hall thought, as he switched on his desk lamp to lighten the gloom, returning to his paperwork.

Hall met with Dobbie, Johnston and Bannistair just after five o'clock. He explained the assignment they were being offered, as well as the possible risks. He then asked Bannistair to give them a short talk on the two poisons, particularly from the pharmaceutical point of view, adding that anyone of them, or even all of them, could be confronted with the deadly threat sometime in the near future.
Bannistair, now on his feet, explained that anthrax, the second poison, was one of the most deadly biological products in the world. In his refined Scottish accent and somewhat nasal tones, he said,

'...and anthrax, going back fifty years or so, was initially thought to be a disease affecting livestock, and only occasionally transmitted to humans. Not so, now it produces severe pneumonia that normally results in the death of the infected victim.' He paused, taking a drink from a glass of water, then continued saying, 'A number of biological products were incorporated into weapons of war during the Cold War, manufactured by both sides, including anthrax. Even before that, during World War II, our boffins managed to produce chemical weapons in a ham-fisted manner. One experiment with anthrax, and using no more than a few dozen small canisters of the stuff at that, out on the tiny island of Gruinard off the west coast of Scotland,' Bannistair stated, 'was so botched up that it rendered the island uninhabitable for more than forty years.' He paused to let the warning sink in. 'Of course there have been programmes for the elimination of these products over many years. There still are, but as with most things military there are always losses of the products. Some of the stuff goes missing in other words. Some of the products may well have fallen into the hands of unstable regimes, for example countries in the Middle East are known to possess sizeable quantities of these illegal, deadly products. By now they may have produced some themselves, but more likely they bought, or were presented with them for purposes unknown. You can never ever be too careful when dealing with biological products. Believe me, one slip is one too many.'

Bannistair finished and Hall thanked him. Hall himself then addressed his team, which now included Detective Inspector Ian Day of the *Anti-Terrorist Branch*. Day had arrived a few minutes after the meeting had started. Hall now introduced him to the others. Day was what was expected in today's security force, tough and uncompromising. He was forty-five years old, tall, and in good physical condition. What hair he had left was grey and cut very close to his scalp. He was good company, and great fun. Hall knew this to his cost, having been the subject of some of Day's pranks in the past. In matters of business however, he knew Day was a good man to be alongside in times of trouble. Day's earlier SAS training confirmed to that.

Hall wrote down on the wall chart the points he wished to bring to the team's attention. Turning around he said, 'You've just heard from Jim some important points about the two possible sources of mass death and destruction, *HCN* and now anthrax. That's why I've listed it as our initial target,' he turned and read as he pointed to the chart, 'Establish Identities behind *Kiremla Ltd.* That, as you'll remember from the briefing, is the company who purchased a large quantity of hydrocyanic acid, or HCN for short. We must focus on what we know of them. Their approach to the acquisition of the product; the mode of transport they used; the accents or mannerisms of the people who conducted the transaction. In short, I want to know everything from their inside leg size, to their choice of aftershave. Everything. They can't have just completely disappeared. Nobody's that smart. They'll have made a few mistakes, believe me. It's up to us to find them.'

The room was silent as the men took in Hall's words. 'Sir,' Mark Dobbie asked, 'do we actually know if the anthrax is in the country at this time or not? What I mean is, we know that the HCN is out there somewhere, but the anthrax, has it been brought in yet?'

'Good point Mark. No we don't know that anthrax has been illegally brought into Britain, at least not yet. However we've reports from some of our foreign security sources that it may soon be, and possibly disguised as anything from hair spray, to after shave.'

Jim Johnston spoke next. 'Sir returning to the HCN. Why don't we just pull in that Zenecal lot? Bring them into the Yard, then put them under some pressure? It'll sure as hell make them focus their minds on that transaction to Kiremla. It's got to be worth a try don't you think?'

'You're right Jim,' Hall replied, 'only I'm planning to do it a little differently. I want Ian to lead a raid on their premises,' he looked towards Day as he spoke, 'although we've still to ask him if he'd like to join us or not?' Hall said smiling.

'Try and keep me out Sir,' Day replied speaking for the first time. 'From what I've heard so far, this sounds like a real interesting case, or cases I should say. I've got to agree with the Commander though,' he said looking at the others. 'I think a full raid on the place will concentrate the minds of the people in that organisation, whatever it's called. Excuse me for not being up to speed on the names and places just yet. I only heard about my involvement from my chief an hour or so ago,' he said with a smile. 'It's been my experience that when people, or organisations, are subjected to an unexpected, high profile and jarring, what shall we call it? Yes visit. They are very

125

helpful for the first hour or so; after that they get a bit angry, less helpful and a bit stroppy. You've got to get to the core quick, right to the point, and direct to the boss man. We must make sure the Managing Director is on the premises; that I believe is crucial,' he stressed. 'We can set up some factitious business meeting with the MD, say for example, to consider placing a large order for something they deal in. We can then use the *Prevention of Terrorism Act* once we admit that we're not who they think we are, and that will help with the lack of a warrant if you know what I mean Sir,' Day said looking at Hall. He then continued, 'We then try to question everyone on the premises within the first one to two hours. Starting just after nine o'clock in the morning, just when they are getting down to work.'

The room was silent after Day stopped speaking.

Hall stood up, then said; 'Now you know why I've asked Ian to join us. Ian, I take it from what you've said you'd like to set up the visit?'

'I would Sir.'

Hall looked at the others, who all appeared to be in agreement, then replied, 'That's fine with me Ian, you lead it. We've full access to any resources you need. I want the visit to take place within the next forty-eight hours, no later. Keep me right on who and what you call for. I've got to keep DAC Hughes in the picture as well. OK?'

'Will do Sir.'

'Now Ian bring me a draft proposal for this *visit* early tomorrow morning, around about eight OK? We can talk it through. I can then brief the DAC afterwards, and hopefully get his 'go-ahead'.'

'Fine Sir,' Day replied, 'now I'd like to have a chat with the rest of the team so that we can get to know one another a wee bit better. I find it helps to smooth off the edges once we get down to the real business.'

'Sure Ian, you take the chair as of now.'

The team meeting continued in an upbeat mood for two hours or more, each member promoting their individual thoughts on how best to handle the *visit*. Eventually, when he was sure they'd firmed up as a team, Hall said, 'I'll leave you all to it. I'll close the formal meeting now as I've got to report to DAC Hughes in ten minutes or so. Anyway, welcome aboard Ian, and when you finish here check with Lorna when I'm due back from the DAC. I'd like a quick word with you later.'

Hall left the meeting and made his way to Hughes' office.

After Hall left the room, Lorna, his secretary, interrupted the meeting saying, 'Sir, I'm sorry to interrupt, but Commander Hall will be back in his office around eight forty this evening. I know he said you were to get in touch through me later, but you see I'm due to be picked up by my husband in a few minutes.'

She flushed a little, but Day sensing the situation replied, 'Off with you girl. If your man weren't taking you out I'd be asking you myself. Now off you go and enjoy yourself, we'll manage fine, and this parts off the record anyway. OK?'

Lorna McBride smiled at Day and the others. They were all getting to know the newest addition to their department, and from what they'd seen and heard so far, they liked him. Lifting her notes McBride said, 'Oh, as Commander Hall hasn't fixed a date for our next meeting, I'll raise it with him in the morning and add it to the minutes.' Smiling, slightly flustered, she left the room. It was seven fifty-eight; she'd started at eight that morning.

CHAPTER TWENTY-THREE

Ali Ciddiqui politely declined the wine waiter's offer of the last of the *Vigna Case Nere 1990 Barola Docg.* It had cost him eighty pounds for the bottle. He wiped his lips with his napkin, stood up to allow Hala to leave the table. They'd both enjoyed their quiet dinner and Ali was beginning to think of his due desserts. He'd given her an exquisite pearl and emerald necklace as they'd enjoyed their *Kir Royal* aperitif. He was anticipating being submerged and overwhelmed in her gratitude later.

He asked the hovering waiter, 'May I have my bill please,' causing the *Maitre d'* to suddenly appear as if from nowhere.

Smiling, in acknowledgement of the expected reply in positive terms the suave and impeccably dressed man asked, 'I trust both Sir and Madame enjoyed their dinner this evening?'

'As always, as always. Where better to eat in London than *Grassini's* I always say, and Madame is especially appreciative of your good Italian food.'

Ali's bill was presented to him. He scrolled his signature on it, and passed it back to the young Italian waiter, placing a twenty-pound note on the plate. He arose to acknowledge Hala's return, as the *Maitre d'* pulled out her chair, allowing her to be reseated. Hala smiled as she sat back down.

'The *Baccala with Polenta* was delicious tonight, delicious,' Hala said. 'What more can one ask for?' she added with a warm smile in the direction of the preening *Maitre d'*.

Ali Ciddiqui also sat back down, albeit a little reluctantly. He'd other needs to fulfil, and he was now ready to leave. The *Maitre d'* evaporated as silently and as quickly as he'd appeared.

Thinking he'd better set the mood for later, and hoping it wouldn't be much later, he took Hala's hand and gently kissed it. Seductively he said, 'Hala my lovely, you look so beautiful tonight I can't take my eyes off you. Have you enjoyed yourself?' Without waiting for a reply he continued, 'Was I good to you? Was I more like my old self? I'm feeling like my old self,' he added with heavy sexual overtones.

'I've had a lovely evening Ali, and what's more the gift you've given me,' she said, fingering the necklace and looking into his eyes, 'is so beautiful. It'll be the last thing I'll let you take off me later tonight,' she said kissing him full on the lips. When they finished she added, 'I'll make you so happy, so relaxed and contented that you'll have no wish to leave my bed. Stay with me tonight. Promise me that you'll do that Ali, promise?' She lent forward and kissed him again.

'How can I refuse. Come let's go now, I'm beyond waiting,' Ali stated a little too loud, causing the only other couple still in the restaurant to look round at him. Hala rose slightly after he did, and they made their way towards the exit. Again the *Maitre d'* appeared and wished them a good night and pleasant dreams. Ciddiqui slipped him another large bank note and they left heading for the Chelsea Embankment, and the apartment he'd purchased for Hala some months before.

As the morning shift began at eight am. sharp, the officers and men from Cranston Hill Police Station left on their respective tasks. DC's Butler and Campbell set off in the direction of Washington Street, near the Broomielaw area of Glasgow. They'd been briefed that they should gain entry, by whatever means necessary, to the Kiremla unit in the Isosceles Centre. They were to take note of the condition of the unit, and observe if the contents, if any, had been damaged by the ingress of water. Their Chief Inspector had also added that they should pick up a video film when they were there, and bring it back to the station.

As the two men headed towards the Centre, Butler said to his colleague, 'We get the jobs don't we Colin? You know it must be three or four months since we had something interesting to get our teeth into.'

'You're right Robert. It was that District Cooncil case; the alleged bribery. Remember it Robert? At least it became a challenge, even though the two Cooncillors got off.'

'Aye, usual lack of evidence, or should I say witnesses who'd stand up an' be coonted,' Butler replied.

The pair walked on in silence for a further hundred metres or so.

Butler sighed, 'I don't see any chance of this visit turning out to be the case of the century either. More likely the case of the hour if you ask me.'

The two men now walked down under the oppressive overhang of Glasgow's massive nineteen sixties Kingston Road Bridge which

129

spanned the River Clyde. Butler added, 'Colin if we don't get a master key when we get here, we burst the lock, have a look see, take the film, and back to the station for a cuppa by nine o'clock. OK?"

'Aye, then the paperwork. It's getting worse,' Campbell replied. 'Did y'see that programme on telly last night? Inspector Hercule Poirot it's called. Great it was. That's the kind of detective work I'd like tae be involved in. It's all done in the heed. He's never had to sign his name let alone fill in a form in his life.'

'Noa, a did'na see it. I wis oan that committee last night. *Police, Drugs, and the Neighbourhood* it's called. What a wasted night a can tell ye.'

The men crossed Argyle Street at the traffic lights. 'Ach well, it pays the bills I suppose,' Campbell sighed.

A few minutes later they arrived at the Isosceles Centre. Since the fire had taken place next door it was still barricaded to the public. They went in through the unlocked small wooden door within the main double doors, and found themselves in a badly lit large space. The smell of smoke from the adjacent building hung heavy in the atmosphere. As their eyes became accustomed to the dim light Campbell said, 'There's an office over there. Let's see if there's anybody there?' Going over, he looked through a dirty glass window. The room appeared to be empty. He shouted and knocked the glass window, 'Is anyone there? It's the police, can you hear me?'

A voice from the darkness replied, 'Aye a can hear ye, a can hear ye. Whit ur ye trying tae da? Noak the place doon?'

The two men turned around to see a small, thickset man emerge from the shadows behind them. They introduced themselves, saying that they were looking for the caretaker.

'Am the caretaker! Ma names McPhail. Yer Chief Inspector said ye'd be coming by this morn.'

'Aye, OK then,' Campbell said, then added that they had some questions to ask.

'Go ahead, y'might as well seen yer here,' McPhail responded.

'It's regarding the storage unit; the one where you've had trouble getting in touch with the tenant. Kiremla, is that what they're called?'

'Aye Kiremla that lot. Listen a've found an auld mester key yesterday. A've no tried it yet, so let's ga'it a try,' McPhail said taking off in the direction he'd come from earlier. Campbell and Butler followed, and found themselves in a high ceilinged shed, their eyes trying to come to terms with even deeper gloom than before. Pigeons fluttered somewhere above them.

'This way, roun' here,' McPhail instructed, turning into a long corridor, each side of which was lined with similar sized storage units. Stopping at unit 27 he tried the lock. He twisted and turned it a few times and the door opened. 'Whit did ah tell yae? It's a mester key efter o.'

'Let's have a look,' Butler said, going into the unit, anxious to get it over with. Campbell followed him.

'Is there a light in here?' Campbell asked McPhail.

'Aye there is. If ye'd let me go first ah could've pit it on fur ye,' McPhail replied turning to the left where he pulled a cord, bringing on a solitary light bulb hanging from the ceiling.

'Looks like a load of old junk to me,' Butler said looking around. 'An empty box for an inflatable rubber boat, two pairs of wellies, rubber gloves, waterproof trousers and jackets, but I don't see any fishing rods.'

The policemen looked around but it was clear there'd been no water damage to the unit, or the contents.

'Right Mr McPhail, that's it. If we can have the film now we'll get out of your hair?' Butler said, noticing belatedly as he said it that McPhail didn't have much hair.

'The film still in the camera, an it'll be easier fur a big bloke like you than me tae get up a ladder an get it. There's a ladder jist ootside,' McPhail responded.

Butler went to collect the ladder.

'Ye'll be in the film yersels when ye see it,' McPhail said to Campbell. 'Ye see the camera starts recording as soon as ye pit oan the light. Oh jist a minute,' McPhail said going back to his office, 'A need ta git a new film. He can pit it in when he's up there,' he added. Thinking about what McPhail had just said, Campbell hoped he hadn't said anything he wished he hadn't, as he knew the CI wanted to see the film as soon as they got back. Butler reappeared with the ladder. As he was placing it to get up to the camera, Campbell

131

decided he'd take advantage of his new-found knowledge to set Butler up.

'Right Robert,' he said, 'I'll go up and get the film. You hold the ladder, and don't let it slip on any of those rubber things lying about.'

As Campbell climbed the ladder, Butler said laughing, 'Whit would you know about rubbers Colin? The only rubbers you ever use for are for rubbing out spelling mistakes in your reports.'

'Funny, funny. It's jist as well CI Anderson can't hear you saying that to me. I'm supposed to be your fearless partner fighting crime,' Campbell replied.

'He wouldna know a rubber either if he tripped over one,' Butler replied. 'He wouldna even know how to put one on if you ask me!'

'I'm not asking you anything Robert, I'm only doing my duty up this ladder. Now let's see how to get this film out.' Campbell worked a few minutes with the camera. 'Ah, that's it,' as he flicked the eject switch, and the video film was slowly pushed out of the camera housing. 'I wonder what we've got here,' he questioned with just a hint of amusement in his voice as he put the film in his pocket.

'Pit this film in when yer up there wid ye?' McPhail shouted, handing it up to the Campbell, who inserted it into the camera. He climbed down and put the ladder back where they'd found it. He then went back to McPhail's office.

'Thanks Mr McPhail for your help,' Campbell said. ' Now I'll just get you to sign these papers, he added, holding out two forms. 'This one says that you provided access to the Kiremla Unit, and that it was seen to be free of any water or fire damage. This other sheet is a receipt for the video film. We'll probably get it back to you in a day or so.'

McPhail scratched his signature on each page and returned them to Campbell, who did likewise, passing a copy back to the caretaker for his records.

'Right then, we're off,' Butler stated. 'You might hear from Chief Inspector Anderson in a day or so. OK? Thanks again for your help.'

'Aye, OK,' McPhail said in a gruff voice, 'I suppose a will. Cheerio then,' he said watching the two men leave the building.

CHAPTER TWENTY- FOUR

Ali Ciddiqui had risen early, too early from Hala's point of view. He'd showered quickly, dressed, then kissed her on the forehead saying she didn't need to come into the office till later. She turned over and went back to sleep, as he quietly left the apartment, and took the lift to the ground floor. As he passed the concierge, who knew him as the wealthy diplomat with the good-looking woman who lived on the fifth floor, Ciddiqui said, 'Good morning, how are you this morning?'

'Fit as a fiddle Sir,' the man replied.

Ciddiqui hailed a passing black cab. '52 Pont Street,' he said to the driver through the open window as he got in the back. He was anxious to see the morning newspaper that he knew would be waiting for him. The journey took ten minutes, and it was just after eight o'clock when he arrived at Pont Street. He paid the driver and went into the apartment building, taking the lift to his penthouse flat. He picked up *The Times* and opened his door all in one movement. He flipped through the newspaper until he reached the *Personal Column*. There in the centre of the page, he saw his message:

Water Water, Everywhere

27th April

He closed his door and went through into his drawing room holding the paper. His thoughts were scattered: to the remote Beneagles Hotel in Perthshire; the University campus in Durham; and, closer to home, to Heathrow Airport. As he looked at his watch he wondered if any of the operators had seen the message yet? It was only just after eight o'clock.

'Iraq will be proud of me when told what I've done. Success will be the deaths of thousands of the infidels,' he shouted aloud, pacing around the large, luxuriously appointed room, and anticipating his place in the history of Iraq.

As Ciddiqui bathed in his expected glory in London, in Glasgow, Chief Inspector John Anderson of Strathclyde Police had arrived at his desk in Cranston Hill Police Station. He'd spent the last two hours at a briefing meeting in Headquarters on the subject of Glasgow's growing drug problem, and had now just received his morning's mail. He caught sight first of a faxed *All Forces Alert* document, which he picked up noticing that it was made up of five pages. As he read it at first he thought he was mistaken. But no the name *Kiremla* appeared in it. He could hardly believe his eyes. The name Kiremla Ltd again appeared at the top of the second page. He turned to the beginning again, reading much slower this time.

ALL FORCES ALERT

Following recent AFA's on the subject of anthrax, with the added warning of extra vigilance being required at all sea, air and channel ports, this alert extends the range of products to be confiscated by Her Majesty's Custom & Excise or any Police Force.

Another deadly poison, in liquid form known as hydrocyanic acid (abbreviated as HCN) is believed to be in the possession of a company named:

KIREMLA LTD

(address unknown)

The estimated quantity of the product assumed to be in the firm's possession is approx. 1500 litres (330 UK gallons).

The HCN was released to KIREMLA LTD from the UK sole stockist, ZENECAL CHEMICALS LTD, Hatfield, Hertfordshire, in circumstances that may now be in contravention of HM Customs & Excise Regulations.

It is believed that the above mentioned batch of HCN has been associated with the deaths of six persons of no known addresses in London. An earlier incident in St James's Park, London, resulted in the death of a large number of species of birdlife, following the discharge by an unknown person, or persons, of HCN into the lake.

A person answering to the name Abdullah Kadri, estimated to be 30 years of age, assuming a Turkish identity, and who may be a citizen of the Republic of Iraq, is suspected of carrying out the incident in St James's Park. Kadri may also have been involved in the deaths of the six persons. Kadri has since become the subject of a murder inquiry, his body having been found in London, close to his workplace in Camden Passage, Islington London. Three photographs of Abdullah Kadri are attached, together with dental records, fingerprints, physical details, and copies of his last known employment records. It is not known if Kadri travelled widely within the United Kingdom, or how long he has been in the UK.

The only established associate of Abdullah Kadri, possibly also a citizen of the Republic of Iraq, is a male person, name unknown, described as being large in stature, mid-forties, dark brown hair and sallow complexion. This person may also be assuming the identity of a Turkish citizen. There are no further details available at this time.

Any information in connection with this AFA should be transmitted as soon as possible direct to Commander C Hall, Operation Hydro, Scotland Yard, London.

ALL FORCES ALERT ENDS   *28 March, Scotland Yard, London*

Anderson finished reading the Notice, then began flipping through the photographs, and other details attached to the *ALERT*. He could hardly believe his eyes. He picked up his telephone and pressed his intercom button. 'Have Butler and Campbell returned yet?' Anderson asked.

'Not yet,' Desk Sergeant Stewart McKechnie replied, 'but I'll let them know you want them as soon as they come back in Sir. Oh hold on Sir, they've just come through the door. I'll send them right up.'

'Tell them to come to the Blue Room right away,' Anderson said as he stood up. He picked up the *ALERT* notice, and made his way to the conference room, his mind buzzing with excitement. He was in the process of trying to start the VCR unit when the two detective constables knocked and came into the room.

'I'll do that for you Sir,' Butler offered, 'sometimes it's a bit of a nuisance depending on who was last using it.'

Anderson muttered something to himself, and left Butler to it.

'Sit down Campbell,' Anderson said as he himself sat at the end of the conference table. 'You too Butler when you've finished playing with that thing.'

Anderson hesitated, but only just till Butler sat down. He looked at the two men. 'Well, what did you find at the Isosceles Centre?' he asked the two men, one of whom was looking slightly nervous, Anderson thought.

Farraj Rasid had parked his car in the airside secure car park at Heathrow Airport. It was ten minutes to six in the morning, and he was due to start his seven-hour shift at six-thirty. He'd left his apartment at five-twenty when it was still dark, and had an almost

135

traffic-free M4 to himself all the way to Heathrow. Reaching into the back seat, he picked up *The Times* he'd tossed in there when he left home earlier, and put the newspaper in his briefcase. He shut the door of his Range Rover, and walked towards the control tower. It was still dark, but a grey glow was now visible in the overcast sky. Cloud level of no more than about four hundred metres, he noticed, which usually resulted in aircraft congestion, as incoming flights needed to be spaced out further apart. It was the kind of day he was thinking, that would've given him a perfect opportunity to set-up a possible air disaster over central London, particularly during the peak morning period. As he got in the lift, he was thinking that it wouldn't be too difficult in such circumstances to pass instructions to two or more aircraft, and put them on a collision course with devastating results. Possibly thousands of deaths taking into account the consequential damage on the ground. What could the authorities do to him? Nothing he thought. He'd plead overwork, stress, even distraction; any number of things. It would be hard to prove he'd done it deliberately. Rasid stepped out of the lift at the level beneath the control tower viewing floor, and checked his designated sector on the roster notice before going to the locker room.

'Same as yesterday,' he muttered looking at the notice.

He went into the locker room, took off his coat and jacket putting them in his locker. Opening his briefcase he took out *The Times*. He flipped through it to the *Personal Column*. It was there, the message he'd been waiting on. He could hardly believe it after all this time.

Water Water, Everywhere

27 April

Rasid sat down. There wasn't much to read, but he read it again to make sure. He'd thought about this situation a number of times, and was sure he knew how he'd handle it. He'd been lucky. There was nobody in the locker room when he'd arrived. He knew some of the controllers would arrive anytime now. He didn't have to wait too long. As two of his colleagues came through the locker room door a few feet away from where he was sitting, Rasid pretended to be looking for something in his briefcase.

'Good morning Farraj, cloud level a bit hung over this morning,' one said.

'Good morning - although I'm not feeling to good,' Rasid replied weakly, letting his head slump down on his knees.

'What's up old man? Got a hangover yourself this morning?' asked the other of the two men. 'Been out on the town then last night have we?'

Rasid knew that neither man had much time for him, and knew also that both would've been more than delighted to report him if he'd been drinking. Farraj Rasid never allowed alcohol to pass his lips, so that would never happen.

'No, it's another migraine I'm afraid. Just came on me as I got here,' Rasid replied, his face showing pain, as he spread out his legs and leant back against his locker. 'I've not had three attacks like this in a six month period since I worked in the States.' He grimaced and moaned a little.

'Can we get you anything Farraj? Paracetamol, something like that?' Rasid shook his head. 'Thanks, but it's too late now. Once it gets started I can do nothing about it. I have no option but to lie down.'

The men nodded, and looked at him with some sympathy.

'I'll have to report sick. Couldn't work like this. I'll sit here for a few minutes then report to the Duty Controller.' The men, not knowing what else to do, continued getting themselves prepared to start their shift in the control tower.

Rasid asked, 'Perhaps you'll let the controller know that I can't work today? He'll need to call in a stand-by.'

'Sure mate,' the man nearest Rasid replied, now feeling sorry for his unfortunate colleague. 'I'll let old Roger know, I think it's him who's on duty today. I'll tell him you'll be up in a few minutes to speak to him. OK?'

Rasid continued to hold his head. This was the third time he'd staged a similar occurrence like this in the past six months, and he knew he'd now be subject to a full medical check-up. They'd find nothing medically wrong with him, but with migraine, how could they prove someone was, or was not suffering from that malaise. He'd be put on sick leave with full pay for a week or so. That would allow him plenty of time to plan his strike at Farmore Treatment Plant. More staff came into the locker room, and soon there was a large body of sympathy for Rasid. Nearly everyone it seemed knew someone who suffered from migraine, and how painful it was. All fools he was thinking, who deserve to die. Such thoughts helped Rasid maintain his facial expression of pain and appearance consistent with a severe attack of migraine. At least that was what those around him thought it was.

In all deluxe hotels of the world, planning and organising breakfast to commence at six-thirty in the morning is carried out like a military exercise. Beneagles Hotel, just outside the village of Auchterarder in Perthshire, is such a place. In charge of serving twelve tables that morning, Hamid Pasha had arrived for work at precisely six o'clock. He'd changed into his old fashioned and dignified, black attire, and made his way through to the Strathearn Dining Room where it was expected that some two hundred and twenty-six people would be served breakfast that morning. As usual, most of the early arrivals would be going to play golf on one of the three famous golf courses within the grounds of the hotel. Pasha, as he did each morning when working on this rota, made his way through the dining room checking his tables and serving station, then continued through to the drawing room and bar which was normally unoccupied at that time of the day. He moved over towards the morning newspapers that were located close to the main entrance to the room, suspended from long, round poles to assist hotel guests deal with the large broadsheets. He, as he usually did each morning, picked up a copy of *The Times* and fingered his way through to the *Personal Column.* He stared at the clearly defined message he'd waited so long to see. He could hardly believe it.
Water Water, Everywhere
27 April
At last he thought, our signal: *Ma Ma, Fi Kul Makaan.* A hotel guest came into the room. Pasha pretended he was refolding the newspaper, and returned it to the rack. Smiling he said to the guest, 'Good morning Sir,' before making his way back to the dining room. He was elated. He consciously slowed his walking pace. His time was coming. Soon he'd be free of this undignified servitude. By the time he arrived back at the dining room he couldn't contain the smile on his face.

It is said that one of the most beautiful sights in all of England is the view that awaits the eye of the traveller approaching Durham City. Perched on the top of a steeply wooded hill, Durham Cathedral looks down imposingly on the River Wear, as the river winds its way through the rolling countryside. On occasions the view can been unsurpassed anywhere, as it was that chilly morning. Niazi Bey and Hussein Mabeirig were both short of breath, although their condition had nothing to do with their appreciation of the Cathedral, or the creative skills of the Norman architects. They'd arisen as usual around six in the morning, pulled on their running gear, and set off on their daily ten kilometre run which took them high above the sleeping city. The early morning air was cold and damp. Perfect for running. As usual they ran in silence, and the kilometres passed quickly. As the early morning light grew slowly in intensity, their route took them alongside the main rail line that skirted the city. As they pushed on, a kilometre or so ahead the railway station came into their sight. It was their normal habit to stop at the news stand there and buy *The Times* newspaper. This ritual had taken place every morning, hail, rain or shine, since their recent visit to the air shaft, high up on Skylock Hill. A few minutes later Bey detoured into the station, picked up a copy of the newspaper, and paid the man at the counter. In the meantime, Mabeirig remained jogging on the spot outside the small building. Folding the newspaper, Bey slipped it into the small waterproof rucksack he wore on his back, and joined his flatmate. The men then followed the more formal pathway from the station, down to the edge of the River Wear, and back to the university campus. In a city of learning, with students of varying age and nationalities, their behaviour was nothing out of the ordinary, and no one paid them as much as a second glance.

'Hussein, you can have a look today,' Bey said, as he sat down on the floor, removing his wet and muddy running shoes. 'Here,' he shouted, tossing the rucksack to Hussein who had already undressed, and was standing naked about to go into the shower. 'You may bring the luck of Allah upon us Hussein!'

Hussein Mabeirig picked up the rucksack, and opened the *Velcro* strip at the top. He took out the newspaper, and unfolded it. 'I am tired of this miserable existence. May Allah be good to us soon,' he said as he thumbed through to the *Personal Column*. By this time Niazi Bey had slipped past him, peeled off his wet clothes, and quickly jumped into the shower.

Ten seconds passed in silence as Hussein Mabeirig at first saw, then read the message:

Water Water, Everywhere

27 April

'It's there. It's in it Niazi, It's in today!'

Niazi was beginning to enjoy the warm water pouring over his cold, sweaty body. 'I can't hear you in here Hussein, what are you saying?' he shouted.

Suddenly the shower compartment door slid open and Hussein stood there still shouting, 'It's here, look: *Ma Ma, Fi Kul Makaan*. We strike on 27 April. Look Niazi,' he said holding the newspaper partly inside the shower cubicle.

'Take the newspaper out of here; don't get it wet. Let me get out of here and dry myself,' Bey shouted. He came out of the shower and wrapped a towel around himself, drying his hands in the process. 'Give me the newspaper Hussein.'

Hussein Mabeirig sat down on the edge of the bath still holding the newspaper at arm's length.

'It says *Water Water, Everywhere, 27 April.* That's it: *Ma Ma, Fi Kul Makaan* - our instruction Niazi'

'Let me see it Hussein,' Bey shouted, taking the newspaper. He read the short notice twice. The words he read were the words they'd been waiting for. 'Allah has listened to us Hussein. We've must now prepare to strike at the throats and bellies of these pigs around us. Praise be to Allah.'

They could forget their studies, a cover in any event. Soon they'd be doing Allah's work; they're highest calling. They could then go back home to Iraq, leaving this land of the filthy infidels. Both men could feel their mind racing. They could hardly wait to cause so much agony and death.

'We have twenty nine days Hussein,' Bey stated. 'We have to prepare to the last detail. No mistakes; no loose tongues!' Bey had considered Mabeirig to be a risk when he'd been selected to serve with him. He'd been overruled on the strength of Mabeirig's command of English, and previous exploits involving Mabeirig in Iran. 'Let there be no mistakes. We're at the summit of our individual mountain, and Allah awaits us with open arms. We must go to him, do you understand me Hussein?'

'My life is Allah's to take when he wishes. My purpose only to serve Him. Death to all infidels.'

"That may be Hussein, but more so now we mustn't make even a minor mistake. Do you understand Hussein? Do you?' Bey asked. 'Did you not hear me Niazi?' Hussein replied angrily. 'I'll not fail Allah, or you Niazi. You've my word, I'll be careful at all times.'

CHAPTER TWENTY-FIVE

Ian Day was sitting opposite Chris Hall in Scotland Yard. It was nine forty-five in the morning and Day had come back with the details of the planned 'visit' to Zenecal Chemicals Ltd, at Hatfield. They'd met for a short time the previous night when Day had said to Hall that the team would, if necessary, work throughout the night to finalise the plan.

'Everything's in place for tomorrow morning, Sir. I've just phoned Zenecal, and their MD will see us tomorrow at nine-thirty, together with their accounts and bonding people. In other words, everybody we need to see and speak to. Our cover story's that a Mr Ian Jay of KML Mining Inc. (UK), and his senior staff, would like to know how Zenecal could cope with a large and repeating order for the supply of bone charcoal. We've told them the charcoal is to be used to assist with the colour adsorption of rural water supplies in the North of England. Zenecal are anxious to impress from what they've said. Our team even had me fooled with that one Sir, thanks to Jim Bannistair technical input,' Day stated.

'Sounds good Ian. I'll tell the DAC that we set off at 0800 hrs tomorrow, and all being well we might have something to report to him in the afternoon. Ian, now remember, no heavy-handed stuff. Keep it within the bounds of acceptability and within the book. Those guys at Zenecal are going to be bloody pissed off by our approach once they find out about it. You know as well as I do that the media would love to get their teeth into something like this.'

'Will do Sir. I've briefed everyone on a kid glove approach. We'll get what we want without any blows I'm sure; that's the way it normally works. They'll spill out loads of information, most of which we won't need, but they'll also say what we want to hear. It's the way it works.'

'I hope so Ian, anyway keep me informed as things progress OK?'

"I'd hope by ten-thirty tomorrow morning I'll be able to contact you Sir,' Day said, then added, 'eleven, no later. We'll have something for you by then Sir.'

'Right Ian, now get on with it. I'll see you sometime tomorrow.' Hall stood up then said half meaning it, 'None of you better come back here if you don't pull this off. Tell the team I said that I'll find them some bloody awful beats to walk if that happens.'

'I think I've got the message Sir. See you tomorrow.'

'What do you mean there was only a big empty cardboard box with a picture of a rubber dinghy on it? What kind of report is that Campbell?' Anderson asked.

Campbell and Butler were sitting in front of their agitated Chief Inspector. The minute they'd returned from the Isosceles Centre, Anderson had them brought to his office without them even having the chance to grab a mug of tea.

'What I meant Sir, was that when we looked in the Kiremla unit, it was empty except for that box for the rubber dinghy. There were other bits and pieces, rope, wellington boots, things like that, but nothing else Sir,' Campbell managed to say.

'Right Butler, you're a man of infinite knowledge, or so you've had me believe. What do you think you saw?'

'Just as DC Campbell said Sir. That's all that was, except some waterproof clothing. That's it Sir, oh and the video film. The caretaker said the surveillance camera only works when the light comes on. So whoever was in the unit will have been filmed and recorded Sir,' Butler stated.

Campbell felt sick. He remembered the derogatory comments Butler had made earlier about Anderson. It'd seemed a great idea at the time; now he was shit scared.

'That's what I'm waiting for Butler. Impatiently I may add,' Anderson replied. 'Perhaps you'll be kind enough to start the thing up so that we can all see this rubber dinghy box you two keep talking about. Campbell, close the blinds, and lets see who and what we've got on this bloody video film.'

As the film started, the first images to appear were the usual flashes and numbers, some background noise, and then blank film.

Anderson sighed then said, 'I hope we've got more than that to see for all your efforts this morning'.

The film continued, and the men remained silent, Campbell getting sicker by the minute. Eventually a dim outline appeared, showing the interior of the storage unit. The lighting in the unit improved as the lamp warmed up, and the quality of the film got better. Suddenly two figures appeared from the bottom left hand corner of the screen walking towards the back of the unit.

'That's somebody coming in from the entrance door Sir. The door is on that side of the unit, and there, see in the corner, that's the box for the rubber dinghy I told you about.'

'I can see it Butler, I can see it,' Anderson replied, concentrating on the screen.

The figures continued to move through the centre of the screen, stopping and examining some cylinders. The cylinders were similar in size, like butane gas cylinders, bright orange in colour. They were split into two groups of four and wrapped in a net harness. One of the two figures in the unit tried to move the harness but it was too heavy. The second figure tried to help, but even then the cylinders barely moved up off the floor.

'Must be bloody heavy Sir,' Campbell said forgetting where he was for a moment, then hastily added, 'sorry about that Sir.' He paused, then said, 'Two men can hardly shift them.'

'We don't know for sure yet Campbell whether they're male or female. Can we stop and enlarge the frame on this machine so that we can get a better look at their faces?' Anderson asked.

'Sure Sir,' Butler said, as he operated the hand set, causing the film to pause. He pressed a few more buttons and enlarged the picture. The picture now showed clearly the side of one of the faces. 'That one looks like a male Sir. Now let's have a look at the other one.' He continued to operate the fast-forward and freeze buttons with some skill. 'There, that's the other one Sir. Now I think that's a male as well, or unless it's an awfully ugly looking woman Sir?' he said trying to lighten things up a bit.

'Right Butler I can see for myself,' Anderson stated. 'It does look like two males, about mid-thirties in age, medium build, and dark hair. But neither of you mentioned those cylinders they're trying to move. Didn't you see them?'

'They weren't in there Sir, I'd swear to that,' Butler replied positively.

'OK Butler, move the film on and we'll all see what happens next,' Anderson said, taking a few notes as the film returned to normal speed. They saw that the men had brought a rope with them, which they tied around one of the harnesses. Neither of the men spoke. The bumping of the cylinders on the concrete floor and the noise of the rope being lashed around the harness were the only sounds. One of the two men walked out of vision for a moment or two, then returned with a heavy link chain, dragging it across the floor.

'That's part of the block and tackle Sir. Each unit's got one for lifting heavy items,' Butler said.

Anderson let the comment pass.

The men negotiated the harness and the four cylinders back towards the bottom left corner of the screen before it disappeared from view. The rear and partial side view of a motor vehicle was just visible through the doorway. It appeared to be bigger than a normal four-door saloon.

'Damn,' Anderson said, 'that camera angle isn't much good. Where are they taking the cylinders?'

'Back out the door Sir,' Campbell responded.

'I can see that Campbell, I can see that.'

After a few minutes the men came back into view, and set about the second harness, which also held four orange cylinders. The unit was now virtually empty, except for a large cardboard box, some rope, and wellington boots. When they returned after a few minutes, they began to open the box. They pulled out what appeared to be an inflatable rubber life raft, and carried it out of the line of sight of the camera.

Anderson cursed, then asked, 'What size would you say the box was?'

'As big as I am Sir,' Butler replied. 'You see I stood it up on end to see if there was anything inside. It was empty, but it had 3.70m stamped on each side, the dinghy size that is Sir, not the box.'

'I hear you Butler, I hear you. So the inflatable maybe about twelve feet long. That's quite a big boat. Did either of you see any sign of an engine, petrol cans, anything like that?' Anderson asked.

'No Sir, what you now see on the film is what was there this morning,' Butler said just as the screen went blank.

'They must have turned the light switch off,' Campbell said, 'that kills the camera Sir.' He then asked anxiously, 'Will that be all you want to see Sir?'

'No, run it on just in case they came back in again. We've seen nothing really except for the life raft,' Anderson stated.

'What's the problem Sir?' Butler asked. 'It's only an insurance job, and as we've told you, there was no water damage. What's the fuss?'

Anderson decided that he'd better brief the two detective constables on the information he'd received earlier that morning.

'The reason for the fuss, as you put it Butler, is that the company that rented the storage unit we've just been looking at, Kiremla Limited as they call themselves, are the subject of a AFA that came in this morning. Kiremla appear to have terrorist connections, and may have been hoarding some highly dangerous chemicals in that bloody storage unit. That's why it's important that we get as much from this film as possible.' As he finished speaking the screen lit up again. This time Butler, Campbell, and the caretaker McPhail appeared on the screen.

Anderson watched it for maybe thirty seconds or so while Campbell squirmed in his seat, before saying, 'I don't think I want to watch you two stomping around on video. You're famous enough around here without me sending video film of you both to Scotland Yard. Run the film back and get me three copies of the earlier part only. I want it right away, yesterday in other words, OK?'

'Yes Sir, right away Sir,' Campbell said with relief, as he jumped up and pressed the rewind button on the controller Butler had in his hand. It was the first time he'd relaxed in the last half-hour.

'Get me some stills of the faces as well as the part showing the rear of their car,' Anderson continued, 'and we'll need them all ASAP. And Butler, I want you to go and bring in the caretaker McPhail. I've more questions for him that I hope he's got some answers to. And when you're at it, clear out the unit; all the bits and pieces. Wear gloves so you don't leave any more fingerprints than you've done already. Have everything tagged and bagged for dispatch by train to London. I'll tell you when to send it.'

As Butler and Campbell left, Anderson lifted his telephone. 'Get me Commander Hall at Scotland Yard,' he said to his secretary. As he waited for his call, he allowed himself a brief moment of amusement. He'd never before had the pleasure of saying those words during his career. He looked at his watch. It was only ten-thirty in the morning, and he felt he'd already had a long day. A few minutes later his phone rang.

'Sir, I've got Commander Hall, Scotland Yard on the line for you,' his secretary advised, 'I'll put you through now,' she added in an unusually formal voice.

'Good morning Chief Inspector, this is Commander Hall, Scotland Yard. What can I do for you?'

'Good morning Commander Hall, Chief Inspector John Anderson, Strathclyde Police speaking,' Anderson responded. He paused before he continued, 'Sir, that AFA that you issued this morning concerning Kiremla Ltd. Well Sir, I think I may have some information for you.'

CHAPTER TWENTY-SIX

After the call from Strathclyde Police, Hall was to say the least excited by the information he'd received from Anderson. He asked his secretary to get Ian Day urgently. His telephone rang and he was put through.

'Ian I'm sorry to break into your meeting as I know you're briefing the team at the moment, but listen I've had a call from Glasgow, from a Chief Inspector Anderson, Strathclyde Police. He's picked up a lead on Kiremla in Glasgow.'

'That'll concentrate the minds of these guys at Zenecal tomorrow. What's the story Sir?'

'It appears Kiremla leased a small industrial storage unit up there. According to Anderson the unit was partly emptied of its contents recently. We've also got some video film, and photographs of the guys who emptied the place. Anderson's sending them to us by train, so we should have them late this afternoon.'

'Even better, I'll be able to confront Zenecal with them, maybe even get some IDs confirmed Sir.'

'Anderson tells me, and the film apparently confirms it, that eight cylinders, like butane gas cylinders, each pretty heavy, were apparently taken from the unit as well as a life raft. The unit's now virtually empty, except for some discarded items, which we'll send to *Forensics*. Some rope, cartons, etc. When you're at Hatfield tomorrow, Ian, establish what type of containers they use for HCN, their approximate weight, etc. I've checked back through the notes of the first police interview with Zenecal, and all we've got is their statement that 1500 litres of the stuff was uplifted by Kiremla. No information on what type of container, how many, or the size. See what you can find out Ian?'

'Will do Sir,' Day responded, 'and hopefully a bit more as well.'

As he hung up, Hall looked at his watch, it was 1053, and he had been due to see Hughes at 1045. At least this time I've got something positive to tell him he thought.

Ali Ciddiqui was finishing off his second cup of coffee and musing over an article in *The Times*. The subject was water, or the lack of it in some parts of the world. The *Industrial Correspondent* reported that *the cost of water to the consumer, domestic and industrial alike in the UK had risen dramatically over the past few years.* Ciddiqui smiled thinking there'll be more problems very soon Mr Industrial Correspondent; problems of a kind you've not even thought about. Since he'd become involved in Colonel Safa's planned operation he was more aware of the UK's water industry's apparent lack of security and protection of their natural resources. Security at most facilities he'd seen was at best inadequate, and at worst, no existent. Reservoirs open to the public, no security fencing or surveillance cameras, and only the occasional printed notice stating that swimming was not permitted. However the plan had one failing, he thought. Assuming it was effectively carried out, Baghdad had predicted that tens of thousands of people would die. This was not nearly as many as Ciddiqui would've wished. He'd have relished the opportunity to operate on a much larger scale. The United States of America, with their huge utilities systems would've provided opportunities on a much bigger scale, which would've resulted in massive deaths, not merely tens of thousands. He folded his newspaper, and stood up, stretching his ample body, before going through to his office. It was time that he thought about his departure from London. He'd want to be in London to witness the results of *Ma Ma, Fi Kul Makaan*, but not one day longer than necessary. He was also thinking about the risk should any of the operators survive their part in implementing the plan, although he deemed that unlikely. No matter, he didn't want to be identified by any of them if they did survive. Looking at himself in a mirror he thought, perhaps he should change his appearance; nothing too dramatic. Maybe his hair; he could do that. He could change the colour slightly. My moustache could be removed he thought. Going into his bathroom he picked up a pair of scissors and began to trim his moustache as close as possible to the skin on his top lip. When he'd cut it back as far as he could with the scissors, he washed his face, brushed shaving soap around his top lip, and began to shave carefully. He then examined his face quizzically. Yes, he was already quite different. A touch of grey at the temples would also be very effective, make him a little more mature, but not old. He'd get his hairdresser to deal with that tomorrow he thought. As he continued to look at himself in the mirror he wondered what Hala would say when she saw him later? Who cares he thought, she could easily be replaced. Anyway, he'd no intention of taking her with him when he left London. He dressed quickly and went to his study where he picked up the *Yellow Pages.* He dialled the first travel agent listed. His call was answered quickly and he asked to speak to ticket sales.

'Jan speaking, can I help you Sir?' the girl responded.

'I'd like to book a flight to Yerevan, in Armenia, on the twenty-ninth of April.'

'Would that be a one way or return ticket Sir?'

'One way.'

'Right Sir, just a moment and I'll check that for you,' the girl said. She then said, 'A British Airways franchise airline, British Mediterranean Airways, flies to Yerevan on a Monday, Wednesday and Friday every week Sir. Your date... eh let me see; yes the twenty-ninth is a Monday Sir. They have both *Club* and *Full Economy* seats available on that date.'

'OK, I'll take that.'

'Fine Sir. It's a one stop service flight number BA6721, departs Terminal 4 London Heathrow at 2105 hrs Sir, stops at Tibilisi in Georgia and arrives at Yerevan 0730 local time next day. As I said Sir, they're showing both *Club* and *Full Economy* price seats available at this time. Would you like me to make a reservation for you?'

'Yes, book me *Club*, a window seat please. How long is the stop at Tibilisi?'

'Club Sir, OK. And I see about a twenty minutes stopover, but there's no need to disembark at Tibilisi. The girl hesitated to allow Ciddiqui to take in the information, and when he didn't ask anything else she asked, 'How would you like to pay for the ticket Sir, and in what name?'

'Cash. I'll have it delivered to you later today,' Ali stated. 'My name's Ali Ciddiqui, and would you be so kind as to post the ticket to me at my address,' he said, giving the girl his address in Pont Street, London, and the name on his Armenian passport as he'd have no further use for it after he'd left London. When his travel plans had been finalised, he thanked the girl and replaced his telephone. He wrote down the flight number and times in his desk diary. By the time he'd boarded the flight to Yerevan, the British would've learned a hard lesson he thought. He got up from his desk and looked out the window. He saw people moving in all direction, cars, buses, and black cabs. Those people, the ones that survive after *Ma Ma, Fi Kul Makaan* that is, will take to the streets and demand assurance that something be done to protect their water, he thought. It'll cost millions of pounds, and maybe even billions to carry out the security works, and it'll take time. Time that they didn't have. In his premature jubilation, he decided he'd go to the Carlton Hotel for an early lunch. Afterwards he'd walk through Hyde Park, where the fresh air would do him good after the strain of the past few weeks. Checking the weather outside, he pulled on his jacket and left his apartment. A few minutes later he entered the Hotel, and as usual exchanged loud greetings with the doorman who didn't appear to notice the absence of Ciddiqui's moustache. As he walked through to the hotel lounge he paid little attention to the man sitting quietly near the reception desk. The man however, whose name was Ivan Beria, saw Ciddiqui, and noticed instantly that Ciddiqui had shaved off his moustache, and wondered why? Ciddiqui's apparent lack of caution had always worried Beria, himself a master of stealth-like presence, and he decided he'd report this change to Colonel Safa.

CHAPTER TWENTY-SEVEN

Just after eleven in the morning Hamid Pasha was leaving the grounds of Beneagles Hotel, in Perthshire. He'd been in high spirits since reading *The Times* earlier that morning. He swung onto the back road from the hotel and put his foot flat on the accelerator, lowering the side window as he did so. The old Range Rover surged forward, and the view of the countryside, together with the fresh air, made him feel good to be alive. He was heading back to Braco, a small village where he and Mohammed Bejyi shared a tiny grey cottage. In his haste to get to Braco and to let Mohammed know about the date of *Ma Ma Fi Kul Makaan,* and as he rounded a sharp left-hand bend a few minutes later, he hit a deep pothole in the badly surfaced road. He cursed his stupidity as he fought to regain control of the Range Rover. Gradually he picked up speed again as he drove along the narrow, twisting road. He couldn't wait to get to Braco. Four kilometres further on, and as he crossed a humpback bridge over a burn leading to *Allan Water* he hit another pot hole, causing the Range Rover to shudder violently even more so than before. He again cursed his stupidity, cutting back his speed, but something was now wrong with the steering. He tried to brake but found it difficult. He pulled hard on the handbrake, and pressed the brake pedal. Eventually he managed to stop on the narrow road. Switching off the ignition he got out to have a look under the front of the Range Rover. Instantly he saw that part of the suspension had broken. The weight of the five, sixty litre orange coloured cylinders in the back had not helped either, he thought. Neither he nor Mohammed had felt comfortable with the HCN cylinders in storage in the Isosceles Centre in Glasgow while they were seventy kilometres away. They collected them, and for a while, stored them in the staff quarters behind the hotel. Then Hamid Pasha had become uneasy about the cylinders being at the hotel, especially after one of the waiters jokingly asked what was in them, suggesting that it might be opium from their kasbah back in Turkey. Pasha and Bejyi then decided four days ago to bring the cylinders back to their cottage, one at a time every day. That morning, after doing his breakfast shift at the hotel, and having read *The Times* and the good news in it, Pasha made up his mind to take the remaining cylinders back to the cottage. He'd used an old jib crane in the hotel garage workshop to lift the harnessed group of four cylinders up into the boot of the Range Rover, and then had managed by himself to lift the remaining cylinder and put it in the boot as well. Now standing beside the stricken Range Rover, and looking at the fractured suspension, he regretted his hasty decision. He'd have to leave the vehicle unattended and get help. As he was trying to conceal the cylinders in the back of the Range Rover, a white van came around a bend twenty metres away from where he'd stopped, and had to brake violently to avoid a head-on collision. The van driver cursed Pasha as he now drove slowly past, questioning Pasha's parentage in the process. Having barely recovered from that, another vehicle, this time a police Landrover appeared from the opposite direction. It stopped behind the disabled Range Rover, as the police driver switched on his hazard warning lights. He got out and put on his cap. 'Have we a problem Sir?' Sergeant Jack Wilson asked, moving himself and Pasha onto the nearside of the road, and behind the two vehicles.

'Well yes, you see I hit a pot hole coming over the bridge. I think the suspension's broken,' Pasha said, trying to appear and behave normally.

Sergeant Wilson collected two *Police-Accident* triangular road signs from his own vehicle then said, 'Hold on till I place one of these signs up by the bridge, and the other on the other side further down the road. We'll be a bit safer then. You wouldn't believe how many people get killed or injured outside of their own vehicles in situations like this. You and I, Sir, don't want to add to those statistics do we? Stand in there on the grass for the moment Sir.'

As Wilson walked back to the bridge Pasha felt like running away, but knew he'd have to brave it out. He looked into the back of the Range Rover and saw that the bright orange coloured cylinders were partly exposed. He wondered if the sergeant had noticed them. He decided he'd wait till the sergeant went off to put the second road sign in place, then he'd try to pull back the boot cover and hide the cylinders. Just as he thought the sergeant would pick up the second road sign and walk on, the man stopped at the Range Rover and opened the driver's door.

'We might as well be safe as sorry. We'll put your warning lights on as well don't you think?' he said stretching into the vehicle and pressed the red hazard warning button. 'This is an old one alright,' the policeman added as he paused to look at the interior of the vehicle. 'How old is she Sir?' he asked.

'I've only had it three or four months, but its fifteen years old I think.'

'Has she done many miles?' Sergeant Wilson asked, looking at the bodywork as he walked away with the other warning sign. He was now also wondering about the vehicle's MOT and insurance. He'd already noticed that the tax disc was up to date.

Pasha took his chance. He opened the boot and pulled the folding flap cover over the cylinders. At least they were out of sight. Wilson was on his way back when Pasha said, 'When I bought it, it had over two-hundred thousand miles on the clock. That's about three hundred thousand kilometres and I've maybe added another thousand or so, but it's been reliable up till now.'

'*Kilometres*, oh ah canna count those. I'm a miles man myself. But you're right about one thing. These vehicles are usually very reliable. Best four-wheel drive ever made if you ask me; especially that two-door model you've got. Don't know why they ever stopped making them? Take this one here,' Wilson said gesturing in the direction of his Discovery. 'I drive it through some pretty nasty winter weather up in these parts, and you need a good vehicle to get you through it ah can tell you. I'm surprised that your suspension has gone, but they have to go sometime I suppose,' Wilson said questioningly, and looking closely under the front wing. 'Aye, there it is, a fracture on the right track. That's what's done for you I'm afraid Sir. You'll need that fixed. Now let's see about getting you out of the way here,' Wilson stated as he pulled his radio hand set. 'Are you a member of the *AA* or *RAC* Sir?'

'Not yet,' Pasha replied, then added and lying, 'I'm thinking about it.'

'Well not to worry, a'll call one of the pick-up boys in Blackford. It'll only take them ten minutes or so to get you out of here. But it'll cost you I'm afraid.'

Pasha nodded in acknowledgement.

Wilson consulted a notepad and dialled a number on his radiophone. He spoke to someone who obviously knew him. After some one sided humorous remarks, Wilson switched off the handset and put it back in his Discovery. 'Well as I said Sir they'll be here in ten minutes. Now I must ask you some questions about you and your vehicle Sir if you don't mind. It's the paperwork you see it gets worse every week. And as I've had to call in outside help, if you know what I mean Sir, well that creates more paperwork. Now, can I see your driving licence?'

This was the nightmare that Hamid Pasha feared worst of all. He'd drawn police attention to himself. He handed over his licence and tried to remain calm. He said hoping to gain some comfort; 'I'm a waiter at Beneagles Hotel Sergeant.'

'Ah, the big hoose, aye. Great place the hotel Sir,' Wilson said taking in the information, and writing it down slowly in un-joined letters. 'Out of interest Sir, where are you from originally?' Wilson asked, looking directly at Pasha with the look of certainty on his own face that the Pasha's answer wouldn't be from Perthshire.

'I'm from Turkey, a town called Van. I came here for work,' Pasha replied, using his passport cover identity.

'Nice place Turkey, I went there with my wife three years ago, to a place called Alanya. Flew direct from that Glasgow International Airport. It was very nice I remember. Lovely weather and good beer. Now where was I Sir?' he asked. 'Ah yes, can I see your vehicle insurance and MOT certificate please?' he asked, as he handed back Pasha's driving license. His look this time was of someone who knew that what he was asking for might not be available.

Pasha passed the folded papers to the policeman. Wilson's expression now changed to one of surprise, but to his credit, he remained silent. He continued noting down the particulars in silence, interrupted only by the infrequent passing of other vehicles, and the drivers rubbernecking as they drove slowly past.

'There, that should do it,' Wilson remarked a few minutes later, as though he'd just finished a novel. 'The paperwork we have to do today compared to when I joined the force twenty years ago is something else. Now with you being of foreign extraction, well that will mean even more paperwork I suppose Sir,' he stated with despondency.

Pasha nodded, concerned at the thought of an investigation. He knew he mustn't give anything away, even to this stupid policeman. He was relieved when he saw a breakdown truck drive towards them. He watched as Wilson directed the truck so that it could secure its crane to the front wheels of Pasha's Range Rover. It was then that he realised that the driver was about to pull the Range Rover up a sloping ramp onto the back of the truck. Pasha's immediate thoughts were of the heavy cylinders in the boot. If they moved back against boot door they'd be too heavy and might burst it open. The driver jumped out of his cab and spoke to Wilson, who he obviously knew well. The man then nodded in his direction before stopping at the stricken Range Rover, where he bent down and looked underneath. He saw the broken front suspension and knew he couldn't tow the vehicle away on its own four wheels. It would have to be rear wheels only.

'Is there anything heavy in your boot Sir?' he asked Pasha. 'Things have the habit of falling out when I lift up the front. We don't want to add to your problems do we Sir?'

Pasha had no option but to open the boot. The five orange cylinders in the boot were now visible for all to see, four in a net harness, and one single cylinder. Wilson said, 'Well Gordon it's just as well you asked or I'd have gone ahead and let you jack up the front. That would've caused me even more paperwork ah can tell you Sir,' laughing out loud. 'Looks like you'll have to turn around and take out the gas bottles first Gordon?' He turned to Pasha and said, 'Sorry about that Sir.'

Pasha watched in silence as the driver attached his motorised jib to the harnessed cylinders lifted them up slowly, before placing them flat on the rear of the truck. He repeated this with the single cylinder. Pasha was relieved that neither the policeman nor the driver asked what was in the cylinders. He decided to make himself occupied with personal items in the Range Rover.

'OK, now let's get this vehicle off this road before we cause any further trouble Gordon,' Wilson shouted. 'Sir,' he said looking at Hamid Pasha, 'you jump in the Discovery and I'll take you to Braco if that's where you're heading. Gordon here will take your Range Rover to Guthies in Blackford. You know where they are Sir I'm sure if you live in these parts. You can tell them what you want them to do with it later on. Do you need to have those gas cylinders taken to Braco just now or what?' Wilson asked looking at the orange cylinders. 'I can arrange that for you if you want. Might be a small charge though, considering the weight,' Wilson said with a hoarse laugh that caught in his throat, causing him to spit onto the grass verge.

'Thanks Sergeant,' Pasha replied, 'if you could take me to Braco that would be great. I'll phone Guthies later. They can keep the cylinders till the vehicle's repaired, then I'll collect everything.'

'OK, well that settles that,' Wilson replied, 'lets get you home and I can get back to my station at Crieff, otherwise they'll think I've been playing golf up there at Beneagles,' again he laughed at his own joke. 'Chance would be a thing at those prices they charge, and me just a poor police sergeant,' a comment he found even funnier.

The Defender and the truck then took off in the same direction, the Range Rover being towed and running on its rear wheels only. Pasha hoped Mohammed Bejyi wouldn't see him arriving in the police vehicle, in case he came to the wrong conclusion and reacted accordingly. Wilson and he drove in silence for the short distance to Braco. When they reached the village Pasha pointed to the cottage where he lived. He quickly got out and thanked Wilson again for his help, then went round to the back of the cottage to let himself in. He was now in a state of mild panic mixed with high excitement; not sure which was more predominant. How could he break the good and bad news to Mohammed? First that of *Ma, Ma Fi Kul Makaan?* And secondly, the fact that five of the HCN cylinders were no longer in their hands? Worst of all, that a policeman had now seen the cylinders!

'Mohammed?' he shouted questioningly as he opened the back door. 'Where are you? Where are you Mohammed?'

'I'm in here, I'm here Hamid, in the kitchen,' Mohammed Bejyi replied, slightly irritated by Pasha's excited shouts. Bejyi was finishing a coffee as he sat in the kitchen. 'What's the matter? What's happened that's so important?' he asked.

'Mohammed, *The Times* this morning. It was in there, I read it. *Ma, Ma Fi Kul Makaan!* Our instructions, we have to act soon,' he said with excitement.

'Let me see it. Where's the newspaper?'

'I don't have it Mohammed. I read it at the hotel.'

'Why didn't you bring it back with you, or buy one? You knew I'd want to read it as soon as possible. I can't believe it!' he said turning away from Hamid. 'You know we won't be able to get one here in Braco.'

Pasha now sat down at the kitchen table, his head bent forward, his hands clenched on the table surface. He said, 'Mohammed, I've also got some bad news. I did bring the newspaper from the hotel, but it's in the Range Rover. I left it there by mistake, I'm sorry. You see I had a breakdown on the way back here. I hit a pothole and the car's suspension's broken. It's now in Guthies in Blackford.'

'You're not hurt Hamid; you're OK, aren't you?' Mohammed asked with concern.

'I'm OK; no cuts or broken bones.'

'Good, then you can take the motorbike and go and get the newspaper from Blackford.'

'Mohammed that's not the problem.' Pasha diverted his eyes before adding, 'You see five of our cylinders were in the Range Rover when this happened.'

Bejyi hesitated for a few seconds, then said, 'The people at the garage won't take much notice of the cylinders. Why should they? People transport things like that all the time. That's not a problem. Hamid, go and bring back the newspaper, or go back to the hotel and get another one whatever. But do it now. The hotel is probably nearer than Blackford. Don't worry about the cylinders. I want to see the notice.'

'There's more Mohammed. The police got involved. A police car came just after I'd broken down. The policeman saw all of the cylinders, he saw them Mohammed.'

Bejyi sat down and listened as Pasha told him the whole story, from the time of reading the notice, until his arrival back at the cottage in the police car. He also said why he'd decided to bring the other five cylinders from the hotel.

'What can we do Mohammed? What can we do?'

For once it was the less dominant partner who seemed to be able to remain calm. Bejyi stood up and went to the window. He gazed out at nothing in particular. The mountains of Ben More, Stobinian and Ben Vorlich were all visible, all around a thousand metres or so high, their tops covered in winter snow.

'Hamid tell me, did the policeman pay any attention to the cylinders? Did he ask what was in them? Think hard, did he?'

'No Mohammed, neither of the men paid much attention to them. Only when we went to pull the Range Rover onto the trailer. Only then, that was all. The driver lifted the cylinders out of the boot first, then he pulled up the Range Rover that's all. Little was said about them. I swear to Allah that's all that happened.'

'Then we've nothing to fear. Go and get me the newspaper. I want to read the good news. Forget the cylinders, no one will bother with them at the garage; they'll be safe there. They'll assume they're gas cylinders. The Range Rover will get repaired and the cylinders will be put back into the boot. No one will remember anything about them. Hurry up, get me *The Times.* I want to read the good news.'

Hamid Pasha stood up and embraced his friend on both cheeks. 'You're right as always. I'll go and get the newspaper. I'll also ask how long it'll take to fix the Range Rover. I'll be positive, thank you Mohammed.'

Bejyi began to reconsider what had happened after Pasha left. He had to admit he wasn't as confident about the situation as he'd led Hamid to believe. What else could they do? They must go on. He again looked out of the window. This time he saw the mountains and their snow-covered peaks. His spirits lifted as he now remembered the news of *Ma Ma, Fi Kul Makaan.*

CHAPTER TWENTY-EIGHT

It was a bright, fresh morning in the village of Wilken's Green near the town of Hatfield, Hertfordshire, as the church clock struck nine o'clock. Day, together with his eight-man team, had arranged to rendezvous at the side of the picturesque village green there prior to approaching Zenecal Chemicals. They had left Scotland Yard in two unmarked police cars an hour and a half before, after having gone carefully through their proposed strategy once more.

The plan, code-named *Zentec,* a subsidiary of *Operation Hydro,* entailed Day and three others turning up at Zenecal's premises to fulfil the supposedly business meeting with that company's MD and others. As currently planned, ten minutes or so into the meeting, Day would come clean, and explain to the Zenecal people that he, and his colleagues were not businessmen as they had implied, but were instead police officers from Scotland Yard. To coincide with that event, the remaining members of *Zentec* would arrive at Zenecal's premises.

When both cars parked at the green, the driver of the first car called the other saying, 'Car 1 leaves for Zenecal in two minutes precisely!'

Zenecal Chemicals' Managing Director, Dr John Hardcastle was going through some costing details with his Sales Director, Donald Hamilton. Hamilton appeared to have all the information at his fingertips. Hardcastle said, 'This is a big deal Don, if we can pull this off, then with KML as a committed client, it could lead to some of the bigger water companies looking at our product. You're sure about that cost per cubic metre Don? Can't we trim it a little more, even by another 0.05p considering the quantity KML are considering? We don't want to lose the order for the sake of a few pounds.'

Hamilton shook his head, 'John I've done my homework on this believe me. We've already undercut all the suppliers in the UK; even in Europe. I'm just about comfortable with our offer, I really am. We can't cut any more.'

Hardcastle looked at the young man. 'OK Don, if you're sure, fine. By the way I take it Pat Kelly got back from his visit to West of Scotia Water in Glasgow yesterday?'

'Yes, he did. I've spoken to him already this morning. We had a session on delivery strategy early on. No problems in that direction either John. Pat said he'd join us at the KML meeting. We're all ready to go John. Have your pen ready to let them sign up. No problem,' Hamilton enthused.

Hardcastle looked at Hamilton for a few seconds, thinking that Hamilton was probably right. But sometimes these young guys got carried away, and lost their focus on the main points. He knew that quality, availability of supply, transport arrangements, and most of all cost, were all important. 'You're right Don, but old habits die hard,' he said hesitantly before adding, 'Ian Brown will also be joining us. He's going to talk a little bit about our own financial position. Give some numbers for this year and last. That sort of thing. Let KML know that we'll be around for a while.' He got up from his desk then said, 'I'll see you in the boardroom at nine-fifteen Don. I've also told Ian to be there at that time. It's just after nine now so I'll see you there shortly.'

'OK John, see you then,' Hamilton replied closing the door behind him.

Zenecal Chemicals premises was located in a modern business park on the outskirts of Hatfield. It comprised ten thousand square metres of production facility, as well as a similar sized distribution and storage unit. The impressive frontage housed a three-storey office block that accommodated the company's management and administration personnel. The facility employed several hundred skilled and unskilled people.

Day's car arrived at the security gate at the entrance to the complex. He introduced himself to the man in the gatehouse. He was then directed to one of the visitors' allocated spaces in the car park. Day and the three others then headed towards the main entrance to the building, where they were confronted by another security guard.

'Good morning gentleman,' the guard said, 'what can I do for you all this morning?'

'Good morning,' Day replied, 'we have an appointment with Dr John Hardcastle.'

The guard looked at each of the four men individually then said, 'Right Sir, if you'd make your way over to the reception desk you can let them know who you are, and who you've come to see. They'll look after you all Sir.' He indicating the direction to the large and impressive desk at the rear of the double height entrance hall, where two attractive young women receptionists sat side by side in deep conversation.

Day thanked the man, having noted the man's inquisitive manner when dealing with visitors. He and the others walked over to the desk. As they approached, one of the women in a loud, brash voice greeted them saying, 'Good morning gentlemen. Can I ask you all to complete these forms for me, and I'll arrange your security badges. Is it John Hardcastle you've come to see?' she asked, looking at a clipboard. The other woman handed out four forms before continuing her conversation with her colleague. Day doubted that either of them would remember him and the three others half an hour afterwards. The security guard was another matter he thought. The men completed the forms using their cover identity, and handed them back to one of the receptionists, who then counter signed the individual sheets. Tearing off the bottom of each form, she then slipped the detached part into a clear plastic sleeve with a lapel clip attached, and handed them back to each of the four men.

'Take a seat gentlemen. I'll advise Dr Hardcastle's secretary that you're here,' she said.

Day wondered how long this system of passes had been in place? He looked at his watch. It was nearly fifteen minutes past nine. It'd taken them a few minutes longer than planned to pass through reception. He asked Dobbie to call the second car and tell them they were running a few minutes late.

Johnston got the message, and realised that he was being stalled. He asked, 'Five, ten or fifteen minutes? How much later?'

Dobbie said, 'Ten will be fine Jim,' finishing the call.

Day heard the receptionist's saying into her switchboard mouthpiece, 'You're coming down now for them? Oh, that's fine, I'll let them know.' She turned to Day then said, 'Someone's coming to collect you shortly gentlemen.'

A few minutes later a smiling, attractive and expensively dressed young woman entered the reception and made her way towards the men. 'Mr Jay?' she asked, looking at the men questioningly.

'I'm Ian Jay,' Day replied rising to his feet, taking the woman in from head to toe.

'My name's Dawn Green. I'm Dr Hardcastle's PA. Good to meet you Sir,' she said, shaking Day's hand.

Day introduced the other three men.

With the initial introductions over, the woman said, 'If you'll all follow me gentlemen I'll take you up to our boardroom where Dr Hardcastle is waiting to meet you.' She turned and led the four men towards a lift. When they reached the third floor, they got out and followed the woman to the boardroom. She knocked on the door and went into the room. Two men were standing looking out of the window.

'Dr Hardcastle,' Ms Green said to the senior of the men, 'May I introduce you to Mr Ian Jay of KML Mining, and his colleagues.'

Hardcastle turned and came towards them, his smiling business face now on show, and said a little too loudly as they shook hands, 'Mr Jay how nice to meet you. Let me introduce you to Donald Hamilton, my Sales Director.' Hardcastle turned towards the other man who'd been in the room with him, then added laughingly, again louder than necessary, 'Donald and you will have a lot to say to each other I'm sure.'

'Good to meet you Mr Hamilton,' Day said to Hamilton as they too shook hands. As they did, Day was thinking that this was the man he'd have to put under pressure in a very short time. He turned from Hamilton then said, 'Dr Hardcastle, let me introduce you to Mark Dobbie, Mark is my Chief Process Engineer.' Hardcastle shook hands with Dobbie. 'And this is Colin Price. Colin is our Chief Civil Engineer,' Day continued. Again Hardcastle shook hands with a flourish. 'And finally,' Day said, 'Charles Partin. Charles is our Financial Director - our money man if you like.'

After having shaken hands all round, Hardcastle then said, 'Take a seat gentlemen,' motioning them towards the elegant table. He looked at his PA then added, 'Dawn, would you ask Ian Brown and Pat Kelly to join us now, and we'll have some tea and coffee right away please. Oh, and will you bring me that extra copy of the product file on bone charcoal. It's on my desk.' As his PA left the room, Hardcastle asked generally, 'Did you have a good journey from London this morning gentlemen?'

Dobbie, who'd done the driving as far as Wilken's Green replied saying, 'It wasn't too bad. We made an early start, and got through the usual congestion spots without too much trouble.'

The small talk of traffic problems on the M25 then took up a few more minutes.

The door opened and the PA returned with a file, which she passed to Hardcastle, as two other men quietly followed her into the room. Hardcastle stood up again. 'Mr Jay, this is Pat Kelly. Pat's responsible for getting our products from A to Z and all places in between. As you will be aware, our products are not found on the shelves of *Asda* or *Safeway*, and they're also a bit more difficult to move around. Anyway we haven't beaten Pat yet. He gets it to where it's got to go, safely, on time, and in top condition. No easy task with some of the products I can tell you.'

Day nodded to Kelly, and partly rose to shake hands with the man.

'This is Ian Brown,' Hardcastle continued, 'our Financial Director. Ian's from Aberdeen and I sometimes think he hates to see our products leave the premises in case he hasn't asked enough money for them. A real Aberdonian you might say,' Hardcastle added, again with a forced laugh.

Day shook hands again, this time while seated. He knew that time was running out fast, and that the others would be approaching the building. He was about to disclose his and the others' real identities when the door was opened yet again. This time it was tea and coffee. Another few minutes went by as coffee or tea was selected and poured, and passed around.

The second car having now arrived at Zenecal's main entrance, the other policemen introduced themselves to both security guards, and were now in Reception. Showing their identification, Jim Johnston asked the guard and the women there not to leave the premises. He also told them they were not to remove any items or documentation, and that no telephone calls were to be put through to any member of the company. The administration building was effectively now secured. Plan *Zentec* had begun.

In the boardroom, as Johnston was securing the premises three floors below, Hardcastle and the others were stirring their tea or coffee. Day abruptly stood up, then said, 'Dr Hardcastle if I may have your attention for a moment. I have to advise you that I'm not the Managing Director of KML Mining Inc. Neither my colleagues nor I are employed by a company of that name.' The look of surprise on Hardcastle's face matched those of the other Zenecal management team. Day took out his Scotland Yard identification card and handed it to Hardcastle. 'These men are officers of the *Special Branch* at Scotland Yard, and as you can see from my ID my name is Day and not Jay, and I'm attached to the *Anti-Terrorist Branch.* We're here this morning in connection with the sale and transportation of a quantity of hydrocyanic acid, or HCN as it's also known, from these premises We intend to question you, your staff, and examine your sales and delivery records in connection with this batch of product and its whereabouts.'

Hardcastle and Hamilton both got to their feet. 'This is outrageous. You simply just can't come in here under some pretence and carry on like this,' Hardcastle shouted.

'I'm afraid we can Sir,' Day replied. 'We have a *Letter of Request for Access* under the *Prevention of Terrorism Act* with us. Similar to a search warrant only more compelling. You are at liberty to phone your solicitor if you so wish, but I'm hoping that you won't feel the need to do that Sir. You see I'd like you to co-operate with us without resorting to legal advice at this stage. That's entirely up to you Dr Hardcastle.' Day opened his briefcase and took out the letter he'd made reference to. He handed it to Hardcastle, who accepted it without a word, and read it quickly.

As he handed the letter back to Day he said in a more subdued voice, 'This is no way to treat people. My company and my staff have nothing to hide. We are a reputable organisation, and everything is fully documented and monitored in the approved manner. We've supplied the Ministry of Defence for years. Government records for the distribution of our products. Everything is above board.'

Hamilton, Zenecal's Sales Director, still on his feet, shouted, 'I agree with John. It's an outrage to turn up like this. We're a highly respected firm! My God!' He turned to Hardcastle saying, 'John I suggest you phone the police in Hatfield and ask them what the Hell these guys are doing here, and on whose authority?' The rest of the Zenecal group muttered in agreement before getting to their feet in a show of mutual defiance.

'Hold on, hold on,' Hardcastle said. 'Detective Inspector Day has got sufficient documentation to justify his presence here this morning.' He looked at Day then asked, 'What is it you actually want from us Inspector? You'll have to give us a clue of what this is all about?'

Day stood up and walked towards a marker board at the far end of the room. Picking up a pen, he wrote KIREMLA LTD on the white surface.

Hamilton reacted instantly. 'We've told the police everything we know about them weeks ago. We went out of our way to help. There's nothing left to say on the subject, you must already know that. Have you guys nothing better to do?' he asked sarcastically.

At that point DI Jim Johnston knocked on the door and stuck his head into the room. 'Excuse me Sir, the premises are now secured. Administration staff has been briefed of their position, and telephone, fax and e-mail communications are being monitored. All visitors are being turned away and advised to call again to make another appointment.'

'This is bloody outrageous,' shouted Hamilton. 'What about our business? What about....'

Hardcastle cut Hamilton off, asking him to cool it and listen to what Day had to say.

Day thanked Johnston, who then closed the door behind him. Returning to his seat Day said, 'Dr Hardcastle we're aware that you and your staff have already been questioned regarding this matter. However I must advise you that we're not satisfied with the information you provided. For a start we've been unable to trace your supposedly legitimate customer, Kiremla Limited.'

'What's that got to do with us?' Hamilton questioned aggressively.

'Leave it out Don,' Hardcastle rattled back at his young colleague.

'We've told the local police all we know Inspector,' Hardcastle said, 'everything.'

Day rose from the table and walked around behind Hardcastle. He said, 'I don't think so Dr Hardcastle and I can tell you we're not leaving these premises until we get the information we need.' As the atmosphere in the room cooled, Day continued, 'What we have at present is,' he went to the marker board then added, 'the firm's alleged name!' he underlined the name KIREMLA LTD that he'd already printed on the board. He continued saying, 'We have your previous statement that the quantity of...,' he paused, 'we'll call the product HCN,' he said looking at Hardcastle. 'The quantity issued to Kiremla you stated was 1500 litres, but you didn't confirm in which manner it was shipped. For example, was it in one large tank, or in numerous containers? If so, how many?'

'The police didn't ask that,' Hamilton shouted.

'Don, for Christ's sake shut up will you,' Hardcastle retorted.

Day paused before continuing, 'So how did the HCN leave your premises?' He looked around the now subdued room then said, 'We have that address which Kiremla gave in Croydon, and which we have now proved never existed Dr Hardcastle.' Day turned and looked directly at Hamilton. 'Mr Hamilton, you as Sales Director must have some record of the initial contact with Kiremla, and if not you, who in the organisation would have?'

'It would depend on who was here at the time,' Hamilton said weakly, averting his eyes from Day.

'Zenecal Chemicals is a *Government Registered Distributor of Highly Toxic Products* as I saw from the certificate in the reception area, and also a business that is *Quality Assured* to *ISO 9001*,' Day said. 'I know that those awards entail keeping good business records Mr Hamilton, so find out and advise me who was the person, or persons, as the case may be, that had initial contact with Kiremla.'

Hamilton scribbled a note on the pad in front of him without saying anything and without looking at anyone at the table.

Day walked back to the marker board and wrote down the questions as they'd occurred during his appraisal of the situation. He looked at them, then said, 'Kiremla paid for the product by banker's draft.' He wrote down *BANKER'S DRAFT*. 'They did have an active bank account at that time, and as we now know it has been closed since the date of purchase of the HCN. Now, and this is for you Mr Brown,' Day added as he looked at the financial director of Zenecal Chemicals for the first time. 'How many of your customers pay their bills by banker's draft Mr Brown? Not many I'm sure.'

Brown reddened a little, but offered no further information.

'Shouldn't you have been a bit suspicious of that?' Day questioned. 'It's surprising the draft didn't turn out to be forged?'

Brown belatedly replied, 'Well in business today, you…. '

'We'll come back to you later Mr Brown,' Day replied, cutting the man off abruptly. 'Now Dr Hardcastle, you as I understand it actually met a representative of Kiremla, when they came to arrange the purchase of the HCN. Is that correct Sir?'

'Well, yes I did, but only for a short time,' Hardcastle responded after a short pause.

'We'll need you to give us a description of that person Dr Hardcastle, and perhaps you'll tell us how long you've been using the present security procedures for visitors to your facility here?' Day asked, as he turned to the board and wrote down the words, *SECURITY/VISITORS*. The room was again silent. 'And now for you Mr Kelly,' he said with his back to the man. 'What record do you have of how the product, the HCN, was transported from your premises? By whom and how many external people were involved?' He wrote the words, *HOW DISPATCHED* on the board. Someone picked up their cup of lukewarm tea, rattling the cup and saucer in the process.

The silence then continued for a moment before Hardcastle asked, 'Inspector, I've answered most of those questions before. I've already told everything I know to Inspector Gentiles from Hatfield Police Headquarters when he came here to see me weeks ago. What more can I tell you? I don't see the point of all of this.'

This small sign of aggression from Hardcastle encouraged Hamilton. He stated bluntly, 'John tell them nothing more. We've been through all this before. Let's at least wait till Karen gets back. She'll be here in ten or fifteen minutes and she'll know how to handle this better than us. And personally I wouldn't give them anything without our solicitors being in attendance.'

'Mr Hamilton, whom may I ask is Karen?' Day asked.

'Karen Hamlet's our Company Secretary,' Hardcastle said before Hamilton could respond. 'She's a director, and specialises in company law. That's what Don Hamilton's referring to. She'll be back here in...' Hardcastle paused to look at his watch, 'about half an hour.'

'I see,' Day said, writing a few lines on his notepad. He paused, looking at the man, 'Mr Hamilton, let me put something to you; something that Ms Hamlet will certainly know all about, and something which, whether you like it or not, you seem to have forgotten. Simply put Mr Hamilton, *The Companies Act*.' Day let the words sink in. 'As you must know Mr Hamilton,' he said sarcastically, "Directors, all directors in Zenecal Chemicals, a capacity in which you are currently employed I believe, are all so placed to manage the affairs of the company. This must be done in accordance with the company's *Articles of Association*, as well as conforming to *Company Law*.'

Hamilton looked down at his hands on the table, his face flushed.

'At this moment in time Mr Hamilton, it remains for the directors of this company to prove to me, by displaying sufficient *Records of Sale*, together with details of the address to which the product in question, the HCN, was dispatched. Failure to do so Mr Hamilton will lead to serious repercussions and is a criminal offence, which I hope you understand?' Day asked questioningly, albeit not expecting and not getting any reply.

As he made his way back to the table he said, 'Now where were we? Yes Dr Hardcastle, as you say you may have told the local constabulary everything you could think of at that time.' Day sat down opposite the man. Both men looked directly at the other, then Day added, 'I'm sure you also think you've told us everything. But what you have yet to tell us is in the detail. Let's develop what you've spoken about today. First take the 1500 litres of HCN. How was it shipped from here, and how many containers? One, two, or more? What would be the weight of each container? That is some of the detail we need.'

Hardcastle looked to his side where Kelly was sitting and asked hesitantly, 'Can you answer all of that Pat?'

'I'll have to check John,' Kelly replied, as he scribbled on a note pad.

Day waited until Kelly finished before saying, 'Mr Kelly, DC Price will go with you now to find out what it is you need to check.' He turned to Price and said, 'Colin bring back the documentation, or whatever it is that gives us the information.' He again spoke to Kelly saying, 'When you're at it Mr Kelly, don't forget to confirm how the product was taken away. By truck, van, type, colour. Whatever, OK?'

Kelly nodded his reply.

Day then looked at Dobbie who was sitting opposite the Zenecal Financial Director. 'Mark, no doubt Mr Brown will need to check his files regarding that banker's draft. Go with him and you too Charles. Contact both banks involved in the transaction, at the highest level if you have to,' he added.

As the men left the room Day said to Hardcastle he'd now like to speak to the security guard at the front desk, adding, 'How long did you say you've been using the security measures for incoming visitors Dr Hardcastle?'

'I didn't say Inspector; you didn't give me the chance. I would think however the system's been in place for almost a year now.'

'So at the time the people from Kiremla came here, your reception staff would've obtained signatures and the like?'

'Yes, and I've already told the police all about that. We've got signatures I'm sure, but you've said yourself the company doesn't exist, so what good are the signatures?' Hardcastle looked challengingly at Day.

'How many security guards do you employ on reception?' Day asked, ignoring Hardcastle's gaze.

'Four.'

'Have they all been employed during the period the current security measures have been in place?'

'Yes, and I suppose we can establish which one was on duty when Kiremla's people last visited us,' Hardcastle volunteered, then added, 'before you ask me Inspector.'

As they made their way to the lift, Day smiled at the man, 'You see Dr Hardcastle, we really are now beginning to understand each other.'

When they arrived at Reception the security guard looked guiltily at Hardcastle, no doubt feeling all of this was his fault. The receptionists had even stopped taking to each other.

Hardcastle said to the women, 'Get me a print out of the visitors list on the days the Kiremla people were here. Also, find out which security guard was on duty those days. It would be about two months ago I think. When you've done that, give me a photocopy of the signed visitors passes that day as well.'

Both women reacted immediately, addressing their computer screens and keyboards.

Day meanwhile had again introduced himself to the duty guard; a tall, alert, overweight man called John Watson. As Day had guessed when he'd arrived at the premises earlier, Watson confirmed that he was a retired policeman. He'd been with the Hertfordshire force for over twenty-five years. Watson told Day that he enjoyed working with Zenecal Chemicals, as mainly he worked day shift, leaving him with plenty of time for his hobbies, which were portrait photography, art and golf. Hardcastle, reading a few sheets of paper came over to join them.

'It looks like we have two dates for Kiremla visits Inspector. One here at Reception for a meeting, and the other, the latter visit, direct to the Dispatch Department a week later. It also looks like you were on duty John when they came here on January,' he said looking at the guard.

'Let's deal with the first date. Can we go somewhere where we can sit down?' Day asked.

'There's a meeting room over here,' Hardcastle said, going in his indicated direction.

'Mr Watson,' Day said looking at the guard, more in the way of an order than a request, 'would you join us please?' He added for Watson's benefit, 'Inspector Johnston will see to security, and any visitors in your absence.'

The three men went to a small room and sat down around a circular table. Hardcastle was still engrossed reading the sheets of paper he had in his hands?

'Dr Hardcastle tell me what you've got that's so engrossing?' Day asked in a light-hearted manner.

'Only one person called on us on the January date Inspector,' Hardcastle said hesitantly, and still looking at the pages. 'A Mr I Aireb - a Turk I seem to recall. Don Hamilton was away somewhere at the time so I met with the man. Talked of a small company that he and some business friends had set up to recycle embedded-chips from old computers. Said there was a market for these chips, using them in toys, and household goods. He said that people couldn't give their old computers away, so they, Kiremla that is, had arranged to take them off their hands for a small sum, and everyone was happy. The man added that HCN was an ideal solution for cleaning the chips, as it apparently didn't damage any of the embedded circuits. His English wasn't all that good if I remember correctly. I kind of lost interest in him and his scheme. It seemed small change to me, so I got him to sign the order for the goods, the HCN that is, and told him to come back in a week's time to allow us to get clearance arranged to release the product.' The room was quiet for a moment. Hardcastle knew that he'd just disclosed more information in the past minute than he'd done when the police had called some weeks before. He looked at the security guard. 'John, you must remember the man? He was a cold fish; spoke broken English. Said he was Turkish, but if you ask me he could have been anything for all I

171

would've known. But he had a genuine Department of Trade certificate for producing recycled goods using HCN, so he could buy all the products he wanted from us as far as I was concerned. Do you not remember him John? That was the day we had the fire alarm go off?'

'Um, yes and no Dr Hardcastle. The day we had the false fire alarm was, let me see,' Watson said looking through the desk diary he'd brought with him. 'Yes, there it is. It was the fourteenth of January, and the alarm went off at 1138 hrs and was cleared four minutes later. Yes now I remember the man,' Watson said looking at Day. 'You'll remember Sir I was telling you that one of my hobbies is portrait photography. You see I always try to see into the subject's mind when I set up my camera equipment. I seem to get better quality photographs that way. I also try to guess what they do for a living.' He hesitated, then added, 'Well I sometimes do that in this job as well you see,' Watson said a little embarrassingly. 'It keeps my mind sharp. This morning for example when you came in, I looked hard at you but I couldn't come up with any ideas. It was strange at the time, but well now..., this morning for example, you weren't exactly behaving like a policeman. Know what I mean Inspector? Anyway, the day of the fire alarm Dr Hardcastle had to vacate his room, and the Kiremla man was with him. They both came down the stairs, like you do in those circumstances, not the lift. Well it struck me that the man... Did you say Aireb Sir?' Watson asked Hardcastle.

'Yes, Mr Ivan Aireb, I think he could have been Russian, but you can never tell with all those mid-European states now independent today.'

'Go on Watson,' Day said looking back at the security guard, 'what else do you remember about the man or the visit?'

'Sorry Inspector, I do go on a bit. It's the job I think. You don't get the chance to talk much to people, although you get to see plenty of them in a day. Anyway, where was I? Yes, Mr Aireb. The shape of his head was unusual I noticed. I see things like that. Back of the head and the neck all on the same vertical line. Most people have a slight bump at the back, and the neck usually sets in from the shoulders. Then his eyes were quite far apart, almost, how can I put that? Oriental yes, that's it, oriental. I'd like to have taken a photograph of him. Good strong features, good shadows on his face.

I only saw him for a few minutes, but it was a face you don't easily forget. Anyway, we cleared the alarm - it was a false alarm - and everyone went back to their desks. Dr Hardcastle and the man went back up in the lift. Yes I remember him alright.' Watson paused, as if not sure whether to continue, then offered, 'I could do a sketch of his face and head if you'd like Sir?'

Both Day and Hardcastle looked at the guard for a moment. Day replied, 'Yes Mr Watson, yes, please do that.' Turning to Hardcastle he said, 'Shall we see how the others are doing while Watson here gets on with his sketching?'

CHAPTER TWENTY-NINE

Farraj Rasid came down the steep stair from his top floor flat in William Street, Knightsbridge. Opening his mailbox, he took out a few letters and leaflets from inside. Glancing through what was mostly junk mail, he extracted a formal-looking envelope, with the initials *NATCG* on the franked postage mark.

Rasid was on sick leave following his recent faked migraine. As expected, he'd been called for a medical the day after he'd reported sick - a compulsory requirement within *NATCG* resulting from his absence from duty three times in the past six months. As he climbed back up the internal stairs, he ripped open the envelope. Inside was a letter from the medical division of the *NATCG*, dated the twenty-second of April. It read,

Dear Mr Rasid
I refer to your recent medical in connection with your recurring attacks of migraine resulting in your inability to carry out your normal duties as air traffic controller at Heathrow Airport, London, and West Drayton.
I am pleased to advise you that the results of the medical lead me to conclude that there is no evidence of any adverse cause associated with these recent attacks. In most cases migraine is associated with the debilitating effect of neurasthenia, a general term for fatigue, anxiety and listlessness.
In view of my findings, and considering the nature of your duties, I am recommending to your department head, that your sick leave be extended for a further four weeks from the date of this correspondence on full salary.
Your return to duty may also be subject to a further medical of which you will be notified.
Yours sincerely

(signed) Dr William J Depwell

By the time Rasid had read the letter, he'd reached the door of his flat. Going in, he pulled a chair to the table, sat down and read it again. Perfect he thought. I'll continue to plan *Operation Delta*, and be paid for carrying it out as well. He laughed aloud at the thought. He was also thinking that it was no wonder the British haven't any respect left in the Arab world. He folded the letter and put it in a drawer. Rising from the table he went to the window of the apartment that overlooked William Street. He pulled his curtains across the window closing them, knowing he was overlooked by a high, circular hotel opposite him. He could never be too careful. He made some more coffee and reminded himself that he should, as soon as possible, uplift the HCN, or *Juice of Allah* as he called it. He was aware from his instructions that the product had been placed in a secure mews garage not far from his flat. He'd recently bought a second-hand, dark blue Range Rover, which he parked in the residents' parking spaces around Lownes Square, a hundred metres or so from where he lived. It was a busy area most hours of the day and night. He intended to park the Range Rover there after he'd uplifted the HCN, which he planned to do shortly. Recalling to himself how he'd last gone to check the mews premises, he'd found parked cars blocking the garage and nobody able to help him to move them. He'd decided he couldn't take that chance again. He'd have the *Juice of Allah* close to hand, then he'd be sure to deliver.

CHAPTER THIRTY

When Day and Hardcastle got back up to the boardroom, the others were already seated, including a young, attractive blonde woman sitting next to Hamilton.

'Karen, this is Detective Inspector Day from Scotland Yard,' Hardcastle said. 'Karen Hamlett's, our Company Secretary Inspector,' Hardcastle added.

Karen Hamlet stood up.

'Pleased to meet you Ms Hamlet,' Day said, shaking the woman's hand.

Karen Hamlet nodded her head, but said nothing.

Hardcastle now seated said, 'Karen, Inspector Day and his colleagues are here in connection with that Kiremla issue. The Inspector seems to thinks that we haven't told the police everything we know about Kiremla.'

'Amongst other things Dr Hardcastle, and anyway,' Day asked, 'what was the outcome of my earlier questions? Using my notes as an *aide-memoire* we'll begin with you Mr Kelly. What have you found out about…?'

'Inspector,' Hamlet interrupted, 'before anyone answers any of your questions, may I see a warrant please?'

This response brought a look of inevitability from Hardcastle, and one of *'watch us fix this cocky cop now'* from Hamilton.

Day took out the letter from his inside pocket and handed it to the women.

'Karen, I think you'll find the letter's all in order, I read it earlier. We could have delayed the Inspector and asked for a formal warrant if we'd wished, but I felt we should show willingness to the Inspector. After all we've nothing to hide have we?' Hardcastle stated flatly.

'John I advise you to refuse to continue with this enquiry until we are all legally represented,' Hamlet replied.

Day admired the woman's guts, knowing that her advice to her MD was legally correct. He also knew that if she persisted, he'd be hard pushed to get any more information this morning. But, he was thinking, he'd already asked all the awkward questions, and he assumed that his team had also received some, if not all of the answers, so he said, 'As you please Ms Hamlet. You're within your legal rights to take that course of action. I must however caution that I will still be asking the same questions of Zenecal that I put to the people at this table an hour or so ago. It's your choice.'

Hamilton was first to his feet. 'I told you,' he shouted at Day, 'you just can't get away with treating people, innocent people mind you, in that Gestapo-like manner.' Turning to Hardcastle, still aggrieved, he added, 'I told you John, it's not right.'

Day waited for a pause in the uproar and, still on his feet, said, 'Dr Hardcastle, feel free to make contact with your solicitors. Are they a local firm?'

'Mayfair Inspector,' Hardcastle replied evenly.

'Telephone them Doctor, but with due respect,' Day stated, 'They'll need to have someone here no later than midday. Is that clear?'

Hardcastle nodded in agreement.

'Ms Hamlet, I trust that situation is also acceptable to you?' Day asked.

'Yes Inspector, I've no problem with that. I just hope that the partner in the firm who looks after our affairs in available,' she said looking directly at Day for the first time since they'd met.

'Ken McKenzie's in all day Karen,' Hardcastle said flatly, 'I spoke to him early this morning on another matter. He told me he'd be around if I needed him for anything.' Lifting his telephone, he asked his PA to get their solicitors right away. Hardcastle then stood up, and looking at Day said, 'I suppose we should have a recess Inspector. I'll get some more coffee and sandwiches brought in.'

'Thank you,' Day replied, as he sat down beside Dobbie and Price. As Hardcastle was instructing his PA on the need for refreshments, Day used the background noise in the room to ask the men if they'd had any difficulties getting the information he'd asked for. Dobbie and Price were able to report that they'd had no problems, and had come up with exactly what they'd come for. Day told them to remain seated, and to listen now rather than talk. He walked towards the window, and used his mobile to call Scotland Yard. When he got put through to Commander Hall, he said, 'Sir, Day here. I'm afraid things are taking a bit longer than planned. Zenecal have asked that their solicitors be present for the remainder of the interview. Someone from there should be here in about an hour's time.' He listened to Hall for a few minutes before saying, 'Not yet Sir, we've not reached that point of discussion.' Continuing to listen for a few more minutes he then said, 'OK Sir I'll bring that into our discussions shortly. See you when you get here.' When he'd finished he returned to the table.

Hardcastle was still on the telephone, and Day heard him saying, 'Yes, if you could Ken, as soon as you can please. See you later.' He hung up, and looking at Day said, 'Our solicitor will be here in about forty minutes or so Inspector.' He got up from the table to stretch his legs before saying, 'Refreshments will be here shortly, but Inspector, must we remain in here? Can we go back to our offices until our solicitor gets here?'

'Sorry Doctor, but under the circumstances I must ask everyone to remain where they are, *comfort-breaks* apart, and even then only one at a time,' Day replied. 'I'll be happy, like you, when we get to a successful conclusion and get back to London,' he added. 'I should also tell you that Commander Hall, who's in charge of this case, is also on is way here. He'll arrive around the same time as your solicitor I suspect.'

'We're being held against...' Hamilton shouted before Hardcastle managed to cut him off. 'Don, for the last time, no more please. We do as the Inspector asks at this time, so just sit back like the rest of us.'

Hamilton, unable to leave off, stated, 'It's against the law. Karen, tell them. It's against the law for God's sake. What is this, a police state?'

Hamlet looked at Hamilton, knowing from her recent dealings with him that he was a volatile character. She said quietly, 'Yes Don, we could all make a fuss and get up and leave the Inspector sitting here. We could, and maybe we will in due course, but as John says we've nothing to hide, therefore we might as well co-operate for the moment. Let's' have a cup of coffee and see what McKenzie's got to say.'

Hamilton remained silent.

Coffee was poured, and sandwiches passed around. Nobody in the room spoke for a few minutes. Day decided after his short telephone call to Commander Hall, to take the opportunity to tell those present some background details of the case. He stood up, then said, 'I'd like to use this break to tell you a little more about our inquiry. You see we've reason to believe that Kiremla has already been involved in at

178

least one act of terrorism in London. We believe also that they're preparing to carry out further acts somewhere in mainland Britain. All eyes were on him waiting for him to continue. 'What we know at this time, and hopefully we'll know more after we assess the information we've asked you for, is as follows.' He walked to the wallboard then said, 'It most certainly will be some form of chemical attack using HCN.' He looked around at the faces in the room, then said, 'Some of you may recall the recent incident in St James's Park in Central London, when the birdlife, including some rare species, were poisoned. Well HCN was used, and we traced it back to a domestic location in Camden. The flat owner, male and now believed to be an Iraqi, is credited with carrying out the attack single-handed. It is almost certain that he also fatally poisoned a number of homeless people outside a London Underground station, something you may have read about in the press. Unfortunately, not long after the incident the suspect was murdered. We have no witnesses and at the moment no suspects. He paused to let his words sink in. Continuing he said, 'Commander Hall, a few minutes ago, told me that the information I've just given you has somehow been leaked to the media this morning, and will appear in the early editions of the evening newspapers.' He looked around the room, noticing that he now had their undivided attention. 'We know from the earlier police investigations, that 1500 litres of HCN was uplifted from your premises here, destination unknown. We hope to update that after today in a more positive manner.' He looked at Kelly who nodded. 'Returning to Kiremla, the company itself, we now know that they've recently used storage facilities in Glasgow. We don't know what they stored there, but we're working on that as we speak.' As he said the last few words, he was conscious of some movement at the far end of the table where Kelly, the transport director was sitting. He looked towards Kelly, then said, 'I should stress, we are very anxious to find whoever, or whatever Kiremla represents, and what they've done with the HCN.' That was enough he thought, although what he'd told them was as much as he himself had been told by Hall. He sat down.

Karen Hamlet was first to speak. 'How do you tie up Kiremla and the murdered Iraqi? What's the link?'

'Miss Hamlet,' Day smiled, really stalling, knowing that he couldn't tell her the answer to that just yet, however he said, 'I'm glad you

179

asked that.' He added, 'You see Zenecal are our only real hope of continuity. That's why we're here. Without any link to Kiremla we can go no further. But what do we do? We can't just wait until further acts of terrorism take place.' He looked around the room before he said, 'Any small matter, mannerism, anything you noticed about Kiremla's people, that's what we're after. We must go after them and at the very least eliminate them from our enquiries.' There was general discussion around the table for another half hour or so, although Day noticed that Hamilton remained quiet and preoccupied. The telephone rang and Hardcastle answered it. 'Bring them both up to the boardroom.' He looked towards Day and said, 'Commander Hall and McKenzie have now arrived. They're on their way up here now.'

A minute or so later Hardcastle's PA came into the room, followed by Hall and Zenecal's solicitor, Ken McKenzie. Introductions by Hardcastle and Day were short and sharp, and the newly arrived pair found seats at the table. Hall asked Day to bring McKenzie up to speed with the situation which he did with lucidity, concluding in almost the same words he'd used a few moments earlier saying, '…and that's why we must make contact with Kiremla, at least to eliminate them from our enquiries.'

McKenzie turned to Karen Hamlet and asked if she'd seen the letter that Day had referred to in his résumé.

'Yes, I have it here,' she said, handing it to McKenzie.

McKenzie took a few minutes to read the letter, then asked Hamlet, 'As Company Secretary, do you think there is anything contained in the letter that would breach Zenecal's position in connection with the Official Secrets Act?'

'No, I'm sure there's not,' she replied looking pointedly at the solicitor before adding, 'I was more concerned with the individual; the personal position of some of the members of the board. Hence my reason for asking to have you here.'

McKenzie nodded his head without comment. He re-read the letter before putting it on the table. All eyes were on him. He looked at Hardcastle then said, 'As I see it, the police have the powers to enter the premises under the *Anti-Terrorism Act*, and to interview anyone they wish, anywhere within the building. Provided, and I must stress this, provided that person agrees to be so interviewed. Each individual has the right to refuse to say anything till he, or she is

180

legally represented.' There were mutterings around the table, Hamilton having again come back to life. McKenzie continued, 'If however someone doesn't want to be so interviewed in *open forum* so to speak, then that person is perfectly within their rights to ask for their own solicitor to be present during any private interview. But I must point out,' and he looked at both Hardcastle and Hamilton before adding, 'if the police wish to question anyone, they also have every right under the powers of this letter to do so. That is the position as I see it John.'

Focus of attention turned to Hardcastle again who after a moment or so of pursing his lips said, 'Happy with that Karen? I think Ken has summed it up perfectly clearly.'

'I agree with Ken's interpretation, I just wanted to be sure everyone else at this table was aware of the facts.'

'Well,' Hardcastle said, 'I think the police can now continue with their enquiries.' He looked at Hall and asked, 'Commander, where, and with whom would you like to begin?'

Hall nodded in acknowledgement, then said, 'Thank you Doctor, and you too Mr McKenzie. Let me make it clear that we've no wish to cause any offence or undue stress to you or any board member, or your staff. We also don't want to cause any unnecessary disruption to your business, so Inspector Day and his team will be as quick as possible. You now know the importance of these enquiries. They may prevent a large number of lives being lost, and I'm not overstating that possibility.'

'Yes Commander I fully understand that,' Hardcastle said. 'You and your men will have our full co-operation.'

'Right then Ian, let's get on with it,' Hall instructed, thinking that the next hour or so would be turbulent to say the least.

Hall took no part in the one-to-one questioning, preferring to listen and watch the reactions of those at the table. The interrogations went on for the best part of two hours and twenty minutes before Day decided to call a halt. He knocked on the table to bring some order to the room, then said forcefully, 'I don't think we can go any further today. Thank you all for your co-operation.' He got up and walked around to Hardcastle side of the table and said, 'Our thanks to you too Dr Hardcastle for putting up with our somewhat unorthodox approach, but I'm sure you now realise why we've had to resort to such tactics.' Then addressing Hamilton he said, 'Mr Hamilton I'd like you to come to Scotland Yard to further assist us in our inquiries. You'll be asked to make a statement there in connection with your contact with Kiremla Limited. I also advise you to have a solicitor in attendance on this occasion. I should also advise you Sir that anything you now say will be noted, and maybe used in evidence against you at some future date.'

Hamilton sat with the look of a man about to face the gallows. Having come under some intensive questioning, he was now showing signs of exhaustion. Hamilton had admitted under questioning that he had been approached directly by a man called Aireb, who claimed he worked for Kiremla. Aireb also said that the company was involved in the recycling of embedded computer chips. He had also admitted that he'd accepted payment from Aireb for his help in ensuring that Zenecal Chemical's records of the purchase of the HCN were falsified. He just about managed to ask Day, 'Inspector, can I phone my wife and let her know I'll be late tonight? We were due to go to a dinner party tonight with some friends.'

'You can Mr Hamilton, but I would ask you to make the call from this room. I would also say that in the circumstances, I don't think you'll be joining your friends for dinner this evening.'

Hamilton now looked as if the noose was being put over his head. As he made his telephone call, the others collected their notes and files, preparing to return to their normal duties. More than one of them glanced with mixed emotions towards Hamilton.

After leaving Zenecal's premises, Day travelled back to London with Chris Hall. Hamilton and his chosen solicitor, McKenzie, were given seats in one of the other two police vehicles.

'Sergeant,' Hall said to his driver, 'get us through this traffic as quickly as possible please.'

'Right Sir,' the sergeant replied with some enthusiasm, switching on the flashing red and blue strip light on the roof of the white police Range Rover. As he did so he noticed that the other two police cars behind did likewise.

As they headed to London Day said, 'This *Mr Aireb,* the 'fixer' Sir. We've got a good sketch of him, Hardcastle tells me. You may've noticed the security guard at Zenecal Sir? He's ex-police. Anyway he offered to do a sketch of *Aireb's* head and his face. I picked it up as we left Sir, and Hardcastle confirms it's an exact look-a-like.'

'Good Ian, we need as much as we can get.'

'I'd also like to hold Hamilton for twenty-four hours Sir. I'm sure we'll get a bit more out of him.'

'We did read Hamilton his rights Ian, so yes you can hold him for at least twenty-four hours. After all, he has admitted to falsifying government records.'

'I'm looking forward to seeing Hamilton locked up for a while. He deserves it for his performance this morning,' Day replied. 'I also think a few hours behind bars will sharpen up his memory.'

'Just remember Ian, we've got him on his own admission that he may have falsified Zenecal Chemicals dispatch records in front of his own solicitor, even if McKenzie tried to stop him saying it. We could put him away for that alone, so there is no need for any heavy handed tactics, remember that.'

'Sure Sir, I'll be patient,' Day said, sitting back in the fast moving car.

Thirty-five minutes later they arrived back at Scotland Yard, and went directly to an interview room on the fifth floor. Day phoned Johnston, Price, Dobbie and Partin, and asked them to come and join them. Within a few minutes the men, including Hamilton and his solicitor, were seated at a table looking at a photocopies of the guard's sketch of *Ivan Aireb*.

'Well what do you think Mr Hamilton? Is this a good likeness of the man you dealt with regarding the sale of the HCN?' Hall asked.

'That's like him all right. I'd know him anywhere.'

'Ok, now Mr Hamilton I'm recommending that you be kept in custody for a minimum of twenty-four hours. You'll be taken to Bow Street Police Station where you'll be asked to make a statement. You'll be detained there. Have you anything to say Mr Hamilton?' Hall asked.

'Commander Hall, on behalf of my client, I must object. You have no justification for the detainment,' McKenzie said angrily.

'Mr McKenzie, may I remind you that your client, by his own admission, has confirmed that he may have falsified company records, and so contravened part of the conditions of *The Official Secrets Act*. Do you wish me to make more formal charges at this time, or are you prepared to accept the lesser situation for the time being? It's your choice to advise your client accordingly. I must add however that I shall be investigating the more serious charges at a later date. Well Mr McKenzie, your choice?' Hall stated.

McKenzie and Hamilton jointly discussed the situation quietly for a moment or so. 'Commander,' McKenzie replied, 'my client is willing to be detained at Bow Street for the period you described, but I must add that should he be detained one hour longer, then I shall apply for bail on his behalf. Is that understood Commander?' McKenzie asked, trying to sound more in control of the situation than he really was.

'That's understood Mr McKenzie. Now Inspector Johnston will take you both to Bow Street, where your client will be asked to make a statement.' He got up to make it clear that there would be no further discussion or argument, then recited the date, time and the reason for terminating the interview, all for the benefit of the recorder on the table. Hamilton and McKenzie likewise got to their feet, picking up their belongings and followed Johnston out of the room.

There was a moment of silence after they left. Day said, 'Well done Sir, that fixed the bastard. I feel like throwing away the keys once they lock him up.'

'Inspector, may I remind you that this is still a very serious matter. It is not a subject that should be treated as a personal crusade,' Hall snapped.

Silence returned to the small room.

'Right Ian, now let's hear how you envisage moving on with *Operation Hydro* now after today's events? *Zentec* is now behind us, apart that is for the Hamilton matter,' Hall said.

Day took the rebuke, as he knew he should, and apologised for allowing himself to be being less than professional. He then said, 'As I see it Sir, we've got a number of answers to the questions that've been concerning us for some time. As you know, the lead we had on that subject got us nowhere. Dobbie, Partin and Brown, Zenecal's FD attempted to follow up on it this morning. The account at the NatWest that it was drawn from has been closed for some time, and Kiremla left no forwarding address. The previous address given to the NatWest was a box number, H20, at a publishing company called Bloomsbury Holdings, and located up at Bloomsbury Square near Holborn. Bloomsbury maintains a number of similar boxes for client authors and others. Apparently, someone from Kiremla calls in periodically and empties the contents. When the people at Bloomsbury were asked if they could describe any of the callers, they said there'd been a number of people over the past few months, but they weren't sure any of their staff could give a description of them. We'll go back, take a copy of the sketch of Ivan Aireb with us. It might jolt their memories.'

'OK Ian, it's worth a try,' Hall responded.

Day then said, 'Colin Price was also able to find out two pieces of important information. The type of transport used to dispatch the HCN, and the manner in which the HCN was packaged. It transpires that Kelly, Zenecal's transport director, well he recalls, and wait till you hear this Sir, that three not one, three, different types of hired vans, all white in colour, turned up at the same time to take delivery of the goods. Kelly couldn't remember the hire companies' names, or even if names were painted on the vans, but he did remember one distinctive thing about the van drivers. He said that the three drivers had different accents. One Scottish, Glasgow he thought. One a Geordie, probably Newcastle, and the third, a bit more difficult he said, sounded a little bit West Country. He guessed Bristol, although he said he'd gamble on it being from east of Bristol wherever that is? He also said he had the feeling the drivers, like the vans, had just been hired to uplift the goods, and that none of the men was interested in what they'd come to collect.' Day paused then said, 'Now this is the best part Sir. It seems that the mysterious Mr Aireb arrived at the same time as the vans. Kelly said Aireb spoke to each driver separately, and gave them each some kind of package, probably money I'd guess, before he left. We also now know that Zenecal's records of dispatch are incomplete, as there are no destination addresses shown on Kiremla's dispatch notices courtesy, as we now know, of Hamilton. Therefore we've no lead in that direction but, and it's a big but I'm afraid, we have the regional accents to work on.' He turned away from Hall and looked at the others, adding, 'What you guys don't know is that earlier today we got a lead in connection with the storage of goods for Kiremla in a warehouse in Glasgow.' He hesitated, then asked, 'Did the van driver from Glasgow take the HCN from Hatfield to Glasgow? We'll have to find out, and find out fast. The Commander tells me we've got someone on his way to Glasgow as we speak. We've also got to try and piece something together on the other two vans. Something to work on guys,' he concluded. 'We also need to know how and under what conditions the HCN is being moved around. As you would imagine, a product of that nature is not just packed into a plastic bottle. Colin established that the HCN left Zenecal's premises in a total of twenty-five, orange coloured and internally glass coated aluminium cylinders. Each cylinder contained sixty litres of HCN and the gross weight of each cylinder when full is approximately eighty kilograms. The dimensions of the cylinders are 330mm in diameter, and about a metre high including the outlet valve. In old money, that's about just over twelve inches in diameter, by three foot three inches high. These are not lightweight items we're talking about. They're heavy enough to require two men to lift them; one at a real push.' Day paused for a moment, looking again at his notes; 'Kelly also recalls that the twenty-five cylinders were divided into three lots. Eight were put into the Scotsman's van, and eight went into the Geordie's van. Nine were then put into the van of the guy with the West Country accent.' Day closed his notebook. 'That's it Sir. Summing it up, we've got a named face: Mr Aireb. We've got a link with the Glasgow lead; the van driver. And we now know we're looking for a total of twenty-five orange cylinders. I'm afraid lots of pieces of the jigsaw are still missing though. Oh, and Bloomsbury Holdings, we'll put them under a bit of pressure,' he added.

'Thanks Ian, at least we're going forward, and with those leads we're due a break sooner or later.' Hall paused, reading a note that had just been passed to him. He said, 'I just said we were due a break, and maybe we've struck it lucky already. Jim Johnston's just phoned to say that Hamilton's given a statement at Bow Street. Hamilton's admitted giving a blank copy of a government licence to Aireb, allowing Kiremla to submit an official order for the HCN. He's also admitted he may've misled the police on the HCN issues when they first questioned him. He said he told the police that Kiremla had only used one truck to pick up the HCN. He then apparently held back the dispatch papers until he could falsify them before having them filed.' Looking at the smiling faces in the room, he added, 'We're just fortunate that Kelly, his colleague, kept his own records.'

'Holy shit, that's fantastic,' Day shouted.

'Hold on, that's not all. Hamilton has now signed his statement in front of his own solicitor, so I think we've got enough to keep him for as long as we like,' Hall said, looking at Day.

'Great Sir,' Day said evenly, remembering he now had to moderate his enthusiasm.

When the buzz died down, Dobbie asked, 'When do you expect to hear from Glasgow Sir?'

'We've two men up there now and they're going to have a look at the warehouse where Kiremla rented space. I've asked them to team up with Strathclyde police and interview everybody who's taken space in the warehouse. We'll ask them if they've ever seen any of Kiremla's people. Who knows what that'll throw up?' Hall said. He got up saying, 'I want that sketch of Ivan Aireb distributed to all forces, as well as a description of the those cylinders. Send it as a supplement to the previous *AFA*. Also check out Bloomsbury ASAP. There's got to be somebody there who's seen Aireb. Finally, I want Mazzini, Fred's' *maitre d',* brought back in for further questioning.' He looked at Day before adding, 'Ask him to come in early this evening Ian. I wonder if the sketch will strike any chords? That part of our investigation has gone cold of late. Don't give Mazzini any idea why we want him to come back in. Also, arrange for someone from that new department we've got, *OTIS* I think its called, *Operations Technology Information Systems*. Something like that I think? Ask them to have someone there as well. I'm told they can produce computer-aided images from a very brief description. Let's find out.'

Day scribbled the name *OTIS* in his notebook.

'Right Ian, get on with it,' he said as he left the room.

The first thing to catch his attention when he got back to his office was his in-basket. God he thought, I better get through some of this paper before it gets any worse. As he sat down at his desk, he lifted the top letter off the pile. As he was reading it, his secretary interrupted him. She said that Inspector Day had asked to see him right away. Thinking that Day must've forgotten something he asked her to send him in. Day came in the room, followed by a woman police officer.

'Excuse me Sir, can I introduce you to WDC David?'

Hall looked at the trim, and bright looking woman.

'I hope you approve Sir, but my Chief at the *Anti-Terrorist Branch* suggested that WDC David might be a help to us on *Operation Hydro*. She's done some good work for me there in the past, and we could do with her particular help just at the moment. I'm sorry if I interrupted you Sir, but WDC David has just reported for duty. I thought it was a good time for you to meet her.'

Hall exchanged a few words with the WDC.

Hall, who was now feeling the strain and the lack of sleep, looked at the blonde women standing in front of him. 'Take a seat David, you too Ian. That was strategic thinking on Iain Marshall's part I can tell you. We could do with some extra hands and a clear head right now. Welcome aboard *Operation Hydro* David, but you may not thank us in a week's time. It's a tough case we've got ourselves.'

'Thank you Sir,' David replied.

'With Day promoting you, you'd need to have a good track record for him to do that.'

'Thank you Sir,' David replied again.

'We're quite informal in this group David, so what do we call you?' Hall asked.

'Barbara Sir, Barbara David.'

'Right, Barbara it is on all normal occasions, WDC David on all others. OK!' Hall said making it clear that was a statement, not a question. He added, 'Ian will you introduce Barbara to the team, and would you get some sleep. You look awful.' He turned to David and said with a smile, 'Now DC Barbara David, get to work on *Operation Hydro*.'

CHAPTER THIRTY-ONE

Hussein Mabeirig and Niazi Bey had just finished putting the eight cylinders of HCN into the back of their Land Rover Defender. They then hooked-up a two-wheeled trailer with a circular tank attached to it, and drove out of the garage. The trailer and the cylinders had been put into a dilapidated garage behind Queen Street, in Newcastle-Upon Tyne, a week ago. After going back to close the garage doors, they drove off heading towards Durham. Two days before, Bey had done a deal with the university boathouse caretaker to let them use the boathouse to garage their car for a week or so. A bottle of Hautes-Cotes de Beaune AC 1996 had helped the man make up his mind. Now they were heading back to the River Wear, and as a result of the Easter holiday, the campus would be quiet. Neither man anticipated any problems as they drove towards Durham. When they drove into the cathedral city, they then took the riverside track to the boathouse. They'd given a lot of thought to the difficulties involved in getting the HCN down into the air shaft up on Skylock Hill. They had decided to transfer the HCN from the cylinders, into a single tank, which they thought would be easier to deal with. They also planned to dump the empty cylinders into the River Wear afterwards.

As they got to the boathouse, Bey reversed back towards the double doors. 'Hussein, before we unload anything make sure there's nobody around,' he said. It was getting dark although there was enough visibility for the two men to look around. Certain that they were alone, they began unloading the cylinders. Apart from their heavy breathing, neither man spoke during the task. Eventually, with the cylinders now positioned vertically alongside the trailer, Bey set about loosening the left-hand screw and valve plug tops. Meanwhile, Mabeirig assembled the suction system he'd devised. It involved a simple bicycle pump and some clear plastic tubing. When both men had finished what they were doing, Mabeirig put one end of the tubing attached to the suction system into the first cylinder. With the aid of the pump, he then created suction in the tubing, causing the liquid HCN to be drawn into it. Bey lifted the other capped end of the tube just above the level of the tank fill point, and as soon as the liquid in the tube reached that point, he removed the cap and put the tube into the tank. The HCN now flowed into the tank of its own accord. It took just over two hours before they'd emptied the last of the cylinders, and although Ciddiqui had warned them not to allow the HCN to come into contact with their skin, he'd conveniently omitted to tell them that the fumes could also be lethal. Mabeirig screwed on the tank cap before they set about carrying the now empty cylinders down to the river's edge.

'These cylinders are much easier to move when they're empty,' Mabeirig joked as he single-handedly pulled two cylinders onto the pier.

'Keep your voice down Hussein,' Bey said irritably, 'people walk this riverbank all the time. We've been lucky so far. Now I'll put the Land Rover in the boathouse while you put the cylinders into the river. Make sure the tops are open so they'll fill up with water and sink. Put the base of the cylinder in the water first, hold it down for a minute or two till it takes in some water, then it'll sink.'

As Bey manoeuvred the trailer and the Defender into the confined space of the boathouse, Mabeirig manhandled the cylinders up on to the pier. He then slid them, one at a time, into the River Wear. Eventually all of the cylinders were disposed of, but what the men had failed to appreciate, was that as the cylinders filled with the water, the fumes from within the cylinders leaked back out towards them. Each of them breathed in a heavy dose of the deadly HCN this way, particularly Mabeirig, as it was he who'd held down the cylinders until the fumes had been forced out by the incoming water. They locked up the boathouse and walked back to their flat in the university campus, stopping to buy two Indian meals from their local curry shop. Back at their flat they ate hungrily without speaking, each man full of his own thoughts.

CHAPTER THIRTY-TWO

When Franco Mazzini arrived at Scotland Yard he was taken directly to an interview room. Chris Hall was already there, anxious to move on.

'Mr Mazzini, thank you for coming in again at short notice,' he said, shaking Mazzini's hand.

'It is nothing Commander. I do anything to help catch Abdullah's killer you know that.'

As yet Scotland Yard had not disclosed to the media that Kadri was probably involved in the incident in London's St James's Park, although the early edition of the *Evening Standard* carried a story saying as much. The story was based on a leak from a London hospital, the *Standard* stated.

Hall asked Mazzini to take a seat, then said, 'The reason I've asked you to come in again Sir is that we're very anxious to make contact with any of Abdullah Kadri's friends. I know you've said previously that he didn't seem to have many, but I'd like you to take a look at this sketch. Is the face familiar in any way?' Hall said, handing Mazzini a copy of the Zenecal Security Guard's sketch of Ivan Aireb. Mazzini put on his spectacles, and studied the sketch for a few minutes. 'No Commander, I never seen this man. You think he's the man who killed Abdullah?'

'I didn't say that Sir, but are saying that you don't recognise the face?'

'No, I never seen the man before,' Mazzini said, then added, 'you know Commander we never see any of Abdullah's friends in the restaurant. He says he had only one. I tell you that before. Once I think I see a man shake hands with Abdullah near the restaurant. A big man, Commander, but it was dark at the time.'

Hall took the sketch back despondently. He then said, 'Well maybe Mr Mazzini you did see someone who can help us to find the Abdullah Kadri's killer. I'd like you to meet some of our technical people Sir. They're called by some new name now - *OTIS* and *WADS* I think. The first means *Operations Technology Information Systems* and the latter simply means *Witness Albums Display System:* a digital database of suspects. I was going to have them at this meeting, but they've correctly said that you'd be better going to them as that's where all their fancy electronic equipment is. I'm hoping, with your help Mr Mazzini, that *OTIS* and *WADS* might come up with something.'

'I try Commander, I try.'

Hall could see the man was desperate to help. He said, 'Good Mr Mazzini, let's see what we, and our technology can do.' He stood up then added, '*WADS* will let you look at various types of faces, heads and body shapes and sizes, and let you decide on a general view of the man you saw. *OTIS* will take it from there, OK?'

'Sure Commander, I do anything to help you, you know that. I try very hard to remember the man,' Mazzini said with a look of concentration on his tanned face. 'He was big man, you know what I mean? Big, heavy, like maybe he enjoys too much good Italian food Commander. I try, I try.'

Hall pressed the call button on his telephone then said, 'Cathy would you ask someone from *WADS* to come up and collect Mr Mazzini please. They're expecting him now.' He offered his hand to Mazzini saying, 'Thanks again for coming in Sir. Maybe you can produce another face and a body for us to look for?' His telephone then rang. He excused himself and asked Mazzini to go through to Reception where his secretary would look after him. As Mazzini closed the door behind him, Hall lifted his telephone. His secretary said that Strathclyde Police in Glasgow were on the line. He looked at his watch it was four twenty five. He said he'd take the call, and covering the mouthpiece, he asked her to make sure Mazzini was looked after until *WADS* came to collect him. He then said, 'Hello, Commander Hall, Scotland Yard speaking, what can I do for you?'

A female voice with a friendly Scottish accent said, 'Sir, I've got Chief Inspector Anderson, Strathclyde Police for you. I'll put you through now.'

After a slight pause, a voice said, 'Good evening Commander, I hope I'm not disturbing you at this time of day, but as you know I've got a couple of your men up here helping us with the Kiremla situation! I thought you might like an update on our progress Sir, if you know what I mean?'

'No Chief Inspector you're not disturbing me, and yes I'd like an update as you put it. I was wondering when I'd hear from them to tell you the truth. By the way I've just received the video film and photographs you sent me. Thanks for that, they arrived about twenty minutes ago. Haven't had the chance to look at them yet, but I will shortly. What do you want to tell me Anderson?'

Anderson coughed clearing his throat, 'Commander you're a busy man so I'll get to the point. Your men and I, together with two of my local DCs, went to the warehouse where Kiremla rented space. The Isosceles Centre it's called. That's a posh name for an old dilapidated building. We brought the caretaker into my office a hour or so earlier, not that that proved to be of any benefit at all.' Anderson coughed again before continuing. 'He's an old sea-going man he says, brought up on the high seas, and a bit *thrawn* as we say up here in Scotland. A bit, how can I put it Sir? Reluctant to be helpful to the *law and order brigade* if you know what I mean. Anyway Sir, we all went back to the warehouse with him, and that's when we started to get some results. He, the caretaker that is, got quite nervous with all the *polis aroun,* as he put it. He must've some illegal whisky put away somewhere in the building if you ask me. You see Sir, there's a whisky bond across the street from the Centre...' Anderson stated as if that explained the whole thing.

'Chief Inspector just tell me about Kiremla, that's my main interest,' Hall stated impatiently.

'Yes Sir, yes well I'm coming to them in a minute. But you see it's all tied up in some way. What I mean is this Sir,' Anderson said excitedly. Hall decided to give up, and just listen as Anderson continued with his progress report. When he finally put his telephone down Hall noticed that it was five o'clock, and dark outside. He looked at his notepad on his desk where he'd written down the main points of the Anderson's telephone conversation.

> *A white hired van, from a hire company called*
> *Arnold Park Motors.*
> *Eight cylinders, like bottled gas cylinders, in two*
> *groups of four in the Kiremla storage unit.*
> *The van driver, from Glasgow, had asked*
> *for help unloading the cylinders and some other*
> *things from his van into the Kiremla unit.*
> *The caretaker refused saying he'd a bad back.*
> *Two men visiting the unit next door offered to assist.*
> *The men had now been contacted, and were*
> *due to come into Cranston Hill Police Station*
> *in Glasgow that night.*

The security video cameras throughout the
centre had been non-operational on the day
due to a fault.

Hall cursed as he re-read the last item. Always the bloody same he thought. The two men who'd helped the van driver might be helpful. They must've picked up something from the driver, however small he thought. Looking at the name of the van hirer firm, *Arnold Park Car Hire* he thought that someone there must have dealt with whoever made the booking. He stood up and stretched his body to release the tension that had built up over the last few hours. It'd been an eventful and trying day, and it was just after five o'clock, but at last he was getting somewhere. He knew that Day was still around, and that he'd still to buy birthday gift for his wife Amanda. He decided he'd leave on time for once, and take Anderson's video film and photographs home with him. On the way he'd stop off and buy Amanda's present.

'Lorna, I've had enough for one day. I'm off to do some shopping, some *retail therapy*. I'll see you in the morning,' he shouted through his open door. 'Make sure Day gets a copy of my notes on Anderson's telephone call. They're lying here on my desk.'

'Sir, DAC Hughes would like to see you right away. He's been on the telephone twice while you were speaking to Chief Inspector Anderson,' his secretary replied. 'If you ask me he seems to be feeling a bit left out. Would you like me to tell him you've left for the evening?' she questioned.

'Shit - I forgot about the DAC, no wonder he's upset. Lorna tell him I'm on my way now. With any luck I might still just make the shops before they close. They're open late tonight I think?'

'Yes, seven o'clock every night now Sir. Leave your desk, I'll tidy everything away. You better go up and see the DAC right now. I'll see you in the morning.'

'Thanks Lorna. Oh, I'll be in early tomorrow. Don't put things away where I won't be able to find them,' he said putting his head around the open doorway, and smiling in an attempt to take any hint of sarcasm out of his statement.

'Off with you, or I'll phone DAC Hughes and tell him you went to Harrods when you heard he was after you,' she shot back at him as he left.

Hall came out of Hughes' office two hours later, all hope of shopping gone. Going back to his own office, he passed by the *OTIS* department and spotted Mazzini, and some of the operators staring at a couple of split computer screens in front of them. He went in and joined them, and Mazzini seeing him coming said, 'Commander Hall, this technology is wonderful. I now recognise him anywhere I tell you. I only see him once, but that's enough. His hair, the moustache, and the build, all just like my poor dead father. Too much pasta I think Commander.'

The technician re-focused the *e-fit* shown on the screen, then pressed the scan button to activate some elaborate electronic equipment. A laser printer then produced a full A3 size coloured copy. The print showed both frontal and side views of a man, as well as a full front and profile of the face only, all based on Mazzini's description. Mazzini, who was still sitting by the technician's side, was fascinated.

'Thanks Sir, the *OTIS* technician said as he stood up from his workstation. 'You've been a great help.'

'I do anything to help catch Abdullah's killer,' Mazzini responded, still looking at the print in front of him.

'Thanks Mr Mazzini,' Hall added, 'if you come this way I'll see you back to the main reception where you can relieve yourself of your security pass. You've a restaurant to run, so we'll get you a lift back up to Islington right away.'

'I do anything to help catch whoever killed Abdullah. He no deserve to die the way he did. It was horrible way to die at back of our restaurant. If you need me again Commander I come back.' Mazzini followed Hall towards the reception, where a police car was waiting to take him back to *Fred's* in Camden Passage.

Back in *OTIS*, the technician was setting up his equipment to produce a number of laminate prints of the *e-fit* for distribution to the media. Some would also be dispatched via the normal *All Forces Alert* arrangements.

As Hall was seeing Mazzini off the premises, Detective Inspector Johnston was also involved in escorting some people to the front door of Scotland Yard. Johnston had spent the last hour interviewing three staff members of Bloomsbury Holdings. He was more than happy, as one of the three, a woman, had stated positively that she recognised the face of the man in Zenecal's Security Guard's sketch. The woman had added that a man resembling the face in the sketch, had called into Bloomsbury's office a day or so ago. Johnston was now going back to complete his report on the interview.

.

CHAPTER THIRTY-THREE

Lyall Mews, tucked in behind Eaton Square in London's Belgravia, was deserted at eight o'clock on a damp, grey night. Farraj Rasid drove his Range Rover slowly down to the bottom end of the cobbled lane. He parked outside a garage. Getting out, he stood still for a moment or two. He picked up the sound of Mozart's Piano Concerto No 20. Looking around he saw a dimly lit upper floor flat opposite. The flat appeared to be the only property that was occupied. The delightful sounds of Mozart, a piece of music he knew and loved himself, was being played so loud that he felt sure the flat occupants would hear nothing else. He unlocked the garage doors, pushing them inwards. He then reversed the Range Rover into the garage, illuminating with his reversing lights a number of orange cylinders as he did so. Once he was in, he turned off the ignition, and then closed the doors from the inside. Only then did he switch on the single fluorescent light. He saw the cylinders, nine in number he noted, as well as a lifting device suspended from an overhead beam that ran the entire length of the garage. Someone's done his or her homework he thought. Wasting no time getting to work he unclipped the rear seats of the Range Rover, removed the flexible boot cover and put it on the floor. He then lowered the seats into a flat position increasing the space in the rear. With the help of lifting tackle, he loaded the cylinders into the boot and secured them using two armoured straps. He unfolded a blanket, and covered up the cylinders, before replacing the boot cover. He then switched on the ignition with the garage doors still closed so nobody would hear the engine starting. He switched off the light and opened the garage doors before he drove quietly back out into the cobbled lane and stopped. He then closed the garage doors. As he did so, he could still hear the sound of Adagio for Piano in B minor from the open window of the flat opposite. European music of that quality was one pleasure Rasid allowed himself, although he thought that it was too good for the infidels. A few minutes later he was back at his allotted parking space in Lownes Square. Farraj Rasid was now ready to strike. He smiled contentedly as he climbed the stairs to his flat.

CHAPTER THIRTY-FOUR

The campus was quiet at two forty-five in the morning, and only the pathway lights gave any illumination. The students were asleep, all that is with the exception of Hussein Mabeirig. He'd woken a few minutes before with a severe headache, and was now soaked all over in sweat. He felt he was going to be sick. Getting out of bed, he went through to the bathroom. He was feeling so weak that he had to kneel on the floor alongside the toilet pan. As he did so, he vomited up blood and lumps of the curry meal he'd had a few hours before. He was choking he thought, looking at the blood, and vomit all around him. He fainted and lay unconscious amongst the mess for a few minutes. Regaining consciousness a few minutes later, still lying in the stinking mess of vomit and blood, the intensity of the pains in his stomach caused him to panic. He screamed at the top of his voice, a last anguished cry for help, 'Niazi, Niazi help me, help me, help me,' before being overcome by another wave of nausea. He vomited again; this time only blood spewed everywhere, and flowed freely from his gasping mouth. Hussein Mabeirig knew he was dying.

'Hussein what's wrong with you? What's happened?' Niazi Bey shouted as he went towards the bathroom, stopping in horror when he saw Mabeirig lying on the floor covered in blood and vomit. 'What's happened to you Hussein? Allah help us,' he begged. He knelt down in the gory mess trying to comfort his dying friend. He had to watch in horror as the blood continued to pour from Mabeirig's slack mouth. 'Allah help us. What can we do? Allah tell me, I'll do anything,' he shouted in panic, covered in his friend's blood, blood that appeared to be everywhere. 'Hussein tell me how I can help you? For the love of Allah please tell me?' Bey begged, crying in his anguish. But Hussein Mabeirig's body was limp. Bey knew he was dead. Death had struck at the very core of the plan. As he stood up and looked around him, he shuddered. 'I have to control myself,' he said shaking, 'mustn't lose my objective. Allah will help me. I'm alone, I need His guidance and support.' He decided first to move the body. Lifting Mabeirig by the ankles, he pulled the body out of the bathroom and into the hallway. From there he dragged him into his bedroom, leaving behind a trail of blood and body fluids. By the time he got to the bedroom he also felt unwell. His eyes and his head were beginning to hurt badly, and he had to sit down on Hussein's bed. He was in a state of shock, but in spite of everything his sole aim was to be able to complete his task. 'I must think clearly. Allah help me; please help me,' he pleaded.

Far away from the circumstances that Niazi Bey found himself in, Ali Ciddiqui had woken just before three o'clock in the morning. He was restless and disturbed, the dreams of dark, swirling waters having returned, although that wasn't what had woken him. Getting out of bed, he pulled on his dressing gown. Possibly a noise in the street outside he thought, as he went through to his elegant lounge. He opened the curtains to look out. The street was devoid of any traffic and nobody appeared to be around. He then went to his study, and saw his paperwork and mail lying on his desk in order of priority, ready for his secretary to deal with in the morning. At his desk he scribbled a note to remind himself to pick up his plane ticket to Yerevan, the thought lifting his spirits. He put the cap back on his gold pen feeling better - and pleased with himself for the way he'd set up Colonel Safa's plan, the operations at Alpha, Beta, Gamma, and Delta. His proud thoughts lasted all of two seconds. As he was about to go back to his bedroom, his head was jerked back violently from behind, exposing his throat, which was then deeply cut, almost silently, from ear to ear. His lifeless body and still startled face, the head barely remaining attached to his body, was then carefully allowed to slump down onto the heavy pile rug by the side of his desk. Ivan Beria, as was his professional habit, glanced around the room to make sure he'd left no evidence of having been there, although his training ensured he'd never be that careless. Beria went to the bathroom, washed the blade of his knife, and slipped it back into a tight-fitting leather sheath just above his left ankle. He then retraced his entry route, climbing through the open bathroom window next to the external fire escape at the back of the building. Within a few minutes he'd reached the lane at the rear of the building and walked briskly away.

Commander Chris Hall was as yet unaware of the very existence of either Hussein Mabeirig or Ali Ciddiqui; however he too had had a disturbed night's sleep. He got out of bed as quietly as possible, showered, then dressed quickly. He left a note to his wife saying he'd gone back to Scotland Yard, and that he'd phone her later that morning. As he drove into London, his mind was plagued by the thought that he'd missed something. Last night before he'd gone to bed, he'd watched the video that Chief Inspector Anderson had sent him from Glasgow three times. It showed little more than the interior of a unit in the Isosceles Centre, but something had caught his eye the last time he viewed it. It may turn out to be of little significance, but until he'd checked it he couldn't get it out of his mind. Having then gone to bed, he couldn't sleep. He was convinced that the HCN had to be stored where the hired vans had come from. That put it in Glasgow, Newcastle upon Tyne and possibly Bristol. A red traffic light stopped him. There wasn't another car in sight, which only seemed to add to his feelings of urgency. Instinctively he jumped the lights, then reprimanded himself. 'Hell, I don't need to get booked for a bloody road traffic offence on the way to the Yard. The DAC would love me for that,' he muttered. He drove on, keeping his speed at the speed limit and tried to relax. He put the radio on, tuning it to the local police frequency for a few minutes, but the humdrum tone of the announcements made him feel worse. He was glad when he arrived at the Yard, and went straight to the War Room.

'Morning Sir,' Day said as he met Hall in the corridor. 'Couldn't sleep either I guess? I'm the same if it's any consolation. Can't keep this case out of my mind. I just feel that we're about to get on top of it. You know what I mean Sir?' Day said looking at Hall and thinking this time the Commander looked shattered.

'I know what you mean alright. Look Ian, I'd like to have a word with you in ten minutes. OK?'

'Sure, I'm going to sign off the latest AFA, the one including the *e-fit* sketches. I'll be back in a few minutes.'

Hall carried on into the War Room and went straight to the video machine. As he was about to put the video film into the complicated equipment, DC Treefield from *OTIS* said, 'I'll do that for you if you'd like Sir.'

'Thanks John, I didn't see you round there. I never was much good with these things, even the simple one I've got at home is hard enough.'

Treefield laughed, then asked, 'What do you want to do with the film Sir? Is there something specific you want to look at?'

'Run it to the end then come back to the bit that shows the cylinders being hauled up by the lifting tackle, then freeze it John.'

Treefield slipped the film into the machine, as his fingers glided smoothly over the computer style keyboard. 'We'll let the computer find the end of the film for us first. Ah there we have it.' He touched a few more keys, then asked, 'Is that the part you mean Sir?' On the screen, Hall could see an open door and the rear and side view of a motor vehicle. The cylinders could be seen in mid air in the background.

'Spot on John. Now zoom in on the back and side of the vehicle.'

Treefield touched a few more keys, 'Tell me when you think I've got the view you want Sir.'

As the picture on the screen was enlarged, it became blurred and out of focus.

'That's the spot. Can you sharpen the picture John?' he asked.

'Not a problem. I'll just centre the part we want to look at on the screen,' Treefield said punching the keyboard a few more times, 'just about there, and then we can digitally sharpen the picture like this,' he said as he played with the keyboard.

The screen now displayed a clear, sharp picture of the selected image.

Hall looked at the rear view, and oblique side view of what he'd guessed was a dark green Range Rover, an old two-door *Classic* model. 'Great John, print me a copy of what we've got on the screen.' It just might have been worthwhile getting out of bed at three in the morning he thought with some satisfaction... Two-door Range Rovers were thin on the ground, and weren't manufactured after nineteen eighty-four. As Treefield was producing the prints, Hall recalled with fond memories, the old white *Classic* he'd bought just after he and Amanda had got married. It was twelve years old when he bought it, but both he and Amanda had loved it. He remembered clearly the vertical recessed door handles in the large single door on each side, and the narrow plastic rear bumper with over riders fitted at each end. Now all of these details were being shown on the screen in front of him.

Treefield hit the print button on the keyboard, and a coloured copy of the image on the screen started to come out of the laser printer. He waited until it had finished printing then removed the print. He placed it face down in a scanner and pressed *Scan to File*.

'If you'd like me to enlarge the print further Sir let me know. I have it stored now so it's easy to enlarge any part of it up to a factor of ten.'

'Thanks John.' Hall stood up, still looking at the coloured print. 'John, would you wind the film back, and have someone bring it to me please.' Hall went to his desk and put the coloured print on it face up. He picked up a closely typed report headed *Operation Hydro* from his in-basket. The report was produced every four hours, providing an update of events connected with their investigations. He began to read it.

'Have I come too soon Sir?' Day asked, as he stuck his head around the door.

'No Ian, come in and take a seat. I was just trying to catch up on these reports, but you'll have read them so you can tell me about them and save me some time,' he replied with a smile.

'Where to start - that's the problem Sir! Since you left last night we've had some minor progress. First, you'll recall we had the Bloomsbury Holdings interview set up. Well Johnston was able to get one of the staff from Bloomsbury to confirm that she did recognise Ivan Aireb. He apparently calls at Bloomsbury to uplift mail or whatever about every ten days or so. We've now set up a system with Bloomsbury's manageress that should Aireb call again then she'll contact us while he's still on the premises. We've advised the local force of our interest, and they're arranging to adjust the route of two of their patrols so they overlap Bloomsbury's address. It should give us a quick response should Aireb turn up again.'

Hall let Day continued without interrupting.

'Secondly, the lads we sent up to the Isosceles Centre in Glasgow. Well they've now interviewed some people from a company who rent the unit next to Kiremla. You'll remember from C I Anderson's report that the driver of the white van, when he arrived at the centre asked for help to unload his van. As it happens there were two men in the next unit to Kiremla's, so the driver asked them to help him. It now turns out the driver's a local lad, Glasgow I mean, and apparently lives around the corner from the Isosceles Centre. He told the men he was just about to get some of his mates to give him a hand when these two guys turned up. Anyway, the guys told our boys that they'd helped to unload two net sacks, bloody heavy they said, and each sack had four orange cylinders in it. The driver gave them a fiver each for their trouble, saying he'd made a bob or two himself on the whole thing. And wait till you hear this Sir,' Day said with a bit more excitement in his voice, 'would you believe from the description of the driver the men gave, our lads along with Anderson's boys have already picked him up, the driver that is Sir. Singing like the proverbial canary I'm told. Apparently he's also got a bit of form as well!'

'It gets better Ian.'

'The van driver, Ian Carey, lives a few blocks away from the centre, in Argyle Street. He said that a few weeks ago he was helping to unload a brewer's lorry at a local restaurant.' Day hesitated as he referred to his notes. 'The Jammery, that's its name. Giving a mate a helping hand he claimed. Anyway when he'd finished, some bloke, foreign sounding not Scottish, according to Carey, comes out of the restaurant and says he'd been given Carey's name as someone who might be able to do a job for him. The man then apparently asked Carey if he'd like to make a thousand pounds for a couple of day's work. Carey claims he said to the man it would depend on what kind of work it was. By the way Sir we have a good description of this foreigner from Carey. Well the man tells Carey it will involve him hiring a van in Glasgow, driving it to Hatfield outside London, and then picking up a load there. Carey was then to drive back to the Isosceles Centre in Washington Street, Glasgow, and put the load in a unit rented by a company called Kiremla. He was told the paperwork was all in place. He was to tell the company in Hatfield, Zenecal Chemicals, that he worked for Kiremla. No description of the load was given. The man added that Carey would receive his money when he returned Kiremla's key to the centre's caretaker.' Day paused. 'Well as you'd expect, Carey says he said *Yes*, and the man handed him a key for Kiremla's unit, some paperwork for Zenecal Chemicals, and the deal was done. When Hall didn't ask or say anything, Day continued.

'The rest we know Sir. Carey hired a van from Arnold Park Motors in Glasgow, and drove to Zenecal Chemicals in Hatfield. By the way Carey admitted he'd lost his licence two years ago, only three times over the limit he claimed, and had to borrow one of his mate's to hire the van. He also borrowed a credit card to pay for it. Anyway he drives to Hatfield, picks up the load, and drives back up to Scotland. Takes the load to the Isosceles Centre, and meets the two guys in the unit next door to Kiremla's, and asks them to help him unload the van. He then hands the key back to the caretaker, who gives him a sealed envelope which had the following message written on it, *Give to person who hands in key to Unit No 6, Kiremla Ltd*. Carey opens the envelope, and counted his money. Twenty fifty pound notes Sir! He took the van back to the hire firm, someplace just outside Glasgow he says, and asks them to get him a taxi to take him back into town. He walks away, job done, one grand richer Sir.'

'Are Strathclyde Police still holding Carey in Glasgow?'

'Yes Sir, but all they've got on him is an admission of driving without a licence, so they can't hold him too long. Twenty-four hours at the most Sir, Scottish Law I'm told.'

Hall looked at his watch. It was ten past four in the morning. He was thinking that he'd like to question Carey himself. He got up and picked up the coloured print off his desk. He handed it to Day saying, 'Ian this photograph shows the side and rear of the vehicle used to take the HCN cylinders away from the Isosceles Centre. Carey's white van brought them to the centre, whereas this vehicle took them away. Where to is the question?' He watched Day studying the photograph then added, 'The vehicle arrived at the centre with a driver and passenger, two males it's believed, on the sixteenth of April according to the records kept by the caretaker. The men, who unfortunately weren't clearly filmed by the security camera while they were in the unit, uplifted the cylinders and drove off. The interesting point is that the vehicle is an old two door Range Rover I believe. We'll get Forensics to take a closer look at the photograph, let them check out the photograph with the real thing. There must be a few of those old four-wheel drives still around the used car showrooms in London. Between having Carey in custody, and a vehicle to target, we're getting a bit closer to the whereabouts of the HCN. Now, go on Ian, what else has been happening since I went home for a few hours sleep? Oh when I remember Ian, I'd like to speak to Anderson in Glasgow as soon as he reports for duty this morning. I take it he'll have a copy of the AFA with the *e-fit* of Aireb?'

'He has Sir, I just sent it.'

'Good. I wonder when he gets to his desk in the morning?'

'From what our lads up in Glasgow tell me Sir, he's at his desk no later than 0700hrs every day he's on duty. He also expects his day shift people to do the same, including our lads, although the shift start is supposed to start at 0800hrs.' Day added, a smile appearing on his face, 'They also tell me he's got a bit of a reputation Sir. His lads call him *The Water Rat.* Some chase or other that Anderson did during his beat days, when he pursued some villain for two miles through the Glasgow sewers. Can you imagine? Anyway, Anderson was supposed to have been up to his neck in sewage chasing the suspected housebreaker, and then performed a rugby tackle on the man, bringing the man down Sir. They say the smell from his uniform lasted for two months,' Day said, laughing for the umpteenth time.

'You know you never change Day, you're still like a bloody schoolboy,' Hall said, although he did smile. 'When I talk to Anderson in an hour or so I'll try not to remember that story. Now go on, what else has happened?'

Still laughing, Day replied, 'Well Sir you'll recall that Mazzini the restaurant manager at *Fred's* had our computer people busy till quite late last night.'

'I know, I was there Ian. We finally produced a face and profile of the deceased Abdullah Kadri's friend. The disappointing bit is that the *e-fit* face doesn't look like Ivan Aireb. There's no similarity whatsoever.' He handed the *e-fits* to Day, who looked at them, and then said, 'You're right Sir,' he said still looking at the images, 'they're not the same person however much we'd like them to be.'

He handed them back to Hall. One face displayed a man with a broad nose over a dark moustache, with large eyes that were almost black. The other showed a smallish head, pale skin, shaved scalp, cold light blue eyes, and a narrow long nose above small thin lips. 'If Mazzini and the guard at Zenecal Chemicals are both correct, then we're looking for two distinctly different people Ian,' Hall said.

CHAPTER THIRTY-FIVE

Around the time Hall and Day were discussing the *e-fit* images, Niazi Bey was driving towards Vaskerley. The body of Hussein Mabeirig, covered by a blanket, was in the back of the Land Rover Defender. When he arrived at Vaskerley at four-thirty in the morning, it was blacked out, and the single street was deserted as he drove through. When Bey had become convinced that Hussein Mabeirig was dead, he'd spent an hour deciding what to do. Initially he'd panicked, assuming he'd die as well, however the nausea left him. He knew he'd have to get rid of Hussein's body, and decided to take it to Vaskerley, *Location Gamma*, and drop it down into the air shaft. He assumed that it'd remain undiscovered until at least after he'd deposited the HCN, the *Juice of Allah,* into the shaft in a few days time. Once he'd made up his mind he acted quickly. He'd gone to the boathouse, unhitched the trailer from the Defender, and driven back to the campus. He'd then gone back to his apartment and collected Mabeirig's body, which he wrapped in a blanket. Luck was with him, and he managed to bring the body down the fire escape stairs unseen, and put it into the Defender. Regaining his breath, he set off towards Vaskerley, and the air shaft on Skylock Hill. Now as he drove quietly through the village, he turned to the left as the road changed from a tarmac surface, to that of a hard flint track. After a few minutes the track ran out and the grassy slope became steeper as he began the ascent of Skylock Hill. Engaging the lowest gear drive, and deciding to switch off his lights to avoid being seen against the black countryside, Bey headed up into the bleak hills. A half moon shining through a heavily cloudy, black sky was the only light. The vehicle struggled as it climbed the rough, grassy hillside, lurching and groaning until it eventually went up and over the ridge that shielded the air shaft. He could now just about make out the stone structure of the shaft at the foot of the hollow. A few minutes later he was alongside it. He parked and got out into what was now bitterly cold air. He could hear the sound of rushing water deep down in the shaft, interspersed by the occasional creaks and groans of the Land Rover's engine as it cooled down. He walked around the shaft then stood in its moonlit shadow for a full five minutes to make sure that nobody had followed him. Opening the back rear door, he picked up the hacksaw and two replacement blades, and the handle of the wheel jack. The tools in one his hand, Bey closed the door and climbed up the vertical side ladder of the Defender and onto the roof. Reaching up, he pulled himself up the ladder fixed to the stone shaft. At the top he sat down to get his breath back. He no longer felt the cold. The roar of the water beneath him was much noisier now. He touched the icy cold metal padlock fixed to the grid cover of the shaft, and wished he'd brought gloves. Moving around until he was as comfortable as possible, and adjusting his position to allow himself the maximum amount of purchase, he began to hacksaw the padlock clasp. He noticed from his watch by the light of the moon, that it was five past five in the morning.

Dawn was still an hour or so away as Mohammed Bejyi climbed onto his motorbike. He switched on the ignition and kick-started the engine. Noise and exhaust fumes surrounded him as he opened the throttle and drove towards the cottage's open gate at the end of the path. It was five forty-five. He had only fifteen minutes to get to Auchterarder, and start his shift at six o'clock sharp. It was dry for a change he noticed, as he steered the bike through the gate and out onto the deserted street. Opening the throttle fully, he disappeared into the gloom, the cold air stinging his face. He'd be glad to get the Range Rover back from the garage he thought. Guthies Motors in Blackford had telephoned last night to say that the Range Rover was now ready to be picked up, and that the damage was less than first thought. He planned to go there and pick it up sometime around four-thirty this afternoon. He cursed as a small car that had appeared from nowhere suddenly swung around a bend ahead of him, headlights on full beam. The car narrowly missed him as it shot past. Pasha and he tried to keep themselves to themselves at the hotel and didn't encourage any of the other staff to become too friendly. Now, as he huddled down over the bike's fuel tank, he wished he'd asked another waiter to pick him up this morning. He cursed the cold, damp country, and the infidels who lived in it. He repeated the words, *Ma Ma, Fi Kul Makaan* continuously through frozen lips for the rest of the journey, trying to make himself feel better. Soon in the gloom he saw the seventh tee of the Queen's Golf course on his right. A minute or so afterwards he arrived at the back of the hotel where he parked the motorbike near the staff entrance. Hurrying inside, he slipped his security card through the electronic card reader. He saw that it was five fifty-nine and twenty-nine seconds on the digital clock display on the machine. He hurried on into the locker room, and took off the waterproof jacket that covered up his white shirt and black bow tie. Opening his locker, he pulled out a black waistcoat and put it on. He threw the waterproof jacket into the locker and locked it. The phone in the locker room rang, bringing Bejyi to his senses. He picked it up and heard the demanding voice of Neil Carmichael, one of the Duty Managers. 'Who's that?' Carmichael asked bluntly.

'Mohammed Bejyi, Mr Carmichael.'

'Where the hell have you been Bejyi? I'm short of room service staff this morning. I've got guests complaining that their breakfast's not been delivered to their rooms yet. Get your ass in gear fast, do you hear me?'

'Yes Mr Carmichael, I'll sort it out.'

Carmichael exploded. 'You'll sort it out will you? With assholes like you working for me how can I provide five star service? And you tell me you'll sort it out! Listen Bejyi; get fucking on with it. Do you hear me?'

'Yes Mr Carmichael.'

The line went dead and Bejyi put the receiver back on the wall bracket. It was one minute past six o'clock. He cursed Carmichael who lived in Aberfoyle, near Loch Catrine, *Location Alpha,* hoping that he'd be the first to taste the *Juice of Allah* in a day or two's time.

The hacksaw blade, the third blade that Niazi Bey had used over the past hour, at last cut through the padlock clasp. His hands were now blistered and bleeding, although he now praised Allah for giving him his strength. His tracksuit top was soaked in perspiration. He rested for a few moments, then stretched across and examined the padlock. He was able to pull it out of the securing flange. Then he climbed back down onto the roof of the Defender, the air shaft's top now level with his head, and lifted the hinged cover as far as he could. Holding the cover up at an angle of just under ninety degrees with one arm, he propped the jack handle under it. Again he glanced nervously at his watch, checking that he'd enough darkness left. It was six thirty-five. He climbed down from the Defender, opened the back, and pulled the sheet from Mabeirig's lifeless body. *Rigor mortis* was at an advanced stage, and the body was already stiff. He tried not to think of the heavy, cold *thing* as his friend as he pulled it out from the back and over the rear edge. He got under the body, letting it rest on his right shoulder, and then straining with every muscle he straightened his back and lifted his dead friend.

'Allah forgive me,' he repeated. 'Show me you understand,' he mumbled as he strained to stand up straight. When he managed, he stumbled towards the ladder, using his right hand to steady himself, and his left arm to pull himself and the weight of the body up onto the roof. Continuing, he grasped the ladder fixed to the shaft, saying as he started to climb, 'Show me your mercy and forgiveness Allah, please, I beg of you.' He repeated the phrase as he climbed before he carefully placed the body on the top edge of the air shaft. He rested for a minute or two, saying as he stood beside the lifeless form, 'It is for you Allah that I do this awful thing.' When he'd got himself together again, he put his shoulder under the body, and in one swift movement nudged it up and over the edge of the shaft. He was near to collapsing, overcome with grief, and he had to sit down with his back to the shaft, sobbing uncontrollably. The realisation of what he'd just done began to sink in. Eventually he got to his feet. He realised he'd have to get off the hill, and back down through Vaskerley before he was seen. He lowered the grid cover over the shaft, positioning the now useless padlock so that it still appeared secure. Gathering up his tools he climbed down, putting his tools in the back of the Defender. He then drove down Skylock Hill, with tears running down his face, and sobbing uncontrollably. The moon, or the part of it that had been visible earlier, was now gone and he could barely see in front of him. He had to regain control and concentrate on making his way back to Durham safely. Wiping his face and nose with his sleeve, he forced himself to focus on the steep slope, and to follow the tyre marks he'd made on the way up. Soon he could see a few lights in the village below. He was in shock, although he'd have been much worse had he known that the Mabeirig's body of was now grotesquely spread-eagled across a water filter within an underground tunnel just beyond the base of the airshaft. The screen filter's prime function, although only a rough primary water filter, was to prevent large foreign bodies, such as cattle, birds, and other wildlife, entering the complex water system. It had worked well in this instance, and Mabeirig's body, having dropped down the shaft, entered the water in the distribution tunnel, and had been stopped by the filter within seconds. In addition, a computer printout, highlighting the partial blockage, was automatically produced in the control room of North Wood Water Treatment Works a few kilometres away. The printout recorded the sudden increase in pressure drop across the filter, as well as pinpointing the location, date and time of the occurrence. The computer itself evaluated the information, providing a full quality check, to ensure that no undue pollution was being detected in the vicinity of the filter. The information was then graded by the computer programme as *low, medium or high risk,* in this instance *low risk,* meaning that the incident could be attended to out-with emergency procedures, but normally within thirty-six hours. In fact it would depend on the time it took for Hussein Mabeirig's body to rupture as a result of the water pressure being exerted upon it, and then the release of the HCN-induced waste and other body fluids. This event would trigger the pollution sensors, and immediate attention would be called for by the complex detection system.

CHAPTER THIRTY-SIX

'Good morning Commander, how are you this fine morning?' Chief Inspector John Anderson asked Hall cheerfully when the latter was put through on the telephone. 'I hope it's as fresh in London as it is here?'

It was five minutes past seven on a severe frosty morning in Glasgow.

'Well thank you Chief Inspector,' Hall replied, wanting to minimise the small talk. 'To get to the point Chief Inspector, I believe you may have a male in custody by the name of Carey, Ian Carey? The man was the driver of the van that brought the HCN from Hatfield to Glasgow.'

'Indeed Commander, indeed we do. We'll have him till ten o'clock this morning unless you or I, Sir, can come up with some other charges.'

'We'll see about that Chief Inspector. Have you received an AFA today, together with copies of two *e-fits?*'

'I have Sir, they're right here on my desk in front of me,' Anderson replied, feeling on top of things.

'Do you have video conference facilities in Glasgow, Chief Inspector?'

'Yes Sir, we do. State of the art I'm told,' Anderson responded, again enjoying the positive direction the conversation was taking.

'Good. I'd like you to have it set up, and bring Carey into conference on it. Hold back the *e-fit* images, as I want him to see them at a particular time. Would you do that please?' Hall said in a tone that was an instruction, and not a request. 'When you're ready, say within the hour, call me on this direct line,' he said, giving Anderson the War Room number at Scotland Yard. 'Do that right away it's very important. By the way Anderson, for your information, its just been established from that video you sent me, that the vehicle used to pick up the HCN from the Isosceles Centre was a two-door Range Rover. That'll be confirmed in an AFA within the hour. Now Anderson get back to me as soon as you can please.'

'Certainly Sir, I'll phone you shortly.' Anderson paused, then added, 'A two-door Range Rover you say? Not too many of those still around I suspect. Have you checked with the DVLA Sir, the Driver and Vehicle Licensing Agency, in Swansea?'

'I know where the DVLA is located Chief Inspector,' Hall replied with a little irritation beginning to sound in his voice. 'Now I'll wait to hear from you,' he said replacing his telephone, the line at the other end already dead. As he did, he suddenly remembered Anderson's alleged nickname. He smiled, glad that he hadn't thought about it during their phone call. He got up and crossed over to WDC David's desk. He handed her a copy of a photograph showing the side view of a Range Rover. 'Barbara would you run this through with the DVLA please. Ask them for the registered locations of all two-door versions of Range Rovers throughout the UK. Let them know it's urgent.'

'Sure Sir,' David replied with a smile. 'They should be able to give us that information in no time. I know just who to get hold of there. I'll bring it to you as soon as I get it.'

'Thanks Barbara.'

As he left David to pursue the DVLA, he went to *OTIS* and asked Treefield to set up their video conference equipment within the hour. He returned to the War Room and picked up the two *e-fit* images from his desk. The face of the thinner looking man still troubled him. He was sure he had seen it before, but couldn't place it. Frowning, he looked at the other one, the heavier individual, the one with the moustache, and was reminded of Saddam Hussein, who he'd seen on television the previous night. Just then his telephone rang, abruptly interrupting his thoughts. He lifted it and heard the voice of C I Anderson, Strathclyde Police.

'Commander, I've put in motion our video facility here in Glasgow, and I've got Carey, and two of my detective constables, Butler, and Campbell with me. As you know Sir, the detainee is being held in connection with driving a vehicle without a valid driving licence. He'll be on my right when you look at the screen, with Butler and Campbell on either side of him.' Anderson hesitated, then added, 'If you'd now switch on your facility we can all have a chat Sir,' he said importantly.

'OK Anderson,' Hall responded. 'I'll divert this call to another line and speak with you again in a moment. I've also got the *e-fit* images I mentioned to you earlier. I would like to talk about them to Carey.'

212

'Right, I've got them as well,' Anderson replied, 'I'll wait till you switch on then Sir.'

Hall rang Treefield on his internal line, and asked him to meet him in the video conference room right away. When he went into the room Treefield was already there, and he heard him saying, 'Chief Inspector Anderson, Commander Hall has just come in now Sir, I'll pass you over to him shortly.' Treefield turned down the sound then said to Hall, 'I've put the conference line through now Sir, but the Chief Inspector can't hear us yet. If you'd like to sit over to the left of the table, everything is pre-focused and ready to go. The microphone is tuned in to individual use Sir, not full room use. I've also set-up the record mode so everything seen or said will be put on to a videodisc for record purposes. Anything else you need Sir, just ask. I'll be out of view of the other location, but able to assist you if you need,' Treefield added, moving over to the computer laptop at the far end of the table. He keyed in the operating code, returning the sound to normal. Hall heard the dialling tone as the modem responded to the Treefield's touch, and the large, flat, wide monitor filled with a view of the Cranston Hill Police Station conference room, in Glasgow. Hall saw that one of four men was in the uniform of a Chief Inspector. The man in the uniform said, 'Good morning to you again Commander,' then introduced those around him, who all looked less than comfortable sitting side by side. Anderson however was enjoying himself.

'Good morning Anderson,' Hall responded. 'Chief Inspector, would you ask Mr Carey to look at the two *e-fit* photographs you have with you please?' Hall watched Carey's face closely as Anderson uncovered and passed the photographs to DC Butler next to him, who in turn passed them one by one to Carey. Carey stared intently at each photograph, then handed one back to Butler.

'That's him. It was him who asked me to go to Hatfield and pick up a load, the cylinders,' Carey shouted.

Butler handed the photograph back on to Anderson, who in turn displayed it to the camera in front of him. It was the face that had troubled Hall for some time. It was the alleged Mr Aireb; the face that had been identified by the staff member at Bloomsbury Holdings in London. The face and profile produced from the security guard's sketch at Zenecal Chemicals Ltd, in Hatfield.

'Chief Inspector...' Hall started to say.

He was interrupted as Carey noisily asked, 'Can I go now? I've told yous all I know. Surely yous can do me a favour now?'

Anderson spoke next, trying hard to maintain his composure, said, 'Mr Carey remain quiet please while we're involved in discussion with Scotland Yard.' He gave Carey a hard look before continuing, 'Commander, I trust that the identification of the photograph was helpful. Is there anything else you need the detainee to comment on at this stage Sir?'

'No Chief Inspector, not at this point, but we may need Mr Carey for identification purposes in due course. Keep a long leash on him if you know what I mean. That will be all at the moment. Thank you for your help.'

Anderson adjusted his desk controller and then zoomed in on himself, so that he only appeared on the screen. 'Commander, it's been a pleasure to help Scotland Yard.' He said smiling broadly, 'If I can be of further help, you need only ask. I'll also make sure that the Mr Carey remains available should you or I need him. I'll sign off now Sir, and let you press on down there in London.'

The screen in front of Hall immediately went blank. Treefield stretched over and switched off the equipment. He asked, 'I'll file this film for you if you'd like Sir, and record it's whereabouts in the case disk. Its all disks now Sir, a lot easier to store, and to find what you're looking for.'

'Thanks for your help John, and yes please file the interview,' he said in a positive note.

'If you need to re-run it give me a shout and I'll set it up for you. What you'll see will be a split screen, one half will be the Glasgow end, and the other half of the screen will show you here at the Yard,' Treefield added.

Hall thanked him again, then left the room, returning to his desk in the War Room. As he sat down his thoughts focused on the fact that they now had two positive identifications of Aireb from sources four hundred miles apart. He hoped they would be as lucky with the other unknown and unnamed face; the Saddam look-a-like.

'Sorry to interrupt you Sir, but I've got the information from DVLA that you requested. One page for each separate owner would you believe?' WDC David said, handing over a thick pile of faxed pages. She frowned and said, 'I never thought there'd be so many of them, did you Sir?'

Hall took the pages, about half an inch thick, with a touch of dismay. 'Neither did I Barbara, neither did I. But it was a good model that one. Look while you're still with this, will you separate this lot up into smaller lots. Split the lots geographically,' he hesitated as he thought, 'into say Scotland, and then the major conurbations in England. You know what I mean Barbara.'

'Sure Sir,' David said cheerfully, taking the pile of paper from Hall. 'When I finish that, would you like me to issue a restricted alert with the information to the appropriate stations Sir?'

'Yes Barbara, that would be great, but remember to keep Day informed of what we're up to would you please,' Hall added.

'Right Sir, I'll get on with it,' David said as she walked briskly back to her desk.

Smart lady as well as a good looker, Hall thought, failing to keep a smile off his face. The smile didn't last long. As he glanced at his desktop computer on which his diary for the day was displayed. He saw he was due to meet with DAC Hughes, and the Home Office Minister's PS, Mr Peter O'Brien, at ten o'clock that morning. It was now 0855am and he'd have to put together a report for that meeting. He lay back in his chair and closed his eyes. He was now beginning to feel the tiredness taking over. How could I not sleep when I was in bed he thought keeping his eyes closed just a moment longer?

CHAPTER THIRTY-SEVEN

Once through Vaskerley, Niazi Bey increased his speed. He wanted to get the Defender back into the boathouse before anybody noticed it was missing. He tried not to think about what he'd done in the last hour or so but he instinctively shuddered every few minutes. He felt cold, and turned up the heater, but although it helped a bit, it seemed to cause the nausea he'd had during the night to come back.

Eventually he arrived back in Durham, and took the riverside track to the boathouse. He was feeling shattered. Once he'd put the Defender into the timber building, and re-attached the trailer, he began to relax. He locked up the boathouse, and slowly walked back to his apartment. It was five minutes to eight in the morning, with a slight hint of daylight in the grey overcast sky. He wasn't up to his regular morning run, as his energy level felt like it was below zero. He'd lie low today he decided, although he also knew the hours would drag from now till *Ma Ma, Fi Kul Makaan*. He forced himself to remain focused, saying to himself that he'd run tomorrow. If anyone asked about Hussein, he'd say he'd gone to visit friends in London, and wouldn't be back till the beginning of term. He himself would maintain his discipline, and his promise to Allah. A few minutes later he arrived at his apartment, opened up and went in. The gruesome scene he'd left a few hours before confronted him again. He decided he'd have to clean up in case someone called. As he did, he tried to convince himself that he didn't need Hussein. At one point he considered putting a message in *The Times* to let his activator know his predicament, but his pride prevailed. He alone would serve Allah. It will be his duty and honour to do so. 'Allah give me strength to fulfil your command,' he pleaded, as he mopped up the now stinking mess.

'That's perfect Lorna,' Hall said, handing the corrected copy of his report back to his secretary, having dictated it straight off to her an hour ago. 'Do the changes in the three paragraphs I've marked, and get me three copies please. Oh, ask Inspector Day to meet me here at twelve today, not the War Room? Got that?'

'Will do Sir.'

'Lorna, I've got a meeting at the DAC's office at ten and I don't want to be late again. Would you do the corrections and get the copies ASAP please. I'll blame you if I'm late this time,' he said grinning.

'Good morning Peter,' Hughes said as he extended his hand to Peter O'Brien.

The two men shook hands and O'Brien smiled back, although his eyes didn't convey any friendship or warmth, saying, 'Good morning Michael. You're well I hope?'

'Fine Peter for a man of my advancing years. I'd be a damn sight better though if we could get this St James's thing done and dusted. Sit here Peter,' Hughes said as he pulled a chair out from under the table. ' Chris Hall, who you've met before Peter, will give you an update amongst other things re St James's. Chris will be here shortly.'

'OK Michael,' O'Brien replied sitting down, 'but I do hope we've got some real progress to report since our last meeting? You're aware Michael that both the PM and Her Majesty are still extremely upset by the loss of birdlife in St James's. Unprecedented I'm told! They can't believe we,' O'Brien paused for effect, 'that's you and I Michael, allowed it to happen?'

'Yes I know Peter, I know. But you must understand that there is more to this case than just what happened at St James's Park. You know that for God's sake.'

O'Brien frowned, then said, 'OK Michael relax, the PM does understand that, however Her Majesty, well she's not in the loop so to speak. She's not yet been informed about the threat of hydrocyanic acid, the HCN, as you call it. But you know the PM. He has to take into account the scale of the resources we have on this. He's been asking me daily where we are with it. You know what he's like Michael; he wants action now, right now!' O'Brien looked at his watch, 'Where is this man of yours Michael; this Commander Hall?'

The phone rang. 'Excuse me Peter,' Hughes said, moving back to his desk. He lifted the phone, listened, then said, 'Send him in please.' Hughes returned to the table and added, 'Hall's on his way in now Peter.'

There was a knock on the door. 'Come in Chris,' Hughes shouted.

Hall came into the room and shook the hand offered by O'Brien who was already on his feet.

'Good to meet you again Commander,' O'Brien said, his voice only slightly less unfriendly than a few minutes before.

'Good morning Sir,' Hall replied.

'Chris sit here,' Hughes directed, pointing to a chair at the head of the table, O'Brien and himself seated on either side. 'Chris, Peter wants to know about progress with St James's? The PM's demanding that we resolve the issue *post-haste*. Would you bring Peter up to speed with what you've got Chris?'

O'Brien interjected. 'Before you begin Commander, I think I should advise you that the anthrax situation has gone cold, or so our friends in the Foreign Office now tell us. Apparently the contacts they use in the Middle East, have found no further evidence of any attempts to infiltrate the UK with it.' O'Brien paused for effect, allowing the statement to sink in, then added almost disappointingly, 'and so, that said Commander, what have you got for me regarding the HCN? A cabinet reshuffle is always just around the corner if you know what I mean. I need some positive progress?'

Hall had already decided he didn't like the man. He withdrew copies of his report from his briefcase. Handing them out he said, 'Sir, my report regarding St James's as of one hour ago. It, apart from confirming that the man responsible for discharging the HCN into the lake is now dead, was in fact murdered, also covers the consequential risk of the distribution of the HCN throughout the UK.' Hall instinctively stood up as he started to explain the contents, and walked around the table. He began by stating the results of the investigation into Zenecal Chemicals at Hatfield. As he was about to list the various things uncovered there, O'Brien interrupted yet again.

'Commander, I would appreciate if you would either stand still, or sit in one place while you're talking. This is a serious matter and I personally,' he said, stressing the last word, 'like to see the eyes of people who are speaking to me.'

'Please Chris, just sit at the table,' Hughes said, trying to diffuse the mild friction between the two younger men, 'now go on please. You were on the subject of Zenecal Chemicals, and the fact that the fifteen hundred litres of HCN may've been split up into three separate hauls, that are now probably in Glasgow, Newcastle upon

Tyne, and, you think, Bristol. What do we know of the possible targets?' Hughes questioned, feeling the tension in the room release a little.

Hall sat back down, and specifically addressing Hughes, continued with his report. When he'd finished, the discussion that followed between the three men lasted for an hour or so. As the meeting was drawing to a close, Hall reiterated the conclusions in his report saying, 'As I've said, it's likely from Glasgow that we'll get our first lead. We have a witness there who has identified a possible suspect from one of our *e-fit* images. We also know that whoever picked up the HCN in Glasgow, did so with a two-door, dark green Range Rover. We're currently checking the list of owners of those vehicles up there in Scotland and elsewhere.' Hall looked at O'Brien for the first time in an hour, then said in a slightly lower voice, 'And, as you said earlier, we too have found no evidence of anything other than HCN affecting *Operation Hydro.*'

There was a moment's silence. In a conciliatory voice, O'Brien said, 'I suspect we're getting somewhere at last. I'll report progress to the PM later today.' He looked at Hall. 'Commander I suspect that the progress you've made, which while it will be appreciated by the PM, will only encourage him to demand more. I'm sure you understand the ways of the politician?' he added, with the hint of a smile.

Chris Hall decided not to respond to the obvious barb in the question. He stood up and said to the Minister, 'Good to meet you again Sir, and be assured that every effort is being made to resolve *Operation Hydro.*' He held the door open momentarily, and looking back at Hughes said, 'I'll be back in the War Room, Sir, if you need me.'

As Hall came back into the War Room, Ian Day was on the telephone to County Durham Police Force. As Day listened, Superintendent Peter Dunlop was explaining that one of his detective constables in the force up there, claimed to have recognised the face depicted on a recently received *e-fit* from Scotland Yard. Day was now holding on till the DC was brought to the telephone to speak to him. Day covered the mouthpiece of his phone and asked Hall to pick up another handset. As he did, he heard the man saying, 'Sir, my name is Hugh Falconer. I'm a Detective Constable in the City Division of Durham Police Force. Superintendent Dunlop said I should explain to you how I came to recognise the *e-fit* posted on our bulletin board this morning. Would that be OK Sir?' Falconer asked.

Day checked to make sure that Hall had also been put through before replying. 'Yes Falconer, but hold on a minute, I've now got Commander Hall on this line as well. He's in charge of *Operation Hydro* at Scotland Yard. We're both anxious to hear what you've got to say. Go ahead now Falconer. Just keep it simple. We'll stop you if we want to ask any questions.'

Falconer coughed, clearing his voice. 'Well Sir, I was off-duty at the time. It was a Friday evening around five o'clock three weeks ago. I'd gone to collect my wife. She's a receptionist in a hotel in Durham, The Royal County Hotel down by the River Wear. Anyway as usual, I'm sitting in my car in the hotel car park waiting on her coming off shift when a car, a Ford Mondeo, pulled up alongside me on my right side Sir. The driver, a male around mid-forties, big man, heavy build, tanned complexion, and dark hair. My driver's side window was down,' Falconer paused, then asked, 'shall I keep going Sir?'

'Yes Falconer, go on, we'll stop you if we need to,' Day replied, looking towards Hall who nodded his head.

'Right Sir, anyway the man parked and just sat back in the seat for a few moments with his hands still on the steering wheel, and he appeared to be talking to himself. At first I assumed he was using a hands-free mobile, but I couldn't see any sign of a connecting cable Sir. Could have been a voice activation phone I suppose, but I didn't think about that Sir. Anyway he had a heavy gold watch on his wrist Sir, very expensive it looked. That's really what first caught my eye. He obviously hadn't noticed that I was in the car next to him, at least I don't think he did. Then Sir he gets out, stretches himself as if he's been driving for a long time, and says quite loudly in a slight foreign accent - and these are the exact words he used Sir - *Glory be to Allah*. He stood there in the car park and repeated the phrase five times, like he was praying Sir. He then locked his car and went into the hotel.'

Both Hall and Day remained silent.

Falconer continued, 'There was something about the man that disturbed me Sir,' he said, beginning to relax. 'So much so that I followed him into the building and watched him check in. Again he hesitated before adding, 'You know what they say Sir, once a policeman; always a policeman. Anyway he was about six-three in height, about the same as me. As it turned out, Wilma, my wife was the one who checked him in, so she was able to tell me more about him when I asked her later. Said his name was Sayid Taleb. He had a Turkish passport, and offered it to Reception without being asked. He also asked if he could settle his bill with cash.' Again Falconer hesitated before saying, 'I did get a good look at him Sir. I'm sure that the *e-fit* that came with the last AFA, number two Sir, I'm sure the man's face is as close a likeness to this Mr Taleb as you could get.'

At the mention of number two, both Hall and Day momentarily held their breath. Hall spoke first. 'DC Falconer, this is Commander Hall speaking. You did say number two?' Hall asked, looking at Day.

'Yes Sir, number two that's correct. I've got a copy here in my hands - the number is on the top right hand corner. The Super gave it to me to study before he telephoned the Yard. He wanted me to be very sure before he called if you know what I mean Sir,' Falconer replied.

'OK Falconer,' Hall responded, his mind racing on. It was the first potential identification of the unknown friend of the murder victim, Abdullah Kadri.

'There's more Commander,' Falconer continued enthusiastically. 'You see my wife Wilma's Scottish. She was born just outside Glasgow, on the north side of the River Clyde Sir. A small village called Milton, near Dumbarton. Mr Taleb told her he'd passed by it a few days before he came to the Durham area, and....'

'DC Falconer, forgive me interrupting. Would you ask the Superintendent to speak to me please? Stay there, because what I'm going to say affects you,' Hall said.

'Alright Sir, I'll pass the phone to the Super now.' Hall could hear the man explaining to Dunlop what was happening.

'Commander Hall, Superintendent Dunlop. DC Falconer tells me you wish to speak to me.'

'Superintendent, good to talk to you. DC Falconer has certainly caught our attention with his information. I'd like him and his wife to come to Scotland Yard just as soon as possible.'

'No problem Commander, consider it done. There's a 125 Train leaves Newcastle at 1231. They'll be on it. It gets into Kings Cross around 1543. They can get a taxi and should be with you half an hour after that.'

'Great Superintendent. Would you ask Falconer and his wife to write down everything they can remember about Taleb's arrival at the hotel, and anything else however small. We need it all. Now forget the taxi; I'll have a car waiting to pick them up at Kings Cross. And thanks again for your help Superintendent, I'll speak to you later.' Hall replaced his telephone, as did Day. He then pressed his intercom and told his secretary to have a car meet the Falconers at Kings Cross at 1543.

CHAPTER THIRTY-EIGHT

Ron Talbot, the caretaker of the luxury apartment block in Knightsbridge where Ali Ciddiqui had lived, was trying without any success to console the woman. Hala Najid was staggering around in her distress, her head buried in her hands, and her ashen face awash with tears as she screamed hysterically.

'God, oh my God Ali's dead, I can't believe it, oh God,' she yelled, stomping her feet in frenzy. 'My poor Ali, why Ali?' she pleaded in her sorrow.

'Ms Najid, now Ms Najid please let me help you. How can I help you? What can I do? Come on sit here,' Talbot asked, the shock of what he'd also just seen in his voice. 'I've phoned the police, they'll be here shortly. Just you sit there till they get here Ms Najid. Now there Ms Najid, you'll be fine I tell you. It's a terrible thing that's happened I know. Poor Mr Ciddiqui, I can't believe it myself.'

Hala Najid was not fine, nor would she be for some time. The woman had arrived at the apartment block twenty minutes before, around ten-thirty in the morning as usual, and had collected Ali Ciddiqui's mail from Reception. Talbot would later recall that that in itself was a bit strange, as normally Mr Ciddiqui would've come down and collected his own mail much earlier. Hala Najid had assumed that Ciddiqui had gone out before the mail had arrived, and had taken the lift up to his apartment using the secure floor key. She'd then gone into the drawing room and noticed that the heavy curtains were only slightly opened, which she thought was a bit strange. Her unease increased when she saw that the bedroom door was open, and that the bed was unmade. Going towards the bathroom, passing the study on the way, she saw that that door too was partly open. Knocking the bathroom door she said, 'Are you in the bathroom Ali? Are you OK?' She pushed the door fully open, and went in. The bathroom was empty, everything was in place, and it appeared not to have been used at all that morning. Thinking that Ali Ciddiqui had gone off somewhere at short notice without telling her, she began to feel angry with him. He'd become so secretive lately she thought. She went back to the study and opened the door. Nothing could have prepared her for what she saw. Lying in a dark pool of blood, Ali Ciddiqui and his almost detached head was spread out on the carpeted floor at the side of his desk. His stark, opened eyes appeared to be pleading to her, and his mouth was twisted in a silent scream. At first she'd stared in disbelief at what she saw, and although she'd never remember how, she went back down to Reception. Only then, as she got to Talbot's desk, did Hala Najid scream in terror and in panic. The caretaker had also been taken aback when she returned only a minute or so after speaking to him, but when she started to scream he realised that something terrible had happened. Leaving her in the hallway for a few minutes, mainly because she refused to go back up to the apartment with him, Talbot went himself to see what was causing her distress. When he found the body, one look was enough for him to know that a murder had been committed. Leaving everything in the apartment exactly as he'd found it, he went back down to Reception, and tried in vain to calm Hala Najid. He then telephoned the local police station.

CHAPTER THIRTY-NINE

For some time tension had once again been building up between the Western Allies and Iraq and, trapped like a rat in a corner, Saddam Hussein didn't like it. Like the vermin counterpart, when caught in such a position, he decided to react in the only way he knew how: attack. He issued instructions that were to be secretly circulated to the capital cities of the Western Allies, where he had long since placed men loyal to him; men like Colonel Safa al-Dabobie, based in London. These men were to be recalled to Baghdad for consultation. Saddam had a great desired to be soothed, his ego caressed, and above all, he needed to feel in control of events.

'We leave for the airport in two hours. We'll meet in the lobby in the usual way. We may be gone for some time,' Safa said. Beria replaced his telephone and glanced at his watch. It was ten-past-twelve in the afternoon in London. He had enough time to pack the small number of personal items he valued, together with even fewer items of clothing and then go on to Bloomsbury Square to check the mail drop. People like Ali Ciddiqui used this facility, although Beria smiled at the thought that Ciddiqui would never use it again. He wondered if Ciddiqui's body had been found yet, thinking that it was a good time to be leaving London. After he'd packed, and called the porter to take his bags to reception, he made his way down to the hotel lobby planning to get a taxi to take him to Bloomsbury Square. He was beginning to look forward to leaving London. Perhaps Colonel Safa and he were being dispatched to a warmer climate; a change would be a good thing he thought. A black cab pulled up at a wave of the hotel doorman's outstretched arm.

'Where to Sir?' the doorman asked.

'Bloomsbury Square, the west-side,' Beria said.

The doorman repeated the destination to the cab driver, and held the cab door open for Beria to get in. Beria sat back as the vehicle sped off into the busy London traffic. Checking his watch again he noted that forty minutes had passed since Colonel Safa's telephone call. Instinctively he sat up a little straighter. After ten minutes he passed the British Museum on his left. Reaching for his wallet to pay the fare, he asked the driver to let him out at the corner of the square. It was a habit he used so that nobody could tell which address he'd gone to. It also allowed him to suss out the area to see if simple surveillance had been set up. He was a careful man, and that care had ensured his survival in the vicious world he lived in. He pushed a five-pound note and two one-pound coins through the open window to the outstretched hand of the cab driver, and waved away the hesitant gesture of change. He deliberately walked in the opposite direction to his intended destination and after walking almost all the way around the colourful square, he arrived at Bloomsbury Holdings.

As he walked into the reception, a young girl in her early twenties asked, 'Good afternoon Sir, can I help you?'
'I hope so?' Beria replied questioningly, looking beyond the girl for someone more senior should she prove deficient. 'I maintain a mail box here, under the name of Kiremla. Would you check to see if there's any mail? As quickly as possible please, as I don't have all day,' he added gruffly.
The girl addressed her computer screen, typing in the name *Kiremla.* She then asked Beria for his authorised name.
'*Aireb,*' he murmured quietly through the voice aperture in the glass screen between him and the girl.
As the girl keyed in the name of the box owner and the authorised claimant, she saw a message on the screen that she'd never seen before. *Advise Superior. Delay departure of caller.* She read the screen message again before reacting.
'Sir, I'm having trouble with my computer. I'll have to speak with my manager. Will you please hold on a few moments till I sort it out?' she said, playing the intended part more by chance than intention.
'I don't have time for this,' Beria shouted, causing more than one face in the large office to look in his direction. One such face instantly recognised him as Mr Aireb and moved into her planned action. 'Bring me your superior please, I'm in a hurry,' Beria demanded of the young girl.
The girl hesitated, again unintentionally delaying Beria, or Aireb as she thought, and became more flustered. 'I'm sorry Sir, but I must get some help with this, I won't be more than a minute or two.' she stated.

'Get on with it then,' Beria said in frustration, now wondering if he should've bothered to make this call. He watched as she went to the back of the room, stopping alongside a more senior woman whom he recalled seeing on previous visits. He relaxed a little assuming the matter would be quickly resolved, but he did again check his watch. It was now just after one o'clock. He looked urgently in the direction of the woman and girl. The woman was on the telephone, and appeared to be trying to avoid eye contact with him. One or two other people at desks nearby were also looking in her direction, with the odd glance at him. Beria's survival instincts suddenly kicked in. He knew he'd been compromised. He about-turned and went back outside, failing to see above him the recently installed CCTV camera that had recorded his every word and action. As he left, the woman on the telephone said, 'He's just gone Inspector. I think he must've guessed that something was wrong. I'm sorry.'

'You've both done well Mrs Cockburn let me tell you. I don't think we've had sufficient time yet to get our men into place unfortunately,' Johnston said to the woman, 'but we've had a positive sighting and also good video film to work with. I'll have someone down there shortly to pick it up. Don't let anyone touch the camera until my man gets there - not even the maintenance man OK? Anyway, thanks for your quick response. If the man should return today or whenever, don't worry, we'll have men around the premises for the next day or so. Thanks again,' Johnston concluded. The woman replaced her telephone and then told the young girl to come with her to the rest room. Both of them needed a strong cup of tea to calm them down after the events of the past ten minutes.

Beria left Bloomsbury Holdings, coming out onto the square, then quickly made his way to nearby Holborn tube station. Any station would've done. He took the escalators to the Piccadilly Line, and got on the first westbound train. Fifteen minutes later he got off at Knightsbridge, and walked back to the Carlton Hotel. He'd decided he'd not mention the Bloomsbury incident to Colonel Safa until they were well on their way to their next destination, of which as yet he knew nothing. At the hotel he waved to the doorman, who was helping a guest into a taxi. Going through the hotel lobby, he took the lift to the fourteenth floor. Checking the time, he saw he'd twenty minutes to spare before meeting the Colonel in the lobby. As he sat down in his room for the first time that day, Beria was feeling a little uneasy about the incident at Bloomsbury. Had he, or more than likely someone else, compromised the operation? Had he left it too long to dispose of Ali Ciddiqui he wondered?

CHAPTER FORTY

Johnston put his phone down after speaking to Bloomsbury Holdings and went straight to *the Boss* as he often put it. He was in luck. Hall was back in his office looking through the list of owners of two-door Range Rovers in central Scotland.

'Is *the Boss* in his office Lorna?' Johnston asked Hall's secretary.

'He is Jim, and he's on his own just now would you believe. Hold on a moment and I'll tell him you're here.' She pressed the speakerphone on her desk.

'Yes Lorna?'

'Sir I've got Inspector Johnston. He'd like a word if possible?'

'Send him in Lorna.'

'You've to go straight in Jim. Oh would you like a coffee? I'm about to make some for the Commander.'

'Black, no sugar thank you Lorna, I'm still trying to get some of this weight off.'

'You'll be lucky! If you do tell me how, will you?'

Johnston laughed, then knocked on Hall's door.

'Come in Jim.'

'Good afternoon Sir, and it might even get better,' Johnston enthused.

'Now hold on Jim, what are you so cheery about? Good news I hope?'

'Bloomsbury Holdings Sir, the post box address used by Kiremla. I got a call ten minutes ago from their Senior Manager, a Mrs Cockburn. She called to say that Kiremla's Mr Aireb had turned up there, checking his mailbox apparently. As we'd arranged, she tried to delay him till we got someone round there, but Aireb took off without warning, and without waiting for his mail.'

Hall looked at Johnston, hoping there was more, as his first reaction to what he'd heard was negative rather than positive. 'Aireb must now know that we've something on him. He'll be even more careful than before Jim. I'm not so sure what you've just told me is all good news.'

'Yes Sir I'm sure you could be right but we've now got a good few minutes of film of him from the camera we installed there. We should get better photographs than the *e-fit* we're using now.'

'True Jim. Get Treefield involved. Once we've got those, alert the air and seaports. Aireb may try to leave the UK so we've got to be ready. Get the photographs made up fast and get them circulated Jim.'

'Will do Sir.'

'On another front Jim, I'm having a look at this list of two-door Range Rovers that WDC David produced. Take a look at this,' Hall said handing Johnston the pages of the owners in central Scotland. 'I can't believe there are that many still around, there must be twenty-six there alone!'

Johnston took the pages, noticing that the names and addresses were grouped into cities, towns and villages. He replied, 'It looks like a simple job to get the local police to check them out. They should be able to do it inside forty-eight hours, making allowances for people being away and whatever. Would you like me to co-ordinate it Sir?'

'Yes Jim, that's why I brought it up, but keep David in the picture. She's done a good job so far producing this. I'll let Ian know what's going on. Get on with it Jim, we need to nail this thing. We've got too many fronts at the moment, all going at the same pace, and none fast enough for my liking.'

'OK Sir, will do. I should have that film in the next hour or so, together with the prints from it. I'll send you copies, and I'll have them e-mailed to Heathrow, Gatwick, Eurostar and the Channel ports,' Johnston said, getting up to leave.

'Don't forget Stansted, Luton and the City Airport Jim, those airports also have flights to Europe.'

'I won't Sir, leave it with me,' Johnston replied, closing the door.

Hall looked at his desk clock. It was twenty-past-one. He pressed his speakerphone, 'Lorna, no more calls or visitors for the next two hours. Just keep everybody away for a while.'

As Hall shut himself away for a few hours work, Day and WDC Barbara David, together with the Detective Inspector Allan, Lucan Place Police Station, Chelsea, began questioning Hala Najid. Day and David were there following a surprise phone call from Lucas Place twenty minutes before. This was the third interview in as many hours since Najid had arrived there. Earlier that day, just a little over fifteen minutes after Hala Najid found Ali Ciddiqui's body, three police officers, two of whom were from the Serious Crime section at Lucan Place, and the third, a beat constable who regularly patrolled the area around Pont Street, arrived on the scene. They were later to be joined by further police personnel, who set up a incident unit in Pont Street at Ciddiqui's apartment. When the police first arrived, they questioned both Hala Najid and Talbot, the caretaker, Najid having eventually composed herself. The officers decided that both Najid and Talbot should be taken to Lucan Place Police Station, where they could make statements, and if necessary, where Hala Najid would receive some counselling. When they got there, Hala Najid, with her head bowed, was escorted into the building, Talbot following behind. They passed through the public area, and were then directed to separate interview rooms, in Najid's case, accompanied by a WPC. As Talbot, the caretaker at Pont Street, came into the building, his attention was caught by the *e-fit* face pinned up on the station bulletin board, headed *Have You Seen This Man?* Must've be mistaken he thought, surely that couldn't be Mr Ciddiqui? It couldn't be! When it was his turn to be interviewed, Talbot had said to the two officers sent to interview him that he thought he recognised the face pinned up on the bulletin board. At first they treated his claim light-heartedly, but one took Talbot back out to check it. Looking at the face for the second time, and taking in all the features of the face, Talbot stated he was certain it was the face of Mr Ali Ciddiqui. The officers advised him that the *e-fit* had only been on the board a few hours, but Talbot said that it didn't matter if it'd been there for a year or two, or an hour or two. As far as he was concerned, the *e-fit* strongly resembled the face of the man who'd been murdered in Pont Street an hour or so ago. Talbot was eventually taken back into the interview room and told that the station's Chief Inspector would speak to him shortly. When the Chief Inspector arrived a few minutes later, together with two further plain-clothed officers, extra chairs had to be found to seat everyone.

'Mr Talbot, I'm Chief Inspector Bowie. I've been advised by my interviewing team that you claim the man murdered at the apartment block in Pont Street, where you're employed as a caretaker I understand, bears a strong resemblance to that *e-fit* face displayed on our bulletin board. Am I correct Sir?' Bowie asked.

'Yes Chief Inspector,' Talbot replied, 'in fact I'm more than sure of it.'

'Mr Talbot, did you read the notes attached to the *e-fit*? Apart from looking at the face, did you read the rest of the notice?'

'Well yes and no, I must admit. It was the face that caught my attention. But I did see something about terrorists I think.'

'It did mention terrorist activities and more. In fact Mr Talbot the notice displays the face of a wanted man. From what I've been told of the man murdered at Pont Street, he didn't have a moustache. The *e-fit* clearly shows a man's face, and the man has a moustache over his top lip,' Bowie stated.

'I know Sir, that's what threw me for a bit, but you see, Mr Ciddiqui shaved off his moustache a few days ago. I remember saying to him that he suited being without it, if you know what I mean Chief Inspector.'

Bowie stood up, then said to one of the two plain clothed officers, 'Turner, I'm of the opinion, whether Mr Talbot is right or wrong about the similarity of the murdered man and the *e-fit*, that we should notify Scotland Yard immediately. We also now have two of our own men who've been to see the corpse saying the same thing. From what I'm aware of, time is of the essence, and it's much better to be safe than sorry. Contact the Yard now DS Turner. Let them know what's happened down here, and keep me informed. Now, what do we do with this woman, Ms Hala Najid? Is she in a fit state yet to be asked to comment on the *e-fit?*'

The other plain-clothed officer said he'd ask the WPC who was with her if Najid was well enough and left the room.

Bowie checked his watch and announced that he had another appointment. Before leaving he said, 'I'll leave it to you, Turner, to move on this with Scotland Yard. And let me know what Najid thinks of the likeness of the *e-fit*. If she's able to have a look at it, that is. OK?'

'Yes Sir, I'll get onto the Yard now.'

Fifteen minutes after receiving a call from DS Turner at Lucan Place, both Day and WDC David had arrived there. They were led to the interview rooms, and questioned Talbot, who was steadfast with his story and his belief that the *e-fit* was an exact likeness to Ciddiqui. Day and David then went to see Hala Najid. Only a few minutes earlier she'd seen the *e-fit* photograph, and confirmed that it did resemble Ali Ciddiqui. She broke down again and they had to wait for her to recover. They questioned her for another two hours, with a break of thirty-five minutes in the middle, during which they'd gone to the scene of the crime. When they got to Ciddiqui's apartment, *Special Branch Prints* officers had just completed their work. Both Day and David had been allowed to have a superficial look around, including the opportunity to view the body before it was moved to a mortuary. They agreed that the dead man's features, with the exception of the missing moustache, did bear a strong similarity to the *e-fit* produced with the assistance of Mr Mazzini, the restaurant manager, the employer of the other murder victim, Abdullah Kadri. When they returned to Lucan Place, they continued with their interview of Hala Najid, and became increasingly aware that the woman knew very little about of her dead employer's business operations. It was equally clear to them that Ciddiqui was not involved in any ordinary business; the complete opposite seemed more than likely.

CHAPTER FORTY-ONE

The black S Class Mercedes 600 smoothly made its way through the traffic congestion heading west en route to London's Heathrow Airport. Sitting in comfort in the rear, and shielded by heavily darkened windows, sat Colonel Safa al-Dabobie. Ivan Beria accompanied the driver in the front. As the big car turned off the motorway towards Heathrow, Beria began to wonder where they were heading. His mind for the past thirty minutes or so had been focused on the earlier events in Bloomsbury Square. It was approaching twenty-five past two in the afternoon and in a little more than five minutes they'd be at the airport. With any luck, an hour later they'd fly off to an unknown destination, as was Colonel Safa's way. Beria tried to relax, thinking of the pleasures of first class air travel, the destination being of little consequence. As he allowed his mind to drift, Beria was unaware that ten minutes earlier at Scotland Yard, Johnston had picked up two high definition photographs of him that Treefield had produced from the security camera film from Bloomsbury Holdings, although Johnston used the name Aireb. Johnston had selected the image showing a full frontal of the man, together with an enlarged facial shot. He copied the photographs to Hall, together with the uncut film. Johnston then had the photographs scanned to disk, together with a memorandum instructing an AFA to be issued as *Extremely Urgent.* He was aware that this normally ensured that the document would be distributed within the hour.

Day was facing Hall in the War Room in Scotland Yard, and had just finished recounting the events of the past three hours. When he'd telephoned Hall an hour earlier from Chelsea Police Station, Hall had asked him to come back to the Yard as soon as possible, and to bring both Talbot and Hala Najid. The latter two were now being detained, albeit with their permission, a few metres away from where Hall and Day were sitting.

'Ian, I've asked *Fingerprints* to give me a preliminary assessment of their findings at Pont Street. Anything that ties up with Kadri, Zenecal, Kiremla, that sort of thing. They've said they may have something in the next hour or so if there's anything worth having.

I've also got DC Falconer and his wife coming to see me. They are due around four o' clock, and it's five to four now.'

'That's what happens when you're enjoying yourself Sir,' Day responded, although his attempt at humour was lost on Hall.

'You'd better hang around, Ian, to meet Falconer. As you know he also claims to have seen the man who's face featured on the *e-fit*, and who we are now almost certain is the murder victim.'

'OK Sir, and I'll tell Barbara David that should *Fingerprints* come up with anything while we're tied up with the Falconers, that she's to interrupt us.'

Seven hundred and fifty kilometres north of London, at around four o'clock in the afternoon, Mohammed Bejyi finished his shift at Beneagles Hotel. He was going back to the staff changing area to pick up his jacket and crash helmet before heading home. As he turned into the back-of-house corridor, he met Mark Carmichael, the Duty Manager. They were alone. As their eyes met the Carmichael said, 'You're all the same. In late and away early, and you do nothing in between. If I'd my way you'd get fired on the spot.'

Bejyi was taken aback. He replied defensively, 'Mr Carmichael, I've worked very hard today. As you know we are very busy at this time, with much to do...'

Carmichael was in no mood to be polite, especially to a lowly waiter. 'Don't you talk back to your superior. Do you hear me, you useless little pile of shit? You're suspended for a week that fix you...' Carmichael shouted, his voice vibrating the length of the corridor. 'I don't want to set my eyes on you for a week. Do you understand, do you?'

Bejyi looked at the man's heavy and sweaty red face, and decided that he'd better say no more. As he tried to go past Carmichael, the irate man shouted again, 'I'm fed up with you. Don't come back at all if you're not going to work harder than you've done in the past. Do you hear me Bejyi?'

Mohammed Bejyi walked away, and went through into the changing rooms. He was relieved that Carmichael didn't follow. Opening his locker, he took out his leather jacket and his crash helmet, and made for the exit. A minute later he was heading towards Blackford to pick up the repaired Range Rover. When he arrived there he saw the sign for Guthies Motor Engineers Ltd above a tired-looking façade of a building. The building comprised a small office at the front, and a steep-pitch-roofed workshop with a full-length open side door. The interior seemed to be full of cars and vans in every state of disrepair. Bejyi spotted the Range Rover parked at the side of the office. He stopped the bike alongside it and pushed open the glass door to the office. A bell rang somewhere in the back of the building. A young man in blue overalls appeared, rubbing his hands with a dirty piece of cloth.

'I've come to collect my Range Rover,' Bejyi said, turning and pointing in the direction of the parked vehicle.

'Oh right,' the man replied, 'I'll get the keys for you Sir. I'll also get Mrs Guthie to make out your bill,' he added going back into the workshop. As he disappeared, a woman emerged simultaneously.

'Good evening Sir, I'm Mrs Guthie. I believe we've repaired your motor car for you. Now tell me, are you VAT registered Sir?' she asked.

'No I have to pay VAT as well.'

'That's a pity Sir, you have to pay it and aren't able to claim it back. But there we have it. One rule for the rich and one for the poor I always say. Now let me see,' the woman said continuing to look at the book on the desk in front of her. 'We have to charge you for picking up the vehicle as well I see. Then the repair.' She touched a few buttons on a small calculator then said, 'That makes the total one hundred and thirty-four pounds, seventy three pence to be exact Sir,' looking up at Bejyi and smiling.

Bejyi opened his wallet, and took out one hundred and forty pounds. He handed the money to the woman.

'Thank you Sir, now if you've any problems, bring your car back to us. The work will be covered by our guarantee for twelve months, remember, so don't worry about it. Now here's your receipt, which is also your guarantee, your change and your car keys Sir. Don't forget those; you won't get far without them,' the woman said laughingly, as if she'd told a very funny joke. 'Now drive carefully won't you,' she concluded.

Bejyi took the change and the keys, and muttered a grudging, 'Thank you.' He went to the Range Rover and opened the boot. The five cylinders were still there. He closed the boot, and asked the young mechanic to help him lift the motorbike up onto the roof rack, where he secured it. He thanked the mechanic, got into the Range Rover and drove off towards Braco. Now he had to think of how best to break the news of his suspension to Hamid Pasha when he got home. At least they now had all the cylinders together, Hamid would be happy about that he thought. He switched on his full beam as he drove out of the tiny village and into the dark night. As he did, he was thinking that Hamid would come up with of something; he always did.

CHAPTER FORTY-TWO

The time in Berlin's Tegel Airport was fifteen minutes past six, local time, on a dark and wet night. A blustery north east wind blew across the main runway, causing the British Airways Boeing 757 to lurch crab-like as it touched down. The flight had left London Heathrow just over one hour and twenty-five minutes earlier, and Colonel Safa al-Dabobie and Ivan Beria had occupied club class seats 3A and 3B. Apart from some minor turbulence en route, the flight had been uneventful. As the aircraft taxied to its appointed gate, Beria's thoughts again returned to the events earlier that morning, though they no longer troubled him. He felt safe on German soil; a feeling he'd always experience there since his training at Pottsdam in what was then East Berlin in his youth. Colonel Safa had hardly spoken during the flight, preferring to doze instead. He had however made it known that they'd be changing aircraft in Berlin, and flying on to Amman in Jordan later that evening. From that sparse information Ivan Beria knew that they were destined for Baghdad in Iraq. When they arrived in Jordan, they would be met at Queen Alia International Airport and taken to a hotel to spend a few hours. They would then be taken on by car some two hundred miles or so east, and across the Jordanian border into Iraq, avoiding the current Allies' *No Fly Zones*. From just inside the Iraqi border, they would be picked up by military helicopter and taken the last four hundred miles direct to Baghdad. It was a trip they'd done many times before from London, although never via the same European capital twice. It was the way Colonel Safa al-Dabobie liked to travel to ensure that his carefully contrived image remained intact. Beria was suddenly jolted back into the present when the aircraft shuddered to a stop alongside the flexible pier at the terminal building. He unfastened his seat belt and stood up. He allowed Safa to ease past him into the aisle in front of him. Opening the overhead luggage compartment he pulled out both Colonel Safa's and his own hand luggage, before joining the rest of the passengers making their way off the aircraft. Beria continued to remain detached from Colonel Safa, ensuring that he could maintain his peripheral vision in focus at all times. They followed the airport signs displaying the route for transfer passengers to other airline gates, avoiding the need to go through customs and passport control, their luggage being automatically transferred to a Jordanian Airways flight from Berlin to Amman later that night. After a walk of ten minutes or so they arrived at the terminal building and went into the Jordanian airline's palatial Oasis Club. They were unaware that back at London's Heathrow airport, and at all other UK international air and seaports terminals, armed Special Branch officers were now manning the various passenger channels through UK passport control. Ivan Beria had only narrowly escaped.

Hall stood up and offered his hand saying, 'Thank you for making the journey DC Falconer, and you too Mrs Falconer. What you've told us has been most helpful. The visit to the morgue, although gruesome for you Mrs Falconer, was also important. Your identification of the deceased, the alleged Mr Taleb, and the real Ali Ciddiqui, is a major breakthrough for us. Now we can focus on the latter in the South, and the former in the North, knowing of course that he's one and the same person. Now I'll get a car to get you back to Kings Cross Station. Inspector Day will take you to it.'

DC Falconer and his wife rose from the table, and collected their coats. Falconer turned towards Day and said, 'When you come up to Durham tomorrow Sir you'll get our full support in any way you need. Superintendent Dunlop will see to that.'

'Thanks Hugh,' Day replied, 'I'll be there around nine-thirty or so in the morning. OK?'

'Someone will pick you up at the Durham Station,' Falconer said as Hall ushered him, his wife, and Day out his office.

When Day returned five minutes later Hall said, 'Ian, the visit to Durham. You must try and find out what Ciddiqui, or Taleb as he called himself up there, was up to. And why was he in Scotland? Whatever it was it's got to be related to the HCN, I just can't get past that.'

'You're right Sir, both those questions need to be answered.'

'Now where is WDC David, surely *Fingerprints* found something for us at Pont Street?' Hall asked, pressing his intercom. 'I need some good news before I go home. We've still to interview Ms Najid and that caretaker, Talbot.'

His secretary responded on the intercom, 'Yes Sir?'

'Lorna find Barbara David please, and ask her to come and see me ASAP.'

Hall got up from his desk. 'Have we asked Mazzini yet to look at the body?'

'Not yet, Sir, we will do shortly,' Day replied a bit too quickly to conceal his omission.

'Hurry it up Ian. Let me know what his reaction is once he's seen the body,' Hall asked. He walked around the room, then yawning added, 'I hope I can still find my house when I try to get home, and that Amanda and the kids still remember me when I get there?'

'Mohammed why did you get involved with Carmichael? You know he doesn't like us.' Hamid Pasha shouted. 'We were instructed to remain passive here, and not to draw attention to ourselves at any time. Now look what you have done; you're suspended for a week.'

'I'm sorry Hamid. I didn't do anything to cause Carmichael to suspend me I promise. Carmichael has never offered us friendship, you know that.'

'No matter Mohammed,' Pasha emphasised in a more controlled voice, 'you caused an incident, and other people, other waiters, will notice that you're not there over the next week; an important stage in our planning.' Pasha initially panicked when Bejyi had come back to their cottage and told him what had happened earlier. Now he began to formulate a plan. Time was running fast towards *Ma Ma, Fi Kul Makaan*. He remained quiet for a few moments during which Mohammed knew not to disturb him. When he did speak he said, 'Mohammed go and pack your bag. We'll leave this place and move nearer to locations *Alpha* and *Beta*. We'll find a place to spend a few days until we've carried out Allah's wishes. Go and pack and I'll do the same. We're expected to strike our targets no matter who or what tries to stop us. Now we'll leave here tonight. Take everything, we'll not be back in here again,' he said with distaste.

Bejyi had not expected such a rapid departure, and while he and Pasha were gathering together their possessions he asked, 'Hamid what if someone comes to ask for us, one of the other waiters for example? They'll tell everyone we've left.'

'Mohammed, trust me. I'll tell the woman who runs the village store that we've gone to Edinburgh for a few days. You know what she's like. She'll then tell everyone, especially anyone who asks. They'll not miss us until we've carried out the strikes in the name of Allah and by that time we'll be far away from here. We'll be heroes in the eyes of the people of Iraq. Now come and help me put the other cylinders into the Range Rover. We'll take the motorbike as well as we may need it. Leave it on the roof rack.'

Bejyi bowed his head towards Hamid Pasha, his hands locked in prayer. 'You are truly a servant of Allah, as well as a wise one. I knew you'd resolve my problem and you have. I'm fortunate to have such a friend to guide and advise. I'm blessed by Allah there's no doubt.'

They went to the shed at the back of the cottage where the other Three cylinders were stored, and put them with the others in the Range Rover. They also threw in a rubber dinghy, plastic oars, two wet suits, and an assortment of tools; all the things they'd collected from the Isosceles Centre. When they came back, they packed.

That same evening Hall had met both Hala Najid and Talbot, and was convinced that neither had any idea what Ciddiqui may have been up to. He'd asked Najid and Talbot to make statements, and as he left the interview rooms he'd felt sure that there would be little, if any, content in these. In the woman's case he thought, after listening to her repeated rambling, probably nothing except about her relationship with the deceased. Hall however was to be proved very wrong. He'd only just got back to his desk when his secretary brought him a four-page fax, marked *Urgent*, from the Chelsea Police Station. He flicked through it, and was about to put it to one side for reading later that evening, when he saw the word *Glasgow* on one of the pages. The fax contained the statements Najid and Talbot had made earlier that day. It was the latter's typed words that caused Hall to pause. Talbot had apparently stated that he'd recently come across a few airline boarding pass stubs that had fallen out of Mr Ciddiqui's waste bin, although that wasn't the name on them. The stubs had the name Sayid Taleb printed on them, one from London Heathrow Airport to Glasgow, and another a few days later from Newcastle to London Heathrow. Talbot was even able to provide the date of the London to Glasgow flight and confirmed that they were with British Airways. It seemed that Talbot was not unlike most caretakers in charge of exclusive apartments, in as much he knew a lot more about the owners and tenants than most would have wished. Hall picked up his phone and asked his secretary to put him through to WDC David. British Airways he thought might be able to add some further information on this Sayid Taleb. He also now thought that Day should carry on up to Glasgow from County Durham. He'd wait and see what David could get from BA first, but things were opening up a little, he felt.

'David where've you been?' Hall asked looking at the video cassette in the WPC's hand. 'What's that you've got?'

'Sir you'll not believe this. This film is something else. Just wait till you see it.'

'Well don't keep me in suspense. Put it in the bloody machine and let me see it if it's all that important,' Hall added. 'Go on then, get on with it. Oh, and while I'm watching it will you get on to British Airways and see what they can tell you about one of their passengers. A Mr Sayid Taleb,' Hall said, spelling out the name as David wrote it down on a notepad. 'Flew to Glasgow from Heathrow, then from Newcastle back to Heathrow; the dates are on this piece of paper.' Hall handed her a slip of paper.

'OK Sir, but this film will stun you when you see it. *Forensics* found it in Ciddiqui's video recorder,' David said as she pressed play, and made her way back to her desk.

The film had been run back to the start and took a moment or two to get to the beginning. Hall sat back, and waited for the film to start. When it did, to his surprise the first image that appeared was Saddam Hussein in full military uniform, including ammunition belt and pistol, standing on a podium in front of several thousand people, in what looked like a Football Stadium. Flags were flying everywhere in celebration of Hussein's birthday. It was the year two thousand and two, and there was hysterical shouting from every corner of the stadium. Hussein raised his large hands to the sky and the crowd became silent. He placed his hands on the podium top with his fists clenched. He spoke in a controlled voice, his dark eyes flashing as he gazed around, using words such as *Western Allies*, and *USA* throughout his speech. The camera scanning the crowd showed it reacting to the words, screaming for death to the infidels, and for glory to Allah. As the people appeared to be on the edge of frenzy, Saddam would control them with his hands. The film then cut to show a dark room in what appeared to be a military college, and the camera zoomed in on a man in the uniform of a Major General. The man sat with his hands on his desk, in front of a book-lined background, looking straight into the lens of the camera. He began to speak saying, '*Ma Ma, Fi Kul Makaan*'. He paused, then repeated, '*Ma Ma, Fi Kul Makaan*'. The film then faded before a string of dialogue in Iraqi followed on before reaching the end of the film.

What the hell was all that about? Hall asked himself, somewhat taken aback with the intensity of the short film and the Major General's murderous look towards the end. Why would our Mr Ciddiqui, or whatever he called himself, be watching that lot? He pressed his intercom button.

'Lorna ask Treefield to come in here please. Oh, and I'll be going off soon. Do you have anything outstanding for me?'

'No Sir, everything's in hand right now. A good chance to get some sleep I think,' she said, knowing that he hadn't slept for hours. She decided to avoid telling him at the moment that he had a meeting with the DAC Hughes at ten the next morning. That could wait until tomorrow she decided.

A moment or two later Treefield knocked the door.

'Come in,' Hall shouted. 'Come in John. Look I'd like you to take a look at this film for me. Then make three copies when you're at it. Also,' he added, 'see if you can find out where it was recorded. And the sound's a bit odd. Has it been dubbed for example?' Hall let DS Treefield write down a few notes before he continued. 'Check if it's been spliced, you know, made up of bits of film that sort of thing. I want to know if it's genuine. And have the dialogue translated. And John,' he said using the Sergeant's first name again in an imploring manner, 'I will need all that first thing in the morning. Seven or thereabouts.'

'OK Sir, I've a few things to do then I'll get right on to it. You'll have it in the morning when you come in,' Treefield stated firmly, picking the video film up and making his way back out of the room.

As Treefield left, Hall pressed his intercom again. 'Lorna you'll get me in the car for the next forty minutes, then at home if you need me. I'm out of here. See you in the morning. Oh when I remember. I need to speak with Day as soon as he arrives in Durham tomorrow. Will you take a note of that please?'

'Right Sir,' she replied, not telling him that she also was about to depart for home after working a fifteen-hour day. 'See you in the morning Sir.'

CHAPTER FORTY-THREE

Hamid Pasha and Mohammed Bejyi awoke the next morning in the small village shrouded in a mist, and at last the rain had stopped. The men had left their rented cottage in Braco, Perthshire, around seven the previous evening, and had stopped at the village store where Hamid Pasha took the opportunity to tell the storekeeper that he and Bejyi were going to Edinburgh for a few days. He knew Mrs MacGregor, who owned the store, would take delight in letting everyone who came into the store know where they'd gone. They'd then driven towards Glasgow, through a mixture of rain and sleet as they travelled south. As the foul weather worsened, they drove into the village of Gartocharn and spotted a bright, welcoming small hotel. Pasha decided to check whether there were any rooms available. Soon both men had been comfortably accommodated, and their Range Rover parked in the car park at the rear. They'd eaten well before going to bed and arranged to meet at eight fifteen for breakfast the next morning.

Pasha had arrived first and he glanced through a morning newspaper. Bejyi joined him a few minutes later and the men chatted about the previous night's weather, and how it might affect their plans.
A young waitress appeared from the kitchen. 'Would yous like some breakfast?' she asked, looking at the two men.
'Can I have some coffee and toast please. Can I smoke in the dining room at this time?' Bejyi asked
'No problem Sir. We allow smoking when we're this quiet,' the girl replied, 'and I'll get your toast and coffee right away. What about you Sir?' she said turning to Hamid Pasha.
'Coffee and toast please,' Pasha replied.
The men sat quiet for the next few minutes, Bejyi drawing deeply on his cigarette.
'Your coffee and rolls,' the girl said appearing back from the kitchen, adding, 'I'll bring you milk and sugar Sir in a moment, and here's some butter and marmalade for the toast.'
'No milk or sugar thank you. An ashtray please will be fine,' Bejyi said.

'Yous two are easy to serve,' the girl said smiling. 'I'll get the ashtray right away.' She went to a nearby table, lifted an ashtray, then placed it between the men saying, 'There you go. Enjoy your breakfast.'

When the girl had gone, Pasha said, 'I think we should stay here for another night, and use this place as a base to work from. This morning I checked the map for locations *Alpha* and *Beta,* and this is an ideal spot.'

'OK Hamid.'

As they ate their light breakfast, they chatted about what they'd do later that day. The excitement of what was ahead of them was however close to the surface and their respective stress levels were rising fast, all of which could be seen and heard in their mannerisms and voices.

Their stress level would've been far higher though, had they known that back at Crieff Police Station, less than an hour's drive from where they were sitting, Sergeant Jack Wilson was reading his Station's copy of an *AFA*. It had just been faxed to him from the Central Region Headquarters, in Perth; the subject matter was *Two-Door Range Rovers*.

In Durham, Niazi Bey was out on his usual run, and it was over twenty-four hours since he'd dumped Hussein Mabeirig's body. It was extremely cold, with hard ground frost. As he ran, his thoughts were focused on the next few days. Could he carry out the operation on his own he wondered? He thought of the weather he was running through and wondered what if it snowed? Would the old Land Rover Defender make it up Skylock Hill? His mind raised doubt after doubt, trying to unsettle him. As he approached the upper railway station on his way back to the campus, he came onto a stretch of the run that he and Mabeirig had raced each other every day. He subconsciously raised his pace and with it his confidence. I can do it he thought. What I did yesterday caused me great stress, but I can do it alone, and so will the Land Rover. As usual, he was out of breath when he reached the newspaper shop in the station where he normally collected the morning paper. He wasn't prepared for the newsagent's first question.

'Where's y're runnin mate this morning then? Not up for it, eh? Too cauld eh?' the man asked aggressively.

'He's away for a few days,' Bey said as he gasped for breath, 'back next week.' He took the outstretched copy of *The Times* and paid for it. As usual, he rolled up the newspaper tightly, then ran off on the final stretch of his run back to his apartment. But, the waiting was getting to him, and he was dreading the remaining hours on his own. Location *Gamma* was with him every hour of the day and most hours of the night. As he came down the hill into Durham, he was thinking that he'd be returning soon to Iraq a hero - and life would be easy after that. He'd be honoured in his village, and his parents honoured for producing a worthy son. *His Excellency* no doubt would want to see him and to thank him for his actions. His mind rambled on, and before he knew it, he'd made it back to his apartment. He went in, and closed the door behind him. The harsh silence of living alone, together with recent events that had taken place in the apartment, meant that thoughts of death were all around him. He took a shower. He knew he had to stay alert, be occupied at all times, but the stress was building up for Niazi Bey.

By comparison, Farraj Rasid had managed to remain composed over the past few days, in the knowledge that he'd carefully planned his actions. He was ready for the cause that he'd accepted as the highest honour. One more day of waiting, just over twenty-four hours. Location *Delta* drew him like a powerful magnet.

Rasid had spent most of the morning at the gym not far from where he lived. He'd spent most of his time there since being put on sick leave by his employer, but time was now lying heavy on his hands. How to get through the next day was what he focused on, almost wishing he was back working. Now as he went through another exercise, his thoughts went back to his work at Heathrow. He knew he'd never be back. I should've made a technical mistake one day. Intentionally he thought. Let a *747* disappear from the radar screens for a few moments, just enough time for it to get in the way. Two of them would've been nice. Eight hundred infidels killed in one small mistake that would've been good. I could've blamed it, on the stress of the job. I could've claimed compensation, several hundred thousand dollars. I could have said my superiors worked me too hard; not enough rest. My migraine would've been a good back-up story. Rasid again got to his feet but his patience was all but exhausted. As he pounded on the treadmill, he consoled himself thinking that he'd been given water to destroy, and with it the infidel who drank it. He reprimanded himself, thinking he mustn't become distracted. Allah deserved his whole being and his full attention. The death of the infidels in any form would satisfy him. Coming off the treadmill he sat down. His thoughts this time went back to the strange telephone call he'd had earlier that day from the Department of Social Services, or so the caller had claimed. He'd been asked to confirm some details concerning his National Insurance number. The caller had been less than friendly and the questions related to sickness benefits he was due. It had left him feeling uneasy. He got to his feet and looked out the window, down on fast-moving London going about its business. He felt his stomach twist in anticipation, but he knew that the stress was getting to him. It could have been much worse though, if he'd known that it wasn't the DSS who'd called him earlier. Farraj Rasid had unknowingly, been speaking to an investigative officer from the Home Office. An irregularity had been noticed in a past year's tax return Rasid had submitted when working in the United States some years back. During further investigation there appeared to be misleading information concerning Rasid's past circumstances. The US tax authorities also noticed that he'd received full security clearance to work with the US military and then with their Civil Air Traffic Control organisation. Rasid's file also showed that he'd requested proof of this security clearance to pass on to the *National Air Traffic Authority* in the UK when he applied for a job there eighteen months ago. In spite of the public perception, the US and UK government departments, particularly in matters of security, traded all information between them. Although the matter had not been initially designated as anything other than an *irregularity*, details had been faxed to all related US government departments. The Central Intelligence Agency automatically relayed the concerns to their UK counterparts, which triggered the telephone call to Rasid earlier in the day. The officer had first spoken to the *NATA,* and established that Farraj Rasid was based at Heathrow Airport, and currently incapacitated on sick leave. The Home Office decided, in the circumstances, that perhaps someone should visit Mr Rasid to verify that he was what he claimed to be. But first, they had to establish was Rasid still living at the address on his file.

As the operators were beginning to feel the strain, Chris Hall had returned to Scotland Yard, refreshed after a good night's sleep. WDC David had been his first target that morning, pushing her for news of British Airways information on Ali Ciddiqui's alias - Sayid Taleb - ticket purchases. His attention was then drawn to his in-tray. In it, as promised by Treefield, was the translation of the soundtrack of the video film he'd seen the previous night, as well as three copies of the film. He read the translation of Saddam Hussein's birthday speech, which it turned out DC Treefield had had done by a friend at the University of London Foreign Language Department. It contained the usual amount of screaming at the infidels, and made repeated reference to the Western Allies and the President of the United States of America. Treefield had also left a note to say that the film was one hundred percent genuine and hadn't been tampered with in any way. As Hall tried to make some sense of it, his telephone rang. His secretary reminded him of his meeting with the DAC, telling him it been put off till midday.

An hour later, WDC Davis returned with the information from British Airways, including details of a false passport and drivers licence that Ciddiqui had used for the car hire from Hertz. She'd also managed to obtain details of the distance travelled by the car while rented to Mr Taleb. Hertz told her Taleb had left some clothes and boots in the car he'd left at Newcastle Airport, and that the contact address and telephone numbers given by Sayid Taleb didn't exist. At first Hall seemed preoccupied, even when she told him she'd arranged for the clothes and other things to be brought back to Scotland Yard. Hall suddenly became more interested in knowing why the hired car had done so many kilometres since Taleb had picked it up at Glasgow Airport. He was more puzzled when David added that a tour brochure and three adult tickets for a boat trip on Loch Catrine in the Trossachs had been found in one of the pockets of a jacket left in the car. When WDC David left, with instructions to let him know when the clothing arrived from Newcastle, Hall wondered why Ciddiqui had gone to Scotland. Why take a tourist trip on Loch Catrine? What was his motive? And who were the other two adults?

Sergeant Jack Wilson's knock on the cottage door got no reply. After going around the back, it was obvious to him that no one was at home. Disappointingly, the main reason for his call, the old Range Rover, wasn't there either. Wilson sighed; thinking for the umpteenth time that a policeman's work is never easy. 'Shit, I suppose I'll have to come back later, or maybe I'll go up to that Beneagles and get them up there,' he muttered. Aye, I'll do that after I call in on Traffic at Stirling he thought. He walked back to his car and drove off in the direction of the M9 Motorway. As he past the Braco village store, Mrs MacGregor watched him from behind her counter. She muttered to no one in particular, 'Well he didna ask, so ah couldna tell him, could ah?' as she continued to jot down items that she'd need to purchase on her next trip to Perth. 'Now where was I?' she asked herself aloud.

When the time came for Hall's meeting with Hughes, he'd decided he'd put the new information as he had it directly to Hughes, hoping to get some alternative reaction to his own. He headed for the DAC's office enthusiastically, and was shown through to Hughes office to take a seat. Hughes was still not back from an earlier meeting apparently. Five minutes later he appeared, still fuming from some Government Minister's remark about the rising crime rate in central London. Hall knew better than to be too anxious to get on with his own report when Hughes was in this mood, so he let him simmer down a bit before beginning. When he did begin, Hughes listened without interrupting Hall's morning update of *Operation Hydro*. When he'd finished Hall asked, 'That's about it Sir, what do you make of it all?'

'Chris we seem to have something that now ties Ciddiqui, alias Mr Taleb, to two, if not three, of the locations where we assume HCN has been delivered: Newcastle, Durham, and Glasgow. Ciddiqui, or Taleb, had been to all three places recently. Fragile connections, but connections all the same.'

'As I said Sir, at the moment Day's in Durham following up on Taleb's visit to the County Hotel there a few weeks ago. I've asked him when he's through there to go on up to Glasgow. The Scottish end is a bit confusing at the moment I must admit. Hertz are reporting that Taleb had done approximately five hundred kilometres when he left the hired car at Newcastle Airport. That's a lot of klicks

Sir; nearly twice the distance from Glasgow to Newcastle! He must've covered a fair bit of ground up in Scotland. Where to and from, I'm hoping Day can shed some light on when he gets up there.'

Hughes nodded, 'What the hell was Ciddiqui doing on a boat trip? Is there a connection there? And the message *Water Water...* What does it all mean?'

'I was hoping you'd be able to tell me Sir I must admit. *Water Water...* well it could be a some coded reference, something far-fetched maybe, say for example to flood London. Damage the Thames Flood Barrier during high tides, that sort of thing Sir.'

'You could be right Chris, and it's better to be safe than sorry. Ask the Barrier people to step up their security. Put them on Red Alert, and let McDade, River Police know as well.'

'God can you imagine the damage and chaos that would cause to London Underground Sir?'

Mike Hughes already knew of the potential chaos of a flood in London from his role as Vice Chairman of *The City of London Doomsday Committee*. He interrupted Hall saying, '*Water, Water Everywhere...*' What if the phrase was taken to its full conclusion, '*.nor any drop to drink?*' Then we'd have a different scenario. What if the real target is the public water supply? Water everywhere, but water you can't drink. We could be looking at a planned strike on the country's water supply Chris. You may be right with the barrier, but the more I think of the distribution of the HCN, at least as we currently know it, Glasgow, Newcastle, maybe Durham, and we're still assuming Bristol, then the more I think about it, I think the public water supply is the target.'

Knowing the DAC well enough to appreciate how his mind worked, Hall sensed that Hughes was more than convinced he'd touched on the real meaning behind the phrase.

'If you're right about that Sir, then God help us all. How can you stop someone who is hell bent on poisoning reservoirs? How do you protect them? There must be thousands of them scattered throughout Britain. The Government would need to bring in the army to have anything like enough manpower, and twenty-four hours a day! God the scale of the thing would be enormous.'

'If we don't do it now before they - whoever these bastards are - get to them, then we'll need to do it afterwards.' Hughes paused, then added solemnly, 'Only then it'll be to bring in the dead as well, possibly tens of thousands of them. That's how big a problem we could be facing Chris.'

The men were quiet for a moment or two, then Hughes said, 'Chris move on the barrier situation. Of the two possible scenarios, I hope you are right. That would be the lesser of the two evils. Regarding the water, well I'll call the Minister of Home Affairs, and get him to set up a meeting today with MI5, and who ever else he thinks will be helpful. You know this all makes the St James's Park incident seem like a trial run. I wonder how long we've got before they strike, whoever they are?'

The men looked at each other, both feeling that maybe the last seconds were already ticking away. They got to their feet simultaneously.

'I'll let you know how Day gets on up north Sir. I still feel our major break will come from that direction. I hope it is sooner and not later.'

'Get on with it Chris,' Hughes replied, as he motioned him to the door.

WDC David looked at the list of identified two-door Range Rovers now checked out by the police, after a massive task force had been put to work throughout the UK and Northern Ireland. The number tallied with about 87% of the total. All owners had been interviewed and details of the vehicles and their use logged for future reference. So far no known vehicle searched had contained HCN, although it appeared from the various post scripts that a number had been found with goods that the owners couldn't explain. David knew that the local police forces would deal with those matters under a separate investigation. She completed her daily review of the vehicle search on her computer and printed three copies of the summary sheet. She signed the top copy, putting it in her out-tray to go to Hall, then one for the bulletin board, and the third copy she'd put in her own daily file. She was about to lift the file when she spotted Hall heading in her direction.

'David have we received the Ciddiqui's clothing from Newcastle yet?'

'No Sir, it's on its way - I know that. Inspector Johnston asked Traffic if they'd pick it up at Euston on its arrival. I'll let you know as soon as we have it.'

Hall's mind was moving on as she finished speaking. He'd spoken with Day within the last hour, telling him of the video film and the coded message, *Water, Water...* but unlike Day, he hadn't committed himself to either the DAC's interpretation of the message, or for that matter his own. It made him wonder whether there was a possible third meaning that they overlooked. He was brought back to the present by David saying, 'Sir this is a copy of my daily summary on the two-door Range Rovers. We've still a little way to go before we can say they've all been seen and checked.'

Hall looked at the sheet of paper. 'We've only a few left David, in a small number of areas. I want you to fax all of those forces - do it in my name; send the faxes to the Chief Constables in each force. Tell them we need confirmation that ALL vehicles and owners, and I mean ALL, have been checked within the next twenty-four hours.'

'Will do Sir.'

'Oh, and finally David, you may have to go up to Scotland to assist Inspector Day. I've asked him to go up to Glasgow when he's finished in Durham. I'll let you know in an hour or so once Day contacts me.'

'No problem Sir, I've never been there. I'll maybe get to see Dunblane. That was the name of my house at school, and I've always wondered what is was like.'

'David it won't be a bloody holiday you're going on! It'll be hard police work if I know Day. He'll keep you going twenty-four hours a day once he gets you up there believe me.'

David reversed her smile. 'Sorry Sir, I didn't mean it like that. Just thought that maybe I'd pass through the place, that's all. I'll get this fax ready for signing in the next few minutes.'

Sergeant Wilson, having been to Stirling, now turned off the A9 heading for Beneagles Hotel, driving past some golfers on both sides of the narrow road leading up to the hotel. He then turned into the hotel driveway, passing a long row of parked cars ranging from top executive saloon cars to the latest Bentleys. Wilson glanced at them as he slowly drove past. The games that people play he thought. He drove on up to a roundabout, and instead of taking a right to the main entrance, he carried on till he arrived at the staff area. As he parked, he said getting out of his car, 'Some day when I retire I'll maybe bring my Elizabeth here for the weekend. Now that would be just nice. We'll go right up to the front door and let the boys unload our luggage, that's what we'll do. Right up to the front door.' He walked towards the staff entrance, thinking he'd better get back to work for the time being. Going through to the security desk, he asked to speak Mr Carmichael, the name on the duty roster posted at the desk.

Within a few minutes Wilson was back in his car feeling a little uneasy for a reason he couldn't quite explain. Carmichael had just told him that he'd suspended Mohammed Bejyi, and that Hamid Pasha, his colleague, hadn't turned up for work that morning, and to make matters worse, they hadn't heard from them. Wilson sat in his car for a few moments as he thought through the situation. He looked at his watch. It was close to midday and he thought he should take a run back down to Braco and get this thing cleared up sooner rather than later. He whistled nervously as he switched on the ignition, and reversed out of the car park onto the Braco road. Wilson covered the distance from the Hotel to Braco in just over five minutes, an indication of his urgency. He parked outside the cottage, but as before, the Range Rover wasn't there. He knocked the front door and waited. Still nobody answered the door. Wilson went around the back of the cottage and noticed how untidy it was. The cottage looked abandoned. He looked through the kitchen window but the room was empty. No cups, fruit, plants or even a newspaper lying around. He walked back around the front and looked into the living room window. A few bits of furniture here and there, but nothing more. Wilson glanced around. The nearest building to the cottage was a small store across the street. He crossed over and went in, causing a bell to ring. He closed the door behind him, and walked to the counter. A woman with grey hair, who Wilson would later describe as being, *in her late sixties and clairvoyant*, appeared from the rear of the shop.

'You'll be asking after the two boys from the cottage then I guess Sergeant?'

'Aye we could start with that,' replied Wilson, 'that would be the young men who work up at Beneagles I take it?' he questioned, watching to see her reaction.

'I dinna know why you went past this mornin'. I could've telt you 'oors ago,' she responded, straightening up some morning newspapers lying on the counter top as she spoke. 'They've gone doon t' Edinburgh for a few days they told me. That's where they are, Edinburgh.'

Wilson heard all of this with irritated finality. He'd missed them, and it would be a few days before they'd be back with that vehicle. He asked, 'Did they take their car away with them then? It's not in the drive.'

'If you'd a caur would you no take it with you?' the woman retorted. 'Of course they went away in their caur, although it's a bit bigger than some of those sma' caurs you see t'day. Aye they left the other day, just efter tea time it was, an Mr Pasha, the quiet one, he came in himself, bought some o' those razor blades, the new kind, to tell me where they wis gaun. Edinburgh he said, just for a few days.'

Wilson looked at the woman. 'I'll have to ask you a few more questions if you don't mind?' he said in his best friendly manner, although he felt less than friendly at that moment. Unfinished business Sergeant Wilson didn't like at any time, and when it involved two absent persons, a vehicle that was the subject of an AFA, then Sergeant Wilson would be a restless policeman for the next few days.

'Well you can ask, but I'm maybe no able to answer thim,' the woman replied.

Ian Day looked out of the window of the train as it entered the tunnel on the approach to Queen Street Station in central Glasgow after having left Newcastle upon Tyne about two hours and forty minutes earlier. He stood up took his coat from the overhead storage space. As the train slowly approached the end of its journey, he made his way towards the front as it passed out of the tunnel and into the station in the heart of Scotland's largest city. Day knew he'd be met at the station, and then taken to meet Chief Inspector Anderson, Strathclyde Police, Central Division, at Pitt Street Headquarters. The train edged slowly into the vast, steel arched, glass-covered station, then shuddered to a halt. Someone in front of Day pressed the *Door Open* button, and with a hiss of compressed air the door moved outwards and sideways. A rush of people jumped out making their way towards the platform barrier further into the station. There was noise of every kind from meeters and greeters to announcements from the *tannoy* system of trains arriving and departing and of luggage and freight trailers edging their way through the busy concourse. Day spotted a policeman and headed towards him. As he got close, the policeman looked at him, then asked, 'Detective Inspector Day, Scotland Yard?'

'That's right Sergeant, I hope you've not been waiting too long?'

'Not at all Sir, train's right on time,' Sergeant Campbell McLaren replied, shaking Day's hand warmly. 'Come this way Sir, the car is just over there,' McLaren said in the easy manner of someone who's had no difficulty parking in the middle of any city centre restricted area. Day followed at the quick pace of the sergeant, seeing the white, red and yellow striped police Vauxhall Senator parked fifty metres away. Soon they were heading through the busy streets and in less than four minutes they arrived at Strathclyde Police Headquarters. The car passed through a ramped security vehicle entrance to a sub-basement, where Sergeant McLaren parked.

'I'll take you up to the conference room on the third floor Sir. I believe they're waiting for you.' After the solitude and the two and a half-hours' rest on the train, Day could sense his pulse rate beginning to climb again. He was back in action, and time was of the essence.

As Sergeant Wilson left the store in Braco, Hamid Pasha and Mohammed Bejyi were leaving their hotel in Gartocharn. They were heading towards the tiny village of Stronachlachar on the west shore of Loch Catrine, sixty kilometres north of Glasgow. After they'd had breakfast at the hotel, they'd discussed their next steps in great detail, with Pasha convincing Bejyi that they should bring forward the final part of their planned action. The outcome was that they'd put everything in place a day earlier to minimise the risk of anything going wrong. Pasha had had second thoughts about their quick departure from the cottage and the suspension of Bejyi from his job at the hotel. In addition, he was concerned about requiring police assistance with the Range Rover, which had drawn attention to them. He'd decided they should take the HCN and other heavy items to the designated locations, and conceal them there. They'd then drive back to the hotel and park the Range Rover in the rear car park. They could use the motorbike the following night to travel to locations. Bejyi had reluctantly agreed after much discussion and only after Hamid Pasha had said that the police might put up roadblocks to look for them. Having committed themselves, they were now on their way to put two cylinders of HCN close to draw-off sluices near the Loyal Cottage, just beyond Stronachlachar. After thirty minutes or so they approached a large stretch of water, which they identified from their map as Loch Catrine. The surrounding countryside seemed to be scattered with lochs. Loch Lomond they'd glimpsed on passing shortly after leaving their hotel, then Loch Ard, closely followed by Loch Chon. Loch Catrine, their target, Location *Alpha,* was stretched out before them. From their maps they identified their position, and followed the sign to Stronachlachar Pier. As Ali Ciddiqui had done a few weeks before, they passed a number of water authority properties on the edge of the loch before arriving at the pier. The pier and the adjacent car park were both deserted, as was the driveway along the shore of the loch towards Loyal Cottage. They drove slowly on, prepared to play the *tourist card* if they were stopped. The cottage eventually appeared through the thick rhododendron trees that made up the all year groundcover around this area of the loch. After looking around to check they were not being watched, they parked at the side of the path, and unloaded two of the orange cylinders, rolling them into the dense foliage out of sight to a casual passer-by. Carefully noting the location, Pasha tied a small yellow ribbon to a tree opposite. A few minutes later they had turned around and were heading towards Millguy, and Location *Beta,* they came across some roadwork's, that Hamid Pasha had spotted on the way to the Stronachlachar. No one was working at the site so he stopped. He told Bejyi to come with him, and then they lifted the roadwork sign and gathered up the red and white tape strung between and around the rough groundworks, putting all of it into the boot of their Range Rover.

'Hamid why do you want these things? They'll be missed! Why do we need them?' Bejyi asked, when he got back into the vehicle.

'You'll see soon enough,' Hamid replied with a dry smile as he drove off. They drove on in silence and after thirty minutes or so reached the outskirts of Glasgow and the ancient Burgh of Millguy. The drove passed steep grassy banks high on their right hand side, which Bejyi said, looking at a map, were one side of the reservoirs. They continued down towards the village of Millguy, passing some of the remnants of Victorian suburbia. After further consultation,

Bejyi pointed out the plan's intended entry point to the reservoirs, saying, 'The entrance is just around the next corner to the right.'

Pasha pulled over to the side of the road, allowing some light traffic to overtake them. Looking back and across the road, they could see the gate leading up to the reservoirs exactly as described in they're briefing notes. The simple chain, and little more than household padlock attached to it. He smiled, checked his rear view mirror, and swung the car around to face the gate, then drove into the side street that skirted the south end of the reservoirs. He drove on till they came to a T junction and turned right up a hill. They were now heading north and soon able to see the waters of the reservoirs on their right, little more than five metres away. They drove for a kilometre or so, the waters of the reservoir remaining on their right, until the narrow road turned left and made its way steeply uphill. Again Pasha swung the vehicle around to the right, then parked on the grass at the bottom of the hill.

'Mohammed your day of service to Allah is here at last. Come now, but be slow and deliberate. Don't do anything quickly and don't make eye contact with anyone who passes by.' The men got out and opened the boot. Pasha told Bejyi, 'Help me take the cylinders out one at a time. We'll place the six of them flat, side by side on the grass bank to the left of that gate,' as he pointed to a rusty metal gate. He then lifted the red and white works sign, the heavy waterproof groundsheet, and the other pieces he'd picked up from the site near Loch Catrine. As he and Bejyi put the last of the cylinders on the ground, Pasha placed the inflatable dinghy and oars on top of them then covered everything with the groundsheet. He then positioned the sign, the props and tied the tape around the area.

'That's it Mohammed. Nobody will pay any attention to these things. They'll assume, as normal, that it's road works waiting to happen,' Pasha said. They got back into their Range Rover and drove off heading back into the Millguy. He was sure nobody would touch the cylinders, or question why they'd even been put there. The items could probably lie there for weeks before anyone questioned their purpose. He was in high spirits. He checked the time. It was five o'clock in the evening. 'We've not long to wait. Now we have to buy a small trailer. We'll find one in the village I'm sure.'

'Why do we need a trailer Hamid?'

'Just wait and see.'

Five minutes later they pulled up at a garage on the road behind village, and bought a second-hand, two-wheeled trailer. They also bought some heavy rope. Pasha paid for the items in cash. Coupling the trailer onto the rear of the Range Rover, they drove back to the road works site they'd created a few minutes before, and parked opposite. Uncoupling the trailer, they pushed it towards the taped-off area. They lifted the groundsheet, and then with considerable effort they put the trailer beside the cylinders, then pulled back the cover. When Pasha was satisfied that it appeared as normal as would be expected, he and Bejyi drove off. Despite the fact that they were on a public highway, close to houses with a village nearby, no one had paid the slightest attention to them. When they got back to Gartocharn, they parked the Land Rover in the hotel car park as far out of sight as possible. Pasha knew that they were now finished with it. It had served them well, but it was a liability. It would be a few days before anyone paid much notice to it, again the way of the infidel he mused. They'd remove the motorbike from the roof rack tomorrow, and use it on the night of *Ma Ma, Fi Kul Makaan.* The men were now on a high, feeling that their mission was more or less completed. It was, except for some minor details; details such as that they still had to discharge the HCN, the *Juice of Allah,* into the infidels' water supply.

CHAPTER FORTY-FOUR

Day was ushered into the conference room at Strathclyde Police Headquarters in Glasgow, where he was introduced to the Assistant Chief Constable, Neil MacKenzie.

'Detective Inspector good to meet you. I hope you've had a good journey up from Newcastle?' MacKenzie asked pleasantly, moving Day towards the other men in the room. 'Let me introduce you to Chief Inspector John Anderson from our Cranstonhill Police Station. John's just been in touch with Commander Hall.'

Day shook hands with Anderson. MacKenzie introduced him to the others in the room, although most of the names Day instantly forgot.

MacKenzie then said, 'Please be seated everybody, we've got some urgent things to get through in the next hour or so, so let's get on with it.'

Day tried to settle into the meeting, which he sensed had been well under way by the time he'd arrived. On the far wall of the room hung a large-scale map of part of Glasgow, starting from an area just north of the River Clyde and stretching well out into the surrounding countryside from what he could see. Suddenly he became aware that MacKenzie was speaking to him, although he was heading towards the map. Day heard him say, '...so with that information from Scotland Yard, we've set up road blocks here, here, and here. In fact any road leading anywhere near Loch Catrine will blocked.' MacKenzie turned to face the others in the room and added, 'Bear in mind if anyone plans to cause serious contamination of the water in the loch, they'd require some large, heavy transport, and that way they'd be forced to use the main road network. We know it was a ten tonne van that was used to bring the HCN up to Glasgow and although that's not a large vehicle, it would still require a reasonable road surface. In short, it wouldn't be suitable for cross country stuff or anything like that.'

Day was at a loss as he heard about roadblocks around Loch Catrine. 'If I may interrupt Sir, why has Loch Catrine taken on such a high profile? What's so important about it compared to the other lochs on the map?' he asked.

MacKenzie looked at Day as it dawned on him that there was no reason why Day should have known the answer to the question he'd just asked. 'Inspector Day, let me apologise for not bringing you up to speed with *Operation Hydro* since you left Newcastle, which I know is just about three hours ago. This morning, after you reported back to Commander Hall, telling him about Mrs Falconer's statement that the alleged Taleb, or Ciddiqui, had been to Loch Catrine in Scotland to look specifically at the waterworks. Well Commander Hall tied that up to a coded message the Yard acquired, the phrase, *Water Water*.... It started alarm bells ringing loud throughout the Scotland Yard. The Commander called his Deputy Assistant Commissioner who now firmly believes that we have the makings of a terrorist attack on the water supply throughout United Kingdom. The DAC telephoned my Chief Constable with this information. Hence the reason we're all here now.' MacKenzie paused, then added, 'You see Inspector, Loch Catrine serves the City of Glasgow and surrounding areas with one hundred million gallons, just under five hundred million litres, of fresh water every day.'

Day felt his face flush as the scale of the problem sank in. Instinctively he muttered, 'God....'

'Yes, we'll need his help as well,' MacKenzie concluded.

CHAPTER FORTY-FIVE

At North Wood Water Treatment Works in County Durham, the shift engineer was studying the printout of his duty schedule for the next five working days. The schedule was produced automatically by the computer programme that served the sophisticated digital controls and sensor equipment regulating and monitoring the flow of water through the plant. It was the 'state of the art' in terms of technology, and the engineers took great pride in maintaining it to the highest standard. The engineer-in-charge, Bill Dobson had worked at the plant since it had been commissioned four years ago and was familiar with all of the major items of equipment listed in the schedule. Now, as he glanced over the list, one item caught his eye and caused him to check an on-screen message. The message made reference to a mechanical screen filter close to the air shaft on Skylock Hill. The message puzzled him, as he knew the filter had been serviced only five days earlier. He punched some more data into his computer hoping to get further details. Nothing changed, just the same on-screen message appeared. Dobson made the assumption that it must be a faulty sensor, and decided to check the sensor readings. On the computer screen in front of him he scanned through a system flow chart until he found the section of the system where the filter was located. He then pulled down a schematic diagram showing the screen filter in the distribution tunnel and zoomed in on the appropriate sensor. The computer instantly responded giving him a set of design operating parameters, alongside the actual operating conditions at that time. Dobson compared the numbers, which fluctuated erratically as he was looking at them. He'd expected them to be erratic, but not as wide ranging as they were showing. He turned towards one of his engineering team and asked, 'George, have we any reported problems up at Skylock? I mean in the last forty-eight hours or so?'

'Skylock? No, not that I know of Bill,' the man replied, as he stretched over to lift a file at the side of his desk marked *Site Action*. 'Forty-eight hours did you say?' he asked, flipping through the few pages that still remained in the file.

'Around that, yes.'

'Well there's nothing listed under *Medium or High Risk* over that period - that's for sure, but you know the computers as well as I do. They've a mind of their own sometimes.'

'Hmm, we'd better have this checked out I suppose. What's puzzling is that the reported defective component was fully serviced only five days ago. I instructed it, and the numbers I'm now getting on the screen are all over the place, well outside the design parameters. It reads like a blockage of some sort. I think I'll get Austin's boys go back up and have a look,' Dobson concluded, as he watched the flow rate rise and fall every few seconds.

'Austin's out with his team at the moment Bill, on emergency at Stanley. That burst we had at the new shopping mall site, where the digger cut both the power cable and the water main. Bloody idiot of an operator if you ask me, I hope they fired him.'

'I'd forgotten that. Poor Austin, I suppose he's been at it all night,' Dobson said looking at his computer screen. 'Well I suppose these readings are not too serious at the moment. It can wait a few more hours. I'll let him get some sleep and book it into his work schedule for the day after tomorrow. It's probably a faulty sensor reading anyway.'

The men returned to their normal duties, examining the stream of numbers that flowed smoothly along, line after line, row after row, page after page on the screens on front of them. As they did so, the now bloated body of Hussein Mabeirig, caught in the screen filter at Skylock Hill, had reached the stage where it was suppurating from every orifice. Only the sensors interfacing with the computers seemed to want to know that.

WDC David had signed for receipt of the clothing and boots found in the Hertz car Ali Ciddiqui had left at Newcastle's Airport car park. She took the items directly to Hall. The contents of the pockets of the Ciddiqui's Barbour jacket had been put into a sealed white envelope.

'Lorna, is the Commander free?'

'Yes, Barbara he's just off the phone. Just go through, I'll buzz him and let him know you're on your way.' She looked at the heavy waterproof jacket David was carrying and asked with a smile 'You expecting it to rain in there?'

David laughed, 'With *Operation Hydro,* who knows what can happen? It just might,' she said going through to Hall's office.

'Come in Barbara, I can hear you before I can see you,' Hall shouted before she'd opened the door. 'I see you've got your raincoat with you. Wise woman the way our weather is at the moment. What've you got for me? Put the jacket on the table,' he said motioning to the large table to his right. 'Put the boots on the floor they're not too clean.' David did as she'd been told and was left holding the white envelope.

'Now what've we got there?' Hall asked looking at the envelope.

'This comes with the jacket and boots,' David replied. 'It's the things they found in the pockets, at least that's what it said on the receipt I signed.' She handed the envelope to Hall.

'I hope whoever emptied the pockets also put all the fluff, grit, paper and anything else that was in them into the envelope,' Hall said, taking his letter opener to open it. He looked inside, holding the envelope vertical to ensure that nothing could fall out. 'Yes, we've been lucky, everything including the spare buttons.' He'd put on thin, clear rubber gloves and carefully extracted a brochure. The colourful brochure described the wonders of a steamer trip on Loch Catrine. Until the other day he'd never heard of the loch, and now from the discussion he'd had earlier that day with Day, it kept turning up. He'd put his phone down after speaking to Day and fortunately decided to check Mrs Falconer's reference to waterworks. He discovered that the loch was in fact a very large reservoir that served Greater Glasgow. He went straight to Mike Hughes, and things had moved on apace since then. Now, as he flipped through the brochure, he noted the location and scale of the loch and the connection it retained with the Royal Family. He put the brochure back in the envelope. 'Let me see the boots please Barbara. Plenty of dried mud on them and some gravel stuck in the treads of the soles. All that should get the boys in *Forensics* a bit excited don't you think.' It was a statement, not a question. As he took the boots from David he noticed they'd been badly scuffed around the toecaps. 'These have done some rough hill walking by the looks of them,' he said. He looked at the jacket and the other odds and ends on his table then added, 'Take the whole lot to *Forensics*. Tell them I'll need their full report ASAP. They'll know what's required. I expect them to tell me which parts of the country Taleb, or Ciddiqui, whoever he called himself, had been to when he was wearing these boots. Also the car he hired. Get Northumbria Police to a look at it. The tyres, the mud on the underside, that sort of thing. Also the inside, see if their *Forensic* people can come up with some *DNA* samples of recent occupants, other than Taleb or Ciddiqui. Everything, I want the works. Oh, and I don't think there's any point you going up to Glasgow now. Stay here and co-ordinate *Forensics*, that'll be more useful.'

'Right Sir,' David replied, lifting up the boots and other things and making sure nothing fell out of the envelope as she left the room. Hall now decided that Day should remain in Scotland as long as he himself thought necessary. He and the team must now concentrate their efforts on their investigations of the other possible HCN-threatened locations, although they seemed to lead to dead ends at the moment.

CHAPTER FORTY-SIX

The sound of the doorbell startled Niazi Bey. No one had called at the apartment since Hussein Mabeirig had died and his first reaction was one of panic. He eventually opened the door and his heart nearly stopped. A policeman stood there. He then realised the policeman was speaking to him, although as yet, he hadn't heard a word the man had said.

"Are you alright Sir?' the young policeman asked, taken aback by the reaction he'd seen on the man's face when he'd opened the door.

'Yes, yes, I'm sorry. I was asleep. I'm alright,' Bey said, but the policeman didn't think he looked it.

'I'm sorry to have startled you. It's just that there's been a break-in to the University boathouses Sir, and we're asking anyone with any goods there to check and see if anything is missing. I believe you have a vehicle,' he paused opening his notebook then continued, 'ah, let me see, yes, a Land Rover Defender, Registration PYV 529 H. Is that correct Sir?'

The policeman, looking at Bey repeated, 'Are you sure you are alright Sir?'

Bey felt he'd pass out at any minute. His head was spinning, and he felt sick.

'I'm a bit shaky that's all. I got up too quickly I think.'

'Well I'm sorry about that Sir. Perhaps you should lie down for a bit. I'll come back later?'

'No, no I'm fine. Do you want me to go to the boathouse now?' Niazi Bey asked, desperate to get whatever it was the policeman wanted checked out of the way. Surely all he'd want him to say was that nothing had been stolen from the vehicle? He wouldn't even ask what was in the tank attached to it, would he? Again he felt faint at the thought.

'If you feel up to it Sir, yes that would be a help, but only if you feel up to it you understand?'

'I'll get my coat,' Bey replied, seeing that it was raining heavily. He picked up his car keys as well as the keys for the apartment, noting as he did so that Hussein Mabeirig's keys were still lying on the hall table. He made his way out of the apartment, locking the door behind him and caught up with the policeman, who by now was heading towards the river.

As Bey drew level with him, the policeman looked at him to make sure he was in a fit state to accompany him on the short walk. He was reassured when, even in the dim light, he saw that the Bey had regained a little colour - in fact the man had a sallow skin colour, he noticed for the first time, almost the makings of a good suntan he thought. He said, 'Sir, I also should've asked you if your flat mate, Mr Mabeirig - is that how you pronounce it? Mab-eir-ig? - Is he available at this time? Just in case he's got some personal things down in the boathouses.' The policeman had stopped walking and stood as if he may have to go back to speak with Mabeirig before they all made their way down to the river.

'Eh, no…, no, Hussein, he's not here at this time. He's gone to London to visit some friends. He won't be back for a few days,' Bey stammered. In his mind's eye he could still see the cold stone walls of the air shaft, the iron grid on the top, and the black circular shaft dropping into the bowels of the earth. And the noise, the unsettling noise of rushing waters beneath. Niazi Bey suddenly felt he'd be sick at any moment. He'd thrown Hussein into that abyss. Allah forgive me, he silently pleaded, the sickness already in his mouth. He could say no more.

The policeman had started to walk again towards the river. 'Fine Sir, you can do the check for both of you if that's OK?'

'Yes, yes.'

'Right Sir, let's go to the boathouses then.' After a few minutes they arrived at the edge of the River Wear, both wet through. The river was running full, and apart from the noise of the rain splashing on the surface, the area was quiet. Bey could see a number of people already gathered at the first boathouse, and one or two waved some acknowledgement towards him as he walked past. The policeman walked on towards the next one where the Land Rover was parked. Bey could now make out the figure of the boathouse caretaker standing there, looking in their direction. The doors of the building were partly off their hinges, visible even fifty metres away. It had only now dawned on Bey, such had been the state of his mind over the past ten minutes, that he hadn't asked if his Land Rover had been stolen. Trying to seem unconcerned, he asked, 'Officer, did you say that my car had been stolen?'

'No Sir, not stolen, but they did break into it. Did you have a radio in it?'

'No, nothing like that. It's an old vehicle; a working vehicle and neither my friend Hussein nor I had much time to listen to a radio.'

The walked on in silence and as they approached the boathouse. Porter the caretaker shouted, 'Mr Bey, I'm sorry about having to bring all you people out here in this weather, but no doubt as you've now heard, we've had a series of break-ins earlier tonight. Your Land Rover was broken into. They left the lights on and I think your battery's gone flat.'

By now the three men had entered the building and Bey could make out the shape of the heavy groundsheet he'd used to cover the tank on the trailer. It lay crumpled on the ground. As far as he could make out the trailer was still attached to the Discovery. The policeman was now holding the door of the vehicle open, inviting him to go in and check the contents. He was a little put out as Bey ignored the gesture, and went towards the back, looking at the trailer or so it seemed.

'Would you like to take a look inside Sir?' the policeman asked pointedly.

Niazi Bey was relieved to see that the trailer and the tank were OK and he relaxed. He went back towards the front of the boathouse, looking closely at the damaged lock on the door of the Land Rover.

'We can get your battery charged up back at the university building Mr Bey,' Porter stated, trying to be helpful.

Bey got into the vehicle and looked around. He knew that there'd been nothing to steal in it. He made a show of looking everywhere in the vehicle, even in the tool kit contained in the boot.

'Seems OK, nothing missing that I can see. Nothing worth taking, more to the point,' he said with a finality that made the policeman look directly at him.

'Take your time Sir; make sure,' the policeman said assuringly. He then asked, 'What's in the tank Sir?' as he moved towards the trailer. 'Did you have anything in it? Anything that somebody would steal?' He knocked the steel tank with his knuckles. 'They'll take anything Sir,' he added.

Bey quickly got out and went round to the side of the trailer. He slapped the tank a few times, and noticing that Porter had left the building said, 'It's liquid fertiliser for the cricket grounds. It's still there by the sounds of it. I let the groundsman use the Land Rover to bring it from another site. But it's OK, the tank sounds full.' Bey was now desperate to take the focus of attention away from the trailer and the tank. He said, 'Apart from the flat battery, and the lock on the front door, I think everything else is fine.'

The policeman looked at Niazi Bey, 'Right Sir, I'll get my report made out on the damage to the vehicle. You'll want a copy of the report for your own insurers I'm sure. You can come by the station from tomorrow morning onwards and pick up a copy if you like?'

'That won't be necessary officer. It's an old Land Rover and once the battery is recharged that'll be fine.'

'Aren't you going to make a claim to have the door lock repaired?'

'No. I've only got Third Party, Fire and Theft.'

'As you wish Sir, but if you change your mind, you know what to do. Now Mr Porter,' he said addressing the caretaker who'd just returned, 'if you and I can have a few minutes then I'll be finished here,' adding a touch sarcastically, 'until the next time eh?'

Niazi Bey went back to the Land Rover pretending to examine the damage. He didn't want to leave until the policeman did. The policeman questioned Porter for a few more minutes, writing down everything he said. Bey wondered what he was asking, and did it concern him? He'd ask Porter. Going around the back of the Defender he tried to open the metal cap on the tank, but it was still tightly shut, something that Hussein had made sure of the night before he'd died. He then checked the sides of the tank to see if any attempt had been made to burst it. It had some old dents and scrapes, but nothing new. The policeman, who was now facing him on the other side of the trailer, startled him by shouting, 'I'll be off then. Don't forget now, if you need a copy of my report, you know where to find me. Goodnight Sir.'

Bey stood up, and trying to look at ease, replied, 'Goodnight officer, thanks for your help, but as I've said, I won't need it.'

'OK Sir, but you never know,' the policeman replied, as he left the building.

Bey relaxed. Going to Porter, who was examining the broken hinges on the boathouse door, he asked, 'Did you manage to answer all the policeman's questions Mr Porter?'

'What's that? Ah yes, that I did Mr Bey,' Porter responded hastily. 'Nice young man that. Not like some o' them who'd give you the impression that they think it was an inside job, if you know what I mean Sir.'

'Did he ask about Hussein and myself Mr Porter?'

'He did Mr Bey. He asked why you'd your car here parked in a boathouse, that he did. And how long you'd had it in here?'

'What'd you tell him Mr Porter?' Bey asked, still trying to remain as causal as possible.

'I just told him the truth Mr Bey, like you told me. I said you'd had it broken into a few times, up at the campus, and as the boating crews are all off on Easter holiday, I'd said you could leave it here for a week or so. That's what I told him.'

Niazi Bey felt as if he had been punched hard in the stomach. Bey had tried to give the policeman the impression that Land Rover didn't really matter that much, and now the man would begin to wonder again about the possible insurance claim? Had Bey ever reported any of the previous break-ins? Porter might have drawn attention to the situation instead of diverting it. His mind raced on before he asked, 'Would it be possible for you to have my battery charged tonight Mr Porter? I mean by midnight?'

Porter looked at his watch, doing a mental calculation. 'On the fast charger it'll take five hours! Yes, that should be enough to get you going Mr Bey. Five hours should be enough.'

'Would you do it for me right away? Oh, and by the way, I've found another few bottles of that wine you like. I'll bring them round to your flat when the battery is ready,' Bey offered. 'And,' he added, 'I'd be grateful if you could drive me over here with the battery when it's charged. Could you do that?'

'For some more of that wine I'd do almost anything Mr Bey, almost anything. You come on round at say…' he paused, again taxing his mind, 'at just before midnight. The battery should be ready by then. Just remember to bring the wine, that's all,' he laughed at his own joke.

'Thanks Mr Porter, and I'll bring the wine.' Bey was tempted to put some of the HCN into the wine before he handed it over, but discarded the idea on the grounds that it was pointless. Niazi Bey had decided to begin his operation at Location *Gamma* as soon as possible. He felt uneasy about the policeman. And Porter hadn't helped. He decided he'd leave as soon as they got the battery back in the Defender then set off early, and position himself and the HCN close to the target. That would remove any outside chance that he could be stopped. A surge of excitement ran through him now that he had decided to begin. For Niazi Bey, *Ma Ma, Fi Kul Makaan,* had begun twenty-four hours early.

CHAPTER FORTY-SEVEN

Like Niazi Bey, Farraj Rasid had also given way to his mounting impatience. He'd locked up his flat in Knightsbridge in the late afternoon, gathered up some personal items he wished to keep, particularly his music collection, and left. He'd not be back.

He planned, after successfully carrying out his operations at *Location Delta*, to return to London and take the first morning Eurostar, First Class of course, to Paris. He'd remain in France for a while. He'd stay in a small hotel off the Champs Elysée; somewhere discreet but high in quality. He'd read the newspapers, study the headlines French and English and bask in the pleasure of knowing he'd caused them. He could almost see them already: *Countless deaths by poisoning near the famous City of Oxford.*

As he now joined the M4, Rasid pulled his Range Rover out to overtake an ageing black cab, and accelerated smoothly and swiftly along the outside lane. He had to remind himself to be careful of the speed limit on this stretch of the motorway, as he didn't want to be stopped by the police. He was thinking he'd miss his Range Rover when he'd gone, as he intended leaving it in the car park off Basil Street in Knightsbridge where nobody would pay much attention to it. No chance of buying one in Iraq, he mused. He was now heading to Bray in Berkshire. He'd made a last minute booking to stay in one of the rooms of a highly regarded inn there, overlooking the River Thames. It would be his last night in England. He'd leave the next day, the day of *Maya, Maya Fe Kul Makaan,* around mid-morning, and drive up towards Oxford. He'd stop off for lunch at some village pub, before gradually making his way to Farmore Advanced Water Treatment Works in the early evening. It was thirty minutes since he'd left his apartment in Knightsbridge and he was beginning to relax as he left London behind, the strain of the waiting slowly easing away.

Two Special Branch officers stood side by side on the landing outside the dark blue painted door of Farraj Rasid's rented apartment in William Street, Knightsbridge. They'd already rung the bell twice. 'Shall we try the neighbour's?'

'I suppose so, but I did say we should've phoned the guy to make sure he'd be here when we called.'

'Press that door bell there,' the senior of the two men said, pointing to the brass push button adjacent to the door across the landing. The nameplate above the bell stated *L. F. Spielberg (Mrs)*. The man pressed the bell, which could be heard ringing in the apartment.

They heard someone moving about in the apartment and then static from an overhead speaker. A woman's voice, with a heavy Jewish accent asked, 'What do you want then?'

'Sorry to trouble you Ma'am,' the senior officer said, noticing a small aperture for a security spyglass or a small camera lens in the door. 'My colleague and I are from The Home Office, and...', he took out his ID card and held it up just in front of aperture, '...we called to speak to your next door neighbour, Mr Farraj Rasid. He doesn't appear to be in though,' the man stated.

The men heard heavy chains being detached and, after some bolts had been slid open, a small woman in her late sixties stood in the open doorway.

'What do you want to speak to him about?' she asked with a degree of distaste.

The men hesitated, taken aback by her directness. 'It's a private matter Mrs Spieilberg. We need to speak with Mr Rasid,' the junior man replied.

'You've missed him. He left half an hour ago.'

'Would you know when he'll be back Mrs Spielberg?'

'How should I know, how should I know? I only wish he'd never come back, him and his loud music. Keeps me awake half the night. And he's an Arab,' she added distastefully.

The officers glanced at each other.

'Maybe he's gone for good,' she continued. 'He put a lot of things in that car of his. Never finished looking in it all the time. Treated it like a woman, never away from it. Mind you I don't know if he'd be any good with a woman. Never saw any woman going in there,' she said with a gesture towards the dark blue door. 'Maybe he wouldn't know what to do with a woman if you ask me.'

'Mrs Spielberg,' the senior officer asked, trying to restrict the conversation to Rasid's whereabouts. 'What sort of things did Mr Rasid take to his car?'

273

'Oh a few things. And a suitcase, one of those soft ones you see people putting on aeroplanes.'

'A suit carrier Mrs Spielberg?'

'Yes, a suit carrier, if that's what you call them. That, and two small holdalls. Put them all on the passenger seat he did. Didn't put them in the boot though. He must be hiding something in there if you ask me.'

'Did it look like he was going away for a few days Mrs Spielberg?'

'Away for good I hope,' she retorted.

The other man asked, 'What make of car does Mr Rasid drive Mrs Spielberg? Do you know the make, or type?'

'Blue, like his door there,' she replied, gesturing towards her neighbour's door.

'Do you know the type, or the make of car Mrs Spielberg?'

'A big one. Too good for him if you ask me. Bloody Arabs.'

'Do you recall seeing the name of the car Mrs Spielberg?' the senior officer asked painstakingly.

'Parked it right across the street he did, right across the street. Bloody cheek if you ask me.'

'The name of the car Mrs Spielberg. Did you ever see the name or type of the car?'

'A Rover. That's it - some kind of Rover.'

'Did it have a number Mrs Spielberg? Say, a Rover 75, or some other number?'

'No, no. It had another name in front.'

'A Land Rover? Was it one of those Mrs Spielberg?'

'That's it. A Range Rover I think. Dark blue it was. Too big and too good for him.'

'Thanks for your help Mrs Spielberg. You've been of great assistance to us,' the senior officer said.

'Do you want me to tell him you were looking for him when he comes back?'

'Eh no, there's no need to do that Mrs Spielberg. We'll get in touch with Mr Rasid ourselves. Thanks again.'

'Hope he doesn't come back if you ask me. Bloody loud music night and day.'

'Thanks Mrs Spielberg,' the junior officer said as the men made their way back down the narrow stairs. At the bottom the senior officer said, 'No wonder Rasid plays his music so bloody loud. My ears are killing me listening to her as it is.'

They got into their car and drove back in the direction of their office off Whitehall. As they sat in the traffic in the Mall, the junior officer was racking his brain about something that Mrs Spielberg had said earlier. Suddenly it came to him. 'That's it, that's it John. I've got it. Remember that *All Forces Alert* supplement that came from Scotland Yard a day or so ago about Range Rovers? Do you remember it?'

'I remember something about it, but I didn't pay too much attention to it. Yard's always sending out waste paper if you ask me.'

'Well John it was related to an earlier *AFA*. About someone who'd put poison into the Lake in St James's Park. It's the Range Rover connection, and that chemical poison, HCN I think it's called. That and the fact that Rasid's from the Middle East.'

'Traffic gets worse every day if you ask me,' the senior officer said, as he tried to make his way into the stream of cars, taxis, buses, and motorbikes going around Trafalgar Square.

'You must remember it John?' the younger man repeated. 'It caused a great stir at the time. I think some tramps got their hands on some of the stuff and drank it. Killed them it did, killed them all.'

'Yes I remember it. But don't go jumping to conclusions. In this job you go by the book. The book tells you to take each step at a time. Tick the boxes as you go. You soon find out what's what. Don't get too far ahead of yourself that's a big mistake. You could miss something if you do that Andy,' John O'Sullivan, Detective Sergeant, Special Branch, said to his younger colleague, Detective Constable, Andrew Taylor.

'I know John, I take your point, but there's something about this lot that gives me a funny feeling. The Range Rover; Rasid's got one. The Iraq connection; he's from the Middle East, and the water thing; well who knows? I think we should check it out a bit further, don't you John?'

'Look Andy, come tomorrow we'll give this Mr Rasid another call. If he answers his phone we make an appointment to go and see him. Ask a few questions, tick the boxes, and we should have all the right answers. No sweat, simple as that.'

'What if he's not there John?'

'We do it the next day, or the next. What's the difference?'

Detective Andy Taylor, Special Branch, frowned. 'OK John, you're the boss, but I'm going to call up the file on that case. I think our Rasid is not going to be around for a while. It'll only take an hour or so. Might be worth it.'

'Andy if it makes you happy, you go right ahead my son. But it's unconnected if you ask me. Oh God, this traffic. Lets put on the blue light and get through it. What you'd say John?'

'You're the boss John, you're the boss.'

Sergeant Wilson had just arrived back at the police station in Crieff, Perthshire feeling more than a bit restless. A bad night's sleep and unfinished business had that effect on him.

'Sarg?' Constable Peter McKechnie shouted anxiously to him as he came through the door.

'Yes, Peter, what's happened now? Somebody rob the local *Co-op*?' Wilson replied, trying to lighten himself up as much as anything with his own humour.

'No Sarg, worse than that. The Chief Constable wants you to call him right away. His secretary says it's urgent. I tried to get you on the radio, but the reception was bad.'

Wilson had a feeling he knew what the call was about. 'That bloody Range Rover I bet,' he said thinking aloud.

'Can I have the good news now,' Wilson shouted back, still trying to shake himself out of the depression that had overtaken him since his visit to the village store in Braco.

'What's that Sarg, good news? I don't have any Sir,' McKechnie replied missing the point.

Wilson picked up his telephone and fast dialled Headquarters in Perth. It was instantly answered and he asked to be put through to the Chief Constable's office. He was asked who was calling, and when he replied the line went silent. A secretary's voice then said, 'Hold on Sergeant Wilson, and I'll put you through to the Chief Constable now.'

After a short silence, a voice boomed down the telephone, 'Wilson, this is Chief Constable Petrie. I believe you're trying to locate a vehicle, a Range Rover I think? Is that correct?'

Wilson stomach took another twist. 'That's correct Sir, I still am. Registered under the name of a Mr Hamid Pasha, a Turkish fellow lives in Braco.'

'Good Wilson. Everything all in order then I hope?' Petrie asked with a hint of expectation in his voice.

'Well not quite Sir,' Wilson responded, 'you see the owner, and the vehicle it seems, according to the local store keeper in Braco that is, has gone down to Edinburgh for a few days.'

Wilson had barely completed his last sentence when Petrie erupted. 'You mean you've still got this bloody Range Rover driving about, as yet unchecked, and you're sitting there on your bloody arse? What are you waiting on Wilson? Get out there and find out where the hell in Edinburgh the bloody car is. Do I make myself clear Wilson? Do I?'

'Yes Sir, I'll get onto it right away.'

Silence followed for no more than a few seconds, but it seemed like two minutes to Sergeant Wilson. 'Wilson, I've been given a proverbial rocket from Scotland Yard no less. They're asking me why it is that we've still got a bloody Range Rover unaccounted for in our region. They're asking why, me Chief Constable of Perth and Kinross Police, why I'm holding up a full scale national inquiry. I'm now asking you Wilson. Why is it we've still not checked that Range Rover? And I want an answer bloody quickly. Do you understand Wilson? Am I making myself clear?'

'Yes Sir, I'll get onto Lothian Police right away. I'll get back to you very soon Sir.'

A brief pause, and then in a slightly calmer tone, 'Right Wilson, but be bloody quick about it. This is a national thing and the Perth and Kinross Constabulary isn't looking too good at the moment. I'll get in touch with the Chief Constable of Lothian and let him know you'll be down there. He'll get you any co-operation you need. Now get on with it Wilson, and phone me when you've got something to tell me.' Petrie hung up the telephone without waiting for an answer.

Sergeant Jack Wilson sat at his desk stunned. He was responsible for running one of the smallest police stations in the country and he was being accused of holding up a national inquiry. He looked around. Young McKechnie was standing, opened mouthed, at his doorway.

'You OK Sarg?' McKechnie asked hesitantly, 'Everything OK Sir?'

Somehow Wilson knew that everything wasn't OK! He had a feeling that it was anything but OK!

The meeting in Scotland Yard had just broken up. At Hughes' suggestion the Commissioner had called the meeting within an hour of Hughes advising him of the latest events in *Operation Hydro*. Now the representatives, who included the Home Affairs Minister, representatives from MI5, OFWAT, and the privatised water companies, were being conducted back towards Scotland Yard's main reception area. All of them appeared to be leaving the building with more concerns than they'd had when they arrived. The major problem discussed during the meeting had been how to protect the number of water treatment plants scattered throughout the country, not to mention the reservoirs with thousands of kilometres of shoreline. The privatised water companies, who had more to lose than the rest, said it was impossible to do it in the short term, and that it would require a huge number of army personnel to patrol the properties alone, never mind the reservoirs. They also said their security systems would need to be upgraded beyond anything they'd been before. That would take time and money; lots of money. The message they were trying to put across was that, *It'll cost millions, and it'll take months, maybe even years.* Some of the companies expressed feelings that maybe the Scotland Yard and the security services were over-reacting to the potential danger, saying that after all it was only 1500 litres of this HCN. *A drop in the ocean,* they said. They had added that, *It'll have little impact when combined with the vast quantity of water stored in any one lake or reservoirs anywhere in the UK.* The arguments had got stronger, and stronger. At least one major company even advocated that; *There was a case for doing virtually nothing.*

As normally occurred in these situations, the Minister of Home Affairs, a key member in the department which had a major say in the price of water in the UK, and the water industry representatives found it difficult to agree on a way forward. The problem, as far as Hughes could see, was *who's going to pay for this additional protection of the water supply?* The answer to that question that appeared to be coming to the surface during the meeting was as usual, *the public,* and not *the water companies.* The Commissioner eventually closed the meeting with one major point reluctantly agreed upon by all parties. The army, as of six o'clock that evening, would provide twenty-four hour cover for all water treatment plants serving major conurbations. All other areas of the country would have to remain *at risk* meantime. The Minister for Home Affairs advised that anything further commitment at this time would involve looking at existing budgets for all other public services. Cuts, for example the Minister claimed, would be required in Transport, Health, and even Education, and to implement them would take weeks, even months. He also advised that the police throughout the country would have to step up their efforts to find the HCN in the three previously identified areas of the country, Bristol, Newcastle upon Tyne, and Glasgow. It had been a *three steps forward, two steps back*, kind of meeting Hughes felt.

Later that same day Ian Day had been driven to Glasgow Airport to catch a British Airways flight back to London. Before leaving the Strathclyde Police Headquarters, Day had taken part in a videoconference with Scotland Yard, with Hall chairing the discussions. Hall had already heard from Hughes that the conclusions of the ministerial meeting held earlier in the morning were, *apart from some Army units being located at all major water treatment plant facilities, the police were to step up their efforts to locate the HCN.* Armed with that limited, and disappointing knowledge, he'd asked Assistant Chief Constable MacKenzie if he felt that Day could contribute much more to their effort up there. MacKenzie had replied that he'd like to keep Day up in Glasgow for as long as it took to close down *Operation Hydro,* however he added, 'Commander I understand your position. We'll have him on a flight back to London within the hour. And thanks again for his valuable assistance.' Mackenzie had made it clear that he was very appreciative of the information picked up from Mrs Falconer, in Durham. The woman, a Glaswegian, had apparently had a lengthy discussion with Ciddiqui, alias Taleb, when he'd stayed in Durham a few weeks ago. During the conversation Taleb had told her about his visit to Scotland. When she'd told him she'd been born there, he became even more effusive about the country and the scenery. He'd been particularly pleased with his boat trip on the *S.S. Sir Walter Burns*, the small ship that sailed on Loch Catrine. He'd also told her he'd stayed at a small hotel in Aberfoyle. As a consequence, the police now had a fairly clear picture of Taleb's trip. Taleb had spent a great deal of time around Loch Catrine and the surrounding area. Doing what MacKenzie had said, was still the question.

Hall wondered why the woman hadn't told him all of it earlier when she'd accompanied her husband, DC Falconer, to Scotland Yard? Like getting blood out of a stone he thought. However his pressing needs now were for similar positive progress to be made in England. He said to MacKenzie, 'From what you've just told me I think it would be more advantageous if Day returned to London. We've still very little to go on here. I think we need all the help we can get.'

MacKenzie agreed, and thanked Hall once again for his support. He said, 'Detective Inspector Day will be with you in a minute or so.'

'Thanks,' Hall replied, then asked, 'One other thing, those security checks on the registered two-door Range Rovers up there. Could you chase them up? There are still one or two unaccounted for I believe.'

'If that's the case I'll have heads rolling,' MacKenzie stated sternly. 'I'll get in touch with my counterparts, the other ACC's, and make sure we get that sorted out without further delay. Leave it with me Commander.'

'Good to speak to you MacKenzie.'

'You too Commander. Talk to you later.'

A few moments afterwards Hall spoke to Day and relayed *Forensics* initial findings about Taleb's clothing and the boots he'd used during his travels. The mud it seemed had a specific chemical content found only in the West Central Scotland. Highly carbonised apparently. In addition, *Forensics* had found evidence of another location, but it was proving a bit more difficult to identify. He also told Day about a call he'd received yesterday from Special Branch in Whitehall. One of their officers had reported that a male, with Middle East origins, who was driving a dark blue Range Rover, might be a help with their inquires. The officer also confirmed that the man was last seen in the Greater London area.

'That said Ian, I think it's better that you get back here ASAP. I don't think interviewing the van driver, Carey, again will prove much more than we already now know, so cut that short. We can detain him anyway under the *Anti-Terrorist Act* in any event, so just get back here Ian.'

Day had been picked up at Terminal One, Heathrow immediately he'd exited the Arrivals building, and was back in Hall's office thirty minutes later. Hall was passing on some addition information on progress with *Operation Hydro.*

'Yesterday, Ian, I put a call out on all blue Range Rovers in London. *Traffic* will stop and search them, and if clean, the owners will be given a circular green disc to put on the windscreen, middle top, centre.'

''You'll not be popular in the rush-hour Sir, I'm sure you appreciate that.'

Hall knew the downside, he'd already heard about the traffic jams in Knightsbridge, but he felt right about doing it. He was being asked to step up his actions; the commuters would have to live with it. 'Ian I'm up to speed with the Scottish situation, and it's encouraging. Tell me, what about progress in Newcastle and Durham?'

'I was hoping you weren't going to ask me that Sir. Everything I got in Durham related to Scotland. It seemed that Mrs Falconer didn't think to ask Taleb what he was doing in Durham. But we do know he was there, but what the hell for is still a mystery.'

'It's the same here. Nothing has come up on Bristol, and nothing further has happened in London, thank God. That's why I've asked you to come back. I want you to go through all our active and non-active information. Right from the beginning, leave nothing to chance. Every lead in this part of the country has gone cold, *Dead* if you prefer. Look what happened to Kadri, then Ciddiqui, or Taleb, and the mysterious Aireb must be lying low. What next?'

'It's not for the want of trying; everybody, including yourself Sir has worked his butt off I can tell you.'

Hall nodded his head in agreement, 'I still think our next lead will come from Glasgow. We know Taleb he covered a huge area when he was there. Doing what's the big question.' Hall got to his feet and paced around the room. 'Ian, I've a theory that whoever has the HCN won't attempt to poison an entire reservoir. Not enough HCN and too much water you see. It's only a theory, but what if they, whoever the hell they are, what if they plan to poison the water as it enters the distribution system, the public water mains in other words. They could do it within the reservoirs quite easily I'm sure.' He started to pace around again, 'It would have an immediate impact. We think of these public water pipes as being huge, but the water content in them is nothing compared to the quantity of water in a reservoir.'

Day conjured up an image of large water pipes underground, passing through streets lined with houses. He said, 'If what I'm thinking is correct Sir, you're saying if the HCN is dumped close to the outlet pipe of a reservoir and some poor sod who lives nearby fills up a glass of water from his tap and drinks it, then he'd be dead in seconds. God, that's horrible, there are countless thousands of people who live next to reservoirs for God's sake.'

Hall nodded, then said, 'They, whoever have got the HCN, would only need a few hundred litres of the stuff to achieve that. Think about it. How would they go about it?'

'OK Sir I've got the picture. I'll get the team together and we'll brainstorm it for a day or so. See what we can come up with.'

'That's no good Ian. We might not have that amount of time to play with. We have to hit it now. Get the team busy on it now, and I'll join you in half an hour. I want to be able to form a strategy based on that concept. OK?' Hall knew he was asking a lot, but he'd no option.

'See you in half an hour Sir.'

'Before you go Ian, get onto the Special Branch. Ask for Taylor, Detective Constable Andrew Taylor. See what else he's got for us, it might be useful.'

'Right Sir,' Day said, closing the door behind him.

Hall was expecting the full forensic report on Taleb/Ciddiqui's hired car later that day. He'd already been told that at least twenty-odd people had been detected from DNA deposits taken within the vehicle. Strathclyde Police were now taking DNA samples from anyone who'd ever worked, driven, or even cleaned the vehicle. The car had been introduced into the Hertz pool in Glasgow only two days before Taleb uplifted it, and as far as records showed, it had never been driven outside the West of Scotland. Before that is, Taleb had taken it Newcastle. It was just possible he'd picked up someone, maybe more than one, during the time he'd had it. The Hertz staff at Glasgow and Newcastle Airport, their mechanics, car wash people, and previous renters would all be checked and cross-checked to eliminate as many as possible. It was a huge task. From the DNA samples it would be possible to determine the sex, age and origins of the people who'd been in the car since it had been put into service. The car had registered only one thousand two hundred and thirteen kilometres on the dial in that period and Taleb had accounted for about five hundred of those. Forty-one percent of the total in fact, during the period he'd had it.

Hall's telephone rang. 'Yes Lorna?'

'It's the Chief Constable of Lothian Police calling from Edinburgh Sir. Shall I put him through?'

''Yes please.'

Clabby introduced himself. 'Commander, I've just opened up an action here in the Lothian Region, focusing mostly in the city of Edinburgh. The action based on our powers of Stop and Search laws that we have up here will focus on two-door Range Rovers. I've instructed this action following a request from my opposite number in Perth, who advises that a vehicle of that type and make, one of only two up here in Scotland as yet still to be checked I believe, is heading for Edinburgh as we speak.'

'It seems that road traffic in Edinburgh and London will cease to move about the same time today Chief Constable. I've recently done the same thing in London, only we're looking for a blue Range Rover.' Hall went on to describe the colour coded disc system he'd introduced, adding that the system needed a very quick response time to make the action worthwhile. 'Twenty-four hours at the longest before it would become ineffective.' he said.

The Chief Constable listened, asked a few questions, then said he'd try and adopt the same system. They wished each other well, and hung up their telephones. After the conversation, Hall was left with the feeling that although he and the Chief Constable of Lothian Police may've stopped the traffic in London and Edinburgh, he himself was stopped in his tracks until his team could produce more active leads. The telephone rang again. He walked through to his secretary's office and said, 'Who is it this time Lorna?'

'Sir, *Forensics* for you. They've been holding for a few minutes.'

'I'll take it,' he said, turning around.

Hall listened to the man at the other end for a few moments, then said, 'Right away.' He put the phone down, and went off to *Forensics* in the basement.

CHAPTER FORTY-EIGHT

Day called a meeting of his team within a few minutes of returning to the War Room. He quickly summed up his earlier meeting with Hall, and relayed the message that DAC Hughes had brought back a short time before. The message was clear. *The police must step up their efforts to find the HCN.* The looks on the faces of his team said it all. They had Day's sympathy; he knew they'd have to re-assess the information they had in case they'd overlooked some small detail. 'Barbara, I want you to get back on to British Airways. Ask them to produce from their passenger records a list of flights made by Ciddiqui, or Taleb. Any one of those names; where and when. And ask how the tickets were paid for, charge card, cash, whatever. That sort of thing.'

'Will do Sir.'

'And Barbara, ask if there are any flights that've been booked in advance in either name. Both names OK? We need to be able to put together a better picture of Ciddiqui or Taleb habits. We now know that the Armenian Embassy he said he represented denies any knowledge of him, or so they now claim. So who and what was he? Where did he come from? We need to know that.'

'Yes Sir, I'll check it out,' David replied.

'I'm not finished with you Barbara. I also want the remaining names of the owners of the two-door Range Rovers that we haven't been able to make contact with. I want the names, addresses, and colour of the vehicles and the expiry date of the current or last tax disc for each vehicle.'

More scribbling, then David said, 'Right Sir. Anything else?'

'That'll do for now, but I want it taken to the Commander inside the next half hour.'

David left the group meeting and went to her desk.

'Now Jim, I've set up a meeting with a DC Andrew Taylor, Special Branch. He's expecting you as of now. He seems to think he may've touched on something of interest to us, connecting a dark blue Range Rover and an Iraqi who just happens to work at Heathrow airport who is on sick leave at the moment. It also seems that the man hasn't been available for routine questioning. See what it's all about Johnston, but do it quickly please, OK?'

'Will do Sir,' Johnston responded.

'In addition Jim, the forensic report on those things from the Hertz car in Newcastle will be with me shortly. I want you to go through it with me, after you've had your meeting Taylor.'

'Yes Sir, I'll be back ASAP,' Johnston said as he left the room.

'Now Mark. For you I've picked the most difficult task. I want you to go sailing, at least the Commander does,' Day said, a smile crossing his face.

'I'm a terrible guy for getting sea-sick Sir,' Dobbie interjected, part in humour, and part in honest trepidation considering the way the weather had been when he'd arrived at the Yard earlier that day.

'Maybe this will cure you then Mark. Anyway, I'll be getting in touch with Superintendent McDade, River Police, and CI Bannistair, our pharmacist. I want the three of you to join me on a trip up to Enfield, to the Queen Anne Reservoir. They must have some sort of boat that'll get us all about. You know what they say about London's water, it's been recycled a few times, so just don't drink the stuff if you fall in.'

'If you say so Sir.'

'I've asked McDade and Bannistair to come up here in a few minutes, so you can sort yourselves out re timings. When McDade and Bannistair get here we can discuss what I've got in mind. In the meantime phone Themes Water and ask for their permission to get out on the water first thing tomorrow morning. The Commander has mentioned to them the non-toxic dye we plan to put in, and why. Ask if they can provide a boat, a reliable one, one without holes in it. Oh, and some life jackets as well, I don't want to lose any of you guys out there just yet,' Day laughing.

'Right Sir, I can feel my stomach becoming queasy already just talking about it.'

'You'll get over it I promise. It's all part of *Operation Hydro,* and if we don't get it sorted out soon, we'll all be more than bloody sea sick I can tell you.'

'Yes Sir,' Dobbie replied seriously. 'I'll phone Themes now, and see you and the others when they arrive.'

WDC David left Hall's office after reporting the outcome of her telephone conversation with British Airways. She'd received confirmation that a Mr A Taleb had travelled between London

Heathrow and Glasgow on a shuttle service on the fifth of February and between Newcastle and London Heathrow on the ninth of February. This information tied up with the ticket stubs that Talbot, Ciddiqui's apartment caretaker, had mentioned. She'd then been told that a Mr A Ciddiqui had pre-booked a single *Club Class* ticket on a BA franchise airline, British Mediterranean Airways, Flight number BA6721 to Yerevan, the capital of Armenia. Ciddiqui was booked to leave London Heathrow at 2100hrs, on Monday, 29th April. When David had given him that information Hall, aware that Ciddiqui wasn't going to show for the flight, wondered about the significance of the date. Why had Ciddiqui planned to leave the country in three days time, two days after the date in the video message *Ma Ma, Fi Kul Makaan*? The man had been obviously involved in the HCN situation although they'd yet to prove it. Had he begun to feel things were closing in on him, or was it something more sinister? It was the only date Hall had and he decided he'd use it as a deadline for the time being. He went back to the War Room where Johnston was now reading the forensic report Day had given him. The report covered the forensic and geologist assessments of the mud on Ciddiqui's clothing, footwear, and the samples taken from the Hertz hired car.

'Jim, locations please. Tell me where did Taleb go? '

'It looks to me Sir that they're saying they think the mud samples can only come from one of two locations in the country. That is, based on the molecular structure of the samples used to make the analysis, the.... .'

'Jim for God's sake get on with it. Where do they think the bloody man went? Tell me that and cut out the crap.'

'Yes Sir. From the two sets of mud samples, one suggests West Central Scotland. Somewhere between the Rannoch moor in the north, and the Fintry hills to the south. The other, from an area in the north Pennines, but south of the Cheviot Hills, in County Durham they think. The gravel and stone samples are a bit more difficult Sir. They can be quarried in a number of places in the UK. But *Forensics'* best guesses are, north of the Fintry Hills north of Glasgow; around the north-west side of Newcastle upon Tyne towards Kilder Water; and the Pennines in County Durham Sir.'

'What about southern England? Nothing from around here?'

'Nothing Sir, all up north it seems.'

286

'Well there wouldn't be. The bloody car never got that far south. The Scottish location we already know about, and both Strathclyde and Lothian Police have that covered. But Kilder Water. That's a massive stretch of water just this side of the Scottish border, if my memory serves me right.' Hall looked at an UK wall map and put his finger on the location. 'It gets worse. Look at the size of that stretch of water. This doesn't make a lot of sense does it? We're talking of fifteen hundred litres of HCN, and from what we know it was split into three separate amounts and sent to three widely diverse locations. Jim we're missing something, I know it. What effect would five hundred litres of the bloody stuff have on the quantity of water contained in Kilder? Or Loch Catrine, even if they put the whole fifteen hundred litres into only one of them?' Hall walked around the room, then back to the map. 'None I guess, and I'm not a bloody scientist. That's also what the water companies told the Commissioner. They think we're over-reacting to all of this. Maybe we are Jim, maybe we are.' Hall slumped down on a chair. 'Unless they injected the HCN into the public water supply in such a manner that it gets to the public only partially diluted. How would they do that, that's the question? You'll be seeing Day shortly. I want that thought developed as far as possible Jim, OK?'

'Yes Sir, but I do agree with you, how else would that insignificant quantity of HCN have any impact on Kilder? No chance Sir.'

Hall nodded in agreement, then got up and walked around the room. Johnston interjected saying, 'Sir I went to see DC Taylor at Special Branch. He said the US Tax authorities found something not quite right about Farraj Rasid, the guy with the dark blue Range Rover. Apparently Rasid, who actually was born in Iraq, had lived and worked in the USA on student exchange scheme for a long time. Clean bill of health until recently.'

'Tell me the bit that's of interest.'

'Yes Sir. It seems that Rasid, who is now employed as an ATC, an Air Traffic Controller Sir, at Heathrow Airport, is off on sick leave....'

'I know that Johnston, Taylor told me that on the telephone the other day when we spoke. What's the point of the story?'

'Well, Rasid filed an incorrect US Tax Return way back, when he was working in the US. It appears that he didn't report a substantial amount of money - five hundred thousand dollars to be exact - which passed through his bank account. Albeit for only twenty-four hours Sir.'

'So what happened Jim? Get to the point.'

'The US tax people, the IRS as they call them over there, they want to get their tax from him for the interest he received for the period he had the money in his account. They tried to trace him but failed. In the US the IRS are obliged to notify the FBI of such truncations, something to do with money laundering. Anyway it seems the money was viewed as being laundered and it was established that initially it came from an off-shore bank account, based in the Cayman Isles, just off the coast...'

'I know where the bloody Cayman Isles are. What else Jim?'

'Sorry Sir, anyway the money comes from this account and goes to Rasid for all of twenty-four hours. He then issues a cheque the next day for the same sum, five hundred thousand dollars, and this is the point of the story Sir, to an Ivan Beria.'

'And? Is that it?'

'More or less Sir, but the twist is in the tale, if you'll forgive the pun.'

'Johnston...'

'Yes Sir. The twist is that Beria cashed the cheque here in London. We know this because the American bank that Rasid used in the USA at that time told the story to the FBI. Oh, and because our lads at Special Branch contacted the US Security people when Rasid came here to work, usual security check it seems - it got noted on his file. So naturally when the FBI goes looking for Rasid, the first thing they do is make contact with our Special Branch. They say they're looking for Rasid, whom they understand is living and working in the UK, and then ask our lads to pay him a call, ask him a few questions. As it happens, when Taylor gets to Rasid's last known address, it seems according to a friendly neighbour that is, that Rasid left in a hurry, and looked like he was going away for some time.'

Hall thought through what Johnston had just told him. He could see the fiscal problem Rasid had created for himself and the reason the FBI would've been brought in. A similar scenario would've probably happened in the UK. So the man may've been into drug trafficking or something like that. But that was pretty common, and appeared to have nothing to do with *Operation Hydro.*

'Anyway Sir, out of curiosity, and we're getting to the sting in the tale now, I asked Taylor if he knew which bank in the UK had cashed the five-hundred thousand dollars cheque for Beria. Taylor said the UABK, the Union Arab Bank, in Threadneedle Street, London, Sir.'

'The Bank of England will also know well Johnston I'm sure what you've just told me. You can't just move sums of money that large on a whim,' Hall said hesitantly, a bit unsettled by the story, although he couldn't understand why.

'When you asked me about the forensics report a few minutes ago Sir, well,' Johnston hesitated, 'that's why it took me a while to get to the point of the report. You see it'd just dawned on me that the man who purchased the HCN from Zenecal Chemicals Ltd, a Mr Aireb, had an account at the UABK. We found that out when we were investigating how he'd paid for the product at that time. He used a banker's draft from UABK to pay Zenecal Chemicals.'

Hall looked at Johnston. It did seem to be too much of a co-incidence, but there was something about those names. He was also thinking how does an Iraqi get to become an air traffic controller at Heathrow airport? If he's involved in laundering drug money, what the hell else is he up to? Hall's mind eventually struck a chord. The name Johnston had said. Aireb, what was it he was thinking? Then he got it!

'That's it Johnston, the name, one is the reverse of the other. AIREB and BERIA that's it Jim, that's it. Do you see that? Jim I want you to go to that UABK and ask them, tell them more to the point, that we want a copy of the authorised signatures of both Aireb, and Beria.'

'Yes I do Sir, your right, they're reversed, but it's now nine-thirty. The bank won't be open now till tomorrow morning.'

Hall closed his eyes. 'Sorry Jim, I'm on a twenty-four hour clock at the moment. It's time we all went home for some sleep I guess. You can get onto the bank in the morning, and bring the signatures to me as soon as you have them. I'll get our handwriting people to have a look at them. Off you go Jim I'll see you in the morning, goodnight.'

'You too Sir,' Johnston replied, leaving Hall's office.

As Johnston left Hall's telephone rang. 'Sir, I've got Superintendent McDade and Mr Bannistair here for the meeting. Do you want me to tell Inspectors Day and Dobbie to join you as well?' she asked, more as a reminder than as a question.

'Yes Lorna, and tell them to come ASAP.'

When the men arrived, Hall explained to them what he wanted them to try and do at Queen Anne reservoir. After discussing the possibility for twenty minutes or so, and although he could see some doubt in their faces, they all agreed they'd give it a try.

'Commander, what if the whole thing's a failure, the results of no consequence? What do we do then?' Bannistair asked.

'We pray Jim, we pray.'

The men broke up in a pensive mood.

Farraj Rasid wiped his mouth with the heavily starched napkin, a well-satisfied look on his dark skinned face. 'A wonderful dinner monsieur,' he said grandly to the tall, handsome *maitre d'hotel*, as the man motioned his nearby waiter to take the empty plate away.

'Thank you Sir, I'm glad you've enjoyed your dinner. Will Sir be joining us in the dining room for breakfast tomorrow?'

Rasid hesitated, 'It'd be my pleasure be assured, but my plans for tomorrow may not allow for such a pleasant start to the day,' he said.

'Whatever you wish Sir. We're here to make your stay a pleasant one in any way we can. If there is anything else you would like me to get for you, an Armagnac perhaps? A cigar?'

Farraj Rasid smiled, but refused the offers. He signed his bill, went to his room on the first floor, overlooking the silent, running waters of the River Thames. He opened up a map of the area, located Bray, then the network of roads from Bray to Farmore treatment works near Oxford. He'd a choice. The M40 or the minor road network through some of the small villages in that part of England; villages that would be affected by his actions. He chose the latter. He decided he'd breakfast early in his room and leave around eight o'clock. He could then drive through the narrow lanes, see where the people lived; people who would be dead the following day if all went to plan. He'd plenty of time and that would be a more picturesque route to *Location Delta*. It was midnight before he switched off his bedside lamp. Rasid was asleep within minutes, the events of the next twenty-four hours having no impact on his physical or mental well being.

As Farraj Rasid had switched off his bedside light, Chris Hall was reading a memo he'd received from WDC David on the subject of two door Range Rovers. From her researches it appeared that of those vehicles registered in the UK, only nine hadn't been accounted for, eight in England, none in Northern Ireland, none in Wales, and he could hardly believe it, still one in Scotland. It was the latter that caused him the concern. His thoughts centred on his telephone call with Lothian Police's Chief Constable earlier that day. 'We must get that bloody vehicle up there checked out in the next twenty four hours,' he shouted. He thought of the work being done by the Traffic Police at that time, the stop and search of all Range Rovers in and around London. He'd heard an hour or so ago that the traffic jams in Knightsbridge were getting worse not better. But what else could he do? They had to find the HCN and traffic jams were a small price to pay. He got up, rubbed his eyes, and walked towards the window. The streets glistened from a recent rain shower. He was exhausted and yet progress was minimal. Thinking back to his meeting an hour or so ago with McDade, Bannistair, Day and Dobbie, he wondered if they'd be able to prove his theory. Would Themes Water come through and allow them to discharge five hundred litres of non-toxic, colorant into the draw-off at Queen Anne reservoir? He knew their Quality Control committee would be meeting even at this late hour to decide. Day would find out tomorrow he thought. It was a long shot he knew, but maybe, just maybe it would work. If it did, then it would give an indication of how widespread the effect of just five hundred litres of HCN would be. He'd come to the conclusion that the water companies had been correct in their assertion that one thousand-five hundred litres of HCN was of little consequence in a large reservoir. The amount of HCN they were looking at in comparison to the mass of water was negligible. But, and it was a big but, he now believed he knew how the HCN could be discharged into the water supply to create maximum impact and countless deaths. If he were correct, the action tomorrow at the Enfield's Queen Anne reservoir would confirm it. It would then be possible to make a reasonable estimate of the impact on the population and what steps the authorities would have to take to prepare for it. It would also lift the complacency of the water companies about the threat to the public supply. How many deaths he wondered would they need to justify some serious action to protect their major asset? Ten, one thousand, twenty thousand, just how many? He switched off his desk lamp, and took his jacket off the hanger, putting it on as he left the room. He could see that most of his team had gone home for the night, although Day was still bent over his desk studying some paperwork.

Goodnight Ian, see you in the morning.'

'Good night Sir.'

It was just after midnight.

Porter had just fitted the battery back into the Land Rover, and was clutching the bottle of wine that Niazi Bey had given him for the prompt repair.

'That'll get you going again,' Porter said, as he opened and closed the door of the vehicle, observing the door light coming on and off. 'Get you to the top of Mount Everest this vehicle would. Great British invention if you ask me, although the bloody Americans own them now; Ford would you believe? We could do with a few more British inventions today I can tell you.'

'Yes Porter, I'm sure you could,' Bey replied, hoping to get rid of the man quickly. 'I've a few more things I'd like to check here before I go back to my rooms. I lock up if you like. Let you go off home Mr Porter and enjoy the wine.'

'Very good Sir,' Porter replied, heading to the doorway. 'I'll leave you to it then. I'm sure your Defender will be fine and thanks again for the wine. I'll enjoy this I can tell you,' he replied, holding out the bottle as he backed out of the door.

As soon as Porter left, Bey locked the door from the inside. He'd no intention of allowing anyone else to come into the space over the next hour or so. He checked that the trailer and the tank of HCN was properly attached, and for the umpteenth time checked he'd all the equipment he needed to pump the liquid HCN into the air shaft. He muttered the names of the items as he touched each one individually; pump, armoured hose, the heavy wrench to secure the hose to the pump and to open the draw-off pipe on the tank, extra fuel, torch, and a gas mask. He'd bought the mask after Mabeirig had died. He believed the fumes generated by transferring the HCN from the cylinders into the tank had caused Mabeirig's death. He'd no intention of repeating the mistake. He lifted the holdall he'd packed earlier that day with everything he'd need till he reached France - his intended destination when he had carried out his action at *Location Gamma*. From there he'd return to Iraq. When he was satisfied that everything was in order, he set his watch alarm two hours on, and eased back the seat to a reclining position. He'd sleep for a few hours, and leave the boathouse around three in the morning to drive to Vaskerley, and be up in the hills before daylight.

CHAPTER FORTY-NINE

Chris Hall drove to his home in Micham, South London, put his car in the garage and went into his house quietly using the back door. Amanda his wife and their two children were asleep upstairs. He glanced through the mail lying on the hall table - nothing of interest. Going into the kitchen, he poured himself a glass of milk. He sat down at the table and tried to remember how long it was since he'd had dinner there with the family. Nearly three weeks he guessed. It was just past one o'clock in the morning, Saturday twenty-seventh April. He leant forward and put his head on his hands. Ten minutes later his wife Amanda woke him.

'Come to bed Chris, you're exhausted. You'll need some rest. Come on upstairs,' she said quietly, kissing his neck. 'Enough for now, come to bed. You're exhausted, look at you.'

'I think we've failed Amanda. I think we're too late.' He slumped again at the table saying, 'I hope I'm wrong, I just hope to God I'm wrong.'

'You've done all you can I'm sure. Get some sleep now, tomorrow's another day. Come on now,' she said, helping him to get up from the table. They went up to their bedroom, and within a few minutes he was fast asleep. While he slept, Amanda lay awake; worried about her husband, their children, and trying hard not to think too much about what Chris had just told her.

Beep, Beep, Beep, Beep. Niazi Bey awoke with a start. He didn't know where he was. 'Allah preserve me,' he said quietly, before realising he was in the Defender inside the boathouse. In the dim light he could just make out the time on the clock on the dash; three o' clock in the morning. Instantly he was wide-awake. This was the day he'd waited for. His thoughts returned to Hussein. Although the sun had yet to rise he got out of the car and put a prayer mat on the damp ground. He wanted to pray before driving to Vaskerley. Allah will understand he thought as he knelt facing east. He bowed forward until his forehead touched the rough ground, then recited some words from the Koran asking for guidance and help. When he'd finished, he lifted the mat and put it in the Defender before opening the boathouse's double door quietly. The smell of the damp night air struck him. The river, a metre or so away, was running fast but silent, as if somehow expecting something sinister to take place. Although it now was just after three, Bey's survival instincts were on a high. He listened hard to make sure no one else was around, then going back into the boathouse he started up the Defender. The engine barked into life, shattering the silence. He engaged first gear, and eased out of the boathouse onto the pathway at the river's edge. He stopped and went back to lock the doors, then threw the key into the middle of the river. Getting back into the Defender, he drove slowly towards the main road. He'd get to the air shaft while it was still dark. He planned to spend the day walking the hills, safe in the knowledge that he'd everything ready and never too far from the shaft. His spirits were high. He was ready to deliver the *Juice of Allah* to the infidels.

Chris Hall awoke with a start. He was perspiring heavily, his breathing laboured, and his heart was pounding. He sat up in bed, his head resting on his raised knees.
'Chris, Chris what's wrong? Are you OK? What's wrong with you? What is it?'
'I'm fine Amanda, it's alright. Just a horrible dream that's all. I'm fine honestly love. I'm fine.'
'Can I get you anything?'
'No, I'm fine love. Awful dream that's all. But I'm fine,' Hall said, his breathing and his heartbeat struggling to get back to normal. He tried to remember what the dream was about and then the images returned with vivid clarity. Images of him in the middle of a reservoir. He was being drawn into a huge water draw-off tower, and as he plunged down into the cold black depths, he awoke. Looked at his hands, he realised he was still shaking. Glancing at the alarm clock he saw it was almost quarter to six.
'You go back to sleep Amanda. Now that I'm awake there's no point me lying there when I might be able to do something useful. I'm fine really, I am. Go back to sleep love, I'm OK.'
Amanda Hall had already slipped out of bed and pulled on her dressing gown. 'Chris don't think for a minute that I'd let you leave here without some breakfast after the last few minutes. I thought you were having a heart attack. You've been pushing yourself too much over the past few weeks, working non-stop. You'll make yourself ill

and where would the children and I be then? Living on some police pension? Is that your idea of looking after your family?'

Hall knew his wife was right. He had been putting in far too many hours, days, even nights on *Operation Hydro*. It'd been an unrelenting battle. He and his team, all experienced police professionals, had struggled to collect every single piece of information they could.

'You're right love, I'll back-off a bit. You and the kids mean too much to me. I couldn't be without you all. The problem is when I'm awake my mind goes on and on. I feel we're getting somewhere now, and that we'll soon be able to reach out and touch the people we're after. Can you understand that Amanda?'

'Chris I know you too well to think that you'd work nine to five. But just ease off on yourself a little, please, for us and for yourself. You'll still get there, I know you so well, you will.' Amanda bent down and kissed her husband. 'Go and have a shower, then come on down and I'll have breakfast ready for you before you go. I love my man, and I just want to keep him. Go on now, have your shower.'

Hall got out of bed and stepped out of his boxer shorts. 'You're right love, you're right. I'll try to adjust my schedule, and remember what you've said. Honest I will. I might even remember that I haven't been the perfect husband to you either lately. Missing out some of the services you used to enjoy nearly as much as I did if I remember correctly,' he said with a smile.

'Well I was beginning to think you were going elsewhere for that, or one of your WPC's was doing more than just helping you check out some thugs,' Amanda replied half joking, half seriously.

'Come here,' Hall said trying to catch his wife as she went out the bedroom.

'Shoo… You'll waken the children. Just come home a bit earlier tonight and maybe, just maybe, we'll see if you can still remember how to play the part.'

He picked up his shorts and playfully threw them at his wife.

'Have your shower, then come down and have some breakfast lover boy. I'll look forward to tonight as well,' Amanda said winking at her husband as she closed the door quietly. She was feeling slightly better; at least he was behaving a bit more normally again and his sense of mischievousness had returned. She was also thinking though that she'd have to be a bit harder on him. It was all very well him chasing up the career ladder at a fast rate of knots, just as long as he didn't fall off. She made up her mind to regulate his work rate a bit more in the immediate future, for all their sakes. She busied herself in the kitchen making breakfast for both of them, noticing that it was already almost six o'clock.

DI Johnston, with the aid of some in-house knowledge, had traced the home telephone of the personal assistant of the manager of the UABK in Threadneedle Street in the City of London. Now, just after ten o'clock on Saturday morning, Johnston was heading to meet the manager in the bank premises. The mere mention of Scotland Yard had been more than enough to gain the manager's instant attention. Johnston was now being ushered through into an ante-room off the manager's office, past a few staff members who were working although the bank was closed to the public. In the ante-room a large, low brass coffee table placed on a Persian rug was the most prominent feature. A grey leather sofa and two matching chairs made up the rest of the room's furniture, with an abstract grey painting hung on the innermost wall, depicting a play on words using the letters UABK. It was a cold, clinical room; not one intended for lengthy occupation. Johnston sat in one of the chairs, and looked around. He wondered if anyone ever came here and asked if they could have an overdraft. Not likely, he thought as he glanced at the frosted security window. More likely to deposit an oil well or two would be more like it he imagined. The interior door opened quietly and a small, dark and well-groomed man in his late forties came into the room. 'Good morning Detective Inspector Johnston,' the man said in perfect English, 'allow me to introduce myself. My name is Shakhar Bhatia, I'm the manager of this branch of the Union Arab Bank. How can I be of assistance to you, and to the great Scotland Yard?'

Johnston rose to meet the man. 'Good morning Mr Bhatia,' he said shaking the man's hand.

'Please be seated Inspector,' Bhatia said, motioning Johnston to return to his seat. 'Would you like some coffee, tea, or mineral water Inspector?' the man asked, adding after a slight pause, 'It would be my pleasure.'

'Water please,' Johnston replied, 'just a glass of tap water would be nice thank you.'

The man pressed a buzzer close to where he was sitting and said looking at Johnston, 'A man after my own heart Inspector. You have good water in the United Kingdom. It is a pity to have to spoil it by putting coffee, tea, or anything else into it. We should all drink more pure water than we do.' The interior door opened again and a young woman dressed in a dark business suit came into the room. She smiled at Johnston, then looked at Bhatia.

'A large jug of tap water Miss Farrash,' Bhatia instructed.

'Now what can I and the UABK do for you Inspector?' Bhatia questioned as the woman left the room.

Johnston sat forward in the soft leather chair, clasping his hands together. 'Well Mr Bhatia I'm not sure how much your PA told you regarding my telephone call earlier this morning Mr Bhatia?' he asked questioningly and, seeing little response in the man's eyes, he continued. 'Putting it simply Sir, Scotland Yard is interested in two of your account holders. We'd like to get copies of their signatures for analytical purposes.'

Bhatia withdrew a gold cigarette case from his jacket pocket, opened it and offered Johnston a cigarette. Johnston declined. Bhatia took one out of the case, lit it, and inhaled deeply before responding, 'My PA mentioned that Scotland Yard wished to come and ask me some questions. That is all she told me Detective Inspector.' The interior door was knocked faintly. 'Come in please Miss Farrash,' Bhatia said. Both men waited until the woman had placed a silver tray on the low table. The tray held a crystal water jug and two crystal glasses, some lemon slices, paper napkins, and two clear plastic coasters. 'We will help ourselves Miss Farrash,' Bhatia said instructively. The woman nodded, and smiled at Johnston before leaving the room.

'Now Inspector,' Bhatia said as he poured water into the two glasses, 'let us get to the purpose of your visit. You want this information from the bank in connection with two of our customers. You say analytical purposes Inspector? Can I ask to what purpose Inspector?' He paused fractionally before continuing, 'You do understand Inspector, we have a confidential trust with our customers, and that we do not as a rule provide information about them to any outside agency.' Bhatia hesitated, then added, 'If I may be so bold as to describe Scotland Yard as an outside agency? That is the UABK's policy Inspector Johnston. I do not make the policy, but in my position, I have to implement it you will understand.'

Johnston watched the man sip his glass of water, and as he placed his glass back on the table said, 'Sir, there are two ways we can play this. One way, the hard way is by the book. Believe me we can and will make you provide us with the information, all within the fiscal laws of Her Majesty's Treasury.' Johnston let his words sink in. 'The second way is the easier of the two Mr Bhatia. Provide me with the information we want now, and I will leave you to get on with the rest of your morning. Now you choose Mr Bhatia. What is it to be? The easy way or the hard way?'

Bhatia lifted his glass again, and after drinking the last of the water, he placed it back on the tray. He got to his feet, cigarette in hand, as Johnston watched him struggle with his decision. 'Detective Inspector you leave me little choice. What can I say to you to assure you that this Bank, the UABK, wishes to co-operate fully with Scotland Yard, and of course HM Treasury. It would be more than my job is worth, should I not comply fully with your requirements.' Bhatia drew hard on his cigarette, and stubbed it out in an ashtray as he exhaled. 'You have the names of the account holders Inspector?' he asked as he turned towards Johnston.

'You have made a wise decision Mr Bhatia. This will save us all much time and distress I assure you. 'The names are,' Johnston said, spelling out the two names, 'first *Mr Ivan Beria,* and second *Mr Ivan Aireb.*'

Bhatia withdrew a gold pen and a small, thin note pad from within his jacket. His face was expressionless. He wrote down both names on the note pad, and lifting a nearby telephone he keyed in a number. 'Bring me the customer agreement form for each of these named accounts Miss Farrash,' he instructed, reading out the two names. He replaced the telephone then said, 'Inspector, forgive me please? Would you like more water while we wait a moment or two for Miss Farrash to locate the information you've asked for?'

'Thank you, I would,' Johnston stated, holding his empty glass forward for the other man to refill. The noise of the water being poured, and the quiet swish of the air conditioning filled the silence.

Bhatia made busy with his cigarette case and lit another cigarette in an elaborate manner, inhaling deeply as his action came to an end. Johnston heard a knock on the door, and Bhatia said abruptly,

'Enter.' The door opened and the woman came back into the room. 'Ah, Miss Farrash, you have located both documents?' Bhatia asked as he glanced at the papers the woman held in her hand. He took both papers, making a show of reading the contents, then said as he offered them to Johnston, 'Detective Inspector, would copies of these signatures meet your requirements?'

Johnston took the two pages, glanced at the signatures, and the printed names above each signature. 'Yes Mr Bhatia, copies of these pages would be fine thank you.' He noted that the dates on each page differed, but far as Johnston was concerned after only a quick glance, the handwriting on both pages was of one and the same hand. 'Miss Farrash, give the Detective Inspector a copy of each please, then return the originals to each file.'

Johnston handed the papers to the woman and she left the room as silently as she'd entered. When she returned a moment or so later, she handed Johnston the photocopies of the pages, together with a large white envelope. Johnston thanked her and slipped the pages into the envelope.

'Thank you for your co-operation Mr Bhatia,' Johnston said, 'I'll make sure my superiors are made aware of the bank's willingness to assist in this matter.'

Bhatia smiled with his mouth only. 'It has been my pleasure Detective Inspector. Miss Farrash will see you out.' He added, 'If there is anything else the UABK can do for Scotland Yard you will, I trust, let me know?"

'Yes Mr Bhatia, you'll be first to hear I assure you. Thank you again for your assistance.' Johnston left the bank and crossed Threadneedle Street towards the waiting police car. It was approaching eleven o'clock. He'd be back at the Yard in ten minutes or so. He was sure that Hall was correct; *Beria* and *Aireb* were one and the same person. 'I wouldn't mind putting a few bob on it you know,' he said as he got in the car.

'Did you say something Sir?' the driver asked, looking at him through his rear view mirror.

'No Sergeant, no nothing really,' Johnston replied, looking out through the side window.

CHAPTER FIFTY

At seven-thirty in the morning, three and a half hours before Johnston was being driven back from Threadneedle Street, Superintendent McDade, Bannistair, Inspectors Day and Dobbie, together with George Michael the reservoir superintendent had slipped their moorings at Queen Anne Reservoir, Enfield. It was barely daylight. The men were dressed in wet weather gear, including life-vests. With the five men and a five hundred litre plastic drum on the open deck, the boat was lower in the water than normal. The drum held a non-toxic coloured liquid, which Themes Water, somewhat reluctantly the night before, had agreed to let the police discharge into the reservoir. The water company knew that if and when the coloured fluid reached their customers, appearing in their kitchen taps and bathrooms, then the outcry would be hard to contain. They were however aware of the security problems at board level, and had taken into account the potential for disaster should terrorist actions take place anywhere in the UK. On that basis, they were prepared to allowed the experiment to go forward in an effort to establish the impact that a similar amount of HCN would have on their own distribution should that ever happen. To find out how widely the colorant had been distributed, they only had to wait till the telephones started to ring at their call centre. They'd ask the callers for their address, and instruct them to fill an empty, clean bottle with the discoloured water from their tap, then arrange to collect it. It was also decided to blame the discoloration on essential mains maintenance works, telling the callers that the water was still safe to use if boiled. Once collected, the water samples would then be analysed. Themes would then be able to establish whether the quantity of five hundred litres of non-toxic colorant, had it actually been HCN, would've been lethal to those drinking the mixture. In most cases, the colorant would normally prevent people from drinking the water, whereas HCN, a clear, albeit almond scented liquid, wouldn't raise too many eyebrows.

The boat ploughed through the grey water, buffeted by the wind and the heavy rain that was affecting the London area at that time. Occasionally a wave broke over the bow into the boat to add to their discomfort. No one spoke, or even tried. Superintendent Michael steered the boat in the direction of the draw-off tower in the middle of the reservoir. He'd decided to take the boat to the up-wind side of the tower, as he knew that the craft would have to remain ten or so metres away from the structure, otherwise the boat itself would run the risk of being drawn into the draw-off. Had his passengers, apart from McDade who understood the manoeuvre, been as aware as he was of this possibility, they've been more frightened than they were. When Michael estimated he'd come as close to the tower as he dared, he made a full one hundred and eighty degrees turn back into the wind, positioning the boat in his preferred location. Keeping the bow of the craft into the wind and white topped waves, Michael cut back the engine to little more than idling speed, making sure he kept enough power at hand in case of emergency.

'Right lads, I'll hold her here till you get that stuff into the water,' he shouted at the top of his voice to make himself heard above the sound of the wind and the rain.

Bannistair, who'd been waiting on this instruction, reacted quickly. He fed a flexible lightweight, one hundred millimetre diameter plastic tube over the stern of the boat in the direction of the draw-off, allowing ten metres or so to float on the choppy surface close to the intake to the partly submerged tower. As he did so, Dobbie stretched out of the stern to make sure the tube remained clear of the boat's propellers. The tube was fixed to a hand-operated pump, which Day had clutched all the way from the mooring, and coupled to the drum. With the boat held in position by Michael and Bannistair satisfied that the tube end was in the optimum position, McDade and Day took turns to operate the pump, discharging the coloured fluid into the draw-off tower.

After some ten minutes or so, the pump started to draw air indicating that the cylinder was empty. Bannistair shouted to Michael to pull away, and started to pull the hose back into the boat. Michael's gave the twin engines full throttle heading back to the mooring at the reservoir's pumping station. The boat, even five hundred litres lighter than it was when the men had gone out, struggled to make headway as it headed into the worsening conditions. Waves broke over the bow constantly, soaking the men through. Michael eventually throttled back the boat's engines and the non sea-going policemen relaxed. Once tied up, the men clambered up onto the deck of the small pier, pleased to feel the solid footing beneath their heavy rubber boots. They waited till Michael joined them, then headed towards the pumping station office. Once there they removed their wet outer garments, their mood a mixture of excitement after the event, and tension as they awaited the results. Michael switched on his kettle, which he'd filled before he left, to make them tea. As he put out an assortment of different coloured mugs, Michael told them it had taken them five minutes to make it back from the tower. He explained that in that time the water and the colorant from the draw-off would now be passing through the treatment plant before going into the public water mains. He checked his watch, then added that at this time of the day it would be another five minutes or so before the call centres would receive any telephone calls, if in fact that happened, reporting discoloration. He told them to find a chair and sit down as he poured out the hot, welcome tea, and handed out biscuits from a tin. As they drank their tea, they felt the heat returning to their chilled bodies. Michael's estimate was thirty seconds out. Four minutes and thirty seconds had elapsed when the telephone in Michael's office rang, startling all in the room. Michael answered it. It was a call from Themes Customer Services at the call centre, advising that their telephone lines were *Hot.* The coloured fluid had reached members of the public - how many was as yet unclear, but had it been HCN, which had no colouring, then deaths would have been mounting from that moment onwards. It was now up to Themes Water's chemists to analyse the samples when they'd been collected, and determine the parts per million of discoloration. This level would then be compared to the previously calculated known fatal level of HCN in the water supply. They would then deliver the good or bad news to the Scotland Yard. McDade phoned Hall on his mobile as arranged, and told him of the partial success, if it could be called that, of the operation so far. He added that Themes hoped to have the full results before the day was out.

'I don't know whether to be happy or sad Bob,' Hall replied, 'however we'll now know where we stand in terms of *is the situation critical?* Or, *is it being overstated?* Give the lads my thanks will you Bob?' Hall added, 'You got some weather to go sailing this morning. It was bad enough driving in to the Yard, but out there on the water…Well I can only imagine. How are my landlubbers doing? Manage to keep their breakfasts down did they?'

'Well Dobbie was very quiet, but give him credit, it was a bit choppy out there.'

Hall smiled at the thought. If McDade thought that, then it must have been bad! He said, 'I'll see you all when you get back Bob.'

Hall and Johnston were seated in the War Room, awaiting the arrival of the Yard's handwriting expert. Hall was comparing copies of the signatures of Ivan Beria and Ivan Aireb. Like Johnston, he felt now having seen the signatures that they were by the same hand. His phone rang. Picking it up he heard his secretary say, 'Sir, David Penn, the graphologist has arrived. Will I show him in?'

'Yes, bring him in now Lorna.' He stood up to meet Penn, whom he'd dealt with on more than one previous occasion. The man had an amazing eye for detail, and if anyone could spot a forged signature, it would be David Penn. The man was a civilian, not a policeman, a criminologist as well as a graphologist, and spent most of his time at his desk in Scotland Yard. As he came into the room Hall said, 'David come in, good to see you again.' Hall introduced Penn to Johnston then added, 'We haven't had the pleasure of your good services for some time David.'

Johnston and Penn shook hands, and Penn said jokingly, 'That's true Commander. You know why? Most of the villains today use computers; they don't write anymore.'

The three men laughed at Penn's ironic and revealing humour.

'Take a seat David, and have a look at these will you?' Hall said, passing the photocopies of the signatures to Penn. He also placed photocopies of the signatures enlarged to twice the normal size on the table. Hall explained the situation generally although not in detail, as Penn was not in the secure loop of *need to know* persons involved in *Operation Hydro*.

The three men examined the signatures; Penn more rigorously than the others. He turned the pages upside down, sideways both ways, using a pocket microscope to scrutinise them. He said, 'Commander, I'm fairly certain the signatures are by the same hand. Ninety-five percent certain I'd say at this time. Let me take them back to the lab and I'll get a better look at them there, but it looks to me that your guess is probably correct. Beria and Aireb are probably one and the same person.' He shuffled up the pages and slipped them into a plastic folder. 'I'll get back to you within the hour.'

'That's great David. It might be academic as we haven't yet managed to lay our hands on either Beria or Aireb, whatever this individual calls himself, but your conclusions will answer a few anomalies we have at present. Thanks for the quick response to my call David,' Hall said, taking Penn back to his reception. 'Speak to you later,' he said as the men parted.

When he returned and sat back down again Hall said, 'Well, well, Jim, maybe, just maybe, Beria and Aireb are one and the same person! Now where does that get us?'

True to his word, Penn telephoned within the hour. He confirmed that in his considered opinion, the handwriting of both signatures was by one and the same person. Aireb was indeed Beria, and vice versa. Hall received the call as he was heading to DAC Hughes' office for an unscheduled meeting and had little chance to relay the information to anyone else. He wondered why the meeting had been called, as he and Hughes were due to meet later that day. He knocked the door to the Hughes' outer office and entered. The secretary smiled and waved him straight through. Hughes was on the telephone, but motioned Hall to take a seat. He was obviously at the end of the telephone conversation, going by his tone of voice, Hughes said, waving Hall towards a chair, 'That's right, get the man and the vehicle up here to the Yard ASAP. Thanks Bob, and pass on my compliments to the village WPC. That was good police work by the woman. I wish we'd many more like her. Thanks again,' he said, before replacing his telephone.

'Good morning Chris,' Hughes said. 'That call was from Bob Murphy, Chief Inspector, Thames Valley Police. It seems they've apprehended a man with a dark blue Range Rover containing nine orange cylinders. The man refuses to give his name. He's thought to be a foreign national, Middle Eastern, but speaks perfect English they say. The man and the vehicle complete with its contents are on their way here to the Yard as we speak. The vehicle was spotted by a young WPC from the Thames Valley force, based in Maidenhead. She was walking her dog this morning before going on duty at eight o'clock. She notices a Range Rover with London plates and no green disc on the windscreen, and telephones Maidenhead, telling them the

305

vehicle's location. Murphy gets a car round to the location on the double, and as they arrive they see a man getting into it. Simple, old fashioned police work, and it looks like it paid off. The man had apparently spent the night in a hotel at Bray and had parked in the hotel car park. When asked what was in the cylinders, he said that they contained propane gas. Easy for Bannistair's lot to check that once we get them here,' Hughes stated.

'If this turns out the way I think it will Sir we're at last making real progress,' Hall said. 'I bet its Rasid we've got. Caught in possession with HCN; I can hardly believe it. That would be the second major step this morning if it turns out to be true?' Hall then told Hughes about linking Aireb and Beria, and the link-up between Beria and the HCN, then Aireb and Rasid.

Hughes as ever impatient, got to his feet. 'You know Chris it's straightforward police work that gets the results nine times out of ten. Make sure your team appreciates that fact. It isn't by any means some spook with a computer who unearths the villains, just solid painstaking police work most of the time.'

Hall said, 'Sir talking about straightforward police work, we're still due to meet later this afternoon I think? Well I hope to be able to tell you the results of the exercise we carried out up at Enfield reservoir this morning.'

Hughes touched his computer keyboard and looked at his screen. 'Yes at three o'clock I see and, Chris, I hope your exercise was a failure for all our sakes if you know what I mean?' Then with more enthusiasm he added, 'We'll also have the man and his Range Rover available for questioning by then as well.'

'Right Sir, I'll see you then.'

Returned to the War Room, Hall spent the remainder of the morning listening to McDade, interspersed with Day's humour, recount his version of the exercise at Queen Anne Reservoir, earlier that morning. As he listened, they were interrupted by a telephone call for Hall. It was the Chief Scientist of Themes Water, a Dr Archibald Walker. Hall went to his room to take it.

Hall picked up his phone and heard the man ask, 'This is Dr Walker speaking. Who am I speaking to? Is that Commander Hall?'

'That's correct, Commander Hall speaking. How can I help you Dr Walker?' he asked tentatively.

'Commander I'm sure you're aware of the tests we at Themes Water are currently undertaking on behalf of Scotland Yard - tests on the water samples taken earlier this morning. You with me on this Commander?'

Hall wondered what was coming next, but he said, 'Yes doctor, yes I know all about that matter. I wasn't expecting any result for a few hours yet.'

The sound of paper ruffling could be heard at the other end of the telephone, and then a few seconds of silence before Walker replied saying, 'Yes Commander, yes we have some preliminary results on the purity of the supply. Let me see...' the man hesitated before continuing, 'yes, the purity has been badly affected by the injection of the trace sample that your men discharged into reservoir. Our telephone lines are still overloaded dealing with public calls of complaint, mainly about the colour of the water, not the taste. But they always do that whenever there is a mains problem, a burst, anything along those lines,' Walker stated flatly.

'Commander, and this is only my very, how can I say, my best guess if I can use that term in these circumstances. A first estimate of the situation if you know what I mean. I'm reluctant to make any statement at this juncture Commander, I'm sure you understand, but my Chairman, Sir James Duncan, has instructed me to do so.'

'I appreciate that Dr Walker, but you must understand I need to have some idea of the possible impact. That information is needed to allow the authorities to make provision for all possible emergencies.'

There was silence at the other end of the telephone, and just when Hall was about to ask if Walker was still there, the man said, 'Thousands, tens of thousands of people Commander. I can't be more certain at this time. It would be a major national disaster of horrific proportions. Even worse than *September the Eleventh.* Nothing like it before, absolutely horrific. It could even trigger typhoid, and cholera.' There was emotion now in the man's voice. 'It is only an estimate Commander, my best guess as I said at this time. Much work still has to go into the calculations, but at this stage it is certain that a real assault of this nature on the water supply, would be catastrophic. My full report will be available for you information in twenty-four hours Commander. Is that satisfactory for your purposes at this time?'

'Yes doctor, it confirms my worst fears. I'll await your full report, but in the meantime, I'll inform my superiors of your findings. We've much work now to do to raise the matter to the attention of the government, health authorities, the water companies, and of course the police. Dr Walker, thank you for your assistance.'

Again Walker hesitated before saying, 'I know that I shall be challenged on this information. I know that, but you see my conclusions are so frightening, so unbelievable from such a simple act of terrorism so easily carried out, that although there will be some errors in my calculations,' he paused, 'let's say plus or minus twenty five percent, maybe higher, but certainly no lower. I'm almost reluctant to confirm the magnitude of the possible disaster.'

'I understand doctor. Thanks again for your prompt response.' Hall replaced his telephone. He paused for a moment deep in thought. Lifting his telephone again, he asked his secretary to arrange an immediate meeting with DAC Hughes.

The driver of the Northumbrian Water vehicle climbed into his works Land Rover Defender. 'Of all the days to have to go up into the bloody hills, we have to have an emergency today,' he said to his mate who was already sitting in the passenger seat. 'Have you got the flask of tea Bob, I think we're going to need it if you ask me. Twenty-seventh April, and bloody temperature would freeze the balls off the old proverbial brass monkey in no time flat. And it's supposed to be bloody spring!'

'Aye ah've got the tea, and some of those caramel biscuits from the canteen that you like Jack. Don't say I don't look after ye.'

'Good man, now let's get this bloody job done as quickly as we can. It's already half-past-two, and it'll be getting dark soon.'

The men drove off from the works depot on the outskirts of Durham and joined the A167 before turning right at the first roundabout onto the A691.

'Is this the same shaft we serviced a week or so ago Jack? It was clean as a whistle at that time if I remember right.'

'Aye Bob, the same bloody shaft up in Skylock. That bastard McKenzie, the service provider as they now call him in his jumped up job, says as we're going out the door that we've to do the bloody job properly this time. Bloody cheek, him sitting in his overheated big office, an' us up in the bloody hills on a day like this, cheeky bastard.'

'You're right Jack, you're right. What's the problem anyway?'

'They say it could be a partial blockage of some kind. We'll see when we get there Bob. Now light me up a smoke will you. The packet's in my coat there in the back. God, look at this bloody rain, bad enough down here on the bloody road. Can you imagine what it's going to be bloody like up on Skylock?'

The men drove on, skirting around Consett towards the small town of Castleside, and out onto the A68 before turning left and heading south. Four kilometres further on they turned right, into a narrow road leading up to the village of Vaskerley. Soon they were climbing up through the village - not much more than a handful of houses. Visibility had dropped to less than ten metres or so due to low cloud cover and the Defender pitched and bucked on the rough, muddy terrain. They continued up the steep gradient, through the wet, thick mist, following a track created over the years mostly by their company's vehicles doing what they were doing now.

'Bloody hell,' the driver shouted as he frantically turned the wheel to avoid colliding with a parked Land Rover that had abruptly appeared in front of him out of the mist. 'Some idiot parked on the bloody track in the middle of nowhere, can you believe it?'

'Yer right Jack. Bloody idiot, and it's got a trailer attached. It's not one of ours. You did well there Jack, not crashing into the thing. Can you imagine what McKenzie would've said had that happened? He'd have us digging pipe trenches for the next six months.'

'Light me another smoke Bob will you, that was too close a call for my liking. Bloody idiot,' the driver said, struggling to get back onto the track. 'And get the tea out Bob, I'll need a cuppa before we climb down that bloody cold shaft. Fair shook me up that did.'

'Right Jack. We're nearly there I think, I remember that last rocky turn we've just past from our last time up here.'

The wipers swept the wet mist from the windscreen and the stone shaft appeared dead ahead. The driver struggled with the wheel until he had parked the Defender alongside the stone structure.

'Thank God for that. Get the tea and the biscuits out Bob. I'm ready for them I can tell you.'

'Coming right up. What a place this is. Still it could be worse, we could be digging bloody pipe trenches.'

'Too right Bob, now come on with that tea.'

Niazi Bey had heard the vehicle approaching long before it reached his parked car. He'd then seen the headlights bouncing through the mist. He stayed back out of the line of the headlights and lay down on the wet grass. He'd been on his way back to the Defender to get something to eat when he'd heard the sound of the vehicle straining as it climbed the hill. Why today of all days he thought? He followed it, staying well behind. He saw the driver manoeuvring alongside the shaft, which he could just make out through the mist. He now spotted the water company name painted on the side. The engine died as the driver switched off the ignition, leaving only the sound of the wind as it blew the swirling mist around the hill and the shaft. He expected someone to come out at any time, but the vehicle, another Land Rover, remained closed and silent. Even the wipers had stopped. He slid down onto the wet grass and lay there for a further ten minutes, wet through and cold. He then heard the doors open and two men in heavy waterproof clothing climbed down onto the hillside. One man opened his trousers and began to relieve himself. Bey lay perfectly still, his head buried in the wet grass.

'Bob, I'll go down the shaft first and have a look. If there's a problem I'll give you a shout, OK?'

'Sure Jack, but hold on, I've got the key here for that padlock on the grid.' Having relieved himself, the man zipped up his trousers and turned following the other voice. Bey watched as both men disappeared into the mist. He knew they'd find the broken padlock in a few minutes. He remembered how hard he'd worked to cut through it few days ago. He didn't have to wait too long before he heard the men climbing the metal rung ladder on the side of the shaft. The first man to the top shouted, 'Aye aye, what's happened here then? Someone's been up here and cut the bloody padlock Bob. Can you believe that? Bloody vandals are everywhere,' the man said in apprehension as much as in anger.

'Who'd want to do that Jack, there's bloody now't to steal down there is there?'

Bey heard the men lift the metal grid from the top of the shaft, allowing it to settle back on its hinges.

'We'd better see what's going on Bob if you ask me. Now attach me to that fixing there and I'll go down and take a look,' the man said, as he passed the rope to his mate after he'd clipped it to his own harness. He put on his hard hat, checked his torch and then swung out, his feet still on the stone edge of the top of the shaft. He allowed himself to sink down the inside of the shaft to test the working of his safety attachment in the manner of someone abseiling down a mountain. He quickly disappeared, touching only the internal metal rung ladder to maintain his alignment.

'Easy now Jack,' the other man shouted by way of encouragement. 'Give me a shout if you see anything odd mate, OK?'

'Sure Bob,' the other man grunted as he sank down into the darkness.

Both men were feeling uneasy and the man sitting on top of the shaft turned to look around, his apprehension getting the better of him. The wind was now howling, and the mist seemed to have lifted a bit. He involuntarily shivered.

After a minute or so of silence, the man down the shaft shouted, 'Bloody hell, what have we got here? What a bloody mess, oh God!' his voice echoing in the shaft.

'You OK Bob, Bob you OK?' the other man asked.

Niazi Bey had decided that Allah was now guiding his hand. As the first man had lowered himself down into the shaft, Bey had made his move to get closer to the stone structure. He flattened himself alongside the shaft. He then heard the muffled voice of the man below. When the second man started to speak in reply, Bey quickly climbed the ladder on their Defender, then the ladder leading to the top of the shaft. He came up behind the man, who was still unaware of his presence. Bey struck the man a heavy blow on the back of the neck, causing him to fall face first down the shaft, his head and body striking the side walls and the inside metal rung ladder as he fell.

'Jack? Jack? What's going on up... ah...' the voice echoed up from the below, as the man at the foot of the shaft realised that something was happening up top. There followed dull thumping noises as the falling man impacted with the man at the base of the airshaft, before falling into the tunnel and fast flowing water. For Niazi Bey the silence returned, although the wind still blew. He climbed down, and made his way back to his Defender to find something to cut the rope still hanging down the shaft, with the more than likely dead man attached. He picked up heavy-duty pliers from his toolkit and went back to the shaft. Climbing up to the to the top, he squeezed and twisted the pliers around the taut rope a number of times before he cut through it. As the rope cut, it and the attached body fell to the bottom of the shaft. Bey sat on the stone wall to gathering his breath. He began to tremble, the events of the past few minutes taking its toll. He then climbed down from the shaft, which was still partly shrouded in mist, and went back to his car. As he passed the water company Defender, the crackle of a radiophone drew his attention. He tried the door handle and it opened. A voice continued to call out a driver number, asking for identification. Bey hesitated, then lifted the phone, partly covering the mouthpiece with his other hand, and in a low, mumbled voice, muttered a few incoherent words. He repeated this procedure three or four times, then switched the phone off. Although he was unaware of it, he'd responded to the works depot where the Defender and the now dead crew had left earlier that day. He was also unaware that following a report from the shift Duty Engineer at the nearby North Wood Treatment Works, the radio call had been made to establish what had caused the earlier fault to manifest itself in the last few minutes to a greater magnitude than before. In his favour for the time being was the fact that he'd answered the radiotelephone, although nothing could be made of his transmission back at the depot. But they'd had a response and assumed that bad weather up on the hills, as it normally did, was making radio reception unstable. The depot service provider Austin McKenzie, who'd made the radio call, in turn telephoned North Wood Control saying that his men were up there in foul weather attending to the problem as they spoke. When he'd finished, he shouted across the office to his line supervisor, telling him to let him know when the men returned, as he wanted to know what the hell had happened.

As the water company personnel assumed all was well at Skylock, Niazi Bey started up the Defender. He put the heater on to full heat. He was soaked through, cold and in shock after the recent events. His whole body was shaking uncontrollably. Stripping off some of his wet clothes, he draped them over the rear seats to dry. He set the wipers at intermittent to allow him to see down towards Vaskerley, then wiped off the condensation on the inside to see out the right hand side towards the other Land Rover. Then he opened the sandwiches he'd brought with him and poured some hot coffee from a thermos flask into a tin mug. He ate hungrily and drank the hot, strong black coffee. He had to stop his body trembling. He poured himself more coffee. He was glad to see that daylight was fading at last, as he'd feel safer in the dark. As he felt some warmth coming from the food and the hot drink, he wondered how long it would be before someone came to look for the two men. Maybe tomorrow he hoped. After a while he turned down the heater and thought about what he'd do for the next few hours. He considered ignoring his instructions to wait till midnight and going ahead with the operation as soon as it was dark. Again he pleaded with Allah to help him to make up his mind. As he was thinking about it, he put his arms across the steering wheel and leant his head forward, feeling overcome by the heat from the engine and the stress of the past hour. He fell asleep.

By the time Hall meet up with Hughes, the latter having been called away unexpectedly to a meeting at the Department of the Environment to report on progress on the St James's incident, it was two o'clock in the afternoon. Hall quickly told him about the preliminary findings from Themes Water regarding the Enfield exercise. Like Hall, Hughes was devastated, as they came to terms with the assessment of fatalities, realising their worst nightmare had come true. 'We need to bring O'Brien up to date on what's happening on all fronts, particularly the Enfield scenario. The PM needs to be aware of it. We'll need top government backing to enable us to counter the threat. At the moment what we've got are half measures. I'll go now to see the Commissioner, bring him up to speed so to speak. Hughes tried to lift their gloom, saying that he'd been advised a few moments ago that the contents of the cylinders in the Range Rover uplifted at Bray did contain HCN. He added that the driver's name, Farraj Rasid, had also been confirmed from the vehicle service handbook. His address was given as William Street, Knightsbridge London. The man had not admitted to anything, and still refused to give his name, his address, or his nationality. The mixture of news failed to lift their spirits. Although it would appear they'd located and arrested one of the known sources of possible carnage, and Rasid was now locked up a few floors beneath them, they were aware that the other two consignments of HCN were still unaccounted for.

'We must think positive about all of this. As far as we know there were three consignments of HCN uplifted from Zenecal Chemicals. We've good reason to believe that two of the consignments went north, one to Northumbria, and one to Scotland. The third one we had assumed was heading to the Southwest, the Bristol area. We may yet be proved right when we get to grips with Rasid?'

'As far as we can be sure of it Sir I'd say yes those were the locations,' Hall confirmed.

Hughes nodded, 'Then I think we can safely say we've found the latter one, and Rasid might be able to shed some light on the other two.' He pressed his intercom and asked his secretary to arrange a meeting with the Commissioner as soon as possible. He then said, 'Right Chris, let's go get Rasid - oh and I'll need a short report from you on Enfield for the Commissioner's meeting, nothing too long, an executive summary of the facts.'

Hall said he'd get it done ASAP.

Hughes called his secretary again to say that they were both going down to the holding cells and that she was to let him know immediately when he could see the Commissioner. Hall had to try hard to keep up with Hughes' pace, as they headed in the direction of the Yard's Detention Centre. When they got there, they were told that Rasid's behaviour was uncooperative and that he appeared to be unstable. As they went into the interview room, they heard him shouting, 'I demand to speak with the Iraqi envoy, I have my rights. I'll tell you nothing, nothing,' he said throwing himself off his chair.

'You have every right to make contact with a lawyer Mr Rasid; we've told you that. We'll bring you a telephone if you wish' said the WDS in charge of the interview. 'Do you wish to telephone? Throwing yourself about like that will do you no good. Shall I get you a telephone book?'

'I don't want your infidel lawyers, I've told you that. I want to speak to the Iraqi envoy. How many times must I say that you dumb whore?' Rasid shouted, kicking the wall in his rage.

The telephone in the room rang. One of the other policemen answered it. He listened then hung up. He looked at the WDS. 'DAC Hughes and Commander Hall are on their way down here right now. They should be here any minute.'

She nodded and pushed her chair back from the table where they all sat. Standing behind Farraj Rasid she said, 'Mr Rasid, you've been advised of your rights in all aspects. You've chosen not to take advantage of the opportunities contained within them. This interview has been recorded and I am terminating the recording at this time. This is Detective Sergeant Laura Laycock...' she paused to look at her watch, '...at two thirty-five pm signing off,' as she pressed the stop button on the recorder. Apart from Rasid, all the others stood up. There was a knock on the door, and a policeman opened it to allow both Hughes and Hall into the room.

Rasid started shouting again as he looked at the senior policemen. He said, 'I keep telling these fools that I will say nothing to you, or anyone else. Nothing until I can speak to the Iraqi envoy. Now will you do as I say? I'm entitled to my rights.'

WDS Laycock interrupted the outburst, introducing herself and the others to Hughes. She then said, 'Sir, you can be sure that Mr Rasid has been informed of his rights. The interview has been recorded in line with standard police procedures. I'm now recommencing with the interview and the recording at two thirty-nine pm...' Laycock pressed the record button to restart the tape recording.

'Thank you Laycock,' Hughes replied, as he and Hall sat down facing Farraj Rasid. Both men introduced themselves for the benefit of the recording. 'Now Mr Rasid, as you've heard, my name is Deputy Assistant Commissioner Hughes, and this is Commander Hall. We're in charge of the investigation into misappropriation and distribution of a substance known as HCN from a chemical firm based in Hatfield. It appears that we've apprehended you in the possession of approximately one third of the quantity in question. Your reasons for possessing the substance and your intended use of it are unclear,' Hughes stated. 'You've been made aware that you may call a lawyer to assist you in anything that you say and I assume that you wish to do so at this time. Do I make myself clear Mr Rasid?'

'Why must I have to repeat myself to you fools? I'll only speak to the Iraqi envoy not you or your English lawyers. Why am I being treated like this? I know nothing of the substance you call HCN. I'm innocent of everything that you've said. Now I want to speak to the Iraqi envoy. Can't you understand that?'

'If you're as innocent as you say Mr Rasid,' Hall intervened, 'then you have nothing to worry about. You should call a lawyer of your choosing now.'

315

'I want to speak to the Iraqi envoy; that is what I want. Not an English lawyer, but the Iraqi envoy. Don't you understand that?' Rasid asked in exasperation, rocking wildly in his seat.

After twenty minutes of getting nowhere, with Rasid repeating himself and giving no further information, Hughes and Hall left the interview room taking WDS Laycock with them. Hall went off to prepare his report for Hughes, while Hughes and Laycock continued to discuss Rasid.

'We're getting nowhere with him,' Hughes said, summed up the position, then he said to WDS Laycock, 'Take him back to the cells and let him spend a few hours there, and we'll try again later. Keep someone close by just in case he starts to talk, you can never tell with cases like this.'

'Right Sir, I'll inform your office if anything happens.'

Ten minutes later Hughes entered the War Room looking for Hall. When they met up, Hall handed Hughes his requested executive summary on the preliminary finding from the Queen Anne reservoir, Enfield. Hughes nodded his thanks saying, 'Chris I'll need to get back to my office. I've a meeting with the O'Brien at four and the Commissioner has asked to see me at five-thirty this evening. He wants an update on *Operation Hydro* would you believe. I'm trying to swop the timing of these meetings as we speak.'

'Right Sir. If anything else comes up I'll make sure you've got the details before you meet with the Commissioner. Oh, Sir. I'd like to hear what the Assistant Minister's proposals are once he's heard about the Enfield.'

'You will Chris, you will. Now I'm off. Speak to you later.'

As Hughes went off to his high level meetings, Hall called together the other team members of the *Operation Hydro,* to bring them up to date with recent developments. He'd suggested that they go to the small conference room near the staff restaurant on the eighth floor - that way even he, and they, would probably stop to eat and drink something other than biscuits and vending machine coffee. The meeting lasted almost an hour, focusing on ideas for tracking down the missing suspect, namely Beria, or Aireb, whoever. An intercom message eventually interrupted them. *'Commander Hall, please contact the War Room as soon as possible.'* Hall excused himself, lifting the telephone.

'Lorna, what's the problem?'

'Sir it's a message from Durham Police. It seems they've received a report of an incident from the water company up there. I'm typing the details just now, but they did ask for you to get in touch with them ASAP. If you're coming back here now I'll have the details ready for you.'

'Right Lorna, I'm on my way.'

Hall told the team what he'd just been told, then suggested that they returned to the War Room. When they got there, Hall's secretary had put two copies of the details of the telephone message from Durham Police on his desk. He asked Day to come with him into his room. Hall handed a copy to Day, both men silent as they read the information.

'Ian this is probably a wild card, but we never know do we?' he said, looking again at the page. 'I mean this comment here about North Wood Water Treatment Works, wherever that is? The reported blockage, well it could simply be a broken underground pipe, the residue then blocking the flow. Who knows? It seems the local force decided to react in view of the new water security status that the DAC was talking about. Water companies are now required to advise the local police of any unusual events that take place in their systems and distribution networks, and I mean any, hence this message from Durham.'

'Covering their posterior Sir, and I suspect we'll be inundated with calls of this nature,' Day said with a wry smile.

Hall nodded, putting the message back on his desk. 'I'll speak with them first, then if I think that there's maybe more to it, I'll let you know.'

'OK Sir, I'll get back and sort out our priorities now that we appear to have removed the threat around London, at least for the time being. That WPC did us all a great favour spotting Rasid's Range Rover. I must phone her up and ask her out for a drink. I like a smart girl like that.'

'Get on with it Day, she'll be half your age. Now off with you, I've work to do.'

Day laughed as he made his way out of the room.

Hall asked his secretary to get him Chief Inspector Ian Percy, Durham Police. Within a few minutes both men were deep in conversation. Percy elaborated on the plain words of the telephone message lying on Hall's desk, drawing a more complicated picture than had first appeared. As they came to the end of their conversation, Hall thought of sending Day back up to the North-east immediately he'd finished speaking to Percy. Now, as he thought about it more, he decided that both he and Day would go there. It was ten to six. They could catch a flight to Newcastle, and be at North Wood Treatment Works just after eight o'clock. It couldn't be that far away from Newcastle he thought as he thumbed through an ordinance survey map lying on his desk. From what Percy had said it wasn't an overreaction. There did appear to be something that the water company was concerned about. At least with Rasid in custody in Scotland Yard, as well as one cache of HCN in their possession, he felt that the level of risk to water facilities in the southern part of the country had now diminished for the time being. He lifted his telephone. 'Lorna would you ask Inspector Day to come to my room immediately please.'

CHAPTER FIFTY-ONE

Niazi Bey had slept for over two hours. He awoke with a start, hearing the noise of the intermittent windscreen wipers on a now dry windscreen. It was dark. The mist and cloud had gone and a partly cloudy, black sky replaced the earlier gloom. The moon, partially visible through the clouds, lent strong, black shadows to the air shaft. Bey checked the time. It was eight-twenty. He had less than four hours to wait till midnight. Allah had given him his answer. He'd wait till the appointed time, and deliver the *Juice of Allah* with honour. He'd be going home soon, he thought, a hero in the eyes of his friends. He gazed unseeingly out of the windscreen at the dark night. A flash of light caught his eye then quickly faded. He focused on the spot for a moment or two, his senses now on high alert. Yes, he saw headlights, two sets, about two kilometres away, bouncing up and down as the vehicles negotiated the rough, steep incline of Skylock Hill.

As it had happened an hour or so earlier, the depot line supervisor of the water company in Durham had become increasingly concerned when he continuously failed to make any further radio contact with his crew at the air shaft. He'd decided that there must be a serious problem. He'd first checked with the North Wood Treatment Works, asking the Duty Shift Engineer what the status was with the reported blockage at the shaft on Skylock.

The Engineer had shaken him when he replied, 'As I said to you earlier, it's worse now than when your men went up there, whatever the hell they've done. We're reading a thirty per cent reduction in flow right now. I'm having to remain on duty and having to divert from other sources to make good the supply.' Dobson paused, then asked, 'What's their latest report? What did they find anyway?'

The supervisor had hesitated, then said, 'That's the problem Bill, I can't make any contact with them. It's as if they've disappeared. I got one garbled response about three hours ago and that's all. I better get a recovery team up there right away. I'll keep you informed.' He replaced the telephone. 'I don't like the sound of this,' he said as he went out of his office. Looking around for anyone who was still there at that time of night, he shouted, 'Does anyone know if Austin McKenzie is still around?'

'Aye, he's at a meeting upstairs with some people from Cramlington. Something to do with this new *State of Alert in the Water Industry* announced by the government,' a voice shouted back.

'Would you get him right away, tell him it's an emergency. It might be more than that so ask him to come down right away.'

The supervisor then selected five of his men saying, 'Look I want you men to form two teams. Take a couple of vehicles, and emergency kits. I want you to go to the shaft at Skylock. I'll come with you. Now get ready right away. We leave when McKenzie gets here, OK?' The men went off to gear up without question, knowing from the sound of the supervisor's voice that something was wrong; something affecting some of their workmates.

Now, less than an hour after explaining the situation to Austin McKenzie, and leaving him to notify the men's families that they'd been called out on emergency, the line supervisor led his two crews, up the steep slope of Skylock Hill. As he sat there in the passenger seat of the front vehicle, he was thinking of what McKenzie had told him about the new *Water Protection Act* implemented in Parliament that same afternoon, and hence the visit from the suits from Cramlington. Apart from notifying the men's families, McKenzie would now also have to notify the police of the emergency in case it was found to be other than a mechanical failure or a natural defect. It was this latter telephone call to the police that had instigated the call from Chief Inspector Percy, Durham Police to Chris Hall at Scotland Yard.

The beams of the headlamps of the two water company Defenders were what Niazi Bey had spotted a few moments ago. Cursing, he thumped the steering wheel, now more than sure that it could only be someone coming to look for the two workmen lying dead at the bottom of the airshaft. I should've acted quicker he thought, right after dropping the two infidels down the shaft. I've failed so often I deserve to die like a dog he accepted humbly. He now watched the oncoming vehicles making slow, continuous progress up the hill and knew he didn't have enough time to discharge the HCN into the shaft before they got there. He was convinced it was somebody coming to look for the two men. They'd find the Defender, then the men at the bottom of the shaft. He cursed his stupidity, and pleaded for Allah's forgiveness, praying for an opportunity to redeem himself for his mistakes. As he looked down on the approaching vehicles in a state of spiritual calm, he shouted aloud, 'I'll take them with me to Allah. They'll grovel in the dirt like dogs at his feet. They'll be left in the wilderness, to rot in hell. Allah will forgive me and I'll be taken into paradise.' With newfound conviction, intentionally keeping his lights switched off, he waited two or three minutes praying continuously. He then aimed his Defender at the oncoming vehicles and floored the accelerator. The Defender bounced wildly, the trailer and tank of HCN still attached, but he managed to drive it straight at them. With the dark, black sky behind him, Niazi Bey screamed at the top of his voice, believing that he was heading for eternal paradise. 'Death to the infidels, the enemies of Allah, death to them all,' he screamed, as the Defender bounced and lurched from side to side on its downward suicidal journey.

The depot line supervisor was sitting next to the driver in the leading water company Defender, and realised that they must be getting close to the air shaft. He stared into the dark but his night vision was not as good as it used to be he was thinking. Suddenly their headlights picked out the shape of another vehicle hurtling downhill at great speed and heading directly at them. 'What the fuck's that? What the fuc... Is the bastard mad? Turn right for Christ sake, turn before he hits us,' the man shouted to the driver sitting next to him.
The driver, who had also just seen the approaching vehicle, tried desperately to turn to the right down the slope, and away from the impending crash. He nearly made it. Bey's Defender struck them a bone shuddering blow on the rear near side, ripping bits of the bodywork off both vehicles in the process and shattering the rear and side windows. The supervisor, who would relate later that he was amazed he was still alive, realised they were now precariously poised on the two offside wheels, plunging diagonally downhill. He tried to shout to the driver but couldn't find his voice due to the pounding they were going through. His head hit the inside of the roof and knocked him unconscious before the defender turned over, then careered down the side of Skylock Hill. When the vehicle slithered on its roof to a screeching, bouncing halt about five

hundred metres away from the point of the collision, the sound of broken glass marked the end of the Defender's journey.

As Niazi Bey had set his sights on the first of the oncoming vehicles and was within twenty metres of colliding head-on, he realised the driver was trying to steer out of his path. Cursing, he swung left to meet it, but bounced wildly off line, causing both vehicles to impact with only a glancing blow. Bey, with his seat belt unfastened, was nevertheless ejected straight through the windscreen of his Defender and, as would be established later, suffering severe lacerations to his head, face, neck, as well as the upper parts of his body. In the post-mortem it was also discovered that when he'd hit the ground, his head had taken the full force of the impact on a rock outcrop protruding through the grassy hillside. He had died instantly. The trailer, with the tank of HCN still attached, now broke free. It bounced over the vehicle, spinning and bouncing downhill for a further two hundred metres. The now driverless Defender spun out of control, before rolling over six or seven times, and finally exploding, and burning out where it stopped.

As these events were unfolding, the second water company vehicle, unaware of the impending doom that lay ahead, had continued making its way uphill. Now its driver and crew could only watch in horror at the drama played out before them. It was as if something had fallen from the sky. The driver braked hard and skidded to a halt. The men remained rooted to their seats for a few more seconds before the crew leader screamed, 'Get out there and get those poor bastards out of their Land Rover before the fucking thing blows up. Get out for God's sake. Move, move.' The man grabbed his radiophone and called his depot. He made contact with McKenzie and tried to explain what had happened, but he too was now in shock. He eventually managed to ask McKenzie to send an ambulance to Skylock and to call the police. As the man attempted to describe the mayhem, McKenzie tried to calm him then asked him if he thought it was a terrorist attack. 'I don't fucking know, it could be. All I know is that we've got one of our vehicles with three people in it, lying on its roof. They're maybe dead for all I fucking know and the other vehicle's on fire. Jesus, the flames!' the man gasped in horror. McKenzie asked if the man knew what had caused their vehicle to turn over and to explain, as best he could, how the incident had started.

In a very shaky voice the shocked man tried to respond. He said between sobs, 'It was another Land Rover I think, not one of ours. No bloody lights on, I remember that. It appeared from fucking nowhere. It crashed straight into the supervisor's Defender. Came downhill out of the darkness at a hell of a speed. We didn't see it till the bloody last minute. It just exploded a minute ago and it's burning right now. If there's anybody inside it they've had it. Serves the bastards right.'

McKenzie confirmed to his man that the police and emergency services were on their way, stressing that nothing at the scene was to be touched or moved until they got there. He told the man to keep his radio line open for further instructions and to make sure that his crew remained with their vehicle.

The man shouted back, 'We're trying to get the supervisor and crew out of the bloody overturned Land Rover for Christ's sake. How can we fucking stay in our vehicle?' He then threw the radiophone onto the rear seat in disgust. McKenzie's voice at the other end continued issuing instructions, although the crewman had left to run downhill to join his crew, who had by now managed to pull one of their colleagues out of the overturned Defender. The man appeared to be alive, although badly cut and bruised. He was in deep shock. The other men, including the supervisor, still strapped in upside down by their seatbelts, were bleeding from facial and head wounds. The men cut them free, and using a ladder as a makeshift stretcher, carried them away from the smoking Defender. Their crew leader shouted, 'That's it lads. We've been told to return to our vehicle and wait there till the police and emergency services get here. Let's carry the boys back up there. We can all wait up there safely till they arrive.'

'You're right Tom. Aye let's do that,' the others agreed, one adding, 'We don't know what the Hell's going on up here anyway; the place could be wired up with explosives for all we know.'

They made their injured colleagues as comfortable as possible, and took turns to ferry them back up the hill, helped by the glow of the fire from the burning wreck. When they'd finished, McKenzie's voice could still be heard on the radiophone. He sounded apoplectic, demanding acknowledgement of his instructions unreservedly, even threatening to have them all fired when they came back. The crew leader picked up the radiophone, hesitating before he spoke, then said, 'Hello base, this is Skylock returning your call. We have three men in need of immediate medical attention up here. Do you read me?' he asked tentatively. McKenzie, relieved nonetheless to hear from the man, spluttered some colourful adjectives, then informed him that medical attention was on its way, and that the men were to stay put by their vehicle, because the police and the army would be turning up in the next few minutes.

'Base what we need up here in a hurry is an ambulance, not the bloody army,' the man shouted back in frustration. 'Don't you understand? Doctors not bloody soldiers for Christ's sake!'

McKenzie tried to explain what was happening, stressing the concern of the authorities. Medical attention would be there within minutes he assured them, telling them to keep their radio line open. He'd just got the message through to them, when the men heard the sounds of heavy machinery all around them.

'Sounds like helicopters,' one of them shouted above the din, as all three looked up into the partly cloudy sky.

'Are they sending helicopters up here? We can hear something like a helicopter, more than one we think,' the man with the radiophone asked McKenzie.

McKenzie confirmed that an SAS unit would arrive by helicopter and that was why they should remain at their vehicle. He emphasised the point saying, 'we don't want any more bodies, is that clear?'

Suddenly, a single beam of white vibrating light flooded the hillside making the men there shield their eyes from its glare. Two more beams materialised from the sky, as the second and third helicopters switched on their broad beam searchlights. As the machines passed overhead the downdraught and the noise were fierce and deafening, adding to the men's alarm. The air shaft was now fully illuminated by the beams, and seemed to vibrate in harmony with the sound of the helicopter rotors. Another Land Rover was also illuminated, parked alongside the airshaft; a reminder to the men standing on the hill why they'd come up to Skylock in the first place. One of the helicopters landed within its own beam of light, and immediately ten, heavily armoured men in full battle dress, poured out from side doors. They ran directly towards the burning vehicle in an ever-widening arc. Two soldiers stopped at a dark, shapeless mound and motioned to some of their colleagues to join them. They'd found the body of Niazi Bey, the driver of the burning vehicle, the man who'd caused the mayhem just under an hour ago. As the other helicopters landed, the number of soldiers on the hillside doubled, then tripled. The trailer with a tank attached drew their attention, particularly as the tank's contents were leaking out onto the hillside. The soldiers cordoned it off. It would be later that they'd find out the contents were a lethal liquid known by the name of HCN, the fumes of which were equally dangerous.

The first of the police officers appeared not long after, then twenty minutes later they arrived in numbers. Hall and Day were with the larger group having been picked up by Derwentside Division of Durham Police at Newcastle's Airport and driven directly to Skylock Hill. An Incident Unit was quickly set up in the village of Vaskerley.

The emergency services, fire as well as medical were now everywhere, the hillside resembling a battle scene. The injured men were attended to and their colleagues were questioned, as the military, and police units strove to ensure that they had no criminal input to the events. The men were then transported back down the hill, well away from the shaft area, which had now been secured by a ring of soldiers. As the crewmen left the hill, three SAS men descended into the airshaft. They found no live terrorists, but they did find the two missing crewmen, both dead, and the partial remains of another body. The remains of the latter person were unidentifiable from all that was left of Hussein Mabeirig.

When the situation on the hillside was brought under control, Hall telephoned Hughes at Scotland Yard to apprise him of the events of the last hour or so.
'Sir,' he shouted above the din in the background. 'I'm speaking to you from Vaskerley, a hill village west of Durham. Can you hear me OK?'
'Just Chris. I got your message saying that you and Day had gone up there. How are things going, some progress I hope?'
'Well it's a mixture of good and bad, the usual thing I'm afraid. The bad news Sir is we've recovered a number of bodies I'm afraid. Two of them are the missing workmen who started the whole thing off. A third adult, male fatally injured in a vehicle crash on the hill, and we

now have the partial remains of another body, which as yet we're unable at this time to say if it's male or female, or if it was even involved in these events. That body was found partially blocking a water filter in an underground water tunnel. As yet we don't know how the body got there, or for how long it's been there. We've also got a few injured water company men who'd come up here to look for their two missing colleagues. All in all it's a real mess Sir. Anyway we've got thirty or so SAS from Hereford and three helicopters to boot. They've secured the place for the time being.'

Hughes listened to the reported carnage, then ask, 'Chris, was there any threat to the water facilities?'

'Well at this point it's a bit of supposition I'm afraid Sir. You see we don't know what the fatally injured person was doing up here on Skylock Hill. He was driving a four-wheel drive vehicle and apparently towing a trailer with a cylindrical tank attached to it. The tank's ruptured and the contents - a clear liquid - are leaking out. I've got someone trying to find out what it is but it's my guess, and here's the supposition Sir, that it's HCN - at least that's what I'm hoping. One of the paramedics who'd been up here earlier on the hill took a sample to a nearby hospital for analysis. He phoned to say that I should get the result in the next fifteen minutes or so, so here's hoping.'

'That would be something Chris,' Hughes responded.

'I'll let you know just as soon as I hear. Oh Sir, how did the meeting go with O'Brien?'

'Quite predictable Chris. In short, now that we appear to have removed the threat of HCN from the South-East by apprehending Rasid, the pressure seems to be off. At the meeting, and after he'd heard the details of Rasid arrest, O'Brien said, and I quote Chris, *'Keep me posted about the HCN Mike, keep me posted that's a good man*, and he dismissed the meeting. Left me thinking, *pity about those poor sods up in the North East, and in Scotland!'*

'Well let's hope we're right Sir, and that Rasid was the only one in possession of HCN down there.'

'True Chris, anyway we've still got all the emergency measures in place for a few more days at least, but I've lifted the Range Rover Stop and Search order, so traffic's back to its normal type of jams here in central London. Look I'll let you get on up there, but let me know when you hear about the tank contents. That would make my day I can tell you.'

'Speak to you later Sir,' Hall replied, and switched off his mobile. He joined Day and some others from the Durham Police Force who were examining the items found on Niazi Bey. Amongst them they found keys attached to a Durham University key ring, and his passport confirming his Iraqi citizenship. Hall's mobile rang.

'Commander Hall, this is David Wainwright, the paramedic you were speaking with earlier. I've just got back the results of the tests on that fluid from the tank. The lab at the hospital is certain it's hydrogen cyanide. They also said that everyone should stay well back from it as the fumes, let alone the liquid, are lethal.'

'Hydrogen cyanide, great David, that's great.'

The paramedic hesitated, then asked, 'Is that what you expected it to be Sir?'

'I couldn't have had a better result David. Thank the lab for me please. That was some quick work on their part. Tell them I appreciate it will you? And I'll see you when next up here in Durham David, hopefully under different circumstances.'

'OK Commander, I'll get back to work now, it's a full house down here I can tell you,' the man said, and hung up.

Hall knew that for hydrogen cyanide read *HCN*. He'd been right after all.

'Ian?' Hall shouted. He quickly explained the situation to Day then said, 'Ian you better get over there and make sure nobody, including the SAS, gets too close to it. Have it cordoned off, and check that it's not leaking into any water sources or such like. If necessary have a soak-away dug to retain the leakage up there. Get over there quick Ian. I'll phone Hughes and let him know the good news.

'Right Sir, will do.'

Hall telephoned Hughes and passed on the news that the tank did contain HCN: approximately five hundred litres of the stuff, based on its measurements. He added that it must now be assumed that an attempted terrorist attack on the water supply had actually taken place. Hughes was elated that they'd now located another consignment of the HCN, and passed on his personal congratulations to Hall and the team for some, as he put it, *superb police work.* When he'd finished his call, Hall went up the hill towards the air shaft. As he did so, he was aware that the success of this latest operation had little to do with his investigations. Events had occurred that were outside his or anyone else's control. The terrorist had made mistakes and had now paid the consequences. Had the terrorist attack succeeded it would've been so much different. He recalled the briefing he'd received on the way from Newcastle Airport, of how the water mains were tunnelled through and beneath the hills he was now standing on. He had explained to him the purpose of the air shaft, and of the countless thousands of men, women and children who relied on the water network for their wellbeing and employment. As he climbed higher, and he could now see the outline of the shaft. Looking at it he wondered how such a structure, and others like it, could be protected in today's world? According to the local police, for the past fifty years apparently the shaft had stood there untouched by anyone other than water company maintenance crew. Now it would need to be protected against all sorts of unforeseen events, but most of all terrorist action. It was the same story with the entire water industry and its precious resources. It created disturbing thoughts. He checked his watch. It was almost nine o'clock. He thought that if he was right about the date; there were only three hours left to find the remaining consignment of HCN. As he continued up towards the shaft his mobile again rang. It was Hughes, saying he was putting him on a conference call. Another person with a Scottish accent also spoke on the line.

Hall listened, as Hughes spoke first. 'Neil, I've managed to get us patched up with my man up there in the north-east. Are you still there Chris?'

'Yes Sir, I can hear you loud and clear. The din has died down a bit up.'

'Right Chris. Chris I've got Assistant Chief Constable MacKenzie, Strathclyde Police Glasgow on the line. I've been telling him of the events of the past few hours, and that apart from the consignment of HCN that went north up to Scotland as we understand it, we've now recovered the rest. Neil seems to think Chris that you should go up there to Glasgow right away and help them out. Take Day with you, I'll sort out the paperwork this end.'

'Congratulation Commander,' the friendly but firm voice of MacKenzie said. 'We'd be very happy to have you up here at this time, as I'm sure you're aware that there's only two hours and fifty-two minutes left till your estimated deadline of midnight tonight?'

'Thanks MacKenzie,' Hall replied, 'and I hope I'm wrong about my deadline I assure you.'

MacKenzie cut to the quick. 'Commander we're not making much progress up here in spite of the efforts and actions that we've implemented. I can tell you the situation is worrying to say the least. Whoever they are, we've either scared them off, or they are lying in wait ready to pounce at any minute, or should I say in two hours and fifty-one minutes from now?'

'We've been lucky so far down here,' Hall replied, 'it could just as easily have been so different I can tell you.'

'Luck or whatever Commander, we could do with some of your luck here, in fact we could do with all the help we can get.'

Hall instinctively looked at his watch. It had just gone nine o'clock. MacKenzie had brought him back to the reality of the situation. One known consignment of HCN was still unaccounted for and from the information they had it was located near Glasgow. He said, 'Sir could you arrange for Day and myself to be flown from here direct to Glasgow by the SAS? There are three helicopters within one hundred and fifty metres of me as we speak. If we can do that then we maybe, just maybe we'll be able to be of some help up there Sir.'

'Leave it with me Chris,' Hughes replied, 'I'll get back to you in a few minutes - however assume I can. Now I'll let MacKenzie and you make arrangements for your arrival at his end,' Hughes said, terminating the connection.

'Thank you Commander, by the time you get in the air I'll have everything set up at this end and let you know the arrangements. In the meantime you can call me on this number at any time,' MacKenzie said giving Hall the number of his secure line, which Hall keyed into his mobile. 'I'll see you in Glasgow shortly,' Mackenzie said, as the line went dead.

During the latter part of that day and early evening, as the water authorities in Scotland became aware that the threats to the water supplies in England had been lifted for the time being at least, they themselves became more concerned and alarmed at the task they faced north of the border. How could they be expected to protect a water supply source that served the Greater Glasgow area, a source that was fed from the combined waters of Loch Catrine, and Mugdoch and Craigmaddy reservoirs at Millguy? Even Loch Lomond could be interconnected. The task was enormous, they realised belatedly. The shoreline of these water sources alone, excluding Loch Lomond, measured close on two hundred kilometres in length. At the command centre set up for *Operation Hydro* in Strathclyde Police Headquarters in Glasgow, MacKenzie had addressed the men and women who'd been charged with protecting this resource. He'd interrupted the meeting which included members of the military, police, health, social, transport, and political representatives from Scottish Parliament to speak with Hughes and Hall and had now come back to the room. They'd spent the past few hours assessing the protective arrangements they could put in place. At best they'd heavily protect the water treatment plants and other engineering facilities. Large numbers of army units were being deployed to ring the plants and other critical facilities. All major and even minor roads in the vicinity of any water facility in the region would be road-blocked by the army and police. The majority at the meeting now felt there was little more they could do considering the geographical locations of the water sources. They had now heard the content of MacKenzie's telephone conversation with Scotland Yard. They now knew that Commander Hall, the man who in the last few hours had been given the credit for locating the HCN in England, was in the air and heading towards Glasgow. Some in attendance at the hastily assembled and appropriately named *Doomsday Meeting*, wondered what Hall could do that they hadn't done already? The mood was one of apprehension, mingled with a feeling of resignation by most of those present. Some even shared the view that it was *a storm in a teacup,* an *over-reaction from London.* As he waited for Hall to arrive, MacKenzie tried to raise the awareness of those present. He started by asking the Strathclyde Passenger Transport Executive representative to go over his strategy for the use of public transport should the worst come to the worst, and thousands of people die as the result of a terrorist strike.

'John,' MacKenzie asked addressing the SPTE Operations Director, John Devine. 'Assume we've around fifteen percent turnout of your drivers tomorrow morning, the rest, because of the emergency that may then have taken place deciding to remain with their families. We've still got to provide hygienic cleaning facilities, fuelling, emergency vehicle repair, medical treatment, and counselling as well. And we've still to feed the ones that still want to eat and dare I say it, water them all. Are you sure that such a level of service as you have implied will exist in these circumstances? What I mean John is, tens of thousands of bodies, some in a very bad state we must assume. Can we transport these bodies using your staff and transport?'

Devine replied unconvincingly, 'Yes, that part of the *Disaster Scenario Doomsday* was feasible as far as SPT was concerned but what about the Roads department? Will the SPT have unrestricted access through them? The Roads people have let us down before! You know roadwork's here, roadwork's there. Most we don't even get told about.'

It mattered not who you asked MacKenzie thought. If part of the plan failed, it had to be somebody else's fault. He'd been through all this before in the *Disaster Scenario*. They were all the same, only this time it could be for real. He welcomed the arrival of Hall and Day. As far as he was concerned they couldn't arrive soon enough. He now knew from a message passed to him that the SAS helicopter unit had agreed to fly them up from County Durham direct to Glasgow. They'd make the journey inside the hour, landing at Yorkhill Quay on the north side of the River Clyde. MacKenzie would have a car waiting to pick them up and bring them to the meeting as soon as they arrived.

CHAPTER FIFTY-TWO

At 2113 hours as Hall and Day were airlifted off Skylock Hill in County Durham, Mohammed Bejyi and Hamid Pasha came out of their hotel in Gartocharn carrying their crash helmets. They'd remained in their room all day watching television, eating room service meals, and avoiding any other contact with other guests. To avoid any suspicion about their Range Rover being left in the hotel car park after they'd gone, they'd already booked for another night with no intention of staying. They were now heading to Stronachlachar, on the shores of Loch Catrine. They lifted their motorbike off the Range Rover's roof rack, then Pasha getting on the bike, revved up the engine as Bejyi got on the pillion. Putting on their helmets and pushing down the visors, they turned out of the hotel car park towards Aberfoyle and Stronachlachar. They were wearing wetsuits under their outer bike gear. It was a cold, damp night, with poor visibility. As they headed towards *Location Alpha,* their initial target, the main beam of the motorbike's headlamp picked out the swirling mist surrounding them as they crested the humps and bumps on the narrow, twisting, wet road. Ten minutes later, approaching Aberfoyle on the edge of the Queen Elizabeth Forest Park, they spotted oscillating blue lights ahead. It could be police or ambulance services they thought, or maybe both, hoping it was the latter.

'Hamid, Police!' Bejyi shouted as they came closer to the lights.

'I see them. Let me do the talking Mohammed. Say nothing unless you're asked. OK.' Pasha shouted, as he throttled back his speed. They could also see a large camouflaged military vehicle and at least four heavily armoured soldiers taking up the middle of the road. A policeman stepped forward, waving a flashlamp in their direction, gesturing them to slow down and stop. The four soldiers also adjusted their positions, and their weapons, just in case they didn't. Pasha cut back the engine, keeping it running on low throttle. He stopped about three metres short of the policeman, making him come to them.

'Evening Sir, sorry to interrupt your journey but we've a security alert in place at the moment. Can I ask you where you're heading?'

Pasha slid up his visor and wiped his nose with the back of his gloved hand. He kept both feet on the ground to steady the bike. Bejyi, behind him, had his hands on to the grip bar and his feet firmly on the rests. If necessary, they could quickly accelerate out of the situation, and take a chance on the soldiers not shooting at them Pasha thought. He also thought that had they been in their Range Rover with the HCN in the rear, their mission would've been over at this point.

'We're going to see one of our mates in Inversnaid,' Pasha said. By chance he'd spotted a hotel on the map there earlier, as he'd checked out the distances to and from *Locations Alpha* and *Beta*. The policeman was busy noting down their registration number from the front of the bike as Pasha spoke to him.

'Not the best night for going over there is it,' the policeman said, 'watch how you go on that road after you pass Stronachlachar. It's not too good a surface; lots of potholes. Take it easy and keep your speed down. Thanks for your co-operation lads,' he said, waving them through the gap between the parked vehicles. The soldiers had retreated a few paces, although they looked closely at them and the bike, as they slowly moved past.

Once through, Pasha opened up the throttle, making sure he remained within the speed limit. Neither man spoke. A few minutes later they came to a signpost pointing towards Stronachlachar, the same road they'd taken a day or so before. They picked up speed once they were out of the small town and Bejyi, now gripping Pasha's waist, shouted, 'You did well Hamid.'

A nod of the head was Hamid Pasha's only response, as he wondered how they'd get back through the roadblock after they'd been to the draw-offs at Loyal Cottage: *Location Alpha.*

The SAS Puma helicopter had received clearance from Air Traffic Control at Glasgow International Airport and was now circling above the River Clyde in its final approach to the landing area at Yorkhill Quay. Hall and Day were strapped into their small uncomfortable seats, just off the floor. The lack of sensation of forward speed and the feeling of descending fast made them aware that they were about to land. The noise of the engines of the large heavy machine was deafening as they were piloted towards the ground. The touchdown, when it came, was smooth. The flight sergeant, their co-pilot, unbuckled his restraining straps then helped them with theirs. Within minutes, Hall and Day found themselves climbing down from the helicopter under the still rotating blades, then being guided towards the more familiar sight of a parked police car twenty-five metres away. As the airman stood back to allow the driver to open the rear doors for them, they thanked the man, and the other crew member for their help.

'Just hope that it's all been in a good cause Sir, that's all the thanks we need. Hope to read all about it in the newspapers tomorrow morning,' the flight sergeant said, before turning and heading back to the black vibrating machine that seemed to be having difficulty staying on the ground.

'Hope you'd a good flight gentlemen; makes a change from British Airway I suppose?' the police driver said as they climbed into the back of the car.

'Great way to travel,' Day shouted in reply, his ears not yet accustomed to the lack of noise around him.

The driver said, 'Commander Hall, I've been asked to take you and the Inspector direct to Headquarters where Assistant Chief Constable MacKenzie is waiting for you. Is that OK Sir?'

'Yes Sergeant, just get us there as soon as you can please.'

'Very good Sir,' the man responded, switched on the overhead red and blue light, and swung the car around at speed. He headed towards an expressway that ran parallel to the River Clyde.

It was now five past ten. If his assumptions were correct they had less than two hours. Did they realistically have a chance hall wondered? Within minutes they arrived at the Police Headquarters building and were taken to the main conference room, where Day had been a day earlier. The room was full of people, some in civilian clothes and others in police and military uniform. Introductions were, of necessity, brief. Hall and Day took the seats they were offered and the meeting continued. Hall was aware that MacKenzie was endeavouring to close the current discussion.

'Ladies and gentlemen,' MacKenzie said, 'I'm sure you'd all like to hear from Commander Hall.' This remark brought a mixture of positive nods, and a few grunts. MacKenzie continued, 'Commander I'll quickly extend our congratulations to you and your team for the way you've brought the terrorist threat in the south to a close.'

Hall nodded his head in recognition of MacKenzie's words.

MacKenzie continued, 'In Glasgow we're hoping you can help us do the same.' He looked around the group of people seated at the table, then looked directly at Hall. 'As we understand it Commander, it's your considered opinion that whoever planned these attacks set a target time of midnight tonight to carry them out. Is that correct Commander?'

Hall could sit still no longer. He now knew MacKenzie was hoping that he'd take the bull by the horns. As he got to his feet he said, 'That's my belief Assistant Chief Constable and we've got sufficient evidence to back up that assumption. We've also got evidence that Glasgow's water supply, namely Loch Catrine, is a target.'

'Preposterous!' a voice shouted out, 'Whoever these terrorists are, they'd need to dump massive amounts of your HCN whatever you call it into Loch Catrine to have any detrimental effect on the quality of the water. This talk of five hundred litres, or whatever affecting our water is just rubbish. Blown out of all proportion if you ask me,' the representative from the water authority responded.

A number of those at the meeting grunted in agreement with the speaker, who had now risen to his feet, his face flushed in agitation. Seeing that he had some support he continued with more confidence, 'If the quantity of the stuff is as you say it is, five hundred litres, then in my opinion, I'd say let them get on with it. It won't make a damned bit of difference to them, or to the people who drink it. In fact in parts per million, that's not even measurable...'

'Thank you Mr Beaker; thank you for your views,' MacKenzie said, interrupting the man.

'I'm sure Commander Hall has heard all of that before?' he responded, asking the question nonetheless.

Hall nodded his head towards MacKenzie, then looking at Beaker and a few of the others who were warming to the man's support, then said, 'You're correct of course in what you say. Quantity to quantity, the five hundred litres of HCN compared to the amount of water in Loch Catrine is a mere drop in the ocean. You're probably also correct in your statement that the mixture in that ratio will do little or no harm to anyone drinking the water. You're the expert, you know better than I do.'

There were murmurs of, *What's the problem then* from some of those around the table, as they looked at one another for support of their conclusions. Hall walked up to the wall map in the room,

335

locating Loch Catrine and taking note of its distance from Glasgow's City boundary. He also picked out the coloured areas on the map known as the Mugdoch and Craigmaddy Reservoirs on the edge of Millguy on the outskirts of Glasgow. He could see the pipeline connections between the reservoirs and Loch Catrine and ran his finger along the line of the water pipes.

He then stopped and looked round, still pointing to Millguy.

'Mr Beaker, does any village or town receive a water supply off these mains before they discharge into the reservoirs here?'

Those seated at the table looked in Beaker's direction.

'Well not really,' the man replied a bit uneasy. 'Maybe the odd small individual connection that was taken off to some farm or cottage years ago, before West of Scotia Water were responsible for the facilities.'

'So when the water leaves Loch Catrine it goes directly down to these two reservoirs?' Hall questioned, still pointing to Millguy.

'Yes.'

'Will you come up here please Ian,' Hall asked Day.

Day rose from the table all eyes now locked on the two Scotland Yard men.

'Ian, tell this committee what you were doing this morning,' *While most of them were probably still in their beds,* Hall thought.

'At seven-thirty this morning Ladies and Gentlemen,' feeling inwardly that it seemed more like two days ago, Day said, 'I was aboard a small boat out on Queen Anne Reservoir, in Enfield, North London. The purpose of the exercise was to put to the test Commander Hall's theory that even a small quantity of HCN, strategically injected into a water distribution system, could prove to be as deadly as a vast amount being dumped into a reservoir.' He paused for a moment to let the representatives absorb his words. Continuing, he said, 'With the assistance of Themes Water, I personally have now witnessed the evidence with my own eyes - and I have to say that there is no doubt that the Commander's theory is correct.'

'The results Ian?' Hall prompted.

'The preliminary results of the test, which we received from Themes Water this morning, proved beyond doubt that 500 litres of HCN, appropriately introduced into the distribution, could cause tens of thousands of deaths and countless thousands of seriously sick people. In addition, the impact over such a short period of time on the public services would be to render them virtually ineffective,' Day said to a now silent and stunned audience.

As the committee came to terms with what they'd just heard and began talking, then shouting, at one another, the meeting became a rabble.

'Ladies and Gentlemen, please,' MacKenzie shouted trying to be heard above the din. 'Order please, order,' MacKenzie tried again with little success. Shouting as loud as he could, he asked everyone to return to the table. Just as he appeared to be making some progress, a police sergeant passed him a note. He read it, then looking at Hall, said, 'Ladies and Gentlemen, for God's sake sit down, sit down please. I've just been informed that West of Scotia Water have in the last few minutes recorded a pollution problem in the water supply from Loch Catrine.' He remained silent till the gathering sat down. The noise level fell to a stunned whisper. MacKenzie continued, 'The problem has been reported from Blareusken Chamber four miles south of the Loch, and it's being confirmed that the water in the distribution at that location is now unsuitable for public use. The pollution has not as yet been identified, nor has the source. A full emergency Red Alert has been issued by the water authority.' MacKenzie paused, looking around the room, then added, 'I've no further information at this time.'

Panic erupted, with some people trying to get out of the room, others trying to use the single telephone and others calling on their mobiles.

Hall and Day were still on their feet at the far end of the conference room, both looking at the map and following the pipe connections and aqueducts from Loch Catrine to the Millguy reservoirs. They located the Blareusken Chamber, at a point where the aqueducts split to follow slightly different routes for nine kilometres or so.

'Ladies and Gentlemen, please?' Hall shouted. 'Please remain where you are, please sit down and listen, please. Listen, we may only have one chance to prevent this situation going critical. One chance, and time is extremely short.'

His words got their attention and they again went back to their seats for the second time in as many minutes.

Hall asked MacKenzie. 'If I have your permission may I continue? The events of the last few minutes make what I have to say even more appropriate.'

'By all means Commander.'

Hall turned again to face the map, placing his finger on Blareusken Chamber and running it down the route towards Millguy, a distance of twenty-seven kilometres he guessed. 'Correct me if I'm wrong Mr Beaker,' now looking at the water authority representative, 'but I suspect that this reported incident at Blareusken will present no real problem to the population served by the Millguy Reservoirs. Will it Sir?'

Beaker again was the focus of attention. Hesitating, he replied, 'Ah, well it all depends on how much time has passed since the problem was identified. You see if large quantities of the polluted water have now been discharged from the aqueducts into the reservoirs before we became aware of it, then we'd have a big problem.'

'Mr Beaker, the sensing, or sampling equipment that signalled the problem at Blareusken... Do West of Scotia Water have similar equipment at any other point in these aqueducts before the point where the water is discharged into the reservoirs?'

'Um, well not at the moment,' Beaker replied. 'You see the equipment is very expensive to purchase and maintain. It's in the authority's engineering budget for next year, I know that. The equipment we have at Blareusken is on loan to us from the University of Strathclyde. It's one of their research projects you see.'

Hall looked at the man for a moment, thinking what he'd just said, then asked, 'OK, so the authority has discovered they have a problem with the water from Loch Catrine. What do they do first? What action has been pre-planned in such a scenario?'

'Well we'd shut down the flow from the loch to the reservoirs,' Beaker replied with some confidence returning.

'Exactly what I was thinking Mr Beaker,' Hall replied. 'Now would you please come and show me where that action would take place on this map.'

Beaker went up to the map, put on his glasses and peered at it closely. He pointed to a spot just north of the reservoirs, 'There, right there,' he said his finger pointing to the village of Strathblane. 'There's a valve house just there,' he added.

Hall nodded, then asked, 'Mr Beaker do you think the valves at that location will be closed now?'

'Yes, they would be closed automatically on the sampling sensor's signal, then manually checked within a few minutes.' He was on known territory now and warming to his task.

'One last question Mr Beaker. How many days' water supply is stored in the reservoirs?'

'Between ten and twelve days - depends on the weather at the time. If it's hot, or...'

'Thanks Mr Beaker,' Hall interrupted as he turned to MacKenzie and asked, 'How quickly can we get to the Millguy Reservoirs? The reason I ask is I think we may only have an hour or so to prevent a catastrophe.'

MacKenzie looked towards his Chief Inspector of Traffic who replied, 'By helicopter Sir, inside fifteen minutes. Depends on how many will be travelling. The helicopter's ready now.'

'Thanks,' Hall said, 'We leave in two minutes. Would you arrange that please Chief Inspector?'

CI Peter Smyth looked towards MacKenzie.

'OK Peter, go and set that up please. We can take five people max, Commander, including the pilot,' he added for Hall's sake.

Hall nodded in response. Hall looked around the room to locate the military representative. He'd forgotten the man's rank, so he asked, 'Forgive me, Kendrick's the name isn't?'

'Major John Kendrick, Commander. How can I be of help?'

'Thanks Major. Major would you have current knowledge of the number and the location of your personnel at the reservoirs?'

Kendrick got up and went to the map. He pointed to the chlorinating station at the southern end of the reservoirs. 'We have a unit there,' and pointing in turn to the east entrance gate, and to a point half way along the south-east bank, 'and there and there. Each unit consists of four men, fully armed,' he added.

'Could you point out the draw-offs please?' Hall asked.

'Mr Beaker will correct me if I'm wrong,' Kendrick said, as he pointed to the two draw-offs, situated just off the walkway skirting the administration building.

'We have in effect two reservoirs Commander,' Beaker responded, coming alongside Hall and Kendrick. 'There's a draw-off here in Mugdoch, and one here in Craigmaddy,' he added, pointing to the positions.

'Thank you gentlemen,' Hall said, motioning the two men and Day back to their seats.

He waited until everyone was seated. Looking around the now subdued room, he said, 'It's my opinion that any attack on the water supply serving Glasgow will be made at the reservoirs. I also believe the incident at Blareusken was meant to draw us away from the real target, namely Millguy Reservoirs.' He had the undivided attention of the people in the room. 'We've got to get to the reservoirs ASAP, and I'd ask the following people to come with Inspector Day and myself.' He looked at MacKenzie and said, 'I trust you'll agree with me on this Assistant Chief Constable?'

'You've got my full support Commander.'

Hall acknowledged that, then said, 'Major, and you too Mr Beaker, would you come with us now please?'

Both men instantly got to their feet.

Hall then addressed the remainder saying, 'The rest of you I would imagine will have other things to do under the current *Red Alert* as it affects your respective roles. I suggest you remain here and plan for the events that will take place should we be unsuccessful at the reservoirs.'

The committee broke up as Hall and the three others rose from the table and left the room. Most members of the committee showed a mixture of relief and regret at not being included in the assault party. It was now five minutes to eleven, with just over one hour to the midnight deadline.

Once clear of the roadblock at Aberfoyle, Hamid Pasha and Mohammed Bejyi had made good progress towards Stronachlachar and Loch Catrine. When they arrived at the pier, they took off the their biking gear and put it, together with the motorbike, behind some bushes. They then set off on foot to where they'd hidden the HCN the day before. In the dark, Pasha eventually located the yellow ribbon he'd tied to the tree, and from there they quickly uncovered the cylinders and the other items. They pulled the cylinders out of the wet bushes as water dripped all over them, then began rolling them towards Loyal Cottage, and the outlet basin. Eventually, they clambered down alongside the draw-offs, alternately lifting and rolling the cylinders as they moved forward towards the crossed-shaped bridge that spanned the outlet basin. The noise of the water rushing out towards the aqueducts and on to the Millguy reservoirs masked any noise they made lifting and rolling the cylinders. By now they were sweating heavily inside their wetsuits. They placed the cylinders on their sides, raising the bottom of each cylinder. When they'd checked that the cylinder valves were facing down towards the draw-offs, they opened each valve and allowed the HCN to flow freely into the rushing waters. 'Death to the infidels. Let them drink *The Juice of Allah*. Allah be praised,' Bejyi said with passion, as he watched the deadly liquid mix with the pure waters of Loch Catrine.

'Let *Ma Ma, Fi Kul Makaan* begin now. Praise be to Allah,' Pasha shouted passionately.

Lifting and tilting each cylinder down towards the draw-offs, they made sure that all the HCN was discharged, before pushing each cylinder into the rushing and thrashing water. Feeling satisfied, and confident that this part of *Ma Ma, Fi Kul Makaan* had been executed perfectly, they made their way back towards the pier. They pulled on their biking gear and crash helmets then got back on the motorbike, and set off back the way they'd come less than thirty minutes before. Pasha checked his watch. It was now ten-twenty. One hour and forty minutes to get to *Location Beta* - the reservoirs at Millguy - and complete their mission. They'd still to get past the roadblock at Aberfoyle if they were to succeed. Pasha contemplated trying to go across country, through the forest that surround them, but one look at the map made him decided against it. He knew they had to get past the roadblock before their actions at Loch Catrine were discovered, otherwise there was no telling what the security check would be like then. He opened the throttle fully and the bike roared through the darkness as fast as the road would allow. Thinking of the alternatives, he decided they'd should take their chances and crash through the barrier if they had to. After a hard and bumpy ride through the Forest Park along the length of the dark Loch Ard, they emerged out into Aberfoyle. Pasha stopped the bike at the junction onto the main road. Raising the visor of his helmet, he turned towards Bejyi and said, 'Mohammed, at the roadblock I'll do the talking again. When we stop there keep your feet on the bike and hold on to the bar. We may have to crash through, do you understand?'

Bejyi responded with a mumbled reply through his helmet, nodding his head in agreement, and thinking if they did, then being at the back of the bike, he was the one most likely to get shot.

Pasha revved up the motorbike and took off again, driving carefully through the quiet village. Again they spotted the flashing blue lights before they reached them. Driving with purpose, Pasha went straight to the policeman as before and stopped. Putting both feet flat on the road, he made an elaborate task of lifting up his crash helmet visor, giving the policeman plenty time to remember him.

'That was quick!' the policeman said with interest, but no real threat. The soldiers posed more of a threat as they hovered on the sidelines, although as before they said nothing.

'When we got to the hotel it was our friend's night off. He'd gone down to Glasgow and hadn't bothered to tell us,' Pasha replied with a touch of sarcasm.

'Some friend eh?' the policeman responded. 'Carry on home then boys and watch your speed. It feels like it might ice up a bit later if you ask me,' he added, rubbing his gloved hands together and stamping his feet on the damp road.

'Thanks, goodnight then,' Pasha said, pulling down the visor. They were still on schedule. He throttled up the bike and took off, quickly disappearing into the darkness, heading towards *Location Beta*.

It was five minutes to eleven when Pasha turned the motorbike off the narrow road that passed through the clutter of houses that made up the village of Mugdoch. They then drove down a steep hill, through a serpentine bend at the bottom of which they'd created their roadwork's site the day before. As they came down the hill, Pasha spotted a number of oscillating blue lights a kilometre or so nearer Millguy in the distance. They didn't expect too many cars on this back road at this time of night, but they were taking no chances. The road works site hadn't been touched. They quickly moved out the cylinders and the other things they'd put there, putting them all in the trailer, then replacing them with the motorbike and their biking gear. Pasha lifted a heavy roll of black, double-skinned polythene, labelled: 50cm dia. heavy-duty storm drain liner.

'Keep this safe Mohammed, I don't want any holes in it,' he whispered in the darkness, as he handed it to Bejyi. When they'd finished loading the trailer, they pulled it towards to a wooden gate leading to the north side of the reservoirs. Bejyi broke off the padlock on the gate, then swung the gate around to let the trailer through. They closed the gate behind them and pushed the trailer along the pathway at the side of the reservoirs. They stopped when they got to the north shore of the reservoir, at the point where the walkway splits Mugdoch from Craigmaddy and where the dividing walkway leads to the control buildings. The men, now in their black wetsuits, pulled on fitted black head covers, making them virtually impossible to see from the south side of the walkway. Some of the buildings on the south side were now occupied and lit up. Alongside them, several police vehicles urgently displayed blue flashing lights. The two men worked silently, ignoring these distractions. The wind gusting around them, reminding them of the exposed location. The sounds of police sirens could be heard in the distance, probably from Glasgow, where the city lights were visible low on the horizon. Bejyi by now had set out the inflatable life raft and began to work the foot pump. Pasha took the roll of storm drain liner to the edge of water. He pulled out a length of approximately five metres and cut it off. Tying a tight double knot at one end, he separated the double skin forming a tube, holding the open end into the wind coming off the water to partially inflate it. He then twisted the open end, trapping the air inside. Keeping the twisted end tight in his hand, he put the knotted end into the water. The air now trapped in the tube kept it afloat. To prevent it drifting away, he weighed down the twisted end of the tube on the walkway with a large rock. He rolled the cylinders of HCN, one at a time towards the floating tube, positioning them carefully, before opening the valve to let the HCN pour into it. As he did this with each cylinder the tube sank deeper into the water. He was careful not to allow water from the reservoir to enter the tube. He was interrupted by the noise of a helicopter approaching. The men stopped working to watch it land close to the building on the south side of the walkway. Pasha signalled to Bejyi to ignore it. He himself had no intention of allowing anything to stop them now, no matter what. He carried on emptying the cylinders, and eventually all six had been emptied into the tube. Carefully leaving a length of the tube empty, he twisted and knotted the end in a similar fashion to the other end, and thus created a sealed air pocket. Picking up a rope, he tied it to one end of the now sealed tube before pushing it into the water at the side of the walkway, making sure it didn't snag on the rocky edge. The tube, now partly

343

floating on the surface, could be pulled easily across the water. Pasha sighed with satisfaction, pleased with the outcome of his solution to the challenging hydrodynamics problem. Bejyi by now had inflated the life raft, and launched it into Craigmaddy Reservoir on the left side of the walkway. Getting into the raft, Bejyi caught hold of the rope that Pasha threw out to him, and tied it to the rear of the raft. Still on the walkway, Pasha watched as Bejyi manoeuvred the raft, bringing the tube into a towing position. When he was sure that they could control the motion and direction, he signalled Bejyi to come back to the edge of the reservoir and let him aboard. Voices across the water caught their attention, but now they were oblivious to all and everything around them. Once seated, they quietly paddled the raft towards the buildings opposite, keeping themselves in the shadow of the walkway. With the raft and the tube now in motion, they moved across the water with ease, Pasha directing their route towards the pod-like concrete structure of the draw-off tower looming upwards in the darkness. The turbulence on the surface of the water increased substantially the nearer they got to the structure, making it difficult to keep on course.

When the police helicopter had landed in the public car park at the side of the administration building, everyone, including the police pilot, went into the adjoining control room. In there they met up with one of the army units, which were busy preparing heavy-duty lamps in line with Hall's recent telephoned instructions. The lamps were mounted on two trolleys, with heavy electrical cables attached. The cables were of sufficient length to allow the trolleys to be pulled close enough to the point where the draw-offs in both reservoirs were linked to the shoreline.

'Major can we get these contraptions out and in place, and lit up as soon as possible?' Hall asked Kendrick.

'The men are doing an earth check on the trolleys at the moment Commander. Give them a minute or two, they won't be much longer. Can't be too safe with electricity near water you know!'

In the control room, Kendrick and Beaker had selected a heavy electrical power source to feed the lamps, closing down a number of large water pumps, with heavy three-phase electrical motors, to provide the supply. Beaker was now in his element, and full of his own importance.

'Ready and able to function Sir,' the army Sergeant who'd been working with the lamps called out.

'Thank you Sergeant. Ready when you are Commander, ' Kendrick stated flatly.

'Get those things out there now,' Hall shouted in reply, 'but don't switch them on till we've got them in place. Also kill the lights in here first, I don't want anybody to see what's coming out. Everyone understand that?'

'Steady old man,' Kendrick said, slightly huffed at Hall's last words. Beaker switched off the battery of light switches on the wall of the control room, throwing the area into darkness. The room now dark, the army unit opened the large double doors and pushed out the two lamp trolleys, one being directed to the left to illuminate the Mugdoch draw-off tower, and the other to the right towards the Craigmaddy tower. It was ten minutes to midnight. As this had been going on, Pasha and Bejyi had reached the shadow cast by the overhang of the top structure of the submerged tower and were having difficulties keeping the life raft and the trailing tube from being sucked into the draw-off. They now attempted to turn the life raft around in the turbulent waters, so that the tube would be closer to the tower draw-off. They'd also have to allow themselves enough leeway to pull clear of the whirlpool effect created by the downward rush of the water once they'd dumped the HCN into the draw-off. As they battled with the currents and the noise of the draw-off, they were too preoccupied with their own struggle to have much time to notice or hear the army unit in the shadows hauling the lighting trolleys into place, only thirty metres away from them.

'Ian you go to cover Mugdoch, I'll go to Craigmaddy,' Hall shouted, both men now wearing heavy flak jackets and protective helmets. 'Mr Beaker,' Hall added, 'will you please remain inside the building Sir. We may need you to start up the water supply again in a few minutes, or to shut it down permanently if we fail.' Beaker looked disappointed. 'OK, power them up,' Hall shouted to the army sergeant standing at the ready alongside the main electrical switchboard.

Hamid Pasha had now managed to get the raft and the partially floating tube into place. A keen sheath-knife in his hand, he was about to cut the rope and let the tube of HCN drift the last few metres into the draw-off.

'Ahhh,' a startled Pasha shouted, as the sudden impact from darkness to the increasingly intensifying stark, bright white light physically blinded him. He was caught partly out of the raft, fixed in the white beam, about ten metres out from the tower, a taut rope in one hand, and a gleaming knife in the other. Due to the angle of the lamps, the shadow of the tower concealed Bejyi, who was rowing strongly to prevent both him and Pasha, together with the life raft, being sucked into the draw-off.

Hall, who when the lights had come on in their glaring intensity, found himself equally taken aback by the glare, and the discovery of a man in a raft at the side of the draw-off tower.

It was a member of the army unit that responded first. 'Halt! Move back from the draw-off immediately or I'll fire. Back off do you hear me?' the soldier shouted. Bejyi was no doubt to blame for what happened next. In shock, he stopped rowing, and the life raft, together with the partially floating tube of HCN were sucked towards the tower. The soldier repeated his harsh warning to back off but the raft, affected by the currents, continued to move towards the draw-off tower. A short burst of heavy automatic fire resounded across the water, chopping Hamid Pasha almost in half before he fell back into the eerily illuminated water, his dark red blood spreading all around his lifeless body, before being drawn down into the draw-off.

'Stop! Stop firing. Stop firing,' Hall screamed. He watched in horror as the black, bulbous tube floated, just beneath the surface, closer to the draw-off. He'd also now spotted the terrified and shocked Bejyi hunched up in the rear of the life raft.

'The bag, the sack or whatever the hell it is, don't burst it for God's sake,' he screamed at the soldiers. 'Get the other man out of the raft before he gets anywhere near it.'

By now several of the soldiers had gone out on the linkway to the top of the tower, and had grabbed hold of Mohammed Bejyi. He gave in with little resistance, in deep shock having seen his friend killed, then being drawn into the draw-off. The body, in two parts, would be recovered later, lodged in a heavy screen water filter, deep below where the action had just taken place.

Hall and Major Kendrick, managed to keep the deadly tube of HCN away from the draw-off, until two soldiers had taken up the oars in the life raft and started to pull away from the tower, dragging the tube behind.

It was well into the night before the army units and the police confirmed that there appeared to be no other terrorists involved in the attack. Bejyi although in shock, had more or less confirmed that he and Hamid Pasha were the only two involved. He also admitted, such was his state of shock that they'd carried out the earlier attack at the Loyal Cottage near Loch Catrine. Their two-door Range Rover was recovered, as was their motorbike, as well as other items they'd intended to use in their escape, such as clothes, false passports, and currency. Their time at Beneagles Hotel was checked, as was their cottage in the village of Braco, Perthshire. The population of the United Kingdom, particularly those living in and around Glasgow, and those in the areas of England who'd faced similar threats, had been spared the horrors of the first terrorist attack ever recorded on the public water supply, but only just. More than seventy per cent of the earth's surface is covered by water. Yet, can we go on calling the Earth the *blue planet*, given that access to clean drinking water is a major challenge for a large percentage of the world's population? The lack of water or poor quality is *the* primary cause of death worldwide. *What price water,* you may ask? The answer: *what price life itself?*

As for Saddam Hussein, he no doubt celebrated his birthday as the events had taken place outside Glasgow, unaware of the efforts his countrymen had put into plan: *Ma Ma, Fi Kul Makaan.* The cost to him however was minimal. Five of his countrymen had died following their cause on his behalf. Had he known, he would probably have cared little about them, thinking only of their failure. Yet they came close to inflicting pain and death on countless thousands of innocent people. Where they failed, others may try again, and succeed. Colonel Safa al-Dabobie and his deadly companion, Ivan Beria were never caught, and live to strike another day.

Marbella, Spain. November 2002

347

ABOUT THE AUTHOR

Bill Higgins, a chartered engineer, was born in Glasgow. He and his wife Ishbel now divide their time between Marbella, in Spain, and southern England, where their daughter Amanda lives.

Bill is currently writing his second novel – a terrorist thriller, involving Iraq, Israel, and the United Kingdom's nuclear submarine fleet.